'Are you thinking you  'Tell me, is that what you wa

'Oh, darling, I'd so n   but I know that's not possibl   , and I don't.'

'Well that's certainly true. I have to get back as soon as possible.'

'You could come back when you get some leave and perhaps I will have a proper house for you to live in. That's what I should love to do, you know. If I could get some local help to get this house put to rights, I think you would be happy to think of coming here for holidays.'

He looked around the living room and I saw it with his eyes. It needed everything mended and made anew. It was shabby and broken down. Even I could feel its sadness. For a moment I wondered if I was completely mad to think of living here alone. But it was a fleeting thought, and as a ray of moonlight lit up the old beams, I was filled with hope.

Brenda Reid was an award-winning producer at the BBC before becoming Head of Drama at Anglia Television. She worked with, amongst others, Rose Tremain, Alan Bennett, Jilly Cooper, P. D. James, Fay Weldon and Lynda la Plante and was also the executive producer of the popular series *Ballykissangel*. Brenda now divides her time between the Welsh borders, her children's houses in London and her village house in Crete.

The House of Dust and Dreams

BRENDA REID

An Orion paperback

First published in Great Britain in 2010
by Orion
This paperback edition published in 2011
By Orion Books Ltd,
Orion House, 5 Upper St Martin's Lane,
London WC2H 9EA

An Hachette UK company

1 3 5 7 9 10 8 6 4 2

A CIP catalogue record for this book
is available from the British Library.

ISBN 978-1-4091-2013-1

Typeset at The Spartan Press Ltd,
Lymington, Hants

Printed and bound by CPI Group (UK) Ltd,
Croydon, CR0 4YY

www.orionbooks.co.uk

For David with all my love

ACKNOWLEDGEMENTS

This is for Iannis, Catherine, Giorgios, Isabel and the many, many people of south east Crete who, since 1980, have made me feel its is my second home.

I owe so much, over many drafts, to my lovely agent, Zoe Waldie at Rogers, Coleridge and White and because of her, Kate Mills at Orion. No one could want a more caring editor, whose every note I wish I had thought of myself. I also thank Jade Chandler and her colleagues at Orion who have done everything possible to help this dream become a reality.

Thanks also to Helen Papadakis for correcting my bad Greek spellings and grammar, and Orion's copy-editor, Liz Hatherell, for looking after my use of the English language. Any mistakes remaining are only my own.

There is of course a British Embassy in Athens and it was instrumental in getting the King and the royal family across the White Mountains to Egypt and safety. However, Hugh Timberlake was not with them – he is entirely my invention.

In the course of my research I read many books and I am particularly indebted to the late George Psychoundakis who was 'The Cretan Runner' and his translator, Patrick Leigh Fermor. I found so much to move and inspire me in 'Crete 1941 Eyewitnessed', edited by Costas N. Hadjipateras and Maria S. Fafalios and 'The Apple of Discord' by C.M. Woodhouse.

Above all I thank my husband David who, with kindness and humour, is my first editor, my sternest critic and not only my best friend, but my inspiration.

Where are your idle afternoons, your mornings bright with
   sunlight?
Your founts, your belfries in the dusk, your churches pale
   with moonlight?
Where are your dove-white houses now, your soft winds
   and your waters,
Your happy throngs, in summer time, your golden sons and
   daughters?

One fiery moment burnt them all, when roofs and walls
   were riven,
And whirled them flaming to the sky and through the gates
   of Heaven . . .
                    . . . Let us live in peace together in a second
   age of gold,
In honour, freedom, fame and wisdom, like the famous
   Greeks of old!

George Psychoundakis
The Cretan Runner
Translated by Patrick Leigh Fermor

The Island of Crete, Greece

SUMMER 1936

HEAVENLY

I first saw the old Orfanoudakis house on a warm, sunlit afternoon; the only sound a lone bullfrog and the cicadas. The village around it was sleeping. It had taken four hours here up a narrow mountain track from the Sea of Crete below; in a donkey cart owned by a fisherman, Petros.

Our companions were his mother, two of his six children and a crate of squawking chickens. When Petros stopped in the village square he pointed ahead to the house, Hugh's family's house; a majestic structure dominating a row of tiny white houses, their windows like mouseholes. I raced up the steps of the wide street and stopped in front of it.

It was dilapidated certainly, but nothing that couldn't be fixed, I felt sure. I turned in delight to Hugh, but he was struggling with our luggage; the sunlight caught a flash of a silver coin in his hand and there was much kissing and hugging and welcoming cries of 'Kalos orisate' from Petros and his family.

I ran down, but my offers of help were waved aside by Hugh.

'Come and see, it's beautiful!' I cried excitedly. He struggled under the weight of the baggage, his face red and sweating.

'It's really old,' I said, 'and just how it used to be, I think, when your grandfather was here.'

'Great-grandfather,' he muttered, gasping for every breath. I was hugging myself with delight and jumping up and down so hard my straw hat fell off and rolled down the street.

And then he was beside me. 'Christ Almighty, Evadne,' he gasps, 'we can't stay here, it's a ruin.'

I looked at the shutters along the front terrace. I suppose they had no paint left and they were hanging off rather precariously. But the front door, open on one hinge, looked welcoming to me and there were crimson geraniums blooming happily in a large stone amphora on a second terrace above.

'Oh, Hugh, don't be such an old pessimist; a lick of paint, a nail or two and it'll be fine.'

Hugh sighed bleakly as he set the trunks down. 'This, Evadne, is supposed to be our honeymoon. We've been married for two years and never had a proper time to ourselves and now are you telling me I must start hammering and painting?'

'Well, Petros said there were no hotels so we'd better make the best of it, hadn't we? Anyway, I bet it's beautiful inside.' And in my eyes it already was.

The steps leading up to the front door were aged and weathered with brown stringy weeds and yellowing grass pushing up through the cracks. Hugh resisted all my efforts of help and, scarlet-faced with exertion, struggled with insistent determination up step by slow step.

As I crossed over the ancient stones of the threshold, an oddly poignant flicker went through me. The day was bright with sun, but inside the large room that awaited me, it was cool and dim. The rays spilling in at the windows on one wall cast an almost romantic light so that, for a moment or two, the room, even with the sagging beams high in the ceiling and the cracked and broken white walls seemed full of all the dreams I'd ever had and, I believe, all those still to come.

I waded through bits of straw, shredded birds' nests and mountains of dust. Here were all the memories of lives lived to the full and yet only the cicadas outside seemed alive.

This morning it is the mosquito that wakes me; that insistently wretched, whiny buzz. I stretch my arm across the sheet, still warm and damp from the heat of the night, but there is only space. No body there. I stumble out of bed and up the rickety stairs, hanging onto the rope. From the terrace window I can see the first crack of dawn break the sky.

I can also see Hugh on the steamer chair outside. His head back, his mouth open and with every breath, a small snore rumples the silence. It takes only a moment to slip out of my nightgown and into yesterday's dress. It's lying on the floor with all the others – no wardrobe.

Thank goodness for stone floors: no boards creak as I creep out of the house. I pause every few steps and listen; the snores are quiet but regular. He can sleep anywhere, my husband. I once found him at an embassy dance leaning against the wall of the ballroom surrounded by chattering matrons who hadn't noticed they had lost his attention.

It is ten days since we came up that mountain path and every day for me has been a delight. The villagers here have opened their arms and their hearts to us. I have, I think, for the first time in my life a sense of belonging. At first we were just a curiosity. No one here has met an English person before. They struggled with our names but were quickly defeated by Hugh and Evadne so we became 'You' and 'Heavenly'.

I laughed but Hugh said rather crossly, 'They must know Evadne was a Greek goddess!'

I remembered what he had told me, the daughter of Poseidon, but I had seen the blank look in their eyes. 'Apparently not, in this bit of Crete.'

'Its probably the way your're saying it. And I don't for one moment think they're calling you Heavenly. It just sounds like it. Personally I'd be quite happy to settle for Mr and Mrs Timberlake.'

I think any visitor; even from another island, is a subject for gossip and astonishment. A day or so ago Irini from a house along the street paused as she was sweeping and pulled at my arm. 'Athens?' she asked. 'Have you come from Athens?' When I said I had indeed lived there, she took hold of the sleeve of my dress and stroked it. 'Like my niece,' she said, 'she went to Athens once.'

Even so early I am not alone out here; as I walk up the path, there are several villagers on the way to their gardens at the edge of the village and they greet me cheerfully; 'Yiassou', 'Kalimera'. With one or two I exchange a comment about the weather, although so far it seems it is never anything but sunny and clear. With every step the sky lightens a little and over in the east I can see the first rays of today's sun. It will be warm in an hour and very hot in three.

The road where our house is leads with wide steps up, up and round and round. Near the top is a *kafenion* called 'il Piperia' and its courtyard is shaded by a huge and very old, pepper tree from which it takes its name.

This is the only bit of the village that Hugh seems to enjoy.

He sits with the local men as they play cards or backgammon and, spurning the thick, sweet coffee they offer, drinks the local wine or *raki*. This tastes to me like cough mixture. I once suggested I accompany him there, but this was greeted with derision: 'Men only, old girl, strictly a boys' club.' He then strode off up the road, seeming not to notice that any woman he passed stared in horror at his bare legs, frantically crossing herself three times as if she had just been passed by the devil.

Further on up, the road branches off to the school and winds around to the other parts of the village. Just as Petros described on our journey up here, there is the cluster of houses forming *Pano Panagia*, the upper village; self contained almost, sitting atop the rest as if keeping a watchful eye. There is *Mesa*, the middle part; by far the largest, containing our house at the edge. Further down is *Kato*, the lower, snugly tucked in at the bottom. I look about me with delight. Two great ribs of mountains enclose this paradise, the slopes gently falling away beneath. Every curve in the land is like a caress; every view is contained in a frame of cypress and olives.

By the time we arrived here from the embassy in Athens, I

was already in love with the island. And in this village, Panagia Sta Perivolia, and the old house I have just left, I have found somewhere I want to call home.

But only yesterday, a letter arrived asking Hugh how he wanted to arrange our return travel: by ferry or flying boat? And I don't want to leave.

In Athens and the embassy it seems there is nothing but talk of war and the German Chancellor, Hitler. One minute he's a friend, the next he's the enemy. Here in the village, life is so much simpler; it is regulated only by the sun and the moon, the seasons and the crops. I have tried talking to one or two of our neighbours and I know, given a chance, I could get to know them, be happy here, but Hugh can hardly wait to be back to the endless round of parties and receptions we have left behind. He loves all that.

I am up in the hills now, not even overlooking the village far below, and the sun is already higher in the sky; it is going to be a very hot day. It crosses my mind that I should have brought my hat, but at that moment I catch my foot on a stone half hidden under a great golden clump of briar, and fall. A horrid, clumsy fall that has wrenched my ankle round.

Oh bugger! As I try to stand, I fall again; it's sprained, I think.

I manage to get onto all fours and peer around me. I am on one of the ancient goat tracks that pepper these hills and although I can see for miles, there is no sign of anyone. I have no idea where I am. I try to think how long I've been walking: an hour? Longer? And in which direction is the village?

Birds are singing and somewhere, far away, the bells of a flock of goats tinkle.

'Hello, hello. Is there anyone here?' I call.

But out here who on earth is going to hear that bat squeak of a sound? I call again for help, this time in Greek, '*Atrape mou!*' and again as loud as I can, '*Atrape!*' and then, sinking back in desperation, 'Oh damn and bloody hell, won't someone *atrape* me?'

The sun is high and beating down on me, and the fall has

left me giddy and nauseous. There is a tremor of panic and I feel frightened and alone.

And then a moment later, 'Hello!' comes from somewhere and after a pause, 'Where you are?' A miracle. Someone is near and they've spoken in English! I wave my arm in the air as high as I can. 'Hello,' I call again, 'I'm here!' And I can see her now, running towards me. She stops when she reaches me, and looks down in astonishment.

'*Panagia mou!*' she says. I'm not sure calling on the Virgin Mary is going to help me much. But at least she's here.

She is young, probably the same age as me but tiny. Stocky, sturdy but with a lively, twinkly face; golden from the sun, with the rosy cheeks of one who spends a lot of time outdoors. Instantly I am reminded of one of the junior nurses I trained with who laughed easily and made everyone's day brighter.

We speak in a mixture of Greek and English and, in spite of the giddiness, I laugh.

'I'm sorry, I don't know your name. No one here speaks English, so how is it that you do?'

'Anthi,' she says. 'It's short for Rodianthi. I'll explain about the English later. And you are Heavenly, aren't you? Everyone knows you.'

A wave of giddiness sweeps over me and I press my head down between my knees.

'You stay here,' she says. 'I must leave you for a little and get my horse. He is tethered further up the mountain.'

'You will come back, won't you?'

She stands now, very still. 'You don't know me yet, Heavenly, but when you do, you will know I never break my word.'

'You are an angel, Anthi. I hope you and I will be friends.'

It seems to take forever, but it is probably no more than twenty minutes before she is back beside me. She is on her horse and goats are skittering around her. I have closed my eyes and tried to shield my face from the sun.

'Heavenly?' she says, and I look up.

She pulls her straw hat from her head and tries to tug it over my hair. It is hard; my hair is wiry and wild and in this heat, all over the place.

'Put the hat over your face if it won't stay on your head, you are already starting to burn.' She clears a large bundle of grasses from the back of the saddle, throwing them down any old how.

'Anthi, I'm sorry but your goats are attacking me!' And as she quickly moves to shoo them away, one starts to eat my dress and the other is hungrily licking my foot.

'I'm sorry about them,' she says as they move away, bells clinking, and we both laugh.

Between us we manage to get me up into the saddle and she jumps up behind me. '*Entaxi*?' she says. 'You are OK?'

'*Entax.*' And I am, just.

And so we travel home, in considerably more comfort than I could have managed alone.

ANTHI

We don't speak much as we move towards her house. Heavenly, I think, is in pain and although she doesn't complain, her body is tense in my arms as I hold the reins around her. The sweat runs in rivers down my face and neck, soaking into the thin cotton of my shift. In spite of her protests I made her keep the hat. She needs lessons in how to dress for this climate. No hat, and her frock, I can see, is fine linen, layered in tiers of palest green and grey, and underneath what appears to be a silk petticoat. Beautiful certainly, costly I am sure, but not appropriate for a ride in the hills on days like these.

I look at her, this strange and rather wonderful-seeming creature they call Heavenly; like something out of a story, come to earth in the hills of Panagia. Her hair is a shining golden red and stands out like a halo all around her face in curls and waves. It must be painful to brush. She is a little older than me, I think, but she looks young. The eyes that look back at me from time to time are the colour of fresh spring grass. I can tell her legs are long and her arms too. In spite of all the finery, I can see that her hands, gripping the pommel of the saddle, are tough hands, working hands.

From the village square and the small hall that serves as our community centre, we ride up the steps to Heavenly's house. As soon as we turn, I see the tall figure of her husband outside, and as we approach I see the anxiety creasing what is a handsome face. Behind him are the Kanavakis brothers, Spiro and Katis, two of the biggest raki drinkers in the village.

They look odd in contrast with the tall fair Englishman; two swarthy, fat shepherds beside a china figurine. He runs down the steps, gesturing the others to follow.

'My dear, what on earth happened to you?' The three of them struggle clumsily to lift her down.

'I feel very silly,' she says, 'but I tripped over, sprained my ankle, I think, and probably would have died if Anthi here hadn't rescued me.'

He carries her through the house and she smiles back at me. She already looks better, just being in his arms. 'Come on, Anthi, we need a drink, we've earned it!' I tether Astrape outside and climb the steps.

I think I had been in the old Orfanoudakis house as a child, but for years it has been empty and shuttered. No one in the village seems to know its story, only that English people owned it and have now come to live in it.

I gasp aloud as I go inside; it seems as if I have entered a cave, so dark and musty, so cool after the heat of the day outside. The room we are in is vast. At one end I can dimly see that there is a wine press and what is probably furniture, but it is piled in heaps in a corner, and what feels like a century's worth of dust rises as we step across the floor. As my eyes grow accustomed to the gloom, I can see there is a faded beauty here, and Heavenly's laughter seems to bring it to life.

There is a high, beamed ceiling and the bamboo struts across it are cracked, the daub and wattle hanging down, moving gently in the breeze. The dust tickles my nose and a stream of sneezes come out.

The Englishman she calls You smiles as he places her carefully on an army camp bed at one end of this great room.

'I can see you are shocked,' he says, 'but my wife insists we stay here in this broken-down wreck.'

'Stop complaining and make us coffee and pour some brandy for your guests.'

The Kanavakis brothers bow hastily, giving embarrassed glances in my direction, and back out of the door, muttering goodbye. I think they have had several brandies here this morning and they are off now, I guess, to the Piperia to have a few more. With their departure I feel curiously alone. There is an unspoken intimacy between this English couple. He is moving around what I guess is some sort of makeshift kitchen while talking over his shoulder to her.

He is a handsome man; his fair hair flops into his eyes and he is clean-shaven. I'm not used to that. But the first thing that is really strange are his trousers. They stop at the knee, leaving his lower legs bare. I have never seen a man's bare legs before, and I turn quickly away, feeling myself begin to blush. My husband Manolis takes his clothes off in the dark, or sometimes sleeps in them. Certainly no Greek man would wear such revealing trousers.

I sit beside Heavenly on the floor and You hands us brandy in cups, but I realise I have been away most of the morning and I have duties and must be gone. I gulp my brandy and rise to leave. Heavenly catches my hand. 'Promise me you will come back soon?'

'I will, I really will.'

I ride away across the horizon, blue and sunlit. Seabirds are wheeling inland. I can see the village below, sheltering in the side of the mountain.

I like this Heavenly, I hope she stays. I can't see her house any longer, but I can see the row of cypress trees nearby. They were planted by my great-great-grandfather, and they always make me think of my father; he loved them. I still miss him so much. He would like Heavenly, I know it. I remember now one night, I was eight years old and I heard him tell my mother I was special – different – not only to my brother and sister but to all the other children in the village. I liked to hear this, so I listened more. 'She could read when she was four,' he said, 'do her numbers when only five. That is special.' My mother said something I couldn't hear and laughed. My father roared back at her. 'Never!' he said. 'This child will stay at school. Go to the college in Heraklion if we can make it happen. Travel the world. Be a proud woman. You and

Ririca' – she's my sister – 'will sew her trousseau if she wants one. Anthi will do better things than any of us.'

But when I was ten my father died and his dreams died with him. My mother and my uncle made what they thought was a good marriage for me and at sixteen, I was the wife of Manolis Manadakis; at seventeen, the mother of Despina; at eighteen, my son Constantinos was born after only six and a half months in my belly; then, at twenty-one, my beautiful Voula was born to me.

I am home now, and as I pass our animal room, the door swings dangerously, straining the broken hinge. For weeks now I have asked Manolis to mend it. Huh! Wait for sheep to sing in tune, I think.

As I dismount, I feel a soreness between my legs. I rub myself there softly. Manolis was drunk again last night and the memory of his violent thrusting in me still hurts.

There must be better ways to show love than to cause this burning? I smell clean, at least. I have learnt to get up as soon as he's done and wash myself, rinse away his mess. He is always snoring by then, the moment he rolls off me, and if I am careful like this there will be no more babies.

I am so late home! These long summer days when I don't go to help in the school are precious. I am not used to idleness. I'll finish hiving the bees and then go to collect Despina and little Voula. They have been with my neighbour, Maria, playing with her daughter Athena. Voula is too young to play but she loves to be with her sister. She will surely be wanting my milk now.

As if she sensed me, I hear a small cry from Maria's house. Quickly I am there and Voula is in my arms. Her dark eyes are open and she is smiling already. I'll take her with me to the bees and feed her there under the olives.

Her soft, warm plumpness is like a piece of heaven in my arms; the milky smell of her, the dark curling wisps of her hair and those velvet eyes I could look into all day. I am lucky in my girls; they came into the world laughing and seem never to have stopped. Even Manolis, when he is sober, can only gaze at them, astonished that these little peaches are the product of his angry coupling between sheets damp with his sweat.

My hat is crammed onto my head and as I bend to Despina, it falls to the ground. I pick it up and as I raise it I can smell a faint, delicious perfume. Heavenly! I remember that red-gold hair of hers, so different to mine. My hair is like a thorn bush. When I married Manolis it was my shining crown, now it already has streaks of silver – twenty-two years old and hair like my grandmother! As we walk to the bees, I remember how buxom I was on my wedding day; round and firm, just how my bridegroom liked me. But I quickly learnt to become what he didn't want – that way he left me alone.

So now I am more like a carrot than a peach – my body is hard, tough. I prefer it this way; muscled from the work, and soft – well, huh! slack – around the belly from the babies. My body, my hair, my thoughts and my heart, they are mine. This is who I am.

HEAVENLY

'Funny little woman.'

'Oh, Hugh, is that all you can say? I thought she was very special, and she did save my life. If it weren't for her, I'd still be lying on the side of a mountain, burnt to a cinder by the sun.'

Hugh loped across the room and patted me gently on the head.

'Oh, dearest, please don't get steamed up. I was worried, you know, but what could I do? I'd no idea where you'd gone and anyway, you know you would hate it if I came running after you.' His eyes are so soft and kind, a pleading in them for understanding, forgiveness. 'Please, let's go home.' He is actually on his knees now, a quiet desperation in his eyes.

'Home? Where's home?' I ask it gently, for his eyes are alight at the very thought of leaving this house, this village.

And here is the problem, and sometimes it seems small, just a little difference between us; other times it is as big as the world.

I don't want to go back to Athens and that embassy life and Hugh does.

This beautiful old house, nestling warmly into the side of the hill, its stones soaking in the golden sun over the mountains and sea of Crete are exactly where I want to be. I see it in the future, filled with rugs and hangings, comfy old furniture and children laughing from room to room.

Hugh sees it only as the ruin it is now. He sees nothing but the holes in the roof. The beams of the ceiling I see rich with

15

the deep blue of new paint he sees as precarious mantraps that will fall at any moment. From the terrace I look down to the still blue sea and think of swimming, while Hugh looks down and sees a life-threatening donkey track as the only way out.

I know that we must make a decision soon.

I dread returning to our life in the British Embassy in Athens; supposed to be our home.

We arrived there a long year ago, from a short posting in Paris, and I had done everything I thought was expected of a diplomat's wife. I learnt Greek. I went to tea parties with the other wives. I took part in endless discussions about hairdressers and dressmakers. In truth I was bored to within an inch of running away. I had read every book in the embassy library . . . well no, not quite true – I had passed by the shelf of motorcar handbooks.

The excitement among the wives reached a peak with the abdication of the King. They all clustered round the wireless to listen to his speech to the nation from Windsor Castle, twittering like magpies. In fact we had known for days that this was to happen, so I found it hard to join in the thrill of it all.

And then there were the never-ending speculations about Wallis Simpson: her hair, her clothes, her shoes, her waistline. All this made me feel like the most frightful snob, as though I was somehow better than them, which is simply not true. I am genuinely sad that I can find so little in common. I would love to have a friend. For one thing, none of them have ever worked. Never, ever earned any money. Well, Nancy, Malcolm Fitzwilliam's wife, accompanied an elderly great-aunt round the Peloponnesus the year before she married him, but I don't feel that quite counts.

When Hugh was asked to come to Crete to sort out some minor demonstrations that were taking place at the tomb of Venizelos, near Chania, it seemed all my prayers had been answered. At first he thought to make the trip alone, but I am afraid I made rather a fuss and he brought me too.

The king had asked the ambassador for help in a potentially tricky situation and Hugh had been entrusted with the seemingly important task of political manoeuvring for the king, who had recently returned from twelve years in exile. I was thrilled to think of us, well me anyway, involved in the real world. This was what I thought we would be doing all the time.

But sadly I was considered to be merely the wife, a minor irritant – 'Send her shopping or to poke around a museum then pack her off to get her hair done and have lunch' – whilst I longed to be part of the team, or at least to understand what was going on. Before we left Athens I read as much recent history of the country as I could find. I knew the importance of Venizelos, who had died only a short time ago and was buried here, in Crete, the island of his birth.

I had come to understand the tension in the air when Venizelos was spoken of. He had tried to turn the country into a democracy, but there was strong opposition from the royalists and he had major battles with General Metaxas, the king's choice of leader. I liked the sound of this Venizelos, but Hugh looked blank when I said so.

'Don't involve yourself with things you don't understand, darling,' he said.

Actually, I think I understood more than some of his colleagues, but of course I couldn't say so; women's opinions are considered to be of little or no worth. For instance, Foxy was puzzled that Venizelos had been buried very quickly.

'You'd have thought a chap like that would have a proper lying-in-state,' I heard him say to Hugh as they played billiards one night in the embassy.

'Dangerous times, these, old boy,' said Hugh, as he cannoned his ball in off the red. (I remembered to stay quiet, and not acknowledge the move. Women were only allowed in the games room on sufferance.) 'Don't forget, not so long ago the communists held the balance of power here. The important thing now is to keep them happy. Not keep reminding them what a good chap Venizelos was; all those social reforms he made are enough as a memorial, don't you think? Give him a damn great funeral in the middle of Athens and all hell could break out. It's bad enough having him stuck in Crete, where he's still causing trouble from his grave. And not too many questions from you, old girl. At least we get ourselves away. Hopefully we can get the business sorted quickly and have that honeymoon we've never managed before, eh?'

I longed for that; time alone together. At last, some time we could give to each other without another meeting, another party, another dinner. It is impossible for me to say this to him, of course, he would be so hurt. Hugh loves the life in Athens, and spends much of his time playing, but he is still my own darling Hugh and that, I'm sure, will always be true.

By the time we arrived in Chania, the trouble was more or less sorted, so we decided to travel across the island and find this old house that had been in his family for ages. One of his grandfather's brothers had married a Greek heiress. She owned two houses in Thessaloniki, and this one in Crete. Travel being so much more difficult back then, they never came here. Imagine! A couple had lived in it for years, in theory to look after it, but when they died it stayed shut up and falling apart, until now. Hugh having no brothers, it eventually came to him. How lucky we are. Ever since we first set foot in it, I have felt happy – as though I belong here.

After Athens, where life was one seemingly endless round of formality, this island was like arriving in heaven. The villagers are so wonderfully welcoming and kind. There is much poverty outside the cities, but everywhere we went we were showered with gifts – it seemed that whatever you had you shared with a visitor. And, oh, the beauty of the hills around us! Crete has only been part of Greece for twenty years or so, one coast looking towards the Balkans and the other to Arabian Africa.

And there is careless history in every stone and fractured pillar. Round every corner not only sweet-scented flowers, but the sudden chink of an ancient pavement under one's feet, preserved for who knows how long while the flocks of goats trod it into the earth.

'Help me up, and get me out onto the terrace. I'm sure looking down to the sea will make us both feel better.'

He sighed and, helping me to my feet, half-dragged me, half-carried me outside. It was painful, more than I had expected; my arm too, was very sore. But in a haphazard way, we were now out in the fresh, sweet air. I was on one of a pair of long carved chairs and Hugh on a stiff upright bench that looked wildly uncomfortable. But even he couldn't resist the lure of the mountains for long and his eyes followed the curve of the crags down to the sea far below. Turning, he gave me a smile, a special Hugh smile and, even though I was hurting, I smiled back.

'That's better, isn't it? Could you be an angel and get me an aspirin?'

An hour or so later we were still on the terrace. The pain was dulled and Hugh was dozing.

The first time I saw him, he was asleep. Well, not so much asleep as unconscious. He was on his way to my ward from the operating theatre at the hospital where I was working. As the porters wheeled him in, his feet were dangling over the edge of the trolley. Mr Timpson Carter had removed his appendix and he was going to be in my care for the next ten days.

'One, two, three, over.' The porters heaved him onto the bed, but his feet wouldn't tuck in tidily. Matron would be here in ten minutes and she'd go wild if the ward, or any of the patients, were in a mess. Hard as I tried, I simply could not get anything right in her eyes.

I was one of the youngest nurses in Greenbridge Hospital and Matron must have been part of the panel that selected me. I can't think why, as she seemed to do nothing but find fault. I'd passed all my first year exams and I loved nursing, but neat and tidy, as she'd like me to be, I was not.

Actually, I've never been much good at anything. I grew up

in the shadow of my perfect sister. Where I am gawky, she is elegant. Where my hair is ginger and crinkly, hers is silky and auburn. Where my skin throws out freckles at the first hint of summer, Daphne's is creamy smooth with a faint hint of a golden blush.

I am hopeless at any kind of sport and I seem to be all big feet and bent knees at dances, a lost cause. The best thing was when I was sent away to school. At Maple House there were lots of girls who weren't up to much, so at last I fitted in. I never lived at home again, so there was a certain relief that I wouldn't be sitting around the house rather pointedly not being invited to tennis parties or dances.

After my father died, my mother had even less time for us. She was on many charity committees and was constantly organising fêtes or sales of work. She was the district organiser for the Red Cross and a gathering of strangers in a church hall somewhere, always had needs greater than mine. She would say, 'For people like us, duty is never finished. It is expected of someone in my position, you see. My life is not my own.' Secretly, I wondered whose it was – it certainly wasn't mine.

She always seemed to be walking in the opposite direction, away from me. I would call to her and she would look over her shoulder at me, smile sometimes, but walk on.

I remember it was a glorious spring day when Hugh Timberlake came into my life. Most of the patients on the ward were elderly, and varied from cranky and fed-up to really miserable and whingey. Hugh was none of these. The funny thing was, I hadn't even looked properly at his face and when I did, I could see he was very handsome. He had shaggy hair, fair, that threatened to fall into his eyes, a straight nose, quite classical, and his skin was a light gold, as though he spent time in the sun. He was altogether delicious.

I gathered his notes together and put them in a folder at the foot of his bed. Hugh Timberlake: even his name sounded romantic. At the top end of the bed he had started to snuffle a little, so I moved round to bend close and listen.

'Sorry, nurse, I think I'm going to be—' And he was, all down the front of my clean apron. I was so busy looking at his green eyes that I completely forgot one of the first rules of nursing: always approach a post-op patient with a bowl in your hand. And now here were Matron and Sister approaching. I stood up, feebly tugging at the sheet. I was taller than either of them, and how they hated it.

'My goodness, what a mess you are, Tyler. Stand up straight, girl!' That was me, Tyler. Just like a boys' school, we were all surnames there.

'Sorry, Sister, Matron,' I mumbled as I uncurled my shoulders and straightened my knees. Matron raised an eyebrow and Sister went 'Tsk, tsk', before moving on.

One of the main things that mattered was always to be clean and tidy, just like the ward. This is the bit I fell down on, day after day. If there was some blood or sick around, it always seemed to end up on me. Once, in Women's Surgical, a bed pan tilted over. I was in the sluice at the time and yards away, but I absolutely swear the urine crept round the corner and aimed for my clean apron. I certainly had a yellow stain, and I'd no other idea how it got there.

I also have a real problem with my hair. It is red and jumps out all around my head. Even when I pinned it up with a helmet of hair clips and squeezed it under my stiff cap – that grim linen semi-circle we made up into its shape each morning – it still sprang out and I'd frequently find strands glued to my face or, even worse, flying around the ward. I had it cut into a bob, but that didn't work either, it seemed to stick out even more. The patients teased me about it constantly. Once, one found a hairgrip at the bottom of his cup after he'd drunk his cocoa.

My hands are all right, although they always appear too big to me. 'Your hands are your best feature, Evadne,' my mother would say, with desperation in her voice. I must be very plain, I thought, looking at the long, broad fingers, if these are prettier than my face.

Hugh Timberlake was on the ward for a fortnight and for

barely a moment of that time was he alone. He seemed always to be surrounded by women. Some were nurses. Plenty came from other wards when Sister wasn't around just to have a look at him; it was rare in Greenbridge to have handsome young men with their own teeth. As for visitors, well there were bevies of pretty girls fluttering around him like butterflies. Staff Nurse had to ring the bell at the end of visiting three or four times before they could be persuaded to scuttle away; manicured fingers waving in the air, blowing lipstick kisses behind them and coquettishly swirling their flowery, frilly and expensive silk frocks.

One day his mother came to see him. I know because he actually introduced me to her. She sat beside his bed and held his hand throughout.

'Mother, this is Nurse Tyler.' Of course I blushed bright red. I didn't know he even knew my name.

She was completely charming and smiled warmly at me as she shook my hand, which she held as she thanked me for looking after her son so well.

I blushed again, of course, and said I was only one of many.

She was what my mother would call a handsome woman. She looked very like him, the same green eyes. She had a lovely smile. It seemed that, after Hugh's father died, she had remarried and lived with her husband in Ireland. She had come over to sort out some family affairs and made time to see her son before going back the next day. She stayed for the entire two hours and kissed him on the forehead as she left.

'Her husband breeds horses,' Hugh said to me as I changed his sheets the next morning. 'I think he looks like a horse. I can't think what she sees in him. She was devastated when my father died. It was so unfair, he'd fought and survived all through the war and then died of the flu. He was quite a hero: he was a major in the East Surrey regiment, decorated at Ypres. And now she's married to this boring chap.'

'Perhaps she needed company. It must be so very lonely to be a widow.'

'Do you know, I'd never thought of that,' he said. 'How wise you are. You're probably right. I was away at Winchester, so there was no one for her to talk to.'

When I was changed over to the night shift, he would sometimes persuade me to linger by his bed, and we would share a whispered conversation. Until one night he said, 'I'm out of here tomorrow, nurse, and I don't even know your Christian name.'

'It's Evadne,' I whispered. I knew he was smiling.

'It's a lovely name; Evadne, the daughter of Poseidon, the sea god. Did you know that?'

'No,' I whispered back, thinking, But I'll never forget it now.

And then I was busy and of course when I went in the next evening he was gone and a grim old vicar had taken his place, wearing his dog collar over his pyjamas and a large cross on his bedhead.

It was one day, about a week later, that I went with Maisie, one of the other nurses, to tea at the Copper Kettle in Greenbridge High Street. It was a treat for us – we usually went to the ABC.

We were lingering over a cucumber sandwich when Maisie peered past me and gasped. 'Don't look now,' she said, 'but that patient just walked in. You know, the good-looking one with all the girl friends'.

I froze, not daring to peek behind me. All I could think was, thank goodness I was wearing one of my sister's frocks and a decent pair of stockings.

He walked right past us, almost touching my chair, and sat at a table across the room. He was alone.

The waitress brought him a menu, but he pushed it aside and I heard him say, 'Just a cup of tea please. Darjeeling if you have it.' And he flashed the waitress that lovely smile he had. As she scurried away, looking pink and flustered, he caught sight of us.

'He's waving us over,' Maisie whispered, 'what shall we do?' As we dithered, I saw him get to his feet and come over to us.

'Hello, girls,' he said, 'what a lovely surprise. May I join you?'

Before I thought of anything to say, Maisie, blushing furiously, was on her feet. 'Here, have my chair,' she said, 'I've got an anatomy lesson in twenty minutes.' And she was on her way out, leaving a shilling on the tablecloth as she went.

I can't really remember any of the things we talked about that afternoon. I just know that half an hour went whizzing by in a flash before there was a shriek and a squeal and a gorgeous girl appeared over my shoulder.

'Hugh, darling!' she squeaked. 'I'm so terribly sorry. Am I unforgivably late?' He was on his feet in a moment and her arms were round his neck. 'Sorry, sorry, angel,' she said. I couldn't hear the rest as I was too busy trying to get up without knocking over the little gilt chair.

'Here,' I said, 'have my seat, I have to go anyway.' And, knowing I was blushing horribly, I was on my way to the door.

'Excuse me, miss,' said the waitress as I passed her, 'that's one and ninepence, if you don't mind.'

Somehow I managed to get out of there. Hugh had insisted on paying for Maisie and me. He pointed out that Maisie had left a shilling towards it anyway.

I walked along Greenbridge High Street in a daze. How foolish to think anything of it at all. He was merely being polite, talking to me while waiting for his girlfriend. I tried to think no more about him and as the days passed in sleep and the nights were busy, I concentrated on the coming exams.

One day, Sister grabbed my arm as I was coming on duty. 'Got a job for you, Tyler. Help out the St John brigade tomorrow afternoon.'

I must have looked puzzled.

'There's a garden party, fête sort of thing at Lady Trout-beck's. Extra pair of hands needed. They usually fork out a good deal for us at Christmas, so Matron said you should go.

Pick up two o'clock from the nurses' home.' Before I could even think of a question, she turned back and gave me one of those awful Sister looks, up and down. 'Try and look a bit decent, will you? Clean uniform, including cuffs, and for goodness sake, comb your hair!'

I was hardly at my best the following afternoon. I knew I'd barely scraped through a rather important viva on fractures in the morning. I'm hopeless at bones and the examiners, two of them, all steely grey hair and grim faces, were clearly unimpressed.

On top of that, the vicar had a bout of sickness in the night, and I'd had to wash and somehow dry my uniform at half past five this morning. It was still damp and creased at five to two, but I had to wriggle into it anyway.

I'd used a dozen massive hairpins and scraped my hair into a sort of bun on top of my head, but as I rushed past a mirror in the hall I could see it was already on its way down my neck and would, more than likely, be on my shoulders by the time I got to wherever I was going.

And then, of all things, oh horrible nasty fate, Mr Hugh Timberlake was standing in the hall. He grinned when he saw me. I gave a flustered smile while trying to hold my hair back up. 'Are you waiting for someone?' I thought I'd better ask.

'You,' he said, 'I'm waiting for you.'

I must have looked completely stunned and inanely said, 'Me? You're waiting for me ?'

'I believe it's you that's coming to do a spot of first aiding at the fete? Well, I've come to take you there.' And he gave an exaggerated bow, then stood up, took my arm, and led me through the great oak door.

He was several inches taller even than me, and I found myself looking up into his eyes. A faint, exciting scent of cigars and eau de cologne emanated from him and gold links gleamed from the pristine cuffs that covered a hint of golden hairs gleaming enticingly.

'I'm not sure I—' I began, but he put his finger on my mouth and led me in the direction of the drive. Parked there was a low-slung grey-and-silver car. He swung open the passenger door and as I moved towards it to get in, it fell off and clattered to the ground. I thought immediately it must be my fault and gasped, 'Oh, sorry.'

He laughed, seeming unbothered, and picking up the door in one hand he somehow managed to twist it back on its gaping hinges. 'It falls off at least once a week. It's a terrible old wreck.' I looked at this beautiful machine and realised it was covered in dents and bumps and scratches.

In a cloud of evil-smelling black smoke, we chugged off out of the grounds of the nurses' home and up Greenbridge High Street.

'Shall I tell you the truth, Evadne?' I nodded, which was a mistake as the movement finished off the bun for ever, and I felt my hair tumbling down to my shoulders.

'Dora told me the St John ambulance lot were short of people and I suggested she ring the hospital and ask her friend the Matron to let you out for the afternoon.'

I was scrabbling around to try and get my hair back up and started to ask, 'Why me?' when I remembered I'd left my cap on the dressing table. I thought I might burst into tears, but he put his hand on my knee, only for a moment though, and said, 'Stop worrying about whatever it is you're worrying about and give me one of those big smiles you have.'

'Have I?' I said, astonished, and he laughed.

'You are a funny one, Miss Poseidon. I don't think you have any idea how lovely you are, do you?'

I shook my head, bewildered, and the last few strands of hair dropped down and a huge metal hairpin pinged off and landed in his lap.

The afternoon passed for me in a daze. Dora turned out to be Lady Troutbeck and he had been staying with her when he was taken ill and brought into the hospital.

It was only later, after I had joined the two jolly plump girls at the St John first-aid tent, that I felt more at ease. Together we fanned and gave seats to swooning old ladies gasping for sal volatile, or put ammonia on wasp stings, or bandaged the odd child who'd tumbled off the swings or the roundabout.

As the crowds drifted away, our little tent was finally empty. Hugh reappeared to take me by the arm to be introduced to Lady Troutbeck. She was seated on a vividly striped lounging chair on the terrace, exquisitely dressed in a riot of coloured silks and clutching a large empty glass. She smiled vaguely at me but carried on talking to the group of pretty girls around her.

'Rather too much gin and not enough "it" I think,' said Hugh as he led me to a small table on the now almost deserted lawn. 'Wait here,' he said, 'don't move.'

He vanished, to reappear a few moments later with two glasses of champagne. We stayed there for ages, until the sun began to go down, and I suddenly realised the time and leapt up. 'I must get back,' I said, 'I'm on duty in an hour.'

He had been engaging and delightful, and more than anything, he made me laugh. Whether he was speaking about his job as a junior civil servant in Whitehall or his family, who seemed to be spread all over the world, or my life at the hospital, everything was a cause for his gentle wit. He seemed so comfortable in himself that, within moments, I felt relaxed and happy too. We also talked a little, as we had done on those long evenings on the ward, of more serious things. He was working hard to pass the Foreign Office entrance exams as he wanted to work abroad; he wanted to be part of an effort to present a positive face of Britain by working in an embassy. He took my arm as we walked back to his car. 'Dear daughter of Poseidon, when can I see you again?'

'I am on nights for another two weeks . . .'

'Tomorrow afternoon then?'

'Well, I am supposed to sleep during the day or I get—'

'Tomorrow afternoon it is then. You can sleep in the morning and I will collect you at two.' As we got into his car, this time without any mishaps, he said with a smile, 'By the way, I love your hair down.'

*

After that I saw Hugh every minute I could escape from the hospital. I was living in a curious world between life and death; bandages and decay, or cocktails and dancing. Rushing from one life to another was, apart from being strange to me, completely exhausting. Sometimes, as I wearily crawled into the nurses' home by the landing window, I wondered how long I could last in this confusion before I started dancing through the ward with a glass in my hand or asking the head waiter at Claridges if his bowels had been open today.

From this moment on, it seemed as though Hugh had rescued me from a dull and predictable life. It seemed that, far from being invisible, I was noticed and even sometimes admired.

The most important thing of all was that I forgot about myself. I no longer stood with my knees bent or my shoulders rounded. I was so busy looking out at the world now that I forgot to look into myself.

This was the greatest gift Hugh gave me – myself. I no longer cared only how others saw me. Through Hugh my confidence grew. He told me I was beautiful. He didn't seem to notice that my hands were the best things about me.

Everywhere we went he knew people. 'You have so many friends,' I said one night as the silver car stumbled me back to the nurses' home.

He waved his hand dismissively. 'You haven't met my real friends yet. Well, Dora Troutbeck, now she's a chum.'

I wasn't sure why, but a shiver of unease flickered through me. Was it that Dora Troutbeck was the one person who didn't seem to like me? She was always charming and polite, but there was a brittle surface there, in her brilliantly coloured garb. A sugared almond, I thought her; pink or cream on the outside and a tough little nut inside. We visited her house often and it was always full of the glittering people that she and Hugh liked.

I dismissed these thoughts, these doubts.

I learned to walk tall, to look at the world around me, and

lose myself in it. I had no need or room for shame or shuffling embarrassment.

And not for a moment did I question this; ask myself if it was what I wanted. Why would I?

I had never envisaged happiness in my blueprint for the future, never experienced it, so for all this I could only thank Hugh. And when one night under the stars he asked me to marry him, I thought I could know no greater joy and said, 'Yes please' without another thought.

ANTHI

'Is it far, Mama?'

Despina's question takes me by surprise. I was daydreaming about the Orfanoudakis house and the time I had been there with Heavenly just a few days ago. Hoping so much that we should see each other again soon.

'You know when you can see our house from the top of the hill, then we are nearly home.'

'I'm hot, Mama, too hot.' Her voice is little more than a croak. I sigh, but do not waste my breath on an answer. Voula is strapped by a shawl to my back and if the rhythm of my walking changes for even a moment she will wake and cry piteously; and that will just be too much because here, a short way from the fields we have left behind us, there is no shade, no shelter, and I cannot stop and nourish her here in the middle of the path.

'Please, Mama, please can I sit on Astrape? Just for a little, little bit?'

'Vespoula *mou*, you know why that is not possible. You are seven now and far too heavy for poor old Astrape. He is loaded down, just as we are.'

We are all carrying home the sacks we have filled with the leaves of the tobacco plants we have just stripped. I think I have chosen the hottest day of the year to harvest the crop. We left the house at first light, the three of us, while Manolis still slept and, only pausing for some cheese and fruit with bread, we have worked until now. Looking at the harsh sun above us, I think it is about four or five o'clock, no time for a rest for me this afternoon.

'How many more corners, Mama?'

Through the sweat dulling my vision I can see her little face, creased and damp like mine.

'Not many, *koritsaki mou*, and then you will see our garden and the tall marigolds will wave their heads to welcome you home.'

Manolis is tending the sheep today. This means that he will be sitting in the shade of a pomegranate tree in the top pasture with a flask of raki beside him. Poor man, how hard is his life! The tobacco will not wait so we have to do it for him.

The seabirds wheel and cry hungrily in the sky, only to remind me that when I get home I must prepare an evening meal and I have picked no *horta* or wild spinach or vegetables today, so it will take even longer.

We have one of the largest farmsteads in the whole of Panagia. That is why my mother arranged this marriage. Me? I would be happy with one garden, two goats and six chickens.

We can afford to hire in casual labourers and travellers from other villages to help us, sometimes. But still the bulk of the work falls to Manolis and, of course, now to me. Apart from the wheat and my bees, I must constantly tend my garden crops: lettuce, radish, spring onions, tomatoes, courgettes and broad beans. I am lucky that our garden surrounds our house; most of the villagers must walk each day to their plots on the edges of the village.

Apart from the wheat and maize crops, the pine trees and the sheep, Manolis and his brother Stelios own more olive trees than anyone hereabouts and, unusually for this area, many and abundant vines. The red wine they produce each year is rich and strong. Stelios is the treader. Since he was a young man, at the end of each summer, he is much in demand from as far away as Palio Kastro to spend a day treading for family and friends. His feet are magic.

31

I am considered better than many, I think, and one reason why, of which I am justly proud, is my horse, Astrape. The only horse around and he is mine, my very own! He is my escape. In my dreams I pick up Despina and Voula and gallop away over the hills never to return. We go to India, Africa, the Americas, wherever we choose. But it is a long time since Astrape galloped anywhere and his name, meaning lightning, is now something of a joke. Maybe once he had some speed in those long black legs, but he is a comfortable, middle-aged mount now and safe as a rabbit for the girls.

We pass the priest's house. He is outside, fat and complacent like a squatting toad. His eyes travel over my body as I acknowledge him. Lecherous old goat!

'Good afternoon, Papa Yannis,' I murmur, but he is too busy staring at my breasts to answer me.

My mother thinks he is wonderful and I blame him as much as her for my marriage. I remember well the night back then when it all started.

My mother had been cooking all day for the celebration of my sister's name day. Toiling at the hot oven did her no favours. Her face had reddened with the exertion and her nose glowed like a beacon.

She is a very thin woman: at least that is how she likes to present herself. She binds her body under her clothes. I know this because I saw her one night when she thought I was asleep.

Ririca favours my mother in looks as well as temperament. She is bony in her youthfulness. Our mother is very protective of her and slaps me hard if she catches me saying she has a nose like a clothes pin.

In the evening all the uncles arrived with their wives and my cousins. The men, as always, sat around the table, the women and children squashed in a corner together. By nine o'clock, the raki was sinking lower in the jugs and the laughter was echoing round the walls of our good room. Even the virgin in the *iconostasis* on the wall seemed to be smiling. There was a noise outside and Papa Yannis came in, rubbing his hands together and calling greetings to everyone. Behind him was old man Manadakis, another fat, ugly creature who was a cantor in the church and often seen visiting Papa Yannis. I wondered why he should be here? He had no connection with our family – certainly my father had disliked him.

My mother grabbed my arm and pulled me with her into the kitchen. It was like a furnace; the great oven through the wall had been working for hours, churning out trays of cheese pies, spinach tarts, a great dish of *pastitsio* and the whole of a goat slaughtered in honour of my sister's day. I thought back to my name day. I had to make do with my two aunts and their daughters coming for coffee and an almond biscuit.

'From now on,' my mother said, 'you will spend time with me in here. You must learn women's duties, and we will start with cooking.'

She marched back into the good room and I made to follow her, holding a tray of honey cakes. Ririca put her hand out to stop me.

'Want to know why you are going to learn to cook?' she whispered, a nasty little smile creasing her face.

'You are obviously going to tell me,' I said.

'You are going to be married to old Manadakis's son.' She was so gleeful to be able to tell me this I could have hit her.

'I am thirteen years old, I am not going to marry anybody.'

'When you are sixteen, silly.' She giggled. 'I heard Mama and Uncle Lukas talking last night. That's why the priest has brought him here tonight.'

I was furious, not only that I was to be married, but also that Ririca should know and I did not.

Our mother was calling for us to take the food in, so there was nothing more I could say just now, but I looked very carefully at the man sitting beside Papa Yannis and tried to remember what his son was like. I hoped he looked better than his father, who sat like a great drop of olive oil, sweating and greasy. His arms, resting on the table in front of him, were covered in a pelt of black hair like a fur. As I moved

33

around the table to pass the food, I caught a breath of his odour; garlic and incense, mixed with about a litre of raki – disgusting!

Late in the evening the Manadakis sons arrived to escort their father home. Just as well, I thought, he was so drunk he could hardly stand unaided. They carried musical instruments with them, a lyre and an accordion, as they had been playing at a wedding in a village across the mountain the day before. There were calls for them to give us music now. They played well; old Cretan songs that Stelios, the younger brother, sang with a clear, true voice. I looked at him curiously as they played; I supposed he was quite good-looking in a rough sort of way.

He was swarthy, dark, with a fine moustache of golden brown strands, curled at the ends. I barely looked at his brother who was so much older. At his age he would be long married, with several children.

When everyone had left that night, I helped my mother clear all the dishes, plates and glasses into the kitchen. Ririca had gone to her bed long before. Clearly, counting the money and gifts she had been given had exhausted her.

'When is my wedding supposed to be?' I asked my mother, as casually as if asking about tomorrow's weather.

As I knew she would, she looked at me in astonishment. 'What do you mean?' she said.

'Why, my wedding to the son of Manadakis, Mama, what else?' I was pleased I could remain so cool and detached, when part of me wanted to scream and stamp my foot in rage.

'How do you know of this?'

'Ririca told me, Mama,' I said sweetly. I knew this would make her furious, so there was a certain delight in saying it.

Her next words, however, filled me with horror.' You will marry Manolis Manadakis when you are sixteen,' she said.

'Manolis?' I almost couldn't breathe. Manolis was the elder of the two brothers. She must be making a mistake. 'I can't marry Manolis, he is much, much too old!'

'He is only forty, Anthi, a fine age; why, he's barely older than me.' She was smiling smugly now, having recaptured her advantage over me.

'Then why don't you marry him?' I said, and for a moment I thought she was going to slap me.

'Enough!' she said. 'You will go to bed now and tomorrow the first thing you do will be to help me clean and clear the mess here. Then you will have your first lesson in cooking.'

'But tomorrow is a day when I help in the school—'

'First things come first. Cleaning and cooking are much more important. When you have time, if you have time, you may continue to help in the school.' She swung round and went through the door, paused, and over her shoulder said, 'That is for now. Perhaps later . . .'

'Yes, what about later?'

'Later will be for your husband to decide.' And she was gone.

Miserably, I trailed after her. In such a few short hours my life had completely changed; my future was decided and all my hopes and dreams pushed away.

Voula is awake now and wriggling uncomfortably on my back. Ahead of me I can see our gate and there is someone sitting on the grass beside it. A drip of sweat trapped in my eyebrow drops free and into my eye, blurring my sight momentarily. But it is her – Heavenly has come to see us!

What wrecks we must appear. She has jumped to her feet and is coming towards us, smiling, the sun catching the gold in the red of her hair and lighting up her face. I am suddenly so happy.

'Here, let me help you,' and she takes the sack swiftly from Despina, who smiles with relief and pleasure. 'What is it? Where are you taking it? Give me another, you look exhausted.' We are drifting towards the fig tree and I drop my sacks and sigh, holding my back to straighten it. At just that moment Voula opens her mouth and wails as if she has been starved for a week.

*

An hour later, the girls are fed, Astrape watered and some carrots, leeks and barley are simmering with some oil and dill. We are back under the fig tree, working on the tobacco leaves with Heavenly beside us, helping as though she is part of my family.

After Despina has checked each leaf for blight, she passes it to Heavenly to pierce with an awl. I then take it and thread it onto long strings. Later these will hang out in the sun by the barn to dry until the autumn when Manolis will press them into bales in a machine Stelios owns. Then he will take them to Sitia and sell them. There is good money to be made from this crop. Manolis likes to stash his money away in English gold sovereigns. He says this is for the girls' dowries, but I think plenty is wasted on the cards.

Heavenly is bouncing Voula on her lap and singing a funny English song about piggies and horses and Voula is laughing and chuckling with delight.

I feel as if I have found a sudden new happiness. In spite of the heat, everything seems to exist in a glow. The crags of the mountains around us shine golden with the flowers of broom, and kestrels hover and shriek above.

Of course, this joyous, dream-like afternoon could not last.

Despina is suddenly on her feet and running across the garden, the *gypo*. 'Papa!' She is shouting and Manolis comes towards us. He does not walk like a man who has worked all day under the boiling sun as we have, although over his shoulder hangs a dead sheep, its mouth open in a stiff rictus, blood slowly dripping onto his booted foot. He stands in front of us, legs splayed, and stares at Heavenly.

'Papa, is it Easter come again? Do we have the roasted lamb?'

He still stands motionless, ignoring his eldest child who is hopping up and down with excitement, and tugging at the loose leg of his *vraka*.

'This is *Kyria* Timberlake.'

'I know who it is, wife, I have eyes.' And he nods his head slowly in her direction. 'You are welcome.' His voice is so cold it is hard to believe his words. But he is a superstitious man and thinks if you do not offer hospitality to a stranger, the meat you eat will be turned into human flesh in your mouth.

'My wife has offered you refreshment, I hope?'

'Thank you, yes.'

He nods again and abruptly turns and strides to the barn. There, on the wall, is the cross-beamed post we use as a hanging straight. Expertly he slings the lamb to fall from this, with the spike at the top through the head.

I see him through Heavenly's eyes. He looks raddled and smells even worse. I hope he doesn't get too close to her. The once stocky body has spread into fat. His still deep, dark eyes are sunken now in the oily craters of his face. The hairs that sprout on his flabby breasts are greying. I don't know what colour the hairs on his head would be as there are none there. Ever since he came home from Sitia, months ago, with a crop of lice picked up, I've no doubt, from some whore's pillow, even he could see the sense in shaving it lest he pass them to the girls and me.

'Why do we have a lamb? What happened?'

'Whatever it was, and I don't know yet, it will give us good food for a while, so I do not expect to hear complaints.'

I sigh. I had no intention of complaining.

As if to compound his brutishness, Manolis reaches for the large knife in his belt and, pulling it out, tries the blade along his thumb. A speck of blood appears; it is sharp enough. With one movement he slits the sheep open from the head downwards. The guts rapidly spill out and fall into a slithering pool on the ground at his feet.

Despina and I are used to such a sight; we are farmers and violent death is part of our daily lives, but Heavenly has shut her eyes tight. This is not something she has seen before, I think. I cross to her and take her hand. She squeezes it. 'Thank you.' She murmurs under her breath, 'I think I must leave you to your family now, and go back to my house. 'When can we meet again?'

I answer quickly, 'If you invite me, I'll come to see you tomorrow, but I will walk along with you for part of the way now, I have to check the bees before sundown.'

'Can I come too, Mama?'

'We'll all go, *koritsaki mou*.'

'Wait, wait,' and she disappears into the *gypo*, returning quickly with a little bundle she must have put together earlier. There is a tattered bit of fishing net, lined with cabbage leaves. Nestling inside are a dozen or so strawberries.

'For you,' she says shyly as she hands them across to Heavenly, who smiles and quickly reaches down to kiss her. Heavenly looks beautiful today, her hair barely covered with a straw hat. Her dress is cotton, simple but still made with the best cloth that surely must have come from Athens. It is finely shaped over her curving body and I can tell no village dressmaker has sewn those seams.

She called goodbye to Manolis, who paused only to turn briefly and spit a gobbet of phlegm that mingled with the mess at his feet. He muttered something that might have been farewell, but I doubt it.

With Voula, as usual, on my back, we walked along together in a comfortable silence. It felt that we had been friends for years.

'What do you think was wrong with that sheep?'

I merely shrugged. 'Whatever it is, I don't suppose I will be told. All I know is that my husband will not be happy about it. Every animal in our flock is precious and he will need to watch carefully for days to see if any of the others show signs of disease. Healthy sheep do not drop dead for no reason. It's also possible that it's meant as a warning to him.' I was in danger of saying more than I intended, when I saw puzzlement on her face.

'My husband is not a popular man in these parts. Oh certainly, he has his own friends – they all drink together in the kafenion they call The Brothers, on the edge of Pano Panagia. But there are not many of them and he makes enemies easily. He is a royalist, and in these parts most people are republicans.'

'Do you mean that someone who disagrees with your husband's politics would deliberately harm his sheep?' She looked astonished.

'It can happen.' I felt I had said enough, but Heavenly wanted to know more.

'I can't really explain it to you,' I said. 'I will take you to meet my *Pappous*, my grandfather, one day and he will tell you more.'

She had lived in Athens and heard and read about our politics. I believe my Pappous would enjoy talking with her. I told her that I did know that General Metaxas ignored the communists completely and it is rumoured around that he has imprisoned many of their leaders. Most of the men in Panagia were delighted when the communists gained power, but not my husband and his friends – they still drink happily together in the name of the king.

'I can't tell you any more. I don't know about England, but here it is not proper for a woman to involve herself in these things – she simply follows where her husband leads and does not question. But my father and my grandfather always treated my sister and me equally with my brother and talked to us of affairs of state. My sister is not in the least bit interested and I am.' I shrug and smile. Voula chortles on my back as if she too agreed.

'I would love to meet your family one day, if you will take me.'

'Oh, I will,' I said eagerly. 'I think you would enjoy my Pappous and Yaya just as I do.'

We walk on together. Above us, the sky mercifully filtered the last, blistering heat of the sun through the scattered clouds. A kestrel wheeled overhead and Despina, with her keen child's eyes, laughed and pointed upwards.

'Look, it has caught something!' She was right, we could see, clenched in its beak, a creature of some sort; now certainly dead. The bird flew swiftly up and away.

'He is taking the dinner home to his wife and babies, just as Papa has done for us.'

I could not disillusion my daughter. To her and her sister, he is like every father in the families she knows; the provider, the ruler of the household. She is long asleep when he chooses to return to the family at night and he rarely comes back, unlike the kestrel, loaded with food for us.

As the sun began to fall westwards towards the horizon, the path divided. Here, at the crooked olive tree, my bees were on the hillside above, and Heavenly's house lay at the other edge of lower Panagia. She hugged each of us in turn and repeated her request that we should visit her the next day. Despina would have gone home with her then, I think, she looked so forlorn at parting with our new friend. Even Voula looked sad as she was kissed. We trudged on upwards towards the hives knowing, all of us, that we had something to look forward to tomorrow.

HEAVENLY

The British Embassy, Athens.

My darling girl,
   *I am missing you dreadfully and we have only been
apart for a few weeks. Every night I find it hard to sleep,
partly the wretched heat, but mainly because I am
plagued by doubts that I am doing the right thing. Why
did I listen when you begged to stay alone? I should have
resigned from the embassy and stayed with you in your
lotus island. But you know, I think I would have gone
mad by the end of another week living with all those Mr
and Mrs Diddlyakis peasants. I think you are marvellous,
darling, to be able to put up with them constantly. I would
have lost my temper before long, and thrown them all out,
or even worse, shot them with one of their wretched rabbit
guns.*
   *The journey back here seemed to go on forever,
making me wish the flying boat had been a possibility.
The crew of this rackety old boat were mostly a good sort,
especially the Captain. He was very persuasive with the
raki flask and it was impossible to say no. I don't
remember much of the night, except falling down the poky
little stairs to the cabins, banging my knee hard and
waking up in the middle of the night with my head under
the bed.*
   *I know I promised, dearest one, and I will stop all this
stuff now that I am back at the office. Truth is, I am*

missing you so much that a glass or two of raki after dinner does make me feel a little better.

All is gloomy here, and the general feeling is that this chap Hitler is going to push everyone one step too far and then anything could happen. I'm sure all that seems very far away to you, there in your little paradise. But I'll write when I can, and will look forward to a note from you if you can manage it.

Foxy and Janet send their love to you, as do I, my angel.

Your adoring husband,
Hugh

He is right; sitting here under the stars of this warm summer night, Athens and that life seem very far away. I like to sit out here with the ramshackle old house behind me. Have I done the right thing? I certainly don't feel lonely, but I am missing Hugh a lot. I ache to see his long legs striding around the village with me. It's so sad that he can't feel as I do. I love all these 'diddlyakis' people, they are so utterly kind to me and I feel so comfortable with them. It seems every farmer or tinker has the look of a Greek god and they all have names straight out of the history books; Hercules, Achilles, Pericles, wonderful!

It was a bleak day when Hugh told us our time in this little village was up and we must go back. At first I just accepted it and started to pack our clothes. But that evening, out on the terrace, under the soft blue cloak of the sky, I felt close to tears.

'Come on, darling,' he said, 'you know you don't really belong here. You go off for a bit of a ramble and damned near break your neck.' He was laughing.

'Oh, how can I make you understand? I feel I belong here more than I do in Athens. I feel so out of things there. I know the other wives are nice, but I honestly don't have anything in common with them. I'm sick of hairdressers tugging at my hair and I can't possibly want another frock for at least ten years. And supposing there is a war with Germany, I'd be much safer here than there, wouldn't I?' I was clutching rather wildly at straws now, but Hugh couldn't disagree.

'Are you thinking you could stay here alone?' he asked. 'Tell me, is that what you want?'

'Oh, darling, I'd so much prefer it if you stayed too, but I know that's not possible. You have responsibilities there, and I don't.'

'Well that's certainly true. I have to get back as soon as possible.'

'You could come back when you get some leave and perhaps I will have a proper house for you to live in. That's what I should love to do, you know. If I could get some local help to get this house put to rights, I think you would be happy to think of coming here for holidays.'

He looked around the living room and I saw it with his eyes. It needed everything mended and made anew. It was shabby and broken down. Even I could feel its sadness. For a moment I wondered if I was completely mad to think of living here alone. But it was a fleeting thought, and as a ray of moonlight lit up the old beams, I was filled with hope.

Parting with him was desperately sad. It was early in the morning, and I think Irini's chickens were the only other living thing awake. He left in the back of Petros' cart; Hugh and several hundredweight of potatoes. He was very game about it as the battered old donkey cart jerked along through the square. We waved until he was out of sight and he was smiling and waving all the time. I knew it was hard for him and as he veered around the corner, I felt tears start to fill my eyes and wondered if he was crying too. I rubbed my eyes swiftly with the back of my hand and walked slowly to the house. The first day of my new life started then.

I have discovered a tiny little church just below, beyond where all the women go to do their washing at the spring. It is called Panagia Sta Perivolia, like this village. It means The Virgin in the Garden and because it is always empty

I feel I can go and sit there by myself anytime. It is so peaceful.

This evening Anthi is bringing someone round to see what he thinks about repairing this house. I would love to be able to do it all myself, but I don't have the skills. I intend to watch and learn, though. I wonder if Hugh will be impressed if I can change a washer on a tap, or build a wall?

Anthi has become a real friend. I love her and her beautiful daughters, although I am not at all sure about her husband, Manolis.

I long to ask her how it came about that she married him. I feel sure that it must have been set up for her. That's what happens here; parents arrange suitable matches and a lot depends on dowries and how much land each partner will bring to the union.

I find it hard to believe that she chose him for herself. Perhaps she wasn't even consulted, how awful!

Anthi seems as happy as I am that we have become friends and we see each other most days. She is very different to most of the village women. Of course, they are amazingly kind, but after a few random questions about how we all are, conversation dries up rather. As if to prove this is true, Irini has just been in with some fruits from her garden; lemons, oranges and figs. We sat on the terrace and spoke about the stars. I tried to have a conversation about the village, some of its customs and about my little church, but she looked rather blank. Clearly anything other than children or food is for men to talk about. She didn't stay long, saying she must get home to her chickens and her children, and scampered away.

It's ages yet before Anthi will be here so I have wandered through the long grass, past the spring and the trees surrounding it and have come to my little church. It is so cool inside, and if I leave the door open I can see down to the sea below. In the distance are two small boats; they are barely moving, the water is so calm.

Hugh likes to sit and watch the sky, I the sea.

He is quite knowledgeable about birds and points them out to me, eager for us to share something.

All my thoughts seem to move in the same direction – towards Hugh. He has done so much for me it is hard to complain, but there is one thing he hasn't done and it troubles me greatly; it is to give me a child.

Tears are brimming up as I think this. Usually I make myself move quickly on to something else in my head, because it is the side of our marriage that is dark, painful and I feel I must keep secret – even from myself.

Ages ago now, when he first 'rescued' me – for that is how I think of my life and myself before Hugh came along and introduced me to his friends – I worried that the only people who seemed to be real friends of his were Lady Troutbeck and her group. Oh, he had lots of acquaintances, for sure, and some who felt like hangers-on, they were all so superficial.

They laughed at my devotion to my patients, and thought working as a nurse was a lark. They all seemed to spend their lives drinking champagne, smoking Sobranie cigarettes and going to either the races or a nightclub.

At first I was swept along with all this, loving every moment and beginning to laugh at myself for caring about what I did. I am ashamed now to think back and remember how I would scour the wards for funny cases to tell them about. I learnt swiftly to turn a sad old lady with a hearing problem and a stutter into a hilarious joke.

'More, Evadne,' they would say, spluttering champagne over each other. 'Tell us more funny stories about that place.'

'That place' was where I went every day, the hospital; where people began their lives by being born, or ended their lives in sad dark nights, often alone.

Certainly I had moments of great unease, usually when trying to sleep. But not enough to stop me dashing to buy new clothes for some party or other and starting all over again the next night.

And then, suddenly, we were married and off to Paris for Hugh's posting to the embassy there; without even a break for us to have a honeymoon. But I was sure that when Hugh had a proper job to do, life would settle down. Quite what I thought that would mean for me, I didn't stop to think. I thought embassy wives were somehow or other important, but apart from learning French, it was a dull round of hairdressers, dressmakers and parties.

I never even quite discovered what it was that Hugh did each day. There never seemed enough time for us to be alone together for me to find out.

And then there was the bed thing.

I love Hugh dearly and, I'm not ashamed to say it, passionately. I love his body, the smooth roundness of the curvy parts, the long strength of his legs, his tight bottom. (Oh I envy him that bottom; especially when I looked at my own loose round one in the cheval mirror in our suite at the embassy.)

The light thatch of golden hairs on his chest is one of my great delights. I run my fingers through it and feel a great tingling wetness of excitement starting between my thighs and moving through my body like a wave.

The first night we were together, really together I mean, in our suite in the Savoy, was a disaster.

The day had been frantic. Our wedding was to happen at Caxton Hall register office in the middle of London at twelve o'clock; a small affair, just us, a few friends of Hugh's, Lady T of course, and three girls I called Minky, Mouse and Boo, who seemed to go everywhere with her. I did ask a couple of the nurses, Maisie and another, but they couldn't get the time away. My mother couldn't come. She had something else on, very important, she said. But I bet it was just another wretched bridge party or a Red Cross bring and buy sale.

I was upset, but only my sister Daphne knew that.

I was sad that Hugh's mother couldn't get there. She had a fall from her horse the week before and had a badly sprained ankle.

She wrote me a letter, which I shall always treasure, saying how very happy she was that Hugh had chosen me rather than one of the 'flighty London flibbertigibbets' he spent so much time with. 'I know you will make him happy,' she wrote. She had seemed so kind when I met her in the hospital, I would love to get to know her more.

My mother had sent the money for a frock, at least, and I raided Harrods with Daphne and chose a sort of floaty pale blue crêpe-and-lace affair that cost sixteen pounds, more than anything I'd ever spent on one thing.

From the start the wedding was not as I had imagined it.

I got there first, which was not how it was meant to be. Then Foxy, who was Hugh's best man, ran up the steps and said he'd lost Hugh last night, and this morning he couldn't find the ring either.

I stood there, looking and feeling completely stupid. I thought I was going to cry but Daphne held my hand very tightly and said not to worry. I thought it was all very well for her, but it was me who had been left at the altar, or whatever it is in those places.

The registrar, who looked surprisingly like Clark Gable, was very kind, but said he had people waiting and couldn't hang about much longer and why didn't we all go to a nearby public house and have a stiff drink or two?

Then Hugh arrived looking flustered and unhappy. He hugged me and said he was desperately sorry, but Lady Troutbeck's car wouldn't start and they couldn't get a taxicab and he'd run all the way from her London flat.

She was there, just behind him, looking even more amazing than usual. She'd dyed her hair jet black and put a lot of white make-up on, with black round her eyes. I thought she looked like a panda, but their friends all cheered and told her she looked fabulous.

I did wonder why Hugh had been at her flat in the first place. He had told me he was having a few drinks with Foxy and some friends at the Savile Club and an early night.

'Don't want to have a hangover on our wedding day, do I, sweetheart?'

We all squeezed inside the small and certainly very

unimpressive room that was the actual 'office'. I thought, momentarily, that I was glad Mother wasn't there, she'd have sniffed loudly, with her nose in the air, and made some comment.

You have to have two witnesses in these affairs apparently, and Hugh had chosen Foxy and Jack Timberlake, his uncle. I'd never met Uncle Jack before, in fact I'd never met any of Hugh's relations.

At last, here was Foxy but where was Uncle Jack?

'I think still stuck in the fleshpots of Calais,' said Hugh, 'or wherever he stayed last night, which certainly wasn't in this country. So, I've asked Dora to oblige and she said she would. She's a brick, isn't she?'

Of course it was kind of her to step in at such short notice, so why did my heart sink into my specially-dyed-to-match-my-dress ballet slippers?

We did the marriage bit, which was over so fast I barely caught my breath and wondered if we were really legally married. But Hugh turned to me with such love in his eyes, I almost cried again.

But standing beside the exotic Lady T in her strange make-up and scarves and Balenciaga frock, I felt like the country girl come to London for the first time. Well I was, wasn't I?

In fact I felt like the timid nurse I was in front of Matron, and I had thought those days gone for ever.

Lady Troutbeck cracked her face into a smile and signed the register with Foxy, then, leaving me standing by the wilted gladioli which some kind soul had placed in the room several days ago, she swept outside into the crisp October sunshine, smiling warmly at everyone except me.

Darling Hugh took my arm and, leaning over, kissed me and told me he loved me. All the negative feelings I was having melted away as he spoke.

'We'll soon be on our own, Evadne, and I can tell you and show you how dear you are to me.'

He put his arm around me and swept me outside and pushed us into the circle of Lady Troutbeck's admirers.

'Sorry to break up this delightful street party,' he said, laughing, 'but we are going to the Ivy for a little champagne, I believe.'

'Aye, aye, Captain,' called Foxy and we all piled into a fleet of taxis that were waiting at the kerb.

Later, much later, we managed to get away from the, by now, extremely noisy crowd. 'Oh don't go yet, Hugh, just another little drinky.' 'Spoilsport, Hugh! Evadne, let him stay and have a bit of fun.'

And more and more calls of the same, so that I felt like the wicked witch snatching poor Hansel into the gingerbread house. But Hugh showed no sign of wanting to stay and we went off to the Savoy hand in hand.

When we got there and Hugh signed the register, (Mr and Mrs Timberlake – I was so thrilled!) the man behind the desk said, 'Excuse me, sir, but a gentleman is waiting to see you.'

We turned and a man uncurled himself from an armchair and leapt towards us on long tweedy legs.

'My dear old fella,' he boomed, and clasped Hugh in his arms. 'Where's the party then? Not too late, am I?'

'Uncle Jack, how marvellous! I thought we'd lost you. Evadne, this is Uncle Jack. Uncle Jack, this is my lovely bride.' And my hand was twisted and tortured in a grip to break my fingers, and pumped up and down.

'My dear lady, what a delight you are. Hugh, you've done yourself proud, old chap.' He was still pumping away so that I thought my arm would fall off in a moment. 'Here let me kiss the bride, eh? Uncle's privilege.'

And I was seized in a warm, sweaty, porky sort of grip and thick, hairy bristles were nibbling at my cheek. I eased myself away slightly and looked at this man. He had beady, blackish eyes, which peered out of pink, jelly-like whites. His hair was dark and thin and combed over the top of his head with loads of oily brilliantine, only it smelt quite expensive, and a thin black moustache lay across his lip, rather as if it had come from a joke shop and might fall off at any moment. I suddenly realised it was probably dyed. This was a vain man and I instantly disliked him.

It appeared that Uncle Jack had indeed got lost in Calais and missed the boat. But he knew we would come to the Savoy at some point so thought he would catch up with us here.

'Time for a little nightcap? Don't send poor old Uncle out into the streets all on his own, eh?'

Hugh looked rather despairingly at me and I thought I had no alternative but to help him out of this.

'Darling, why don't you do just that,' I said. 'I'll go up to our room and I'll see you there in a little while.' I turned away quickly. I really didn't want another rabbitty kiss from this man.

The truth is, I minded quite a lot. I'd looked forward all day to this chance to be on our own and this boring old man had got Hugh, just when I thought I deserved a bit of him to myself.

Nothing to be done except go upstairs alone and wait. I lay on the vast bed and looked around the sumptuous room. I had never seen anything quite so rooted in luxury. I yawned and, within moments, I must have slept for when I awoke it was dark.

I lay still for a moment, no more, before reaching out to touch the sleeping body beside me. 'Hugh,' I whispered. The only response was a great, grunting snore that must have woken him.

'Christ, darling, I'm so sorry.' And the blankets and sheets scrabbled up and away and my new husband sat up and put the light on. I'm glad he did because I instantly realised we were not alone in the room. In horror, I saw the still-sleeping figure on the chaise longue at the foot of the bed.

Uncle Jack was snuggled down under Hugh's greatcoat, snorting throatily and with dribble running down his chin.

Hugh spent most of the rest of the night apologising. I sat on the huge green brocade sofa shivering in my peignoir. I didn't cry, I felt only despair. He hadn't meant it. He'd felt rather sorry for the old boy. Couldn't turf him out on the night streets, could he? Thought I wouldn't mind.

There were no words to express how I felt, so I didn't try.

Hugh finally persuaded Uncle Jack to wake up and he staggered off into the corridor, waving a shaky hand behind him.

'Any chance of meeting up for a spot of breakfast?' he said, just before he disappeared. 'No, I suppose not. Oh well, see you soon. Toodle pip.'

It probably was not the best start to anyone's married life, but somehow, by the end of the next day, Hugh had managed, just, to make me laugh about it.

We left for Paris within the week and I so looked forward to a new beginning, a new start with my beloved Hugh.

I'm not sure what I had imagined embassy life to be like. Paris itself had seemed to be the important thing, with the Eiffel Tower, the Seine, the Louvre and all the places I'd heard of, but life inside the embassy was exactly the same as being in England. Everyone spoke English all the time, except when dealing with the French, who were regarded as rather alien foreigners who annoyingly made demands on one's time.

We had bacon and eggs or kedgeree or kidneys for breakfast, roast lamb and cabbage for lunch (served, naturally, with mint sauce), and steak and kidney pudding for dinner.

I would often escape before breakfast, when I could manage it, and would find a little pavement café where I had my *café au lait*, *croissant*, or *pain au confiture*. I spoke French in the markets and shops, and as long as the weather was fine I walked alone among the beautiful streets and boulevards. I haunted the many art galleries and churches when it was not. No one seemed to miss me from the embassy. Hugh was such a junior diplomat that I don't think anyone noticed if I was there or not. Sadly, even Hugh seemed happy to let me wander around without explanation.

I turned up for any important lunches or dinners, of course. It seemed there were more cocktail parties than there were days in the week, and Hugh encouraged me constantly to shop for clothes or get my hair done or my nails manicured. I was soon very bored.

There were sometimes beggars on the street, especially gathered on the steps of the many elegant churches and cathedrals. I would give them as much money as I could, it seemed so wicked to me to have my hair done again and again when there were women and children so desperately in need. It was the children who moved me the most and it made me long all the more for a child of my own. Hugh would laugh when I tried to talk to him about it.

'Bored with me already, darling? Aren't I enough company for you? Plenty of time for kiddies when I'm properly established. Early days yet.'

But I was unhappy that the lovemaking we indulged in was rare and deeply unsatisfactory.

And then we were sent to Greece; to Athens, and I hoped and prayed all over again that this time we could make a real go of things. But it seemed that, apart from the language, nothing changed, not even the food.

Night after night, I would go to our rooms alone, get into bed alone and try to sleep, still alone. It was only ever the lightest of sleeps, for I was instantly awake when Hugh came to bed, often in the early hours.

I remember one night, when we had been there for a month, when, sad and feeling lonely, I tried to arouse him. I stroked his body gently at first, and then, as I hoped he would do to me, more strongly. My lips joined my hands and I tasted the scents of his body. I was nervous; this was new to me, to take the initiative like this, suppose it displeased him? But to my surprise and delight, murmuring my name, he pulled me closer to him. I felt him stiffen against my body and the pattern of his breathing changed, he was panting and stroking me in return. I was wet and ready for him; it had been weeks since we had made love, months.

He leaned over me and as his part touched my body, he gave a groan and it was suddenly limp again. I reached down and tried to caress the flaccid thing back into life.

Roughly he pushed my hand away and seized it himself. His face was full of angry frustration and he moved his hand frantically back and forth. And suddenly, not yet fully hard, he came and the creamy seed spilled onto my thigh.

'I'm so sorry, so sorry.' And as he turned over I realised he was crying.

I stroked his back; his head now in the pillow, and muffled sobbing was all that I could hear.

'Don't worry,' I said. 'It doesn't matter. There are other days, other nights.'

But inside myself I suspected that this was just the beginning of something that was going to trouble us for a long while, because it was not the first time. On the last few occasions we had tried, something had gone wrong and he was unable to enter me. Often he seemed not to even notice. Sometimes he came, mostly he just faded away, and within moments of turning away from me, he slept.

I would lie, silent and miserable, until finally I too would fall into a sleep.

We never spoke of it. If I tried to raise the subject of our intimacy he would merely look horrified and change the conversation at once to some embassy topic, or a joke, so that he could feel at least he was making me laugh.

He would try again, usually after a cocktail party, but the result was always the same.

During the days, he behaved as normal and always after a troubled night he would be especially kind to me. Often he bought me flowers or chocolates, which was a hollow gesture really as the embassy resembled an expensive florist and I dared not eat the chocolate for fear of adding more inches to my bottom.

His flat refusal to talk about this, which I felt was becoming a big problem in our lives, left me wretchedly sad. His only answer was to drink more each night and fall into bed, incapable sometimes of even saying goodnight.

It was the remorse, I think, that affected me as much as the lack of lovemaking. I loathed seeing the sad eyes, the downturned mouth and the humility with which he invariably approached me. I loved the Hugh I had met, had cared for, and wanted him back; the man that was relaxed, kind, and above all strong and carefree.

He swore every thing would be fine when we got a chance to be alone together.

So I had hoped so much that this house, this village, this time away together would be the honeymoon we had not had. But here, in Panagia now, we had been alone and he still turned away from me each night.

Here we slept together in a ramshackle old bed. It was broken in several places and the mattress, if you could call it so, smelt strongly of the horse that it had lived with, closely. If either of us tried to turn over, asleep or not, it was likely that we would fall out onto the floor. This was not the comfortable intimacy I had dreamed of.

Now he had returned to Athens, to that world of people who seemed like aliens to me. I imagined the high-pitched giggles, the flirtations, the delight at a surprising new cocktail, and, worst of all, the possibility of falling into bed with whoever was nearest and remembering nothing of it the next day. I know this happens sometimes, and I hate to think of Hugh acting like this.

I tell myself to stop. And my head, long used to this prompting from my heart, turns to happier thoughts.

There was a call, and then a small voice saying my name, 'Heavenly,' and then again louder, 'Heavenly!'

A small, sweet face hovered around the corner of the church door – Despina, Anthi's eldest daughter, was peering into the dark interior.

'Heavenly, are you here?'

I jumped up into the light, facing her. 'Boo!'

She gave a shriek and leapt backwards, laughing.

Hand in hand we climbed upwards through the scrub and weeds to the village, where, outside my house, Anthi was waiting with Voula and a man. This must be Yorgo Babyottis, the builder. He held his hat in his hands, turning it roughly but firmly by the brim, round and round.

He was smaller and older than I had expected, with a creased face like a walnut and in the middle, twinkly blue eyes of an astonishing brightness. His moustache was a handsome one and shaped finely over many years This man had been exceptionally handsome in his youth. As if to prove it, his eyes moved swiftly over my form, checking it out. It felt like an automatic glance; he did this to all women, I suspected.

He held out his brown wrinkled hand and I grasped it and smiled at him.

'*Ya*,' he muttered, his head down.

We all looked at the vast exterior of the house. I saw the cracks and the roughness of the weathered stones. Red roof tiles hung loose at one end. I felt a sudden wave of nervousness as I looked at the supports of that terrace, perilously close to disintegration. I remembered the days and nights when Hugh and I had sat there; it could have crashed down on us so easily.

'Come, let's walk round and I'll show you what I'd like to do.'

ANTHI

I think Yorgo Babyottis was stunned by Heavenly, as were all the other people in the village; she and You are treated as though they have dropped in from somewhere beyond the moon. Coming here from Athens is odd enough, but to have come here to live, from across the sea in England, is beyond thought.

We walked round her house together, Despina skipping along behind. As we saw the scale of the work, I began to be concerned. Yorgo was delighted, I think, although he was trying not to show it. He was agreeing to everything she wanted. This worried me. He could see he would be employed on this one job, in his own village, for a long time ahead. All Heavenly could see was her dream coming to life.

Yorgo stood in front of us, turning his cap round and round. 'Kyria Heavenly,' he started, 'of course I can do this work for you. I have much experience of such places.'

I looked at him in astonishment. He spent most of his time making coffins for the old people who die in winter.

Although I had brought him to Heavenly, I had warned her that he was a village man, no more accustomed to great renovation work than any one else here. But perhaps he may know of someone who could handle all this for her? It will be a problem. There is no one I know around these parts to do this sort of thing. The men of the households repair their own homes when necessary; a hole in a roof, a simple outhouse to be built, or a new coat or two of thick white *isvesti* were easily coped with.

Yorgo Babyottis clearly wanted this job, but I could not let my new friend employ him without some serious talking. He was telling her now how he could remake all the windows, doors and shutters.

'But what of the really heavy work, Yorgo?' I said. 'Who will help you?'

Yorgo shifted from foot to foot and looked worried. 'When do you want me to start, Kyria?'

His hat, I thought, would be worn through if he did not stop twisting it.

We all turned to look at Heavenly.

'As soon as possible, I think.'

'Excellent,' he said. 'We will just wait for Kyria Heavenly's husband to come home and I will agree a price with him and I shall start immediately. Well, nearly immediately. I must finish a little bit of this and a little bit of that and then immediately. Nearly.'

Heavenly was still smiling, but it looked a little stiff now – I could see she needed help.

'Yorgo, Kyria Heavenly is an English lady,' I started slowly, 'and in England they do things differently. The ladies deal with everything about the house, for example, so you will expect to get answers and decisions from Kyria Heavenly. Her husband is away at the moment. You will discuss everything with her. Or,' I added hastily, 'with me.'

Heavenly looked pleased that I was helping her with the difficulties of the situation, as well as of the language. Athenian Greek is a long way from the Greek spoken in these villages.

Yorgo finally left. He had at last seemed to understand Heavenly's situation, and said he accepted her as the person in charge of the house. But he looked very doubtful as he walked down the steps. In passing, he had mentioned his nephew, his sister's boy, Christo, who lived in a village near

Sitia and wanted to be an architect. The boy was trying to earn money to help his widowed mother pay for his training.

'I will speak with my sister,' he said. 'Perhaps her boy can come and help me here for a while. Not,' he added hastily, 'that I need much help, I usually work alone, but it's good to give a hand to the family from time to time.'

It was clear to me that Yorgo would need all the help he could get. I felt responsible to Heavenly for bringing him here to help her repair her house. I am learning she is a woman who gives her trust easily, perhaps too easily.

She had wanted to give Yorgo money straight away. I had stopped her. 'Yorgo, you must give Kyria Heavenly a list of everything you will need money for and how much each piece will cost. Then she will give you some of the money to buy these things. You understand?'

Yorgo agreed. He is not a dishonest man, but with a pocketful of money he would be at risk. A bellyful of raki and the first tinker passing through would sell him more ribbons and cloths than bricks and mortar.

As she watched him go, Heavenly came out and joined me on the terrace.

'Anthi,' she said, 'I know you feel responsible, but it is my choice, you know, my decision. You haven't seen, but I can be very fierce when I need. Mr Yorgo will find me as hard as any man to deal with, I promise.' She put her arms around me and hugged me tightly. 'Dear friend, trust me.'

Voula woke noisily at that moment. She had been sleeping in another of Heavenly's boxes, but now she needed food. I picked her up into my arms and, sitting on the army bed, I opened my shift to feed her. Any shyness I felt earlier at baring my breast in front of another was gone. Heavenly seemed such a calming presence that Voula was quickly soothed. Sometimes when she was restless and unsettled, Heavenly held her in her arms and rocked her, singing a song she told me was especially for babies. I liked to see her singing my Voula to sleep.

She is a woman without a child. This puzzles me. What is

wrong with her that, loving babies as she seems to, she does not have one of her own?

Riding home that day, I thought about my friend and her husband in his funny trousers, who is happy to leave her alone here for who knows how long? Months? Years?

Later that night I lay sleepless. Beside me, Manolis is snoring. If only he would go away for a few months or years, I would be happy!

Before the babies came, our marriage had not been a bad one. Certainly at sixteen, I already had better things to do with my life than devote it to my husband. But he seemed not to mind me continuing to help in the school. As long, of course, as I looked after him and the house. But I had started to enjoy the cooking I had learnt from my mother. I especially delighted in the fact that I quickly became better than her. My pastry was lighter, crisper; my roasted lamb and kid were sweeter, juicier; the fruit I picked and dried or preserved in liquor were more delicate, richer. I loved making all this magic happen.

A mound of flour, a jug of oil and either sugar or salt and herbs, with my fingers kneading and mixing, resulted swiftly in delicacies that visiting neighbours or family praised as they had never praised hers. This made her furious and she had no sooner forced me into the kitchen than she was trying to keep me out of it, so mean-spirited is she! She taught me to weave and sew and again my slender fingers worked the wools and hemps into pleasing shapes far faster than her fat stubby ones. The humour I found in all this so delighted me that I begged for more lessons, but she all but threw me out of the house saying, 'Surely you are needed at the school, go, go!'

I was replaced at the oven by Ririca, who thought that as I had mastered these skills with so little effort, so too could she. She was hopeless. I would hide behind the kitchen door and stuff my fingers in my mouth to hide my laughter as my mother scolded her puny efforts. Stodgy *pastitsio*, those delicious layers of macaroni, cream and meat which was my favourite thing to make, would be thrown for the chickens and goats, along with limp cheese pies and vinegary preserves; heavy rancid pastry would be scorned even by the animals and it lay in their stalls until it was trampled underfoot and became part of their bedding.

As is the custom, I saw little of my husband before we were wed; certainly never alone. By the time of the ceremony I was thoroughly sick of my mother and her sisters and Ririca squealing and giggling all over our house as they stitched and sewed for my trousseau. I would have gone to the church in my shift, so little did it all matter to me. I sought refuge with my grandparents whenever I could. They were the only people who were happy for me to talk about the school, the grain harvest, the threshing and all the work in the fields.

Often, during my visits there, I would sit in front of their fire, watching as my grandfather carved a chest for me, from wood he had gathered from the pine forests. These two old people were the ones I loved more than anyone in the world. Soon now I would be the wife of Manolis Manadakis – could I love him even a quarter as much? A tenth? I thought not. I looked at them sitting side by side, their love for each other apparent in every move, every breath. Occasionally, one or other of them would catch my look and smile: their eyes full of the affection they felt for me, the only love in the world I was sure of.

It was my grandmother who prepared me for my wedding night and told me of the things my husband would expect from me. I was astonished. 'Is it true, Yaya, that men behave just as the animals in the fields?'

'Well, yes, child. Human babies are born just like all the other creatures.'

I tried hard to think of this closeness, this intimacy with Manolis Manadakis but it was hard. I shivered to think of sharing a bed with him.

At first it wasn't so bad. Manolis had some redeeming features, I thought. He had beautiful eyes, dark, velvety brown, which at first looked at me kindly. He even seemed to enjoy my company. Certainly, in the beginning, I laughed a great deal, so glad was I to be out of my mother's house. I loved having my own home and Manolis, his mother being long dead, was happy for me to make any changes I wanted.

His demands on my body were concluded swiftly, with the minimum of fuss. In the beginning it was painful, but when my part had grown accustomed to his entry there, it became easier. There were moments, sometimes, when he fingered me to stretch me wider, that his thumb caught my sweet spot and a shiver of excitement would run through me, but it was never more than that. He hastened to start his thrusts in me, usually he concluded in ten, but on good nights he could be done with in four or five. Other than those rare touchings, there was no pleasure for me, but why would I expect there to be?

It was a cold morning in winter, and I had been to the mill to grind the wheat for our bread, that I first was sick. When this happened again and then again and my breasts became swollen and tender, I knew I must be with child. My grandmother said this was so, and nine months later I was gripped with pains all one day, growing stronger and stronger towards the evening. Manolis fetched Kyria Glykeria and she bustled in quickly.

She was all clean apron and tidy neat with her daughter Tassia behind her, smiling vacantly. They set about boiling water, and tearing into pieces a fine linen bed sheet my aunt had so carefully embroidered. The pains were fierce; ripping through me until I screamed.

Tassia sat mutely by my side. She is just a lump of dull flesh, poor girl. No one knows her age and she is known to be stupid. Her mother peered under my shift and poked me with a pad of nettlesoak. I had heard that cloths stewed in nettles, gathered by the light of a full moon, would ensure the safe delivery of a boy child. But fifteen minutes later, a beautiful girl was born to me, Despina.

I was soon back to work in the kitchen and the fields,

Despina always on my hip or by my side. Manolis seemed fond enough of her, as fond as any man would be for a girl child, I thought.

He was keen to resume our mating, and although at first it gave me great pain to take him inside me, I never thought to protest. I was pregnant again soon enough and Manolis was delighted. 'This time you will bear a son,' he said, with such certainty that even I thought he was right.

And then one day the movements inside me stopped and that night my body, swollen and tender, was gripped with terrible pains. A great flood of my waters, streaked with blood, fell from me and onto the stone floor. I was not due for another three months. This was too soon. I wept as Manolis, his face stormy and troubled, rode down and over the hills, through the chill air for Kyria Glykeria.

As before, she brought Tassia, who sat again silently by my side while I sweated and chewed on a length of cloth trying to stifle my screams.

Soon after dawn the child was born. A son indeed, but a tiny, withered old man of a son who was already dead as I pushed him out of my body.

Tassia was sent to break the news to Manolis sitting by the fire downstairs. With Kyria Glykeria pressing down on my belly, causing the worst pain I have ever endured, I heard my husband's great roar through the wooden boards. 'No!' he shouted and again. 'No!'

Tassia slid back into the room, her eyes wide with fear and resumed her place at my side. The afterbirth came away from me. Kyria Glykeria reached for it quickly and, together with the dead child, wrapped it in another of my mother's linen sheets. Drearily I watched from the bed, my hair matted with sweat. As she moved away, muttering to herself, I realised she was leaving the room with her bundle and I whispered, 'Please give him to me.' She turned in surprise. 'Oh, child,' she said gently, 'what use is it to you? Best not spend time with the dead. Leave it to me. I'll do what is necessary.'

'He is my child, my son, let me hold him.'

She shrugged and pushed the cloth towards me, the stuff from my belly as well as the child. I unwrapped him carefully and, my heart full of sadness and my eyes full of tears, I said, 'Hello and goodbye, little man. At least you will never know evil. Have a safe journey, my Constantinos.'

Tassia's eyes were full of excitement and she reached for the little body. I let her take him; I was too weak and full of grief to resist. She rocked him roughly in her arms and as she started to sing to him, her mother pulled him away. 'What do you think you are doing?' she said. 'Creatures like this are the spawn of the devil and bad luck will come to us.' She bundled the body up again, with the afterbirth, and pushed them down to the bottom of her capacious bag.

As she washed me clean I heard the door slam below.

'Your husband has gone to drown his sorrows at the kafenion,' she said. 'Who can blame him? He told me, he told everyone, this child must be a boy. Every man wants a son. It's natural.' She was scrubbing my parts with an infusion of alum and hawthorn. I knew Manolis would blame me for this tragedy. I turned my head and wept into the pillow. Tears for my lost little boy, and for the bleakness of my life ahead.

Within moments, I was alone in the room again. In the corner the tiny crib carved in fine sycamore by Pappous was empty. There was silence. It seemed to me like the silence of lost hope. There was not a sigh, nor a breath, no smile, no laughter, no spirit, just a deadening sense of failure: the failure to produce a son. There would be no going back now, no forgiveness.

In Manolis's eyes I had not only failed to give him the son he so longed for but, as my mother was quick to tell me, village superstition meant I had given birth to something evil. Something so bad that had sprung from his seed, it was as if I had produced a *vrikolax*, a vampire, so I must not be surprised that he was so appalled.

We lived our separate lives under one roof from then. Little Despina would run between us. Mercifully, she didn't seem aware of the scant attention he gave her, but then he was only here to eat and sleep. Occasionally he would take down his lyre from the wall and carry it out to the waiting mule. I guessed on those evenings he and Stelios were playing at a wedding or a feast day in another village. He would return, sometimes days later, stinking of drink and tobacco, his moustache bedraggled and his cheeks dark and unshaven.

In the village no one spoke to me of Constantinos, not even the Papa. This was not a surprise. Bad luck, like bad health, is considered contagious here, so it is pushed away and forgotten. Since Constantinos's birth, Manolis had mostly turned away from my body. I didn't care if he never touched me again. I made sure Despina and I were in our beds before he should come back from the cards or the drink.

But sometimes at night he used my body. I was merely a part of his daily ritual: washing, working, eating, drinking, shitting and fucking, his was a simple existence.

One night I was less careful than usual, turning back to a deep sleep when he had finished with me, and Voula was born, calmly, one winter night after a short labour, and seemed already smiling as she emerged from my bloodied loins.

Manolis was gone for three days after her birth. Another daughter. Another failure.

This is my life. There is much to keep me happy and I am grateful for that. My girls have been my only friends. But now there is Heavenly.

Tying up Astrape and lifting the wriggling Voula down, I realise Despina is singing a little song, almost under her breath. 'Heavenly, you are Heavenly,' it seems to go. I ruffle her hair as we go into the house. 'I think you like our new friend, little one.' Her face turns up to me. 'Oh, Mama, she is LOVELY!' and she skips inside singing over and over, 'Heavenly, you are Heavenly.'

Manolis came home when I was chopping vegetables. He spoke to the children but ignored me. Nothing new.

But when they were both settled for the night, he pulled me to him as I passed the table. 'What was your business with Yorgo Babyottis today?'

'I took him to Kyria Timberlake. She needs help with repairing her house.'

He laughed coarsely. 'She needs a coffin, does she?'

I knew better than to rise to this jibe.

'She will need plenty of woodwork in that place and Yorgo can help her pick a stonemason, I thought.'

'You choose to give work to the communists in our village then, do you?'

Inside myself I sighed. If he chose to, Manolis could make this into an unpleasant disagreement. I pretended ignorance.

'Communist? Is Yorgo a communist?'

'You are not stupid, wife, you know his persuasion, I think. And if you had chosen to discuss this with me, as you should, I could have sent someone better than Babyottis.'

Upstairs, Voula began to cry. I was saved for the moment, and I ran to her. A little later the door slammed. He had left the house and I breathed into Voula's sweet soft neck. 'Thank you, my little one,' I whispered and as she let free the wind trapped in her small body, she was already asleep again.

Later, I sat in the dying rays of the day's sun, and thought of his words. For sure I knew Yorgo's politics well. In the village anyone who is not a royalist, is automatically thought of as a communist.

He had been a friend of my father, and my grandfather is godfather to his daughter. He is also a good craftsman. The wood he works with comes alive under his strong fingers. I know little of the work of stonemasons in these parts but I would speak with Yorgo's wife when we washed our clothes together. Aphrodite is a kind and sensible woman and would be amused to learn her husband was going to be in charge of the renovation of one of Panagia Sta Perivolia's biggest houses.

*

The top of the hill was hazed with early morning light the following day, as the girls and I rode through on Astrape, a large bundle of soiled linen strapped to the saddle.

We passed slowly along on the dusty dirt ridge towards the spring, through vineyards and olive groves and past the small church of St Nicholas. As always here, I can't help looking up. High up into the sky, on the top of the mountain, stands the little church of St Kosmas and Damianus, now rarely used. My father had wanted to be buried there, my Pappous had told me, but my mother had insisted that he be buried in the bigger, more splendid church of St Athanasius, where her family had a burial space reserved. She never visits his grave now, my girls and I are the only ones to tend it.

I smile a little now as I remember discovering, some time after the event, that she had arranged the burial of my son Constantinos at the little church on the top of the mountain. She, of course, wanted him disposed of as far away from the village as possible. She couldn't know how happy this would make me when I discovered it. St Kosmas and Damianus has long been my favourite and I felt that the little spirit of Constantinos would watch over us.

I hear the shrill babble of women's voices coming through the still air towards me, both old and young, and I know I am close to the laundry. I turn off the track and take Astrape gently down through the wooded path.

As I had expected, Aphrodite was already at the spring and briskly scrubbing water through her family's laundry.

She hailed a greeting and, as usual, stopped what she was doing, roughly dried her hands on her shift, and hugged Despina to her warmly.

She loves my girls as her own. She roared with laughter, her ample belly moving up and down under the tight fabric, when I tell her the news. 'My Yorgo? Does he think there is a team of strong stone workers lying around the Piperia waiting for him to call them? He will need to talk to his sister in Sitia.' She grimaced. 'He won't like that. He hasn't spoken to her in weeks. But don't fret, he won't let you down.'

She looked at me quizzically. 'What is this new friend of yours about? There is talk she has come from Athens and before that, Paris in France.' I flushed. I knew there was talk of Heavenly in the village, but I did not want to be part of it. She has showed me nothing but openness and warmth – I would not repay it by gossiping about her life. Besides, I knew little more than the bare facts, as they did; she had come from England, through France and then Athens to our village.

As I went about my work I realised that the women around me were speaking of her, but only praise for her beauty and her ready smile.

They spoke more of her husband, You. They had been surprised to see his bare legs in the village, and were giggling like girls.

Eleni Peridakis called out to me above the hum of voices and the laughter, 'Hey, Anthi, what kind of husband is the Englishman? Why does he leave a beautiful woman like your friend, and go to Athens?' Before I could answer, another of the village women called, 'Does he walk around the Athenian streets with bare legs?'

Another asked, 'Has he left her to stay in that wreck of a house alone?'

I shrugged. I could see there was no point in entering this conversation, so I let them call out more questions, until they tired of the subject and went back to talking about the poor wheat harvest, which I knew for many of them here was a serious problem. No wheat means none to sell to buy other provisions, and none to grind to make the daily bread. There would have to be more bartering, but with little to trade, there would be little to buy. I felt sad for them. We had plenty, thank you, *Panagia mou*.

It is a beautiful autumn day, with the memory of summer in the air. We ride on and collect Heavenly from her house. We are taking a picnic up into the hills to celebrate the last day of freedom. School begins tomorrow, and Yorgo Babyottis is due to start work in the house.

I tether Astrape outside her house. A kestrel hovers as we walk upwards together through the drying heather.

'When Yorgo is busy on my house, do you think it may be possible for me to visit you in your school?'

I was suddenly struck with a thought: 'Not only visit – help teach the children English, why not?'

'Do you think I could?'

'I think it is a wonderful idea. They can have proper English talk, with a real English person!'

I was laughing with excitement. It gave me great pleasure to think of my friend by my side in my school. I was sure the professor would agree – he would only see what a good idea it was for the children.

After my father died, it was from him I learnt a delight in words and language. When school finished each day, I would stay behind and he taught me English. I was a greedy pupil, hungry to learn all I could of the world away from here. In spite of my father's fancies there was, of course, now no chance I should go elsewhere later, for learning. No one from these parts went to the university in Heraklion, and as for going even further say, to Athens, hah! What a joke.

A village girl at such places? What a thought!

My girls will go, though, I swear, whatever else happens. Knowledge will be their wealth, their inheritance from me. The way their father drinks away so much, it may well be all they have.

It seemed natural to me back then that I should stay and help the professor with the growing number of children coming to learn. It was unofficial, of course. The professor had applied many times to the authorities. But his requests always went to the bottom of the pile.

And now Heavenly can come and be an unofficial assistant as well. How lucky is that?

HEAVENLY

Athens   *November 1936*

My dearest Evadne,

  I think of you all the time and miss you painfully.
Sometimes I just want to rush back to Crete and be with
you, but I must remember my life is here in Athens now.
And what a different world away it is! Sometimes it feels
to me that Athens is a separate country entirely; part of
Europe, like London or Paris or Rome. Greece itself, your
idyllic island and indeed all the other islands, still part of
the Balkans; two civilisations trying to exist side by side.

  There are worrying things happening that alarm H.E.
The other day the remains of King Constantine and
Queen Sophia, of the old royal family, were disinterred
and brought back here for burial in the grounds of their
old estate in Attica. Reasonable, you would have thought,
as I did. But ever since, there have been rumblings of
dissent all around. A nasty fire on the edge of Athens
killed many, including children, probably started by the
communists. And many other such incidents. We were
lucky in Chania that the Venezelos problem was hushed
so quickly. There are rumours every day of plots against
the government and even here we are seeing increasing
signs of poverty.

  In Panagia no one spoke of this to us, but the
disastrous wheat harvest this year has crippled the
country. There was a general strike and all the services

here broke down. On one day only the shoe-shine boys were working! But even they were broke as their customers stayed at home.

How I wish you were here beside me now, and we could talk about these things. Do you remember how we used to talk, my darling, in your ward at night? We seem to have got out of the way of that lately. My fault, I know, always something else to do.

But I must be here, to earn the shillings to pay for the bricks and slates for mending broken-down old ruins. And you do seem to be happy there.

I hope it's just that, beloved, and that you are not just happier to be away from me. I long for news of you, your little notes are kept in my bedside drawer and I read them over and over.

Your adoring husband,
Hugh

'Oh, Yorgo, what have you done?' In front of me the small, wrinkled man stood shaking his head vigorously from side to side. He was covered, brow to boot, in grey plaster dust. Well, some dust, otherwise it was flakes, chunks, and even at his feet, some hefty slices. It was falling, slowly for the most part, from the ceiling and walls of my living room, onto the man below.

'*Kalimera*, Kyria.' He paused in the shaking of his head momentarily and peered at me through thickly clogged eyelashes. 'I thought we should start quick, quick, not waste time. I finish Kyrios Manos's coffin before I go to my *gypo*.'

Then, 'Ah!' He stopped abruptly and ran across to the door, tripping on his ladder, which crashed from where it had been precariously balanced against a beam, bringing down with it most of the rest of the vast ceiling. Only the great beams, oaken, rich brown and majestic, were left behind; a mere skeleton of what had been before.

Ignoring this, and the fact that a moment ago we could

both have been killed, he was rummaging now in a sack which was under a heap of rubble.

A large hammer clattered to the floor and then, 'Ah yes!' He stood up, clutching three cucumbers in his grey and filthy hands. He skipped across what was now a building site to stop in front of me. 'For you,' he said, and I think he smiled – it was hard to tell.

'Fresh, very fresh. I picked them this morning for you. Tomorrow, tomatoes.'

I had a ruin of a house to live in, but at least I had three cucumbers. It was impossible not to smile, but truthfully dismay filled my heart.

It was going to be hard to write to Hugh with any enthusiasm about the work here and I kept feeling seriously panicky that I had made the right decision.

Holding the cucumbers, I looked up slowly. 'Why, Yorgo? Was it really necessary to pull the whole ceiling down? Why?'

'To see what was underneath, of course.'

'And what is underneath?'

'It is good. Bamboo, as I thought, and good hemp and sheep wool, all very old, of course, hundreds of years maybe. And there was much else besides. It will be warm in winter and cool in summer. Perfect.'

'And now that you have it down and know this, now what happens?'

He looked momentarily puzzled.

'Now, Kyria, we put it back up again.'

And that was the first day.

Each evening he walked me around what was still standing of the house. With delight and pride he showed me more and more devastation. Each day I wondered anew if I could live in this wreckage for much longer. One day the room I optimistically call my bedroom was piled so high with planks of wood I couldn't see my bed. Unbothered Yorgo shrugged his shoulders and turned to walk away. But this was too much for me. Even to my own surprise, I grabbed him by the sleeve of his filthy pullover, which stopped him dead. His eyes slid around and looked at my hand on his shoulder in astonishment. Quickly I took it away.

'Enough, Yorgo. I have had enough. All I see is my house falling down. Now I want to see at least one sign of it going up again. You cannot work alone like this; you must bring in some men to help you. How am I going to sleep in my bed tonight, buried like this?'

He looked so crestfallen I thought he might cry.

'Come,' he said in a small croak, 'come with me.' And he led me outside to where the old cypress tree stood at the edge of the path to the house.

There was my bed, one leg broken off and, lying on the top, three cats and a kitten were fast asleep, curled up on what I think was my pillow. Yorgo pointed to it with pride.

'See, I move it for you,' he said and shooed the cats off and away.

I closed my eyes and counted to five.

'You want me to sleep under the tree, Yorgo?'

He nodded glumly as he realised this was not, in my opinion, a good idea. I could almost see his mind ticking over.

'Not cold,' he tried. Then, 'No wind tonight, no rain.'

'No, Yorgo. You must mend the bed and bring it back inside. Tonight, I'd better sleep in the kitchen.' This was one room Yorgo had not touched. Yet.

So, with my help, that is what he did.

That night I took a chair outside and sat watching the stars. An unseen music echoed around the village, a plaintiff melody of ancient sadness, of love long abandoned. This was a low moment for me. The first time I felt both helpless and hopeless. I missed Hugh painfully, and regretted that I had urged him away.

It seemed impossible that I had ever thought that, alone, I could turn this wreck, this heap of old stones into a home for us. I recalled my excited dreams of warm tapestries lining the walls, children's voices echoing happily through the great rooms. Where was Hugh now? It seemed far more than a few months since he had gone. His letters always left me hungry for more. Yet what would I be doing there in Athens now? Lying alone in our bed, probably. I looked up as a small cloud rolled over the moon and a scops owl called aloud.

Enough self-pity, I told myself. Tomorrow I will help Anthi at the school and the hope in the eyes of the children will cheer me up.

The village school is a centre of real pleasure for me and I feel lucky to be here. I have been coming several days each week, and the children, now used to me, seem to like me.

It is a long, low building of soft grey stone. Its windows at the front are small, like little rabbit holes, as are all the houses built here. The sun does not shine in, so in the heat of the summer, the rooms inside are always cool. But there is a balcony all around the structure and in spring and autumn much of the schoolwork is done outside. I love the vista from this balcony, sweeping down to the village below, tucked into the curve of the mountain. The olive trees, with their gnarled trunks, some of them over a thousand years old, give a feeling of solidity and safety. Looking way up above, the little church of St Kosmas and Damianus sits on the highest peak, seeming to offer calm protection to all below.

Kyrios Tsimbanakis, the professor who runs the school, is a kind, genial man. If you met him elsewhere you would think, 'This man is a teacher, I hope.' He is much respected in Panagia for he controls the children without any resort to violence. A quiet word of reprimand and the class is immediately still.

There are probably thirty children in the school and gradually they were divided into three groups. The professor looks after the brightest – they tend also to be the oldest. Anthi looks after the middle group and Kyrios Tsimbanakis's wife, whom everyone calls Kyria Titica, looks after the youngest, some of them only two.

The school has become the centre of the community, along

with the church. Mothers leave their babies and toddlers here with Kyria Titica while they work in the fields. Often Anthi's little Voula, who is now beginning to toddle around, will be among them if she has not found a neighbour to care for her for a while.

I was warmly welcomed into this cheerful group with pleasure and interest. Education is the most important thing in villages like Panagia, so helping the children to speak English is a valuable service.

It was decided that I should have any child from any group who wanted to come to me for an hour or so each day; any child who showed the ability to learn some basic English.

This works well for me too. I can be at my house with Yorgo Babyottis whenever I feel the need. I smile at this thought; mostly the further away from both Yorgo and the house I am, the better.

For the first time since my marriage I feel a real sense of myself again. Here I am, performing a service. The children are a delight to me. Almost without exception, their bright eyes gleam as they rise to the challenge of new words or thoughts in this strange English language. They love to say a whole sentence and receive a 'bravo!' from me, a woman who but a short time ago had felt totally useless.

There is just one child who bothers me, a deaf and dumb boy. He is the only son of a shepherd and they live, the two of them, in a cave above the village. I learnt the boy's mother had died three years ago. Each morning his father, Manos, brings the boy into the school and each afternoon he collects him. Dimitri is thought to be about ten but neither Anthi nor Kyria Titica can be sure. He has no papers from his birth.

He is quiet, seemingly responsive, but silent. Whether he takes in and remembers any English at all, I can't be sure but Kyria Titica feels he's happy to be here, so he comes whenever he wants.

He is a painfully thin, angular child who seems almost to be just a skeleton, the flesh on his limbs is so sparse. His dark-brown eyes seem huge in his face, and rough, dark, grubby hair falls over his forehead into them.

One morning I arrived at the school before anyone else. Yorgo had woken me at daybreak with exciting news: he had found some workers to come and help him.

Thrilled as I was at this, I would have been equally excited an hour or so later. I found it hard to return to sleep, so decided to walk through the early sun, just breaking, and take the road to the school over the wooded hillside and up a long winding track. I am so early it is deserted. I pass through the area where the children usually play, which is just now silent, except for the birds singing. There is a figure curled up in the porch. It is Dimitri.

I run towards him and he cringes away as I reach down to touch him. He is cradling his head in his arms but through the torn sleeve of his shirt I can see drying streaks of blood on his arm and a couple of horrible slashes. On his knees, showing through the old cut-down *vraka* that barely covers his legs, it is clear there is dark purple and yellow bruising.

I hear a group of children beginning to arrive, Anthi's voice and laughter. I turn quickly; she sees me and I wave her over as urgently as I can without wishing to distress Dimitri, or alert the children to something being wrong.

As soon as she sees the child huddled there, she says, 'Stay here a moment with him. I'll get help.'

She is back almost at once, with the professor running behind.

I move aside. Dimitri remains motionless in his corner. I can almost feel his desire to disappear. Without any of the children stopping their play, or seeming to notice anything amiss, the professor picks Dimitri up, as gently as if he were an injured bird, and carries him through the back door and away.

Later, Anthi seems strangely reluctant to speak of the incident, only to say to me, 'It's nothing. We will keep him here for the day and the professor will take him to his father later.'

I thought I could sense a different atmosphere in the school. It may have been only my imagination, but it seems much quieter. At break time only a few children are running around outside, most are huddled in groups together. There is little laughter.

I went into Kyria Titica's room and there was Dimitri, still curled into himself on an old army bed, not unlike the ones in my house.

Anthi had followed me in and knelt down beside the boy, stroking his head.

She turned to look at me saying, 'You are a nurse, Heavenly, can you help him?'

I bent down to the motionless little figure. His eyes were closed. As I gently touched him, his eyes flickered open and, seeing me, abruptly closed again.

Gently I rolled up the sleeves of his shirt and moved his arms by turn, slowly and carefully, up and down and round. He didn't flinch. I did the same with his legs and as I finished, he instantly curled himself back again into the cocoon in which he felt secure.

'There are no breaks, which is a good thing, the bruises are bad, but will heal themselves. The cuts are quite deep though, I need to dress them. Wait here with him.'

I went quickly to my room and rummaged in the single drawer of the table there. I had, in the beginning, brought some simple first-aid remedies in, just in case. I had never needed them until now. I had iodine, some swabs and a few bandages. I went back to Dimitri and Anthi rolled him over to help me. I cleaned the wounds on his legs, and what looked like slashes on his arm. Iodine is painful on such raw cuts, but he did not flinch or moan. Mutely he lay still and let me finish.

As I put my old skills back into use, I felt a rising anger in me. 'I can't believe this comes from a natural fall, Anthi. It looks to me as though he has been beaten, and savagely too. Who has done this to him? Is it the father?' I spoke in English so only Anthi could understand.

'No. Not his father, never. I don't know who would do this to a child, but we must find out.'

'I'll go to my room,' I said. 'The children will be back again shortly.'

But there were no children who wanted to learn English today, it seemed, and I was alone. After a while, I stacked up my books and left.

As I walked home, the same way I had come a few hours ago, I looked around the echoing hills. What secrets did they hold? An image flashed into my mind of the dead sheep hanging in Anthi's garden and the swoosh of that knife as her husband, smiling with pleasure, it seemed, slit the belly open so the guts spilled out. Death and its companions were no strangers in these parts. Involuntarily I shuddered. It felt as though a chill wind had suddenly touched me.

Reluctantly, I walked up the path to my house – there were voices and some laughter coming from inside.

'*Yiassou*, Kyria,' Yorgo called to me as I walked inside. 'Very soon now the work can be finished. Soon, soon. You are pleased, eh?'

I looked around. Nothing was changed, it seemed to me. In the living room there was still rubble everywhere, the air thick with dust. My bed, I could see from here, was still in the kitchen, now decorated with a couple of old copper pans and two cats. But today Yorgo was not alone.

There were several other men scattered around the room.

Two I recognised as Hugh's drinking companions on the day of my accident out walking: the Kanavakis brothers; I nodded in their direction and tried to raise a weak smile. Another couple stood at the far end by the wine press. On top of the rubble on the floor there were now several long planks and a couple of tall ladders propped against the walls.

As the men realised who I was, they all went into instant action, picking up the ladders and moving them around, shifting the planks. One man had acquired a rudimentary broom and was briskly sweeping. Basically, this meant shifting the rubble from one bit of the floor to another.

Yorgo stood still in all this activity. Shuffling from foot to foot, he could tell from my face that I was not very impressed by what I could see.

'We will get all the work done very quickly, now I have good, strong help, Kyria. Look.' And he poked the arm of one of the Kanavakis brothers, who obediently flexed his biceps.

'You feel how strong.' But I hastily backed away.

'I'm sure you are right, Yorgo,' I said, somewhat desperately, 'but they don't actually seem to be doing any building, do they?'

'Kyria, of course not at this very moment, you see this is, just now, the time for lunch. They must have a break.'

'A break from what?'

'Ah, you see, a break from thinking about where to start, who is to do what, who is to be in charge of which job and when.'

I waited as he paused, running out of ideas.

'Much thought is required for a house as big as this one. As you will know, an educated kyria such as yourself, that thinking is tiring work. At four o'clock we will start. That is,' he hastily corrected himself, 'we will start again.'

It was hot. I was tired and I simply couldn't argue any more with this Cretan village logic. A battered chair was produced from somewhere and I sank down on to it. Everyone sat on the floor amidst the rubble.

Wine, bread and fruit appeared from various pockets, and from somewhere a half wheel of cheese and a lethal-looking knife.

We ate together in silence. The wine vanished quickly – three bottles seemed to have emptied by themselves when Spiros Kanavakis spoke.

'How old are you, Kyria?' and another said, 'How old is your husband?'

While I stumble over the answers to these rather surprising questions, Yorgo said, 'And how old is your king?' I didn't need to answer as the room then erupted into a discussion about the rights and wrongs of a monarchy and I remembered Hugh saying it was all anyone in Athens seemed to care about.

'About forty,' I said loudly. They stopped arguing and looked at me in surprise.

'The King of England is about forty, I think,' I said firmly.

'Why do you come here? Why are you alone? Why does your husband leave you here? What does your husband do? How much does he earn?'

I was bewildered by this hubbub of interrogation, but I remember Anthi telling me everyone asks personal questions of each other all the time, especially of a stranger. Yorgo, his eyes twinkling over his great moustache said, 'How much does your prime minister earn?'

I breathed a little more easily. 'Oh, millions and millions of drachmas, I should think, but I don't know for sure.'

'Huh,' said the small, rather swarthy one, called, I think, Petros, with a shrug, 'I suppose he can afford to eat tinned meat twice a week if he wants to.'

'Probably,' I said, hastily thinking of the tables heavy with food at the embassy banquets, 'at least twice.'

The questions died away and for a while there was silence.

A couple of men left the house and lay down under the cypress tree, no doubt feeling they had earned a rest after the arduous lunch. The others slowly wandered off, uttering half-heard promises about coming back to help another day.

Yorgo and I were left alone in the middle of the wreckage, now made even worse by the addition of cheese rind and fruit parings. I was about to try and get some sense out of Yorgo and force him to make a plan, a proper plan, when a sound from the doorway caused me to look up. There was someone there, someone I hadn't seen before.

The room was so dusty it was difficult to see him in detail, but a ray of brilliant sunshine came through the high window at that moment and lit up his face. He saw me at the same moment and smiled. He was young, probably only about my age.

He was holding two buckets and as he moved towards me,

still smiling, I saw they were brimful of water. As he reached me, he placed them on the floor at my feet and not a drop spilled. He wiped his hand on the back of his *vraka* and stretched it out to me.

'*Kalispera*, Kyria Timberlake,' he said formally, in a low voice. 'You have a beautiful house, it will be an honour to work on it.'

The ray of sunlight that had lit up his face followed him as he walked. I took his hand in mine and shook it. It was a strong, warm hand.

He was tall and slender, and the first thing I noticed was that he smelt of the sunshine outside and fresh grass. That was the moment it struck me that around the village most people smelt of their animals. It was not unpleasant, I was used to it. But this young man smelt oddly different, clean and sweet.

Beside him, Yorgo was bobbing up and down with excitement.

'This,' he spluttered, 'this is the very Christo, the only one, the son of my sister. He has come to make your house lovely. He is clever and-and—'

'Enough, Uncle,' said the very Christo. 'Kyria Timberlake knows there is much work to be done here and I will try and help, but it will not be quick. It must be rebuilt properly.'

I was so grateful to hear these words. This man would not just pull down walls, I felt sure, he would start to build them up.

As if I had spoken aloud, Christo said, 'First we must get these walls and ceiling back up again.' He looked around him, his eyes the same piercing blue as his uncle's, and only partially hidden by the little steel-rimmed glasses he wore.

'We shall get these ladders and planks together and make a scaffold, so that we can reach the top and start from there. We must make cement.' And he gestured to the buckets of water.

'But first, would you show me around your house, Kyria, and tell me how it is in your imagination?'

'I should love to do that,' I said. I hoped he would know

what I was talking about with colours and textures and feelings.

Together we walked into the adjoining kitchen. As this was almost part of the main room, it was not much better to look at than the living room, but at least the smoke-blackened ceiling and beams were intact. Yorgo hadn't taken his hammer to them yet.

I explained my fears to Christo and he shook his head.

'It's not necessary. My uncle felt it was important to take one room apart to discover its structure and make-up.'

'It seems a pity that he chose the biggest room to experiment on.'

'But that is the most important room in the house, from a structural point of view. If that roof is safe, everything else can rely on it and rest safely on it too.'

'And the bedroom?' I asked as we moved down the stairs and into it. 'Does everything rest on that too?' He smiled again, and thought for a moment.

'Well, I'll look at it and then decide, but I think that was probably a mistake.'

'I'm glad you say that,' I said, and he raised an eyebrow, questioning. 'Well, now I know I can trust you, because I think you are telling me the truth.'

He laughed. 'Perhaps when we look around, I can be truthful about more of my uncle's mistakes, but I hope not.'

'Oh so do I,' I said. 'I long for this house to be finished so that I can enjoy it properly. Your uncle thinks it is acceptable for me to sleep in my bed under the cypress tree.'

He laughed again. 'Well,' he said, 'I often sleep out under the stars when I come away from the town and into these hills. It is possible to sleep well and cleanly. You are quite safe.'

'But my friend Anthi has told me about the wolves here and they sound like a real danger.'

He was laughing again, 'Wolves are the stuff of old grand-mothers' nightmares – there have been no wolves around these hills for many years now. If there were, they would be hunted down and eaten, for sure, and quickly too. It was a bad winter and people in these villages are hungry.'

'Do you stay with your uncle here in the village?'

'No no, I prefer to be alone, to be independent. I sleep up there.' And he pointed way up into the mountains. He saw the puzzled look on my face and smiled. 'In a cave. I promise you it is very comfortable, warm and dry and clean.'

I must have looked doubtful. 'I'll take you and show you if you like.'

I pulled back. 'Oh no, I believe you.'

'Most of the shepherds here sleep up in the caves, you know. It is not a strange thing to do in this part of the world.'

I remembered Dimitri, the shepherd's battered son from this morning, and told Christo about him. He frowned slowly. 'I think I know this family,' he said. 'His father and his grandfather before him fought against the Turks and his uncle and his family were brought here from Turkey in the population exchange. You know about this bit of our history?'

I nodded, although it was a little hazy. I knew it was a major upheaval that had torn families apart.

'If you are interested, you should get someone to tell you about it. Your husband, maybe, when he comes back.'

'Perhaps you can tell me some more, while you are here working on the house?'

'It would be an honour, Kyria. But it is difficult for me to be impartial about this. I am not a royalist and there are two different stories to tell, perhaps more.'

'Can you call me Heavenly? It's what everyone calls me here.'

'My uncle calls you Kyria Heavenly, so perhaps it is better if I do the same?'

We walked on through the house; he was summing up each room in turn, I could feel it. Occasionally he nodded or said under his breath, 'Yes, yes.'

'I believe you came here from Athens and before that, England?'

'You know all about me already, I think,' I said.

He shrugged. 'Not all, no, just a very little. Like where you were before. Your husband is in Athens now, I understand.'

'Yes,' I said.

'There are few secrets here, Kyria Heavenly. Everyone knows everything. Never doubt it.'

'I have no secrets,' I said quickly.

'No matter. They will make something up if there is nothing to tell.'

'I thought, coming from Sitia, you would not be part of this?'

'I don't believe all the things I hear in the kafenion, for sure, but this is a simple place, no one writes letters or reads newspapers; so they only acquire knowledge by talking to each other, and then, of course, a little is added here and a little there and by the end of today, for instance, the village will believe your husband is closely related to your prime minister.'

I laughed at this absurd thought. 'And, of course, eats tinned meat at every meal, I suppose?'

He bowed his head and smiled. 'Of course. They meet in the laundry, the shop, the fields, by the school, in the square and buzz, buzz, buzz, little stories are passed around. Sometimes they start as truths, but if an old widow is feeling vindictive or perhaps just mischievous, these gossipy bits will be made up. Then, a much more interesting story comes along, and the last one is forgotten in the excitement of the new.'

While he was speaking, he had swiftly and athletically climbed onto my wooden boxes. These were all that I had as a wardrobe and chest of drawers. Even though he looked as though he knew what he was doing and had excellent balance, he seemed very precarious. As if he could read my thoughts he called, 'Don't worry, I won't cause harm. I dreamt of being in a travelling circus when I was a child, and practised in the trees, so this is an easy climb.' He clambered down swiftly.

'Your ceiling is quite safe here. This room used to house

the animals and no one would risk danger for them. They are the most important creatures in the household. They'd rather put the grandmother outside in a storm than let an animal suffer. They are much too valuable. It's good to have this as your bedroom down here. It will be cool in summer and warm in winter.'

He paused and then asked, 'How do you want your house to look, Kyria Heavenly? Do you want it to be very modern? Do you want marble on your floors and gilded edges to the steps? Are you fond of wallpapers and paints, brocades and the like? Maybe you want to cover these old walls with new *isvesti*, lose these dirty old stones?'

'Is that how you see me, Christo? As a woman who prefers brick to stone? Marble in preference to wooden floors?'

'You must tell me, Kyria, I do not know you yet.'

I took a deep breath, for clearly this was a testing moment.

'I shall not be keeping animals in the kitchen, you can be sure of that, and if my grandmother were alive and came here she would be treated at least as well as the goats, and she would certainly sleep in the house.'

As I was speaking, he had moved to the wall and was feeling a large stone that protruded into the room. 'Come here, Kyria Heavenly. Touch this stone, what do you feel?'

I let my fingers linger on the surface of the rock before I answered him.

'I feel the warmth of the summer sun from outside. I feel the strength of the sea that is so near. I feel that this has been part of this structure, part of this house, for many, many years.'

'Exactly,' he said and I realised his eyes had closed while he handled the stone. He was still smoothing it under his hands. 'Can you feel the dreams that have been dreamt here over the years? Can you sense the pain of a life lived a little too long?'

'Can a life ever be too long?' I asked.

'If the heart and the mind outlive the strength of the limbs, then maybe, yes.'

We paused, stepped back and looked at each other.

'I believe we feel the same things, Kyria,' he said. 'I think we will not be using marble and gilt. Am I right?'

'Oh yes, Christo, you are absolutely right. Will you make this house as beautiful as it used to be? Once upon a time, someone had a dream of how this house would look, even for the animals.'

'Then we must search for that dream,' he said. 'But first, I'm hungry, let's find my uncle and see if there is any of that cheese left.'

As we walked back through the rooms I tried to tell him how important it was that I should get this house ready for when Hugh comes back. 'I want us to live here, and I think my husband will need a lot of persuading.'

Back in the main room, Yorgo was trying to balance one of the ladders against the wall. Christo sprang across to help him. 'Here, Uncle,' he said, and showed him how it should be done, to make it hold the scaffold plank.

It seemed that within moments the room had taken a different attitude. Suddenly, with the addition of this struc-ture, I could see that building work could begin, that there would be no more destruction. Soon they were carrying hefty buckets of rubble outside. I stood nearby and watched as they carted them down to the ravine.

'We give these stones back to the mountain where they came from,' said Christo.

They worked together for the rest of the afternoon. I think Christo understood how useless I was feeling just watching them for, after a while, he said, 'Do you want to help, Kyria Heavenly?'

'Oh yes I do,' I said quickly. 'Tell me what I can do that will be useful.'

'Oh no!' said Yorgo. 'It is not suitable work for a lady like you. You should rest.'

'Rest from what exactly? And where precisely would you have me rest? I have done almost nothing all day. I *want* to help. Please let me.'

*

By the end of that day, the three of us had shifted at least half of the rubbish and the room, full of dust as it was, accepted the sunshine filtering through the window and the open door and suddenly felt like a different place to me.

At six o'clock we were dusty, grubby and exhausted, but I think we all felt an enormous sense of achievement.

I fetched raki and water and cut up pomegranates and we sat in the fading sun on the terrace drinking together as if we had been doing this all our lives.

I think the arrival of his nephew had re-energised Yorgo and he seemed happy to take second place to this young man who clearly knew what he was doing.

'Oh, Christo, you still haven't eaten. You were hungry and in search of food hours ago.'

He shrugged and waved my protest aside.

'I forgot about food when I started to work. It's always the way. My uncle will feed me tonight and I shall be fine.'

'Aphrodite is roasting fat pigeons. We shall have a feast.' Yorgo laughed and rubbed his hands together. I think he suddenly realised I was there and probably would dine alone for he looked awkward and said, 'Kyria Heavenly, perhaps you would like—' but I stopped him before he could go further.

'I have my supper planned, thank you, Yorgo. Remember you have brought me fresh salad every day, and I have eggs and cheese and cakes from Irini and her cousin. Plenty.'

He sprang to his feet and shaking my hand firmly, said, 'Until tomorrow, Kyria Heavenly.'

And they were gone. The room suddenly felt empty. It was; I was alone.

I ran outside and watched them walk down the mountain away from me, through the gathering mist, Yorgo astride his old donkey and Christo walking alongside. It was a timeless picture, two villagers moving across the horizon of these hills.

As I watched, Christo turned around. I couldn't see the expression on his face, but his glasses glittered in the last rays of the sun. He was too far away, but he waved to me, and hesitantly I waved my arm back.

Later, much later, I found it difficult to settle. Many things were going through my brain. All the events of the day were struggling in my head for supremacy.

Little Dimitri kept coming into my thoughts. I was worried and puzzled. I wanted so much to talk to Anthi, but I would not go there at this late hour. I had to accept that while I loved her and her children, I really did not like her husband Manolis and would not risk his sneers if I arrived after dark. Perhaps tomorrow I could walk over to her house and she would tell me.

I lay in my bed in the kitchen and thought how it would be under the stars. I listened to the dying sounds of the village around me; somewhere far away a confused cockerel was trying to herald an early dawn, a dog gave a desultory bark and some other creature howled at the moon. At least now I knew it wasn't a wolf, and I smiled to myself.

Yawning, I reached under my pillow for a handkerchief and my hand touched paper. It was Hugh's most recent letter and sleepily I started to read it through, but the words blurred on the page and I put it down beside me and closed my eyes.

My thoughts were of my house and of my hopes for it, and the last thing I remember thinking was about Hugh and the thought of him walking in here and his face showing astonishment at how much I had achieved.

ANTHI

There was a haze as thick as a bridal veil over the hills as we rode through them this evening. The dying rays of the sun tried to instil warmth into the hour, but I shivered a little. At my back, strapped close with a shawl, was my sleeping Voula. I put my hand behind me and felt her cheek – it was warm. Despina had gone home with Athena and her friends. I knew Maria would keep her there until my return.

Ahead of me, the professor held Dimitri in his arms as he urged his horse onwards. It was a younger and much stronger animal than Astrape, so it needed little coaxing to tackle the rocks and streams that broke up the path. Poor old Astrape stumbled often as he valiantly attempted to keep up. It was a losing battle and, hard as I tried to push him forward, the gap between the horses was widening and in the mist I could see the professor disappearing from view. No matter, I knew the way to Dimitri's cave well, and the important thing was to get him there quickly, and home with his father; if his father, Manos, was there.

To be truthful, I was not supposed to be here. The professor told me to stay with my girls: 'I can manage better alone,' he said. 'It doesn't need us both to take one child home.'

But I was curious, needed to know. If there was danger for one child in the village, perhaps there was danger for them all?

It was rare for Manos not to collect his son. Was something wrong? After all, I was sure he would never raise a hand to him.

In the surrounding caves in that cluster of rocks the shepherds thought of as home, I would swear no one else would touch him. They are a close-knit community of their own who had lived apart from the village for many years.

Coming down only to seek work, they were diligent and honest. It had taken a long time for people to trust them. Many of them had seen much conflict in their lives. Some had come from Turkey in the population exchange, leaving behind their homes and any hard-won living to return somehow to this island they knew of as their own.

Some had fought against the Albanians and ended up here with nothing but the rags on their backs. Most of them, one way or another, came from another life. Some had chosen to live this bleak, lonely existence; dependent on no one for their welfare. As a consequence they thought of themselves as brothers. If you hurt one, you hurt them all.

That is why I was so sure the injuries to Dimitri had come from outside these barren mountains. There had been no strangers passing through. It must have come from within the village of Panagia. If there was an incomer, the word spreads around our community like the wind. It was the season for the passage of gipsies, I know, and there had been many lately; coopers, carpenter-craftsmen offering hand-carved chairs for sale, knife grinders, legume sellers from the island of Rhodes, sellers of cakes, sweetmeats, ribbons and threads. But these men and their families were known to us all, they had been trading in Panagia for years. They would have no reason to harm a simple shepherd's son from the caves.

Quarrels in these parts were usually simple. They may be long-lasting; years, generations even, but at the core the reasons are straight: among women, almost always the gossip is about the size of a dowry, among men, about property or boundary lines, borders of land. Politics and differences of opinion about royalty can divide whole families for years.

But none of those things would apply to the cave dwellers. What use would they be in an argument about the king, or the ruling of the country?

I shook my head and gently kicked Astrape on for the last half mile.

Underneath me his poor tired old legs struggled to keep moving forwards, but gallantly he pushed on relentlessly. I patted his rump gently. I knew he would never let me down whilst there was breath left within him.

There was no sign ahead of the professor, or his precious passenger.

A faint scent of wood smoke in the soft mountain air told me we were approaching the caves. It sharpened as I pushed upwards, and Astrape whinnied and shook his head.

I pressed him to a halt by a pine tree, bent and twisted from the wind, and there was the professor's horse, tethered roughly to the trunk. He was almost invisible in the evening mist, but Astrape moved towards his old friend and stood, patient and exhausted, beside him.

I went onwards alone. I was mercifully sure-footed on this rough track. I have walked here all my life.

I could hear the professor's voice, although he was speaking low and gentle. Cautiously I stepped forward and into the entrance of a cave.

The flickering light from an oil lamp showed the rough interior. It was simple but quite large and in the chill evening air I could feel warmth from inside. The professor was lowering Dimitri to the ground and I could dimly make out the huddled figure of his father on a blanket under an overhanging rock. As I watched, Manos reached out an arm to his son who whimpered painfully as he stretched to touch his father. I could see, even from where I stood, that Manos's arm was bruised and bloody.

'You'd have done better to leave him in the school tonight.'

'Did you bring him down this morning?' The professor's voice was soft.

'I did. I could do nothing for him here. I see you have dressed his wounds at least.'

'We have indeed. The Englishwoman who comes to the

school was a nurse. Do you want to tell me what happened here last night? I assume it was last night?'

Manos didn't answer immediately, but paused and looked around in the flickering gloom of the cave. I must have moved at that moment for he suddenly saw me and called, 'Who is it? Who are you?'

I stepped forwards into the light.

Holding Dimitri tightly in his arms, Manos stared at me for a moment and I saw immediately that not only his arm, but also his face, was bruised and swollen.

'What are you doing here?' he said.

'Please, you know who I am,' I said gently. 'You know how I care for Dimitri in school; I was worried about him.'

Still he was silent. He was angry and suspicious for sure. The professor did not look pleased that I was here. He spoke under his breath: 'Perhaps this is men's business, not the place for you.' I was stricken. He was right. Of course I should not be here and I turned to leave at once.

Manos spoke and I paused.

'Perhaps it is no one's business but my own.'

The professor spoke again. 'We are only here to try and help,' he said.

'Perhaps we don't want your help,' was the reply.

'But Dimitri needed help, didn't he?' I looked from one to the other.

'If you think I beat up my son, you are wrong. And if I did, it is not for you to chastise me, gossip about me.'

Unwanted here as I was, I had to speak.

'Oh, please, we would never believe that and certainly never let you or your son be the subject of rumour or gossip. It is because we know you would never harm Dimitri that we came. And it is clear that you yourself have been beaten. Is there nothing we can do?'

He laughed harshly. 'You?' he said and looked away.

There was a long silence and I saw that Dimitri had fallen asleep, safe now in his father's arms. A small string of dribble trailed from his baby-like lips; he seemed so vulnerable. It broke my heart to see his battered little face, the painful cuts now drying into scabs. He is a child who cannot speak in his own defence and never will be able to.

'Come, Anthi, we'll not bother them further.'

It was as the professor turned that Manos finally spoke again, the sleeping boy rocking gently in his arms.

'It's not the first time we have felt threatened here. Ever since the sheep started to go missing, some in the village have turned against us. We are the obvious targets. We have little, but down there,' he pointed savagely, indicating the bottom of the mountain, 'something goes missing and it must be us who have taken it! An animal dies strangely, and we must be responsible. It's a rough justice there now. Ever since the mayor died, it has been every man for himself; there is no one to speak for us.'

A picture suddenly came to me: sheep! A violent memory of my husband slaughtering the lamb; the innards slithering out. I didn't know there had been others.

Outside an owl screeched. Close by I hear a great rustle of wings and the high scream of an animal trapped. The abruptness of the silence told us the owl had caught his prey. I stood, unable to move. I felt cold all through me, a sharp stab as if a knife of ice was seeking my heart.

I opened my mouth but no words came. My throat was as dry as a bone bleached by the mountain sun. 'And Dimitri?' I finally managed to ask.

He looked at the boy, sleeping peacefully in his arms, and stroked the top of his head. His gaze penetrated through me, his eyes were like cold steel. 'They came last night and he got in the way. Simple as that.'

He fell into a stubborn silence, making it clear he wished us gone. We turned to leave. We had no place here now.

We didn't speak until we had reached our horses. Darkness had fallen while we were in the cave and there was a strong chill breeze now blowing. I pulled my shawl closer around Voula and shivered.

We parted ways at the bottom of the mountain path, the

professor to his village over the next hill and me to my home in Pano Panagia. He took my hand briefly and warmed it in his strong grasp.

'Titica and I will take them something tomorrow. Dimitri must have shoes and certainly clean bandages. Titica will ask Heavenly to show her how to dress the wounds.'

'What do you think really happened there, professor?'

'Don't look for trouble where there is none. You heard what he said? Leave it at that. I told you not to come.'

'One of the sheep he spoke of came from our flock, not stolen, I agree, but an unnatural death. Manolis is not a man to forgive and forget, do you think—'

'You have always had a powerful imagination. Let this matter rest now. Accept what Manos has said and get on with your life. Look to your children.' And he was gone.

I need to talk to someone who knows the village and the villagers well. Someone who cares about the cave dwellers and who doesn't always assume they are thieves, sheep-stealers. I distrust my husband so completely, he is the first person to my mind to be involved in evil-doing.

Above me the stars looked coldly down; I would get no help from the heavens. Away across the hill, the faint voice of the cantor echoed from the church. Of course, today is the day of a big memorial ceremony for Andreas Mamadopolous, the mayor. He was a good and powerful man in Panagia and there was much grief when he died. Today it is the special ceremony that takes place ninety days after death, and my grandparents will be there. My Pappous was a very close friend of Andreas. There are many here who want him to be the next mayor. With great reluctance he has adopted some of the smaller duties until a new man is appointed.

He, like Andreas, is seen as an honourable man. I must ask him to seek justice for these people. As I urged Astrape forward, I looked again up to the heavens. There was the brightest of the stars, the evening star, always first to shine.

'Thank you, Papa,' I said to myself.

*

I stood at the back of the church with the other women and looked around, savouring the rich smell of incense. The church was packed – Andreas had been a popular man and it seemed the whole village had come today in his memory.

I scanned the faces, looking first among the men. Manolis was not there.

But there was my Pappous, dressed as usual for such an event in his old blue flat hat with the red scarf draped across his shoulder. With his proud silver moustache he could have been a visitor from another century. And there, at the back with the women, was Yaya. I caught her eye and she smiled.

Papa Costas, himself an old friend of Andreas, chanted the closing words of the service; I had got here just in time.

Everyone milled around the entrance and some took my hand or kissed me in welcome. Many asked after the health of my mother and I murmured some reply that I hoped would satisfy. My grandmother bustled close to me and took my cold fingers in hers. Her dear hand was warm and rough to the touch. I took it up to my face and saw her fingernails were blackened. She pulled her hand swiftly away and hid it behind her back. 'Elderberries,' she said, by way of explanation. 'There will be some preserve for you for later.' She reached her hand up behind me and murmured some endearment to Voula, who was stirring now and cooing. 'Here, let me hold her for you, Anthi, she is heavy and you look tired.'

Voula chortled in Yaya's arms – she loved her great-grandparents and it was a while since she had seen them.

'Will you come back to the house with us, Anthi? We understand if you . . .'

Her soft grey eyes were full of love, she would forgive me any lapse, I know.

'Of course, Yaya, I need to ask Pappous' advice.'

She looked at me shrewdly. 'Are you in trouble, child?' she said, her brow now creased into a frown.

I smiled. 'Of course not. But if I were, where else should I go for help?'

She nodded, reassured. 'Come, we shall take some of Irini's

memorial bread and get Pappous away from those wicked friends of his; they would have him down to the Piperia playing *prefa* and we should not see him until midnight.' But she was smiling now and I knew she spoke in jest.

The scent of acacia was strong and sweet in the air and jostled for precedence with the lavender and rosemary that grew in profusion around their door. Yaya fumbled for the key she kept under a stone in the porch. I felt a momentary anxiety for Despina, but I knew she had gone home, would light the lamps and wait for me.

'I have heard this sheep business talked about in the Piperia. It was a hard winter, food is scarce, money is almost non-existent and that makes simple people behave in ways they might avoid in more prosperous times.' Pappous threw another log onto the already blazing fire and sat back. He was drinking his usual raki and I was sipping a hot cordial Yaya had made from wild berries gathered on the mountain.

'Cretans have always been fighters. If they can't take arms for the defence of their country, they'll find something else to rage about. But I tell you, if war comes as they say it will, everyone will want Cretans as friends, certainly not enemies.'

'War, Pappous?'

'I listen to the wireless set Fanis has installed in the Piperia and I'm sure war is not far away.' He paused, puffing at his pipe. 'Years ago, this village was not the happy place it seems to you now. Families fought against families, as they did all across this island. We were Cretans, not Greeks – we still are!' The strong raki slipped down his throat in a single gulp and he held out his glass for Yaya to pour him another, which she did. 'You know, my friends and I grew up believing violence was normal in a village. When our fathers went off for a day's hunting, we almost expected them not to return in the evening. As children we played revolutionaries and soldiers. Our guns were sticks, but we all longed for the real thing. We never knew about sides. We copied what we saw our fathers and uncles and neighbours do – shoot each other. We never questioned why. And nobody told us, so when we were older and got real guns, we were ready to go and shoot anybody.'

Yaya had lit the lamp now and, immediately, excited moths rammed the glass of the shade again and again, and silvery powder from their collisions fell on the table.

'All I do know is that Cretans were one people and the Turks and their followers and descendants were not. Not true Cretans.' He gave a hoarse laugh that wasn't a laugh. 'Aah, so what? It is all history now and should be buried under the stones of time.' His stick was trembling in his hand and, seeing it, he coughed and turned the tremor into a bang: up and down, up and down on the cracked tiles.

'Pappous, I need to ask you something.' He looked at me quizzically. 'Can you not do something for these poor cave dwellers? They have nothing, not even one *stremata* of land between them. It seems so unfair they should be considered target practice for the village men, who have nothing better to do.' Of course he knew what I was thinking and said at once, 'Child, I am too old now to take on all the responsibilities of Andreas Mammadopolous. We speak of this often in the Piperia. There will be a mayor before too long. I hope, a younger man. Until then I do what I can, of course. I'll ask around and see what I can find out.' He seemed momentarily lost in thought and puffed hard on his big pipe. I love the smell it makes, that pipe. It is a ripe autumn smell that makes me think of log fires burning, warm wine and a wonderful *stifado*. This is a stew that my Yaya makes better than anyone in the village. Its rich scent of rabbit and juniper fills the air now and I can see she is already ladling a stone dish full for me to take home. My mouth waters as I think of eating this later, but I must remember why I have come. I must tell them of my fears that Manolis may be involved in this revenge.

As I knew they would be, they are horrified.

'You can do nothing about this, child,' Yaya says at once. Her fingers are nimbly tying a length of hemp around the pot I shall carry away. 'You must forget this nonsense. It cannot concern you.'

But it is to Pappous that I look for an answer. His eyes are creased in what I think is anger and I am right, for when he finally speaks, his words are like sparks that shoot from the fire and will burn as they land.

'She can do nothing about this on her own, Giorgia, but she must know the truth. We must all know the truth. This is our family as well, our name that will be associated with this. It is a bad time, little one, when neighbours, friends in a village, take arms against each other. It was always easier to give in to the invaders. That way you stayed alive. If you fought, as any true Cretan did, mostly you were punished. Your house burnt down, your sheep or crops destroyed. Our family, your family, Anthi, stood against the Turks. My father and I fought side by side on this mountain. In my life I have seen many die here. One time, eight men from Panagia were shot as they lay sleeping. One, who had dug his land daily with my mother's father, was killed by a neighbour of them both. A bullet in the head. BANG!' His shout caused Yaya and me to shudder.

'Another, Yannis Gordopoulos, remember, Giorgia?' He crossed himself three times. 'Yannis was married to the daughter of the man who killed him. He hung his body from a cedar tree as a warning to others.' He paused again. I saw silent tears sliding down my yaya's cheeks. I moved across to sit beside her, near to tears myself at her pain. This was my fault. I dropped my eyes in shame.

'Don't upset yourself, child. It is not wrong to remember the truth. Be proud to be a good Cretan, and that means caring for the poor and helpless in our community. Men, women and children who are, for one reason or another, unable to defend themselves. I will walk home with you. I know you well, you are your father's daughter; you will let nothing rest unsaid. It is a dark night and I prefer you not to walk alone.' I smiled. Even with my own baby here, and her sister waiting, he still saw me as a child myself. I found the thought comforting, and, as I knew he would, he did not dismiss me as being over-imaginative.

The mist was lighter here in the village, but it was thick enough to hide the stars. I looked up and saw the mountains were now completely in the clouds, cloaked like a shroud. I shivered, and not only from the chill.

Pappous sat on his donkey and rode ahead of us through the outskirts of Panagia.

The closer we got to my house, the more apprehensive I felt. 'He may not be here.' I said quietly.

'Child, do not fret. I am an old fool, I know, but I will do nothing to cause your husband's alarm. I shall certainly ask around, with discretion, to see what I can discover, but confrontation without informed knowledge or proof is not the way of a good soldier, don't worry.'

As we crossed the hill, the dim light from our lamp shone through the windows, and I knew the house was not empty.

We tethered our animals and walked through the half-open door. The very first thing I notice is that there was no sign of Despina. On my back Voula was getting fretful and I thought I should have fed her before we left Yaya.

Manolis was in his usual place by the fire that was blazing like the gates of hell. The stack of logs beside the door had dwindled and would not last the night if the fire continued to eat them as greedily as it was now doing.

Manolis, his back to us, did not stir as we came in and I saw quickly that the raki jug at his feet lay on its side, empty.

My grandfather called out a greeting and at his voice Manolis slowly turned his head. Holding on to the arms of the chair to help himself, he peered at us blearily.

'Where is Despina?' I asked.

'Excuse me, wife's grandfather.' It was as if I hadn't spoken. 'I am not feeling quite myself tonight. I have not eaten yet and my hunger is great. You see your granddaughter has other things to occupy her, instead of minding her house and her family. You are aware from her words that she doesn't even know the whereabouts of her eldest daughter, who could be lost on the mountain, for all she cares.'

Fury swept through me at his words, but it would not do

me good to answer him just now. Voula was in full cry and needed my urgent attention. I swiftly crossed the room and sat in my nursing chair in the dark corner at the back. I would not give Manolis the satisfaction of questioning me about exposing my breast in front of them.

My grandfather ignored Manolis and was now refusing coldly his offer of alcohol.

'Not even a glass of my best wine?'

'I will take nothing. I think your wife needs you to tell her where Despina is.'

Manolis poured a glass of the rich, ruby-coloured liquid for himself. First the jug of raki, now the wine; for sure I would be clearing away his vomit tonight.

He shrugged. 'The raising of the children is my wife's duty. Perhaps the child is with one of our neighbours?'

My grandfather's eyes were like black ice as he turned to me.

'Where is she likely to be, Anthi?' he said. 'I shall go and fetch her to you.'

'Thank you. I think she will be with her friend Athena, the daughter of Maria and Michaelis. They came from school together and usually play here or there.' Without another word, Pappous turned and left the house.

Manolis spat in the fire and watched the flame spurt up before he stood and spoke to me. 'Why is Stephanos Karanakis here? He is not the most preferred of visitors in my house.'

'He is my grandfather, Manolis, and he will always be welcome wherever I am.'

'You forget something, wife, this is my house and visitors are only welcome here with my permission. He is a dangerous man in Panagia, and well you know it. He has always been known as an agitator, a communist.' And he spat on the fire again.

My heart was beating fast in my breast. 'At least he is a man of honour. A kind man who does not attack innocent people and children.'

I was shaking as I spoke and Manolis turned and smacked his fist into my face. I reeled back in shock and pain, clutching my baby even tighter in my arms and she began to cry.

'You are hysterical, Rodianthi, and don't know what you are talking about.' His voice was like snake venom, creeping into my heart.

My face burnt and stung, like one of my bees had taken against me, or as if I had fallen in a bed of nettles.

He had taken his hands to me often before, but never with such violence.

'You won't silence me, Manolis. Beat me as you choose, I will speak out.'

His face was ugly in his rage and he was breathing hard. There was little difference between him and the dog that lay panting at his feet. I think he would have hit me again, but my Pappous was standing in the doorway.

'Not there. She is not there.' He had returned just as I was bringing myself together and starting to change Voula. 'Michaelis said she had walked home with Athena but he saw her wave and come on in this direction. He assumed she had come here, to her home, to you.'

My heart thumped wildly again and my voice was little more than a tremble.

'Did you not see her, Manolis? What time did you come home?'

Despina is eight now and a sensible child. She knows her way around the village as well as anyone older and wiser.

He shrugged. 'What does it matter? She is not here and that's it. She'll come back. I'll go to the other end of the village and look. And I'm telling you, if I find her, she will have the biggest thrashing of her life.' He clutched the arms of his chair, making to rise. His head was shiny with sweat and I asked myself, for the millionth time, why my mother had thought him a suitable husband for me.

Pappous and I looked swiftly at each other. Both of us realised, I think, that Manolis was incapable of finding a scorpion in a coffee cup in his state. The kafenion he visits is the only place his steps will take him and if he finds Despina on the way he will drag her with him, for sure, and I do not want my daughter taken to such places. As if to prove his lack of intent, he slumped again into his chair and drank deeply from his wine glass.

'Come, Anthi,' said Pappous, 'we can do nothing standing here. We must go through the village. She is a good and sensible girl. We shall find her in no time at all.'

Pulling my shawl around Voula and myself, I hurried with my grandfather to the door.

'You can leave the baby here, if you want, I shall not eat her.' Manolis paused, belched loudly and continued, 'even though I am near to starving myself. Thanks to you, wife.'

I did not answer but silently put my grandmother's dish of rabbit stew on the table and Pappous pulled the door shut behind us.

The night was full dark now and coming from the warmth of the house, I shivered in the blackness.

'Come, onto the donkey with you. I shall walk beside.'

Gratefully I sat in the hard, worn old saddle moulded over the years to fit my grandfather's rear. For half an hour or so, we walked the rocky paths of the village. Far down below, the light of a fishing boat blinked faintly out at sea, but I was too concerned about my daughter to wonder who was out there tonight. From chimneys the sweet smell of olive wood fires fragranced the air as we passed. We were the only people abroad in the foggy night. Others were warm in their houses with their animals or already sleeping. From somewhere ahead, through the thickening mist, I heard the sweet sound of a woman's voice. She was singing a song I recalled from my childhood – it was Yaya's voice.

Pappous stumbled and clutched the saddle beside me. His great moustache was glistening with the drops it had gathered from the air and his splendid hat was trembling.

I knew he was worried and upset by the events of this evening and I felt guilt that it was I who had caused this. Sometimes it is easy to forget he is an old man.

'Is it my wife?' he said, and then louder, 'Is it you, Giorgia? What are you doing here singing, and so late? What is wrong?'

She was still invisible through the damp mist, but she answered, 'Stephano, I have Despina here. With me.' It *was* Yaya! My daughter had gone to my grandmother. I jumped down from the donkey and she ran into my arms weeping.

'Don't cry. You are safe. We are together now, nothing is wrong.' Pappous ruffled his hand across Despina's head and murmured words of comfort to her.

'I don't know why she came to us, but I am pleased that she thought to do so. She was greatly distressed when she arrived, but I could get nothing from her to tell me why. She hasn't spoken. She missed you by moments only, and I knew you would worry, so I thought I must get her back quickly.'

'I am so grateful. Despina, come with me now.' Yaya was mopping her face. Pappous put his arm around her and she seemed happy to have his support, for she leant against him, almost collapsing.

'Thank you, Yaya, and thank you, Pappous. I will find out what has happened here.' Despina's tears had almost stopped, but she was snuffling and hiccuping into my side and trembling like a feather in the wind. I rubbed her head. 'My darling child, it's all right, you are safe. Pappous, you must take Yaya home, we will all come to see you tomorrow. I can only apologise for the lack of welcome you received in my house.' Both my grandparents hugged me and I felt the warmth and security of their unquestioning love.

Pappous and I helped Yaya onto the donkey. Her clothes felt damp from the misty air and, knowing we could run to warm ourselves, I wrapped my shawl around her in spite of her protests.

'Until tomorrow. We have unfinished business I shall not forget. Take care of yourself tonight.' And Pappous lowered his voice: 'You must not rile your husband in any way; his mood is ugly with the drink. Do not put yourself at risk any further.' As he spoke, his hand gently stroked my swollen, bruised cheek. So he had seen.

I put my hand on his arm. 'It's since the stillbirth of our only son – I can do nothing right for him.'

'*Sto kalo,* child,' he said. 'Take care of yourself.'

The children fell asleep quickly and I lay with them. I was deadly tired with a throbbing head but sleep was far away. I was trying to make sense of the day behind me. Manolis was still in his chair by the side of the fire. He had not looked at me, feigning sleep when we returned. But it was obvious that he was awake, for his fingers were moving through the rough black coat of the dog lying at his feet. He was picking off fat grey fleas that he threw to the floor and ground his foot over. I shuddered each time I saw him doing this. It would be for me to scrub it clean in the morning.

Despina had clung to my skirts desperately, all the way home. From time to time, a great hiccuping sob would shake her body. But she would not speak a word.

This worried me, she is normally full of chatter, but there was something alien in her silence tonight, as though she was afraid. And she shook all the harder as we walked into the house.

She wanted nothing to eat, even Yaya's stew, which usually she would gobble down.

'Did you eat with Yaya?' I asked. She shook her head vigorously.

When we were upstairs I questioned her gently, 'Was Papa here when you came from school?'

She was looking blankly into the far corner of the room and seemed unable to answer me. Her face was milk-white and her eyes looked bruised with tiredness.

'Did you do something naughty to make Papa cross?'

She was in bed now and buried her face in the rough hemp of the sheet, pulling the cloth around her tightly so that she had made a cocoon for herself, not even her face looked out. Within moments she slept.

As I lay with both my girls, worried and unhappy, I was thinking that something was wrong here and I could not understand what it was.

Later, much later, I left them for a moment to creep down the stairs, to see if Manolis had left any of Yaya's stew. I thought it unlikely. But I could not sleep while I was so hungry.

I stopped halfway down. There were voices from the living room where I had left Manolis alone but for his dog. Oh, *Panagia mou*, it was the priest, Papa Yannis! I shuddered as his fat, greasy face came into my mind. There was another voice, which I recognised as coming from Dimitri Kostanakis. He was one of Manolis's friends. I dislike him and his skinny, mean-faced wife.

I had not heard these men arrive, and they spoke together quietly with Manolis, but I could not understand why they were here and not at the kafenion.

I sank down onto the step and sat there hunched forward so I could hear, but it was almost impossible to make out their words.

I heard Manolis shout something that sounded like 'Ignorant communist peasants!' and the sound of his spit hissed on the remains of the fire, his voice slurred by the amount he had drunk. I heard the priest laugh and cough throatily; then a clink of glasses and a slurp of something being poured.

There was a stale smell of cigarette smoke, drink and unclean men. There were no windows or doors open to sweeten the air. The fat priest wheezed on, but I could not tell what he was saying.

I was becoming chilled sitting on the stairs. Manolis had let the fire die to its embers, so there was no warmth in the house now. I wanted to know what plotting was being organised. I felt sure I knew of one family already who had suffered at their hands. Were there to be others? I shivered, my thoughts spinning in my head, I was so tired. Tomorrow I must finish clearing the rest of the fields. We are late this year. The stubble must be burnt off quickly before any rain.

Downstairs, the men were moving towards the door and they were louder, drunken but louder. I heard my Pappous' name mentioned and I trembled. I struggled for the next words but it was impossible. What could they find to say about my beloved grandfather? Then a few words from a broken sentence came clearly to me: 'Englishwoman's house'. And then, shockingly, 'She thinks the sun shines out of that fat English arse. Sure, it's time for her to learn a lesson.'

Who? Who needed a lesson: Heavenly, my dear friend, or me?

These are dangerous men indeed. I felt only fear at the thought of them in the house. I had no feeling in my feet from sitting with them so tightly held for so long; an emotional frostbite that left my extremities feeling swollen and unfamiliar.

I loathed my husband completely tonight and knew I must take care of Despina, Voula and myself more than ever.

The priest and Kostanakis left soon after and, as I moved slowly up the stairs to my girls, the only relief I had was to hear Manolis's snores. Tonight, at least, I would sleep alone.

But it was hours before my stiff body could relax.

I awoke long after the rest of the village and, quickly jumping from my bed, I could not see the girls, but Voula was sobbing from somewhere in the house. My body was slow and heavy today and my yawns seemed never-ending but I got myself together somehow and forced myself down the stairs thinking to see Manolis snoring.

Not so; he had started the fire and was walking Voula round and round the room, rocking her in his arms. He looked awkward and clumsy. His hairless head was already coated in a sweat. 'This baby needs her mother,' he said roughly and thrusting her away from him he pushed her into my arms. Despina sat at the end of the table eating a chunk of bread and drinking water.

I quickly quietened Voula at my breast. 'Will you have some fruit with your bread, Despina?' She shook her head.

Her eyes had not looked up once since I had come down the stairs. Manolis walked round the table towards me and looked at Despina closely. 'She has not spoken this morning,' he said, and he shrugged.

It was as though my child, my sparkling, laughing Despina, had been taken, and another put in her place.

'Speak to me, Despoula, my dear one.' And rising, I moved round and held her in my arms. Our house is not known to be one full of love and perhaps because of this my daughters like to be held, cuddled more than most. This morning was different and Despina was rigid in my arms. I stroked her hair back from her brow. She didn't respond to the touch. I wanted to weep as this changeling child was rejecting my advances. I looked up helplessly at Manolis, but his face was stony.

I took my shawl from the hook under the *iconostasis*. 'Come, we will take Astrape this morning and ride to the school.' This was normally a great treat for them and Voula laughed. But this morning there was no answer from Despina and her eyes were blank, but she did rise and allowed me to push her gently forwards.

'Away in a manger, no crib for a bed . . .'

The little voices went on but they were getting ragged now and there was laughter. Heavenly was here.

'Listen, Despina. You know who is here today? You can go and join in. They are singing the English Christmas song Heavenly taught you.'

This morning she didn't jump down and run in as normal, but clung on to the saddle as if she would never move again. 'Come, Despina, Voula and I will come with you.' There was suspicion in her eyes, but at least she moved to get down from the horse. She clutched my skirt as we went in the door.

'Despina! How lovely. I thought you might be ill.' And Heavenly held out her hand to her. There was a moment of stillness and then Despina moved forward and took it in hers. She looked round the room and I knew she was afraid that her friends might laugh at her. I understand my daughter and her feelings well.

She was a different child this morning and anyone could see it.

Heavenly looked at me, unspoken questions in her eyes; I think she had seen my bruised face, but there was nothing I could say. She nodded to me, and taking Despina with her, moved across to rejoin the group of children. But within seconds, Despina was back clutching at my skirt again.

She was beginning to seriously worry me. Why would she suddenly stop speaking? What had sent her reeling back to babyhood overnight? My arm went around her, and I uttered a silent prayer to the virgin. There was no question of leaving her here without me.

The professor was at the door as we passed by. There were questions in his face as he saw me, but he would not ask in front of the child.

'I'll be here as usual tomorrow. You will stay if I am here, won't you, my darling?' Her face was bleak but she nodded. And with a sense of disappointment and failure, we left the school.

Outside the sky had cleared but the mountains, thundery grey against the deep sky, seemed to tower against a deeper darkness, a threatening, violent darkness. I felt afraid as I rode home through the village. I am not a woman who feels fear. But today I felt the first threads of it weave their way through my blood. With all that I have known in my short life, I have never felt so vulnerable as I do now.

I rode on as if in a dream. I saw flashes of water through the rocks, and a waterfall, a snatch of music, a lit window and someone pulling water from the well in a yard, goats rang their bells as they moved from one graze to another; in the sky a falcon swooped low on an unseen creature in the stubble and a distant barking told me dogs would soon be out scavenging the fields for any nesting creature. All these things were so familiar to me, they were the tapestry of my life, but this morning they seem to have taken on a new and unknown dimension. And there is no comfort for me here.

I looked down at my firstborn child, just there in front of me on Astrape's saddle, and circled her small body with my arm. Then I felt a pat on my head and a sweet cooing. Voula was gently stroking my hair. Her tiny hands came to the front and as she patted my cheeks, I knew I was weeping. Here was the root of my fear, in my girls. And I don't know what is happening to us.

HEAVENLY

My dearest Evadne,

I think we must be living in two separate worlds, you and me. I have to admit I read your letters about the building work going on in the house with some horror, although this chap Christo seems to know what he's doing, which makes a change, but is it really necessary for you to work with them?

The thought of you banging away with a hammer is an amusing one, I agree, but not really suitable for a diplomat's wife.

Your life in the school sounds interesting enough but I hope, my love, you are not working too hard. I like to think of you having lazy days in the sun, not rushing around a class full of smelly brats. Do you have to keep going there? If you are bored, I can ask Janet to send you some silks and whatever bits and pieces needed to make a tapestry? You may enjoy that. I hate to sound stuffy and preachy, darling, but I keep thinking of you and wondering where you get your hair done and things like that. Who does your laundry? Don't tell me you go to that spring place with all the village women!

Meanwhile, life feels very unsettled here. The Germans seem to be full of good intentions and are offering help with the Greek defence programme, but can one really trust them?

They were here for three days and ended up giving Metaxas more than three hundred and fifty million drachmas for armaments, which is not to be sneezed at! On top of that, my old chum from school, Charlie Boot was here (he couldn't make it to the wedding, but you may have met him at Troutbeck? Damn fine fast bowler).

Well, his family are big financiers in the city, and I understand over a couple of million pounds is on offer. Trust a Wykehamist! I gather a chunk will come your way, to help out your peasants in Crete.

Charlie had a bit of a wild time while he was here. Even I had a job to keep up with him! I can't remember if I told you I had a cablegram from Lady T? Well, she arrived here on the twenty-fourth and she is staying in the Residence. I must say, it's wonderful to have her here. She's en route to Egypt. That's where everyone is heading. She's taken a house there with some chums. There's pretty much a feeling of panic, it seems. In the UK, they are all worried about war in Europe.

There's a lot of talk here of northern Crete being a particular hot-spot. I know you are down in the south-east, my love, but I worry that I could look after you better if you were here with me. At the first sign of trouble, those villagers you are so fond of will rush out to fight. I know I've asked before and you never seem even to think about it, but please consider coming back. There's a flying boat once a week or so to the islands. Or Dora says she'd love to have you in Egypt. My darling Evadne, I love you and miss you so very much, please take great care of yourself until we are together again. It seems such an irony that I agreed to you staying on the island because it would be safer and now it only looks like trouble!

Your loving husband,
Hugh

This was accompanied by a rather bleak card, showing an unsmiling Greek royal family. Christmas has come again. Last year it had passed as a day like any other. There was little to celebrate here, the winter was a harsh one. I felt a wave of nostalgia for Christmas in England. The only really happy times were in the hospital, where we would take it in turns to go into the children's ward where sad little souls too unwell to go to their families looked for amusement from the doctors and nurses who were only too happy to oblige.

Manolis was off with his brother, so Anthi asked me to go with her and the girls to her Pappous and Yaya. I think it was in my honour that Yaya had cooked a roasted hare with red wine and sage. I was touched and had a lovely day. I taught them all to sing 'Away in a Manger', although they were puzzled why lying in a stable was so strange to the infant Jesus and his parents – they share their houses with their animals even now.

I left to walk home at the end of the afternoon and suddenly felt very alone. And at home I read Hugh's letter again. I sit very still as I read, listening to the night birds singing to the wind. I am wrapped in many layers, for the night air is chill in these, the last, lingering days of the year. The lamp gutters low, creating a soft glow. The candles have long flickered out. The moon is high in the sky and clouds seem to race across the only stars. I feel an awful sadness come over me as I read. It seems that I hardly know the man who wrote these words. And he certainly doesn't seem to know me!

In the days and the weeks and the months that have drifted past since we were together, his life in the embassy has gone on as before, whereas I feel I have moved forward and embraced a new life in this village. How could he know me as I am now, thinking my days should be taken up with tapestry and needlework? I write to him regularly of my work at the school and here in the house. I thought they were rather jolly letters because I so want to share with him the pleasures of my life.

I always tell him funny things that have happened, like me by mistake pulling down all the wood that Yorgo had just put up! Does he read those letters? If he does how could he imagine that the person who wrote them should be lying idly around in the shadow of the sun? For sure it's interesting to get a view of what is happening in Athens. But it seems centred around his old school chums. I feel he has no idea of how life is away from the capital, dominated as it is for the villagers by the seasons, the weather, the crop yield. There is a fine line that exists here between hunger and starvation. The choice that has to be made between a winter wrap for a child or shoes for the husband. If another baby comes, will it live or die? No one seems sure which is preferable; to live is another mouth to feed, to die means the cost of a funeral and the deep, dark pain of a mother's loss.

I try and fail to find a flicker of jealousy that he is to have a high old time showing Dora Troutbeck the high spots and nightclubs of Athens. I feel only grateful that she will keep his thoughts away from my return.

I have a melancholy ache now, that so easily we seem to have become different people with separate dreams and hopes for a future that lies way beyond any recognisable horizon. Apart from this, the most recent letter from Hugh, I often think back to when everything began to change for me here, and it isn't easy to point to the very moment. Did it start when the serious task of restoring our house became more than a fantasy? That was with the arrival of Christo. Or did it start when I first learnt to look at the village and the villagers as they really are and not with what I recognise now as my rather patronising naivety?

No, it was the day that I found the boy Dimitri huddled in the porch and Anthi couldn't or wouldn't tell me what was going on, I think. That was the day little Despina changed from a lively chatterbox into a silent and reserved child with everything she felt locked up inside herself. But that was also the day I met Christo. I start to smile. Everything began with Christo.

For a start the house began to look as though one day I might live here comfortably. Working alongside Yorgo and Christo, I felt it was not only at the school that I had found purpose in my life. Here in this great and beautiful house I have learnt skills I never thought to have! Christo showed me how to lay a tile on a roof so that it stays there. It's very unusual to have a tiled roof on a village house. Yorgo couldn't believe it could be done. 'They will fall off!' he kept saying. But slowly and patiently, Christo showed us both how to do it and we are now, Yorgo and I, experts in the fine craft of tiling.

He taught me that a turned-over tile would make a proper slope for the rain to pour away. I learned how to chip away at a stone with the right hammer (and to do it slowly and carefully) so that it was a thing of beauty in a wall and not just a support. He taught me how to rub up a stone so that it reflected glints of light to make it shine like a lamp, and he taught me how to polish wood with the wax from Anthi's bees so that it would keep clean and dry, even when left, by mistake, in the rain.

In the beginning I made many mistakes like that. Yorgo would say '*po po*' and look at me helplessly, but Christo would say, 'It is from the mistakes that you will learn perfection.' He never made me feel stupid or clumsy.

One day I realised, to my surprise, that my clothes were all too loose on my body. The work I was doing, some of it quite physical and tiring, and the diet I was living on now, all simple fresh food, made the pounds I had gathered at banquets in Athens fall away. Hugh was right to wonder about my hair. It now either stands out around my head or hangs down my back it is so long! Some mornings I fasten it back with combs or pins or sometimes even tie it into plaits. Occasionally I keep it tidy in a headkerchief like the village women.

Once or twice a week, I wait for dark and walk down to the spring to bathe and wash my hair. There is never anyone there and the clear crystal water sends the day behind me into the past with a quick gasp as the first icy drops hit my body.

I go down to the spring on other days too, for Hugh was right again, I join the village women to do my laundry. I learned so much there: not only how to use a pumice to scrub away a stain but all the gossip. Who was planning a liaison or a marriage, how the progress of a dowry was coming, or a trousseau. Who was ill and with what, and which herbs were being cooked to make a linctus or a poultice. The women discovered I had been a nurse and would call me in to help them with a sick husband or child or to give advice on pregnancy or childbirth. I often told them they had no need of me for, with their strange mixtures and concoctions passed down from mother to daughter, they had managed perfectly well for generations.

Sometimes there is a birth or a death to be celebrated and, here or in the village square, the women gather and talk of the loss or addition to their numbers.

I quickly became absorbed in village life. I was no longer a novelty, a curiosity among them. They accepted me. They were still so kind, bringing me gifts of eggs, lemons and cakes or sweetmeats, sometimes a dish of olives steeped in brine, or the pungent green oil from the first pressing of their olives.

Often the food I remember as a luxury in England – artichokes say, or pomegranates and figs – are commonplace here and grow in abundance in gardens. Meat is scarce unless a sheep or goat has been slaughtered, so tinned meat is regarded as a great delicacy. Irini always seems to make too many dolmades and I find a plate of the savoury stuffed vine leaves or courgette flowers on my doorstep. Michaelis brings me fish when he has a good catch and eventually, recognising I had nothing to trade, accepted a few (very few) drachmas. Vassili, smiling, cut down the grapes from my overhanging porch and in return brought me wine; his wife, Varvara, usually following behind with a jar of sweet raisins or some other delicacy. She is so round and plump and tiny with a small twitching nose, she reminds me of a rabbit.

But while this kindness and generosity is shown me in great profusion from the villagers I am beginning to think of as friends, I no longer look around me only through spectacles tinted with rose pink. I know there are many sides to these hills. As well as offering shelter from the heat of the sun or protection from the harsh winds of winter, they shield those who live here from the prying eyes of outsiders. All is not always well in these clustered dwellings along the rocky paths. A quarrel could spring up from nowhere and suddenly one family will not be seen to be speaking to another. A father and son will fall out over a shooting incident or a proposal of marriage. Occasionally a wife will appear with a bruise on her face or arm. No one speaks of these things.

The shepherds who live in the caves above have a harder life than most. I sit on the terrace at night, wrapped warmly against the chill, and see the lights of fires outside the caves, wondering sometimes who has lit and stoked them high? Which one did little Dimitri and his father Manos sit beside? Which one had Christo lit and sat next to after his day working on my house?

Anthi is reluctant to speak of the darker side of the village. She knows I saw her bruised face; I knew it was that horrible husband of hers. I long to ask her about it, not just out of curiosity, but because I really care. I long to give her a hug. But she keeps silent about it and therefore so do I.

She won't speak of little Dimitri or tell me about the night she went up the mountain with the professor. I did ask her about that. 'It's nothing, Heavenly,' she said. 'Just a silly village row, nothing important at all, it's over now.'

But I couldn't help but notice from that day on that she seemed different somehow, haunted. I know she worries about Despina. The sudden silence of that lively child worries me too.

It is accepted now that the three of us – Yorgo, Christo and me – are working as a team. Sometimes another who knows more about ironwork, perhaps, or glass will join us and eventually these workmen recognise that it is my house and I labour with the men.

It has taken a while to convince Yorgo, of course. At first he was shocked. I was a woman, I should be tending my house. But how could I until I had a house ready to tend? I argued.

'Or working in the fields.'

'What fields? I have no fields.'

'Looking after the sheep or goats.'

'Whose sheep or goats? I have none.'

One day I heard him arguing with Christo. 'I am embarrassed to work with a woman. My wife does not understand it.'

Christo laughed. 'Aphrodite does not give a fig with whom you work as long as you bring home the money. She told me this herself.'

But after a day or so of such muttering he started to order me around just as Christo did. I was content.

The house is beginning to find its shape again. Walls are strong and as straight as being built into the side of the mountain will allow. My bedroom is any room not full of tools, ladders, or sawdust. We look around at the end of each day and one of us, usually Christo, decides where I shall sleep that night, and my bed is moved in accordingly.

I am with Anthi at the school for two days at least, as well as helping with the restoration here. It is good to have the entirely separate life of the school when I am there, but each day I hurry home to see the day's progress. Christo shows me where he wants me to look. He occasionally wears a pair of small wire-framed spectacles, passed onto him by his grandfather, he told me. He peers over them and watches my reactions as I admire the work.

One day I told him his painting was good, excellent even, and he told me, smiling, it had been done a couple of hundred years ago! I didn't mind his joke at my expense. It was the first time he didn't call me the more formal 'kyria'. It was also the first time I noticed how very blue his eyes are in his sun-darkened face.

As he turned away from me, he caught his arm on a piece of rusty iron sticking up from the floor. It ripped the thin cotton of his shirt and as he looked down at it and pulled it clear he saw, as I did, that it had cut lightly through his skin and a line of blood droplets sprang instantly up. His arm trembled and he held it stiffly away from his body in an urge to control the shaking. His face was white, ghostly. I jumped up. 'Here, let me—' I started to say, but he pushed me roughly away and went quickly outside where I heard him retch repeatedly. I looked across to Yorgo who shrugged and said quietly, 'Just like his mother, she could never stand the sight of blood.' Before I could speak Christo was back with us, wiping his hand across his mouth. Colour was returning to his cheeks. His sleeve was buttoned tight over the wound. He never referred to it.

From the day little deaf and dumb Dimitri appeared huddled in the corner of the porch at school, Anthi seemed to change. It was some time after that before she reappeared in the school.

There was nothing strange in that, she mostly only worked two or three days a week. On the days she wasn't there the children would all work together with the professor or Kyria Titica, but this time, Despina did not appear either and she was usually the first to run in whether Anthi were there or not, laughing and clapping her hands.

I walked over to her house once or twice but, apart from the clucking hens and the guinea fowl, it was deserted and if she was working in her fields, I did not know which ones to try. Eventually I decided I must see her. I was worried.

From first light it was a terrible day; the worst I had ever seen here. Rain poured down in sheets; thunder resounded through the hills, echoing off the rocks and crashing fit to bring the village to its knees. Sharp forks of lightning lit the dark clouds and tore them apart momentarily.

In the main room we kept the shutters closed against the torrents. There was a pleasant intimacy working by lamplight with the two men. We talked little. I knew to work alongside whichever of them seemed most to need an assistant.

At midday we paused and sat for a little looking out of the lower doorway at the street that had turned itself into a river. The terrace above, now made strong and safe, sheltered us.

'We really need more time for the new struts to dry and weather,' said Christo, frowning and shaking his head.

'I used old wood,' said Yorgo, 'deliberately, in case this happened.'

Christo smile. 'You see,' he said to me, 'an old carpenter has his uses after all.'

'Not so old,' Yorgo replied. 'Aphrodite tells me we shall have a new baby in the spring.'

I could see him puff up with pride as he spoke, and he looked out at us from under his dark beetle brows defiantly.

'Congratulations,' I said, and he beamed.

'Did you need another baby?' asked Christo, and Yorgo chuckled.

'Well, we like the ones we have well enough, but Aphrodite wants a boy, she says. She's in charge of all that sort of thing . . .' and his voice trailed away.

The rain had slowed and come to a stop as we talked and the wind, which had been gusting the sheets of rain wildly along the village road, blew stronger.

'There you are,' said Yorgo pointing outside, 'the wind will dry it all in no time.'

I hope so,' I said, and got to my feet. 'I want to go to Anthi's house.'

'You can't go alone in this weather, you'll be blown away. I'll take the donkey and walk with you.' Christo had already acquired his own animal from somewhere. He knew I was about to protest, so he quickly added, 'I'll call at your house, Uncle, and pick up the other saw we need for the beams.'

The rain had turned to a drizzle, but we were fighting the wind all the way along the beaten track to Pano Panagia and the journey, which usually takes twenty minutes, took nearly an hour. Christo insisted I should sit on the donkey while he walked beside and guided us along the path.

'He doesn't like this,' he explained to me, 'he loses his sense of direction. With the wind against us he'd have us down the mountain and at Tres Petromas before the morning's over.' Ahead of us the mountains were haze-dark against the lowering sky and the little church of St Kosmas and Damianus was lost today in the clouds. It was hard to speak and even harder to hear.

Around the last of the bends, the donkey stumbled and fell to one knee. Of course I fell with him; both of us hard up against Christo who staggered slightly. Then, holding me tightly around the waist with one hand, he shoved hard on the animal with the other and within moments we were all stable, upright and safe again.

I laughed to conceal my horrible embarrassment and fiddled unnecessarily with my hair. Although one or two pins fell to the ground, the large comb that clasped it held its length tight to my head. 'You are a hero, thank you.'

'Should I let you fall next time? Here, up again.' With what felt like a great heave, I was back on the animal and, a little slower now, moving onwards. There was no other soul in sight. Houses we passed were shuttered fast against the outside world. A child's painted wooden horse clattered and rolled along ahead of us.

'Heavenly!' It was a great shout that ripped through the air to us and I quickly turned, looking from left to right. It was Anthi and she was running towards us from one of the fields. Voula was bumbling alongside, but Despina walked slowly after her, her eyes to the ground.

We all stood huddled for shelter under a pomegranate tree. Although its roots and some of its trunk are in the field, the overhanging branches, bare of fruit now, swoop down and across part of the dirt track.

Anthi looked tired and drawn. Despina, now clinging to her mother's skirt, was still gazing at the ground. She hasn't spoken or shown any sign that she knows who I am.

Anthi looked at Christo and, catching my eye, looked quickly away again. I mumbled an introduction and they briefly smiled at each other.

Christo knew that Anthi has been a good friend to me but Anthi, to my surprise, could barely mumble a greeting in return. This was far from the Anthi I know.

Christo broke the awkward silence and said, 'I will leave you with your friend.'

I was set to move onwards, put a little energy into Anthi and her children, and find out what on earth was going on, when I realised I was still on Christo's donkey. I jumped down and promptly fell over flat on my face, on the dirt and grit of the path. Everyone rushed to help me up, but as Anthi bent to grasp my arm, Voula who had been skipping up and down, lost her balance and tumbled down too.

Christo pulled me to my feet and we all started to laugh. It was only a moment but it had broken the awkwardness and to my relief even Despina gave a small half-smile.

Later that day, I walked back along the same path alone. The storm had cleared itself hours ago and all was calm now. Anthi had insisted I leave while there was still some light in the sky and I trod the familiar track, thinking about the things I had learned today. I was horrified by what Anthi told me she had discovered with the professor in the cave. But it was the unspoken words that affected me most. When she told me about the brigands, or whatever they were called, who had systematically sought out and harmed that innocent family, her voice had quivered and she was trembling.

When I asked her who they were, she shook her head in such vigorous denial that it seemed to me that she did indeed know, but was not going to tell.

Which meant to me only one thing: her husband Manolis was implicated. Or why not tell me? Other names would mean little to me.

It will be a long while before I forget the first time I met him and his obvious pleasure in wielding his knife to slit the sheep open. Anthi didn't notice, but his eyes slid in my direction as the guts and entrails oozed bloodily to the ground.

I couldn't help but flinch from such a brutal, deliberate act and that reaction of mine alone gave him pleasure; a twisted half-smile flickered briefly, bleakly, across his face, which was momentarily turned away from his wife and child. It was the look, the action of a sadist.

I hurried along to get back to the house. I wanted Christo to tell me what was going on here. He was the only person I know to ask. I had an instinctive feeling for his goodness, his truthfulness; he knows everything about these hills.

I pushed my pace into a stride, for the light was fading fast now, and I though for a passing moment of Hugh and his safe and rich life in the capital. I smiled, but not a smile of joy, as I remembered his anxieties about my hair, my laundry. If he knew just how much I am a part of the village here, he would understand none of it, I am sure, but would he care? I knew, with sadness, that his answer would be to walk away. Better not to uncover what is hidden, than to risk confrontation with darkness.

I remembered one glorious early spring day in Paris where I had learnt for the first time that a mother would mutilate her own child to earn more money begging on the streets. I had wept that evening when Hugh asked me about my day and I told him this. He was looking into the cheval mirror in our suite in the embassy, tying his white tie for yet another formal dinner.

'Damn and blast this wretched tie,' he said. 'Evadne, you are so good at this, will you do it for me?' I rose obediently and moved across the bedroom to join him at the mirror. In that moment he realised I was weeping.

'Oh come on, old thing,' he said. 'Nothing to do with us what these wretched beggars get up to. They come from blackamoor land in the first place. They can go back there, can't they, if they don't like it here? Ahh, well done, darling.'

He was peering at himself in the mirror again. 'You really have a knack for these blasted ties. That's something to be proud of.'

Ahead of me was the house. A figure on the terrace was silhouetted against the skyline: Christo. He had waited for me to come home. I realised how happy I was to be here and found myself smiling for the first time today. As I approached, he came down the steps and peered into the gloom.

'Is it you, Heavenly? Are you safe and well?'

I smiled. 'Yes, thank you, I am safe and well.'

Later I spoke to him about the things I had learnt from Anthi and he looked sad and thoughtful. I had joined him on the terrace at first as he seemed in no hurry to get back to his cave, and then we had lit a fire in the living room and sat before it on a pile of blankets.

When the doors and windows are shuttered fast, there is the most wonderful smell in this great room. It is not only from the wood, but there is also a warm, spicy smell of apples which are mounded in a corner by the wine press; small piles of dried grapes and *mousmoulas*, that are scented like peaches, lie on the other side of the press, with apricots, mandarins and lemons piled high beside them.

'You come from a country which has only once, I think, been at war with itself.'

I nodded. 'Certainly not in my lifetime.'

'Here, war and fighting is second nature to us. It comes from the womb as we kick our way into this world. My grandmother, and before her my great-grandmother, always said every Cretan male child born will come out fighting; it is then up to the women in his life to teach him peace. This will always start with his mother. This is why every traditional song that we have sung for generations tells of the same thing – always they are about the one perfect woman, the mother.'

I nodded again. 'Anthi told me some of this,' I said, and laughed, 'Even her own brother, who couldn't wait to leave home, still sings songs in praise of his mother.'

'The Greeks are ready for war,' he said, 'and especially here in the biggest of the islands. We are ready, always, for invasion. And it will come. What no one yet understands is from where it will come.'

'This is what I hear from Athens,' I said.

'The Cretans are masters of invasion, it has happened to us so many times we are always ready. But we don't always fight in regular armies. We get together in groups, small groups, and the hills that surround our villages are the best hiding places. This is what is happening here, now, I think.' I nodded.

'I hear talk around in the kafenions. Times like these, there is the smell of war in the air . . .' He shook his head. 'The army is away fighting in Albania, the people here feel vulnerable, unprotected. It is possible Manolis was involved in something, but also likely that it was a simple fight about a missing animal. Manolis is known as a hothead. He is not a popular man.'

'Poor Anthi,' I said. 'It must be awful to be married to a man like that.'

'She has two lovely children for compensation.'

'Daughters, not the same thing at all. She told me she is considered by her husband to be a failure because she has not given him a son.'

'Then the man is a fool. His daughters are beautiful. He is a lucky man.'

There was a wonderful stillness about him as he spoke. His gaze never left my face. I found this most extraordinary in a man. Usually they look anywhere but in my eyes directly. It is too revealing. But he had none of this anxiety; there was a confidence in his words that, although spoken quietly, told me of the truth in him.

'I hate war, detest fighting. I prefer to save my energy for repairing your house, and think of my studies for building things up, rather than destroying, pulling them down. But I will be ready, and so will my friends to fight any real enemy that tries to take us.'

Only the sharp crackles of the newly chopped log he had thrown on the fire broke the silence. Outside, a creature made a great yowl; a wild cat or some such seeking its night food.

'For many years, the name of Manadakis has been one to fear, not to respect. The word around was that sometimes they could be bought to fight on one side or another. They are not known for their principles. I have wondered what was going on here ever since my uncle Yorgo told me it was Manadakis's wife who had brought him here, to you. Her husband would not like that, I think.'

I gave an involuntary shudder. 'Do you know him?'

He smiled. 'Only from a distance.'

'I loathed him from the first moment I saw him,' I said.

'Your friend Anthi should take care of herself,' he said.

'I saw today that although she wore her headkerchief pulled forward, she couldn't hide the bruising on her cheek. I would be surprised if Kyria Manadakis received an injury like that from a cupboard door.'

My face must have registered the disgust I felt.

'It happens. You cannot stop it, nor change it. To some men it is as natural as breathing or breaking wind; she will know how best to deal with it. From all I have heard she is a strong individual and a determined woman. She persuaded her husband to let her continue teaching in the school, didn't she?' I nodded.

'Then she knows how to get her own way. Care for her as you do, as a good friend should, but don't try to tell her how to manage her husband. Just be watchful. One day she may need you more than now and then you can help her, but until then . . .' He shook his head and stretched his long body the length of the blanket.

'Time for me to go back to my cave,' he said, 'although it is hard to take myself away from this fire, and . . .' He stopped quickly and shook his head again.

'Sometimes I sleep right here,' I told him.

He laughed. 'You do no more than most of the shepherds.'

'I wondered about that,' I said. The fire flickered the flames

124

high and I saw them reflected in his eyes. We had eaten bread and fruit and slices of the cheese his aunt Aphrodite had made. He showed me how to soak the sun-dried tomatoes that Anthi had given me in olive oil to soften them and release their sweet sticky juices into our mouths. He poured a little of Vassili's wine into the only two glasses I owned and I told him that in England people said 'Cheers', when they toast each other.

He told me, when I asked, that he had wanted to speak English well since he was a child. 'Another day I will tell you why, but now it's time for sleep.'

We were speaking in English now. It was a pleasure and a relief to me to use my familiar tongue. I have even started dreaming in Greek!

'When we are together here, why don't we speak in English? It would be good for you and I should love it.'

There was a long moment before he replied. 'We must be careful. There is nothing more pleasing to the village women here than something to gossip about, and if we are speaking a different language to them, well they will invent what they think we are saying, and it might not always be good.'

I answered without thinking, 'Does it matter? Do we care?'

'We have become friends and friendship between a man and a woman is unknown here. They will presume our relationship to be more than what they understand as friendship.' I was just taking this in and considering what it could mean, when he spoke again: 'Also, I don't want my uncle Yorgo to feel excluded, isolated. He is a good man and may be hurt if he doesn't understand what we are saying. However,' he said slowly, looking at me now, 'when we are alone together, like this, perhaps . . . ?'

Quickly I leant across and threw another log onto the embers. My back was to him, he could not see my face. I knew I was blushing. I was trembling inside, but something made me say, 'Do you think we shall have other evenings like this then? Alone together?'

There was a long silence before he answered. 'Yes, I should

like that. But right now I think you should move, or you will fall over and set fire to your hair.'

I turned back to him and, of course, I fell, not badly enough to hurt, but enough to cause him to laugh as well.

'That is three falls today. This is not good for you, all these tumbles, you will hurt yourself.'

I brushed myself down. I was wearing a long skirt I had made from an old curtain I had found in one of the trunks that was in my bedroom. It was thick and warm, but attracted the dust and bits that liked to cling to it.

At the moment it was covered in warm ashes.

'You noticed my falls?'

'Of course I did.' And then into the silence he said, 'I notice everything about you.' Before I could react, he was on his feet and he stepped back quickly into the cluttered and half-built room and moved to the door. 'Thank you for the food. Sleep well. May the angels watch over you tonight.'

I stood and watched the horizon but there was nothing to see. Even the trees couldn't be seen through the heavy mist. Far away, over the ridge into Mesa Panagia, a dog was barking, and, as if in answer to it, a donkey brayed three times.

Later, I went outside to relieve myself against one of the side walls of the house. We all do this and each day one of the three of us takes a shovel and clears the earth. At first this embarrassed me, but it's what everyone does here so it quickly became second nature. When my bathroom is finally done I shall have a lavatory inside. Yorgo is thrilled to be involved in making this happen. We have a picture of a smart English lavatory made by Thomas Crapper stuck on the wall, and every day he gazes at it as if it is an object of magic.

'Who would think,' he said one day, 'that I should be the man in Panagia to install such an invention?'

'And you, Uncle,' Christo said, 'shall be the first man to use it.'

Sleep, which usually comes easily, was evasive tonight and for some reason Hugh's last letter and the thoughts he had expressed there kept running through my mind. I did sleep at last, but it was of Christo I dreamed.

The storms of yesterday were gone by the morning. The next few days were sunny and clear and I walked up to the school with a spring in my step.

The children who come to me are really getting on so well with learning English that with one or two of them, I can hold a conversation. It may be slow and stumbled, and helped along with copious hand gestures, but we can speak to each other about the village, the harvest, or their animals. I had so hoped that one of these bright, quick learners would be Anthi's Despina. But it is not to be. She has not spoken for weeks. I know Anthi is sick with worry. She seems to have so many problems just now that her dear face is permanently creased and frowning.

I wish she would talk to me. I know she has only a few friends in the village and her mother is like an enemy to her.

I met her once, briefly. She visited Anthi one day, unexpectedly, with Anthi's sister, Ririca. What a strange pair!

She reminded me instantly of the matron at Greenbridge. But I think she smiled even less. I found it hard to take my eyes from a large hairy mole on her cheek. The hair on it was so long it blew in the breeze from her mouth when she spoke. Why didn't she pull it out?

As for Ririca, she was skinny; with a thin, mean little face. It was hard to believe they were blood relatives of my beautiful friend.

They sat awkwardly on their chairs, both looking as though they had a bad smell under their noses.

Then the mother said loudly, '*Anglika*?' and I nodded. I spoke to her in my best Athenian Greek and she jumped back slightly. They didn't stay long after that. The mother shouted goodbye in my face and Ririca, it seemed in some embarrassment, pushed her through the door and away.

Anthi laughed when they had gone. 'What a relief,' she said, 'they only came to have a look at you.'

Yorgo and Christo will be here soon. Last week Akis, the ironworker from the forge in Aghios Georgios, was here with them and the doors now all have proper fastenings to strongly close them to the elements. It is a huge, childish pleasure of mine to open and close the shutters and doors, just because I can. One of the doors creaks so I get olive oil and tease some drops into the crack where the lock joins the wood.

Now it is eight o'clock, but there is no sign of them. They are always here before this time and we start our day by taking some coffee together.

Anthi has taught me well how the Greeks like their coffee, and it is certainly different to Hugh's perked drink that was very bitter and always tasted burnt. I felt rather guilty, but not for long, when I threw his percolator away.

Wrapping my long curtain skirt around me for warmth, I walk outside and gaze along the path up through the village.

Christo said I looked like a sparkling firework in this homemade skirt, like the golden sun walking on the street. I think I am considered to be so eccentric here that my wearing window dressing surprises no one.

At first, the village women gathered around me, taking quick pinches at the material, rubbing it to test the quality, and one even said curiously, 'Athens or England?'

'Panagia Sta Perivolia,' I said and everyone laughed. But now, when I wear this golden one or the other I made, they take no notice.

The early morning sunshine sends an arrow of warmth through me and here comes Christo now, urging his donkey along the path towards the house. He looks up and, seeing me wave, acknowledges it with a quick nod and looks straight down again. He sits on the donkey like a jockey, leaning forward, a crop in his hand. Through the thick serge of his *vraka* the muscles of his calves look so strong. His mountain boots encase the leg from the knee down. They look shiny and polished. Does he clean them at night in his cave?

'No coffee. I must leave at once. Yorgo tried to come back with all the supplies alone from Sitia, Aphrodite told me, and of course he had an accident and they are scattered all over the mountainside. He left at dawn to go down and retrieve them. I must go and find him. Will you wait here for Andreas? I have asked him to come today to measure for the windows.'

I take my coffee outside. The wind cannot make up its mind this morning; some moments it whips up the trodden dust underfoot and then there will be an hour or two of calm. Across the horizon down to the sea, clouds are tossing around in the sky but it is still the same azure blue of a summer's morning.

I think back over the last weeks. I feel Christo and I have become good friends, but there is a caution between us. I cannot bring myself to speak of Hugh or think of Hugh. I know that I am pushing away all thoughts and memories of him. When Anthi ever asks for word of him, I tell her the news from Athens but resist saying more.

She is sufficiently interested in what is happening in Europe just now that it's not hard to distract her. I hear myself saying more about Christo; telling her details of our conversations. Once or twice I have caught her giving me odd glances when I talk of him and I make myself stop then, and turn the conversation around to village gossip.

At night, in the darkness, it is then that I allow thoughts of him to swim around in my head. Even as I feel a warm glow at these moments, I am frequently overcome by a dirty little wave of guilt. For I think of him in ways that should be reserved for my husband. I know it is wrong of me to think of him in this way but oh, it can send me to my own private heaven! Sometimes, when we sit by the fire in the evening, I am afraid he will feel the heat from my body and know it for what it is.

At last I see he is coming back, his donkey loaded with all the stuff Yorgo had tried to bring alone.

There is no sign of his uncle. I run down and together we

bring everything inside. I stand alone in the middle of the main room for a moment, catching my breath.

Christo comes quietly into the room. I can feel his presence even before I see him. I know, as I turn, that we are standing too close together. Our eyes meet, interpreting our separate thoughts, and I can sense the knowledge we have of each other.

He scans my face. I hesitate, my heart beating furiously in my chest. I know I shouldn't touch him, but I want to put my arms around his strong body, know I want to stroke his beautiful face. I want to rub my cheek into his beard. I want everything and then more.

We turn away from each other at the same moment and when he speaks his voice is tight. 'Heavenly?' he says. Then again, 'Heavenly? What is it that you want? What can I do?'

At first I can't speak and we stand separate but together.

'*Yia*, Christo, *yia*, Kyria.' It is Andreas, and as quickly as it had come, whatever was in the air vanishes. Within moments, I was making coffee and they were discussing life. My heartbeat slowed and my hand stopped shaking as I took them the coffee. As always, when someone comes to your house for whatever reason, work stops and conversation takes place. I put the coffee and a plate of Irini's cookies on the table for them. Andreas nodded his thanks and carries on talking animatedly to Christo.

It is the middle of the day before Andreas leaves us. He must go to Sitia and buy glass. I had to thrust my energy into doing something, so I began to clear and clean up the house. After a while, I threw the broom down in frustration and swore aloud. It was pointless. All I was doing was moving the dust and woodchips from one place on the floor to another. My eyes were stinging and the air was thick. It was difficult to breathe. It would be better to let it settle and stay there until each room was finished.

I wanted to weep.

Such a short time ago, my life had seemed perfect. Hugh was busy in Athens and I was content to be here. I took pleasure from my friendship with Anthi and her lovely daughters. My days at the school were a delight and gradually this house was becoming a home. I saw it all now through my tears as though all the goodness had been stripped away.

Yes, Hugh was happy in Athens, but if I was there or he here, would our physical life be a growing thing of ugliness between us? I remembered the nights of loneliness. And the days! Oh those dreary days. Would I still be wandering from shop to shop, dressmaker to dressmaker, party to party?

But then again, in this place that I love, that I want to be perfect, I discover there are the same thugs and murderers as in any busy city. And I try to be positive but this house is still a ruin for the most part. Will it ever be right? Even the school seems now full of troubles; the attack on Dimitri and his father, Despina's silence. Lift a stone anywhere, and it is as though underneath will be something evil waiting to pounce.

I sit on the floor before the fire, which I had lit to warm me, and drop my head in my hands. And then there was Christo. What was happening to me?

I remember my sister loved to play cards, Patience, and one day I watched her cheating. I was completely puzzled and asked her why she would cheat herself?

'Because it's no fun if you don't win,' she said, without a flicker of remorse.

'But the winner and the loser are the same person . . .' I started to say and she swung round on me.

'Oh, Evadne,' she said, 'you are an old stick-in-the-mud and too honest. Everyone cheats at something.'

I knew then that was why she would always win eight games to my one. And I vowed that I would always be honest with myself, at least.

So here I am, forced to admit that I am a married woman in love with someone not her husband. I cannot lie to myself. I can make my head think of other things. I can exhaust my body with working, but I still ache for Christo each day in my heart and in every bit of me. I can hardly bear the thought of a day going by without seeing him. I feel as though I am in a strange and dark place, whichever way I turn it will be wrong; follow my heart and I know I will always be guilty, follow my head and a lonely path lies before me. Tears fill my eyes.

As if he had sensed all or any of this, I heard him call softly from outside. And then he was beside me. I was trembling. He paused and looked at me. 'Are you all right? You look strange, flushed.'

He had arrived within my fantasy. I couldn't speak. I couldn't be sure that if I opened my mouth, the right words would fly out. Slowly I nodded my head, and he sat down beside me.

'It's too late to think of working today. It is already dark and you look as though you have had enough.' He threw a log on the fire and stirred the embers until it caught and strong flames were warming us through.

'Shall I tell you a story?' I nodded.

'I will tell you about another uncle of mine, one who went to London, England. I thought it would make you smile?' I looked at him through my drying tears and he reached out his hand and took mine as he told me. His hand was firm and smooth and I worried that he could feel the trembling in mine.

'Many years ago, long before I was born, my Uncle Stephanos ran away to England, to London. He was thirteen and, coming from here, knew nothing of the ways of the world. First he worked as a waiter in a restaurant. For years he saved all his money, living on scraps he found in the kitchens and never going to dances or music halls when his friends tried to persuade him to join them. One evening the owner of the restaurant, who was also the cook, fell and sprained his ankle. So Stephanos said he would do the cooking for that night. He had never cooked anything in his life before, but he loved food, fresh food.

For years he had stood beside his mother in the kitchen and she would let him mix the flour and the eggs for the pastry, stuff the herbed mixture of meat and rice into the vine leaves, or taste the juniper in the stifado.

That night in the restaurant he made only Greek dishes. Well, it was all he knew. He made a big tray of moussaka. He made *gemisto*: large, glistening tomatoes and zucchini were filled with the meat mixture, sprinkled with olive oil and *rigani* and baked. And that night in the restaurant he sweet-talked the customers into trying this new and very foreign food.'

By now I was enthralled; I had forgotten my trembling hand, that was still gently clasped in Christo's. 'What happened?' I ask.

'That was the first night that everything from the kitchen was sold.'

I smiled. It seemed that was all he needed to encourage him to continue.

'Better than that, people came back for more. Every day he had to make as much Greek food as the oven could take and it all went. The customers loved it. Before long he had a reputation across that part of London and there were queues every night. Gradually he saved enough to open his own restaurant. He took a great risk, as Greek cooking was unknown in those days.'

Christo paused, he was smiling with excitement and I don't think he realised he was stroking my hand now.

'He eventually had several restaurants, all over London, and he was a very rich man. Imagine; a young man from a small Cretan village became so successful that he was a millionaire in London!'

'Where is he now?'

'Ah,' he said, 'Of course, he came home to his family, here. He built his mother a beautiful house, and went back to England to make some more money and marry the Greek girl he had met there. He died later, but still his sons come here every summer. You are English, perhaps you know his restaurants?'

'London is a big city. What are they called?'

'Ilios. Each one is called Ilios – sunshine.'

I sat very still. Yes I knew these restaurants. Hugh had

133

taken me there the first time we left Greenbridge and went to London. Christo was right; the food was excellent. Hugh had spoken to the chef and complimented him on his cooking.

Perhaps that was Christo's uncle?

Hugh, Hugh, Hugh. Now he was here in the room with me. If I closed my eyes I could see his face.

'Is something wrong ? You are very white.'

I jumped up and, moving very fast, was suddenly on the other side of the room.

'Nothing wrong, nothing at all. What could be wrong? It's a lovely story, thank you for telling me.'

I was in the dark corner beside the wine press. I could see his face only by the light of a sudden flame. He was puzzled and, jumping up, moved across to me.

'Have I upset you? Telling you a story about London, England? I am so sorry, it was thoughtless. I have made you homesick for your friends, your family.' He was beside me now, very close beside me, and his voice faltered, 'And homesick for your—'

Because I knew what he was going to say and I couldn't bear him to, and I had to stop him, the only way I knew how was to kiss him. So I did.

It seemed as though it were the most natural thing in the world. His lips were as soft and gentle as in my dreams. His smell was so familiar, warm with the flames and scented with the wild herbs he had ridden through.

His hands rose and caressed my cheek, my brow. He gently pulled the comb from my hair and his fingers wandered through my tangles, smoothing them. He pulled away from me, but only for a moment and then his arms were around me and his kiss was strong and sweet and seemed everlasting.

My fingers were moving across his back when he pulled away and looked at me. 'Heavenly, Heavenly,' he said, 'that is what you are to me.'

My breath was fast and hard and while my head was thinking, this is too bold, too soon, my heart and my body were urging my hands onwards, and I was undoing the lacing at the top of his shirt. It was rough hemp and as it parted I felt the intoxicating silkiness of his skin against my hand. I pulled the shirt open further and kissed his chest. He raised his arms and pulled it over his head. Then he took my hand in his and walked me back over to the fire. Still standing, his body close to mine, he looked into my eyes and said, 'Are you sure?'

I nodded. 'I am sure, quite sure.'

Together we sank to the rugs there and his hands were moving more strongly now and tugging at my skirt. Released of all our clothing, I gasped as his firm body moved over mine. His fingers reached down softly and his lips kissed my breasts. As his tongue touched them my nipples hardened. He paused to say, 'So beautiful, my Heavenly,' and then as his fingers moved into the wetness between my thighs, I called his name just once: 'Yes, Christo!' and I trembled with a pleasure I had waited all my life for. The rhythm of our movements together then seemed like the most natural thing in the world; as though we had practised this for ever.

Within moments his breathing was faster, his thrusts harder and deeper and, as he came, his seed spilled into me and he collapsed in the ecstasy I was already feeling.

ANTHI

It was the smell that first pulled me into consciousness, old sweat dried into wool. Then the searing pain as he thrust at me from behind, finding entry where he was not welcome. It is years since I have been wet there, wanting. It was over soon, mercifully, and he rolled away snoring again, leaving me to seek sleep in the damp patch of his spent seed, already cold in the night air.

These nights I am mostly wakeful. Sleep is an elusive thing that only babies and drunks seem able to do easily; in this house at least. My body is so exhausted each night that I drop sometimes wherever I am and sleep like the dead. But only for a couple of hours and then my dreams haunt me and I wake fast: my heart thumping in my chest and I lie until dawn in silent wakefulness. Despina is often there beside me these nights. Sometimes I think she has woken me by stroking my face as if she wants me to share in her own sleeplessness.

She used to sleep fast at night. I could barely wake her for the morning. That was before – oh, everything good was before.

I can't bear to think about it any more. Each day I try and get through without much thought. Thinking is bad; thinking is memory, pain.

Each morning a new day and what will it bring?

I had learnt to love the days: my babies, my school, my home. My new friendship with Heavenly had added so much to my life. I had never had such a friend before. It is not the way of things here. The people you are close to are your family. Your neighbours are the ones you chat and gossip with. But more likely you will be talking with them about the weather, the crops, or the price of tobacco. You do not share thoughts of the world outside this village; life in other places; the life of the imagination. That was what Heavenly and I had in common, that was what made her special in my life.

But since, well since then, there was too much I could not share. Too much fear and far, far too much shame.

I rise and, yawning and stretching these heavy legs, walk downstairs and open the door to the world outside. The sky is red with the rising sun, the chickens are restless, the cock is crowing and there are eggs to be collected, bread to be made.

Sometimes I amaze even myself with what I can achieve within an hour, if left alone. This morning I have fetched water, washed myself, dressed myself and Voula, made break-fast for us all, set the bread to rise, cleaned the grate, fetched wood for a new fire and lit it and prepared the vegetables for the stew that will simmer gently all day on the hob, and put dried beans to soak for another day. Before doing anything though, I bagged together all the laundry.

Despina likes to help me; so she collects the eggs, feeds the hens, sweeps the yard, and has gone up the hill to check on the bees. She is still not the same child she was before. She is growing fast, but it seems to me sometimes that inside her child's body beats the heart of an old woman. It is as though she knows too much of the world. There is suspicion in her eyes. She jumps and turns at the slightest sound, she rarely smiles. She talks again, but very little, not like before, and she will do anything to keep close to my side.

'It's just a phase. She is growing up. She will grow out of it.' Everyone has said so, the professor, even Heavenly. But I am beginning to find it hard to remember the child who laughed every day.

Voula is tottering around now and I can see in her face, her sweet, round, apple-cheeked face, the woman she will one day become. She has an innocent wisdom in her eyes, which are large, shaped like almonds and dark, dark brown. She is a solemn little girl, not given to constant laughter as Despina always was. She is thoughtful, watchful and then, when she has decided who you are, and whether you are a good thing to have in her day, her face will suddenly crease and a rich, sweet chortle will emerge from her rosy lips.

My belly turns over as I look at her; my baby, my angel.

The sun is already streaking through the sky as we do the digging for today. Manolis is still snoring upstairs. Perhaps he had only just come to bed when he took me? Another late night with his friends at the kafenion, I suppose. What are they plotting now?

Within half an hour the onions are set and the broad beans are in. I dig the hole and Voula staggers after me and drops a seed into each. She is very good for one who cannot yet count, and rarely puts more than one seed into each hole. Her baby teeth chew a little on her lip as she concentrates hard on what she is doing. Her fair hair is thickening into curls now that bounce around her face. Apart, that is, from the ruffled, sparse downy patch at the back, rubbed off in her sleep.

Despina is back from the bees and tugs at my skirt. 'Are you coming to the school today, Mama?'

'No, child, but Athena will come for you, so wash your hands and face and get your books. They are in your room upstairs.' She knows now not to argue, so silently and slowly she turns to get the books.

'Heavenly will be there today, I think.' And she smiles and something of the old Despina is there as she skips away. I think, with a pang, that Heavenly is the person she loves most in the world now.

The spring sun is already beating warmly on my back as we struggle with the loaded Astrape to the spring. Voula is singing gently to herself and seems to be counting her fingers. Aphrodite is there ahead of me and greets me with a loud welcome.

When we have finished our washing, we load Astrape with our laundry and put Voula on beside it and walk slowly back up the track.

'What do they know in Pano Panagia, Anthi?'

'What do you mean?'

'There were some women from there earlier and they said something about war. And Yorgo heard some talk of it in Tres Petromas last night.'

'Did Yorgo remember anything more?' I ask, and she laughs.

'When he has taken drink Yorgo doesn't know whether it's Wednesday or April.' She doesn't mention Manolis, so neither do I.

'Your English friend, Heavenly, wouldn't she have some idea? Her husband sends her news from Athens, doesn't he?'

'I'll ask her,' I say as we unload her washing at her house.

Heavenly's house is just a little way above the spring and there is silence from there as I walk closer.

I pause a little before we arrive and look around at my beautiful hills. So quiet, so peaceful, only the ring of goat bells and the cries of birds, dots in the sky as they fly past. Is this peace to be shattered soon? Men crowd nightly into the Piperia to listen to the news from Athens, but they rarely share it with their wives and Manolis certainly would sooner be seen in his grave than go to what he considers to be the haunt of communists. He has his own sources of information, I'm certain, and he would laugh at the thought of telling me anything.

Voula is impatient in the saddle, jumping her little rear up and down and clapping her hands together, calling, 'Helly, Helly.' But Heavenly is nowhere to be seen. There is her donkey, Lotto, acquired for her by Aphrodite's brother.

Then suddenly I hear her laugh. No one in Panagia laughs like Heavenly. It starts from deep inside, and pulses fast and rich as it reaches her throat.

It is answered by a man's rich echo. Someone is happy. I pause and wait a moment. Oddly, I have a sudden notion of intimacy from inside. The closed door seems to divide us into two worlds. It seems wrong to interrupt without warning.

I'm rescued by a shout from below and Yorgo appears at the end of the path.

'*Yia*, Kyria,' he calls up to me, a full bucket clanking in each hand, 'you well today?' And Voula answers him for me, '*Yia*!' and then pleased with herself, '*Yia*!' again.

In the house the laughter has stopped. I tether Astrape, and seeing the door is open a little, I step slowly inside.

Christo is on the top of the ladder and at first I fail to see Heavenly. She is lying against the ladder on the furthest side, one foot raised carelessly on a rung. I'm sure the purpose is to steady it, but her skirt is pulled up and a long tanned leg looks oddly naked and provocative from where I stand.

Her head turns in my direction and I see the sun catch her face and light it up. She is flushed and smiling. I have never seen her look so beautiful as she does at this moment.

Above her, Christo smiles down and, after greeting me, asks her to pass him another brush.

It is several weeks since I have been here and in that time something has happened, something that has changed them both. It's barely a moment before I guess what it is. There is an aura, almost tangible around them, and they seem to shine. It is the sun, I tell myself. But I don't believe it.

Flustered, I offer to make some coffee.

Heavenly moves forward. 'Here, let me.'

'No, if you don't mind, let me do it for you.'

'Of course, if you'd like to.' She has gone back into the living room where, from round the corner, I can see Christo smiling to see her again, as if she has been away a week.

Yorgo is in and out of the room with his buckets, singing softly to himself: songs telling anyone who wants to know how much he loves his mother. He seems oblivious to the electricity in the air that sparks between Heavenly and Christo. Yet I know I am not imagining it. Intrigued, anxious, I stay longer than I mean to. They seem not to notice I am here, so absorbed are they in each other.

The house is changing now every time I see it. Christo is a craftsman, just as his uncle is, and between them the house is slowly regaining its ancient majesty. Heavenly's vision for it is clear now, not at all strange as we had first feared. The simplicity of the woodwork and the plastering are far superior to the rich marbles I've heard are often used in old houses in Sitia.

The stone floor in this room is painted a warm red, contrasting brilliantly with the richness of the old rugs that have not seen daylight since the Orfanoudakis family lived here. And downstairs where the animals lived, is being transformed into rooms, each opening onto the lower terrace. There is a delicate scent of fresh spring flowers. Heavenly must have scoured the hillsides for boughs and stems of early blossom and, even though they are in cracked and discoloured old jars and bottles, their beauty and perfume charge the air.

Christo and Heavenly chat blithely to each other, occasionally including Yorgo, or even me, for a moment's questioning; the angle of a stone, the slope of the floor. But while Yorgo nods in agreement, or I shake my head, it is simply politeness.

I sense their intuitive knowledge of each other. It seems heightened as they work together. It doesn't come from the words they speak, the meaningless phrases, it is simply there.

Yorgo leaves around noon to take lunch with Aphrodite and whichever of his children are around. I wait for a moment and then say in a rush, 'I must go home. See, Voula now needs more food than I can give her from my . . . from me . . .' I falter, suddenly embarrassed to mention my breasts. That's what it is like here today. I no longer feel at ease with them both, as I do when I'm alone with Heavenly.

Taking Voula by the hand and extricating from her tiny fist the hammer with which she was banging the floor, I mutter goodbye and move towards the door. But Heavenly is there ahead of me.

'Stay,' she says. 'Why not take some food with us, we have plenty for both of you.'

'Oh no,' I say, too quickly, 'I must go home now and Voula must sleep. Thank you.'

But I have hardly reached Astrape when she is beside me and holding me so tightly in her arms I can barely breathe. 'I have so much to tell you. I desperately want to see you alone and talk to you. So much is changing in my life and I need, want, to share it with you.'

'I can see,' I say, more coldly than I mean to. 'I am not blind or foolish. The changes are written clearly on your face. And . . . and him.' I nod my head back in the direction of the house.

'Oh dear God, is it that obvious?' And she flushes bright pink; she is so happy, it's hard for me to be angry with her.

'My dear friend, you must take care. You know how gossip flies through this village and there are already questions about the way you work in the house with the men.'

She looks astonished. 'Is that true? I only help here on the days when I am not with you at the school. I can't just sit around and watch them. I would go mad and I am learning so much.'

'I think it's not only about house-building you are learning.' She looks so like a child, just now, caught with her fingers in the honey jar, I can only hug her.

She pulls back and looks straight at me, her eyes shining with truth. 'I am in love with him, and I believe he is with me. I have never in my life felt such happiness before this. Don't tell me to stop because I don't think I can.'

'And Hugh? Your husband? Am I to forget you are married? As you seem to have done.'

At the mention of her husband her face changes into a look of great sadness and she pulls back even further on the path.

I take her hand in both of mine. 'Be careful! This is not Athens or London. If the women here see you appear to discard your husband so easily, they will fear for their own, and turn against you and destroy you without a thought. You are an outsider with strange and different ways to us. They watch you closely and a woman who spends so much time

142

alone with two men in her house is a feast for someone who hungers for trouble in a dull round of work and children.'

She looks not only stricken, but totally shocked. 'I mean no harm. You know how much I have changed since I first came here; you more than anyone. Think of when we first met. I was a foreigner, a stranger all dressed up in linen and silk, a fat old pudding who thought she knew everything.'

She pauses, her eye caught, as was mine, by a flash of silver high above us; an eagle hovering.

'I love this village and all my neighbours. I have felt so free here and I think I have at last found out who I am and how I want to live.'

Tears now freely pour down her cheeks. I have frightened her beyond words and I am filled with guilt.

I hug her to me again. 'I have probably said too much. Of course you are loved and respected here, I meant only that you must take care. Be watchful of yourself. Your happiness shines from your eyes and anyone who looks at the two of you together will jump to the most obvious conclusion. The truth will be hard to hide. Be on your guard. I think Yorgo is oblivious to anything except his family and his work. He is a man and men often don't see what is under their noses. But your neighbours now; Maria, Irini, Sophia, all of them are used to wandering in and out of your house as if it were their own. They will see the glances, the unspoken words before you even think them.'

She rubs the drying tears from her face. 'I know what you are telling me is right. I suppose I have been a careless idiot. Only tell me that you understand? Tell me that you forgive me. I have fallen so in love I hardly know myself. I barely tolerate each moment without him, longing for the sight of him again.'

A wedge of sun shines down between us but I feel only chill. 'There is little I can say to you. This love you speak of is unknown to me and I suspect to most of the women here. Our marriages are arranged for us as transactions; land changes hands and we smile and dance through a ceremony that has little to do with our feelings. We survive, that is all I ask each day. Love is something I reserve for my girls. All I can say to you is, take care. I will shield you from others' judgements in any way I can. But I can't protect you if you blindly walk about in this glow, this – love as you call it.'

Truly, I feel a great shaft of pain shoot through me as I speak. Envy. How I long to feel even a little of something like this. But any thought of even affection for Manolis makes every bit of my body cringe, squeeze up inside, as if I have sucked lemons.

Her fingers grip mine tightly.

'From now on I will only look at Christo as if he is the ugliest man I have ever seen.' And she pulls a face full of such disgust, I can only laugh.

Although I had left Heavenly's house with laughter, it lasted only a moment. 'She must be so careful,' I found myself saying to the little one bundled up in front of me in the saddle.

I had reached Yorgo and Aphrodite's house when I was called to a halt. Yorgo had run out of his door and was waving me down calling, 'Kyria Anthi, stop, stop!' Aphrodite, holding her youngest child in her arms, was behind him. 'It is true. Everything the women from Pano Panagia said is coming true!'

'What do you mean?' They were clearly so troubled both of them that as they spoke to me they could hardly get their words out quickly enough.

'War! There is going to be a war!'

A cold wave of fear rippled through me and I gripped Voula tightly in my arms.

'Tell me what you have heard, what is happening?'

'Guns, all our guns. We have to collect them up and take them to the square this afternoon. The general has ordered it.' Yorgo spoke quickly, stumbling over the words. Aphrodite looked at me. 'All we know is that there is to be a collection of arms today. It is the same in every village. Everyone must surrender anything they have, guns of every kind, rifles, machine guns, pistols, everything.'

'Oh don't be foolish, wife,' said Yorgo. 'No one here has a machine gun.'

Aphrodite hit him on the hand. 'Just listen to me and do what you are told,' she said. 'Your Pappous,' she nodded at me, 'he is to be in charge for now. He is sending Michaelis, and anyone else he can get hold of, round the village, upper, lower and middle, and we are all to gather in the square with our weapons at five o'clock.'

Yorgo looked at me and obviously thought I needed more explanation.

'You see, ever since Andreas Mammadopolous died there is no mayor and—'

'She knows all this. Now, go and tell those neighbours that were away in the fields when Michaelis came what they are to do.' And she pushed him away. She looked at me, exasperated. 'Sorry. Tell anyone you pass and we shall see you later in the square.'

My first thought was the school, but then I remember the professor came from another village. If Aphrodite spoke the truth, other villages would be doing their own collections. And then I thought of Heavenly. I must tell her what is happening. I turned Astrape around and headed back to her house.

Voula wailed when she realised we were going in the wrong direction for food, but cheered up when she saw we were back at Heavenly's house.

A little later she was sitting on a cushion at Heavenly's feet munching happily on a piece of apple and a rusk dipped in milk. We are waiting for Christo, who had gone straight up to the Piperia when Michaelis called with the summons.

We didn't have to wait long. We heard him as he tethered his ass outside and ran up the steps.

'It is not war,' he said, 'yet. But Metaxas is taking a precautionary measure. With the army in Albania, if defence is needed here, there will be no weapons for the volunteers or the conscripts to fight with. There is no need to panic. For all his faults, Metaxas seems to know what he is doing. It is good sense for everyone to dig out the arms they have all got stored away.' Heavenly looked dubious.

'I suppose it is what Hugh calls, "their old rabbit guns",' she said. She looked away quickly. I guessed she was uncomfortable speaking of her husband.

During the afternoon I felt more relaxed in their company. They were so happy together and they included me so warmly, it was impossible to feel otherwise.

Heavenly, proud of the new skills she had learned, didn't mind that I took over her kitchen and provided cold lemonade or sliced fruit while she skimmed and smoothed the old walls with the white *isvesti*.

Christo is a good teacher, or she an able student, for the results are perfect.

Maria, Athena's mother, calls on the way from school to say that Aphrodite has sent word that Despina should go home with them, and she seemed happy enough to do that.

It is impossible to miss the importance of the gathering at five o'clock. Half an hour before, there started first a trickle and then a constant stream of villagers along the pathways and tracks leading to the village square. They came from their firesides, their gardens and fields.

Old Yerasimo is rubbing the sleep from his eyes after siesta. His wife, being woken too soon, bangs her stick angrily along beside him. Vilandis the baker is still covered in flour but, cannily spotting an opportunity for a sale, has a cart full of fresh bread and cakes behind him.

When we arrive in the square it seems as though the entire population of the island is gathered there. Every wall has become a seat for the older villagers. Babies and children are in their parents' arms or on shoulders. Others run alongside. Balls are bouncing, odd games of football and cup-and-stick start, and girls whizz themselves deftly in and out of skipping ropes or jumping hoops hewn from large twigs or, in one instance, a small tree.

There is one thing in common with everyone gathering here: most adults, and even one or two of the children, have a gun. A rough assortment, maybe: battered, rusty and creaking in movement, but nonetheless hauled out of attics or cellars or taken down from walls.

A large table is being dragged along from a nearby house and several pairs of hands lift it onto the stone platform in front of the old village hall, creating a focus for the activities. There is a buzz in the air; nothing so exciting has happened in Panagia for years.

At the back of the platform sits Manolis's brother Stelios, the grape treader. At his feet a large flagon of the product of his trade, half drunk. In his hand the lyre that I know he can play exquisitely. Beside him, the fiddler known as Pipos and his son, on a small drum. Cautiously, and at first rather tunelessly, they begin to play a traditional song and one or two of the younger women, careless of the solemnity of the occasion, link arms in a dance. Young men, eager for any excuse for a party, start to clap them along but are swiftly silenced by a few elders.

Hearing the music and recognising the tune Voula, at my feet, starts to wiggle her little body in an imitation of the rhythm.

'Do these idiots think it is a party?' The thick nasal twang tells me Papa Yannis is here. If he is, then Manolis will not be far behind. What will he say when he sees his brother is part of the entertainment?

In front of the platform is a growing heap of weaponry. While some firmly grasp what they hold, reluctant to part with anything until absolutely necessary, others throw them down swiftly and carry on their conversation as casually as if they were snuffing out the tip of a cigarette.

Coming down the hilly path from Mesa Panagia is my Pappous. Sitting astride his donkey and firmly looking only ahead, he comes to a stop at the front of the gathering and slips easily to his feet, his every movement that of a much younger man.

Order is quickly called for from some of the older men near him and a growing hush sweeps over the crowd like a breeze. Pappous is hoisted onto the platform by his friends; he looks magnificent in my eyes and I feel so proud to be his granddaughter. By his side is the old Turkish *yatagan*, the magnificent sword that is usually hung over the fireplace in his house.

Is he going to sacrifice this for the greater good, I wonder? That would be sad. It had been captured by his great-grand-father in the war against the Turks over a hundred years ago.

My Yaya is nearby and as she looks around, she sees me and quickly smiles.

Pappous raises his right hand in the air and the last whisper dies away.

'People of Panagia,' he says, and his voice carries to the far reaches of the square. 'I am here today instead of my dear friend Andreas Mamadopolous. A man we all loved, admired and respected. I make no pretence to be able to take his place here fully. But until we have been appointed a new mayor, I will do as I can. Most of you know that these are dark times for our country. There is much unrest across the whole of Europe and especially among the Balkan nations. We none of us know from where will come any attack. But clearly our leaders in Athens and our recently restored King believe there is danger for us. We must help. Every one of us must give up our own weapons for the greater good of Crete.'

'I'll keep mine and shoot any enemy that comes near me!' comes a shout from the crowd. This is an answer that moves others to cheer and call, 'So will I.'

An old woman, Toula, whose husband died a year ago when he fell in the river on the way home from a night of celebration at the kafenion, is on her feet and waving a large thick stick in her hand.

'This stick is all I have to guard me at night, now I am alone, but I will happily give it to you if it will help protect us.' And the stick flies through the air and clatters down on the pile below.

'Thank you, Kyria, you are a good woman, but I think you should keep your stick by your side at night now that you have nothing else in your bed.'

There is some laughter, but it fades as his voice rises in anger and he addresses the first speaker: 'It is not an option for you to keep your gun, Kyrios Matalous. If it is not surrendered by the end of this week, there will be only punishment for you and anyone else who chooses to turn their back on patriotism.

'Here, see,' and his hand waves the heavy *yatagan* over his head and rests it down atop the weaponry already there. 'Do as I do,' he says and a cheer rises from the crowd at his gesture.

There is suddenly a disturbance suddenly from the church-yard next to the square. This is the Holy Church of St Athanasius, the church my mother worships at so devotedly with her adored Papa Yannis.

Panos, the simpleton son of the barber, is running out of the gates with a muddy spade held high above his head and his mother behind him, trying to keep up and calling for him to stop at once.

Papa Yannis pushes his way to the front of the gathering and smartly grabs Panos in his outspread arms. Someone else takes the spade from his grasp before he catches the fat priest round the head with it. Panos wriggles and yelps like a trapped animal.

His mother follows and, for a moment, is too puffed to speak. She wipes her sweating face on her apron and falls to her knees at the priest's feet.

'Forgive him, Papa,' she gasps. 'He only wants to help.'

'How can I forgive him when I don't know what the simpleton has done?' he says pompously. Everyone around is agog now.

Still puffing, the barber's wife speaks under her breath so that only the priest can hear. He raises himself upright and calls to the crowd.

'This idiot child was digging up his uncle's tomb!'

There are gasps of horror and the barber's wife slowly hauls herself to her feet. Despairingly she looks around, her hands twisting and knotting her apron in front of her.

Papa Yannis speaks loudly. In his hand he twists the ear of Panos, who squeals in pain. 'Uncle's shotgun and cleaning rod were buried with him, it seems, and this mad boy thought to retrieve them. Does anyone here want to go and finish the job?' There are mutters and groans, but no one steps forward.

'Oh please, Papa, my husband and I will do this and we will bring any weapon we find within the week. Please, Papa, will you come and bless my brother's tomb again when we have finished?' She is practically begging now and I feel only shame to see the way she must so publicly humiliate herself before the priest. He is enjoying every moment of it, no doubt thinking of the extra money he can squeeze out of this poor family. He will, as always, charge highly for his services and this one good gesture of poor Panos will cost his family dearly for some time to come.

This incident has interrupted the solemnity of the occasion and people are shuffling around now, chattering and laughing with their neighbours. Pappous is talking again, but his voice is getting frail and faint and much as I and several others call for quiet for him, it is getting increasingly difficult to hear him. Christo is here now, but no sign of Heavenly.

I am relieved, as they should not be seen in public together, and no one would expect her to have a weapon to relinquish. Manolis is beside the priest now and looking around, checking on who is here, I guess. I duck my head down to speak to Voula and hope he does not see me. He would expect me to be at his side.

The pile of weapons is growing smaller as Michaelis and his friends have started to gather them up and carry them for safekeeping inside the old village hall. They will no doubt be locked and guarded there until the prefecture in Lassithi has time to collect them and dispatch them to where they are needed.

I wait to see my Yaya and Pappous before they leave, but

instead I see my mother. She walks past them, reluctantly acknowledging them only with a nod, and makes her way to Manolis instead. Both of them then scan the crowd and before I can duck again, I am spotted. My mother's beady eyes have seen me and, digging Manolis in the ribs with her elbow, she points me out. Several people turn in my direction.

It is time for me to find Despina and take her home.

I crouch down, grab Voula, who was digging a hole in the dirt with another small girl, and, nudging my way through the people to the edge, walk quickly down the familiar paths towards my home.

Despina is waiting at the side of the path as we approach and she stands up to greet us. 'I'm hungry, Mama!' she says and Voula claps her hands at the thought of more food. I sigh for it is the middle of the Lenten fast and hard for me always to find enough to eat for the girls without breaking it. My family expect me to adhere strictly to the rules as they have always done: no oil, no meat, fish, eggs, milk or cheese. However, the younger women in Panagia secretly break it. How are we to nourish our children without the simplest essentials?

Yaya and Pappous can survive on boiled wild greens and bread and olives, but my daughters would never sleep at night if I imposed such deprivation on them. Manolis pretends to keep the fast and the laws of Lent so that he can forbid me to teach at the school on Wednesdays, but I know that he will eat with his friends elsewhere, for he comes home reeking of garlic and wine.

Taking the girls into the house, I prepare a dish of greens with a stew of lentils and beans with potatoes, tomatoes and herbs. I say a quick prayer to the virgin for forgiveness as I liberally splash in olive oil. Despina will get sore, dry, flaking skin without that, and I will not watch her suffer.

Aphrodite has told me that Yorgo's cousin, who now lives in Albania, is coming with his wife and baby son to spend Easter week with them and she told me that she will be baking as many sweetmeats as she can manage. They are leaving their home in Tirana for ever and coming to live near their family here.

I know she has invited Christo to join them for the feast at the end of Holy Week as he is far from home, but I cannot help but wonder what will Heavenly do if she is alone?

I fear Manolis will make her anything but welcome if I ask her to join us, and I think she will find a way to refuse such an invitation anyway.

My girls eat hungrily. There is barely enough left for Manolis when they are finished so I must make do with some forbidden bread soaked in the juices. But really I am too disturbed to think of food for myself just now. Heavenly today has shocked and frightened me. I care for her so much as a friend and I don't think she has any idea of the real danger she is in. And this man, this Christo. Oh yes, I can see he is charming – he has certainly charmed her. But he is Greek. He will tire of her and move onto another after the novelty of the conquest has worn off – they all do.

The slightest hint of scandal and people like Papa Yannis will look for her to be driven out of the village. And nothing any of us can do will help her.

HEAVENLY

Athens   *Easter 1939*

My dear Evadne,

I cannot begin to tell you of how awful it is here now. War, war, war is all anyone speaks of and our letters are now being xxxxxxxxxxxxxxxxxxxxxxx so I shall be brief. I can tell you that it seems to me now that you are in the best, the safest place.

The Italians now appear to xxxxxxxxxxxxxxxxxxxxxx-xxxxxxxxxxxxxxxxxxxxxxxx.

H.E. insists that we must stick to the Orthodox Lenten fast. So I am now stick-thin and hungry most of the time. However, thank goodness for Foxy, who has managed to find a nightclub or two that defies the protocol and we can get a steak or a good chop, but at a price!

The stock of decent French wine here is terribly depleted and all we can get on most days is some local stuff.

I have the great honour of spending a little of each day with the royal family. Naturally we are worried about their safety so I think xxxxx xxxxxxxxxxx.

I've a nasty feeling that everything I write is pretty suspect.

I send you all my love, darling, take great care of yourself,

Your beloved husband,
Hugh

In many ways it is something of a relief to me that Hugh's letters are censored. For the last weeks the very thought of him stirs appalling guilt in me and I have only skipped through the last two.

I have never known such feelings. I couldn't imagine before that it was even possible to feel like this. Such love, such longing, such desire!

How does anyone live with such depths of passion? I find it so hard to do anything that is not somehow with or about Christo. In order to take my laundry to the spring and get such chores done, I sneak something of his in the pile. Oh the delight of cleaning his underclothes, his shirts! Am I mad?

I know the need to keep everything utterly secret. When she is here, Anthi watches us both like an eagle stalking a mouse. We have learnt to avoid even a glance when anyone is around. For if I so much as catch his look on me, I start to shake. I can feel my face blush when he comes within touching distance. Two days ago he slid on the newly painted floor and I had to hold my hands together behind my back and cross my feet over to stop myself rushing to his side and kissing the bruise. Andreas was in the house and if I had touched Christo, I knew I would groan aloud with desire.

When we are not alone, I have taken to going down to the little church of Panagia Sta Perivolia to sit and write my diary. Only there do I feel safe and I can write the words I long to say aloud. I keep my diary under the stone at the back of the altar – everyone here is far too religious to poke around there, so I know it's safe.

We have been lovers now for two months and four days. I don't need to refer to my diary to know that!

At first we would snatch moments alone together here. We encouraged Yorgo to leave early each evening, saying he should spend more time with his children, his wife, even his animals. Profuse with his thanks he would at first reluctantly, and then speedily, depart.

We fell on each other as soon as he was down the path.

As if starving, we would touch, kiss, taste and smell;

rubbing and stroking flesh with flesh. The juices we made, whether sweat, tears or our most intimate fluids, would mingle and later, alone, I would smell his body and mine on the linen and sleep as sweetly as if we were still together.

As the sun stayed later over each day's sky, we had to decide between the danger of his lingering, when Irini or Sophia may enter at will or, as on many days now, I should go out later in the evening and ride alone up into the hills to visit him in his cave.

Sometimes, passing one of my neighbours on these evenings, I feel the need to invent a reason for my late journey; a visit to the church, a need for some air or, and this one I was especially proud of, painting or drawing a view, a waterfall or an odd-shaped tree to send to my husband in Athens.

This was Yorgo's idea. He had seen one or two of my sketches around the house and suggested Hugh would like memories of the village he must be sad to have left. I loved art in school so it seemed natural for me to take up this hobby when I needed an excuse. Off I would go at the end of the afternoon, clutching my sketchpad to my side, crayons, pencils and pastels rattling in my saddlebag.

I was happy to show this work, that kept me so busily out of the house and away in the hills, to any passer-by who showed interest.

It was Anthi who pointed out to me one day that I had been drawing the same tree for weeks on end. For the next two days I quickly started a variety of sketches that I could be seen to be working on whenever I wanted.

It was when Anthi guessed that Christo and I had become more than good friends, the day of the arms amnesty, that I realised the danger I was in from the gossips around me. At first I hardly left the house, afraid that one of my neighbours would accost me and accuse me of being a whore. Night after night, I would wake from frightened dreams of being pursued by a crowd of angry villagers and told never to return to the place I now loved more than anywhere I had been in my life.

When Christo learnt how I was tormenting myself in this

way he took it upon himself to put my world in proper perspective for me.

We were lying in his cave on a thick and beautiful rug that had belonged to his great-grandmother. Our lovemaking had been more frantic even than usual that night and, as I trembled to the finish and fell back into his arms, I found myself weeping uncontrollably. His strong arms held me tightly, the fingers of one hand stroking a gentle rhythm through my hair, his lips taking up the tears as they fell.

'Heavenly, Heavenly,' he said. 'Why so sad?'

At first I could not speak. He let me lie quietly until I had eventually choked to a stop and then spoke again. 'Please tell me what's wrong. Has someone or something upset you? Is it me? I would do anything in the world for you, don't you know that? Is there word from Athens?'

I sniffed, blew my nose, and rubbed the tears away roughly with my hands. I could not bear to think of Hugh now I was lying here in Christo's arms. As I sniffed I caught a breath of his smell; powerful, intoxicating. He smelt of the outdoors, of wood smoke, the trees around us – cedar and spruce and pine and overlaying all the ubiquitous scent of the olive, even here inside his cave.

'No, nothing from Athens. It is me, I am what's wrong. I am just so afraid. Suppose someone sees us? Suppose we are discovered and I am forced to leave here. I could not bear that now. I belong to you so completely that I cannot live without you.'

'My dearest love. Are you thinking anyone is interested in us?'

I nodded. 'That is what the women do here, they gossip. Of course they must see us and see what I feel for you. What else?'

He was smiling.

'I mean it.'

He stopped smiling at once. He could see that I was genuinely afraid.

'Listen to me. Every day I am out in the village. I am known and trusted here. Believe me, no one out there gives a mule's fart for what we are doing. They have far more to think about, to worry about, than to give us more than a passing glance. They care for the weather, the crop yields, the tobacco subsidy, the tomato harvest, their olives. The price of resin is of far more importance than who their neighbour's wife is fucking. On top of all that now, they worry about the war that is brewing on their doorstep. They listen to the radio each night in the kafenion, as many of them as can get inside, to see what is happening in Albania, not at the end of the road.'

I smiled. Of course he was right. 'Anthi says we are in danger, we must be careful every moment. Are you saying she is wrong?'

'No, she is right to be concerned. We must take care. We do take care. We must keep our lives to ourselves, of course. If we were to flaunt ourselves publicly, if we walked the streets hand in hand, then a nose or two would sniff in our direction. But if we behave with discretion, as we do, and be quiet with our love, then Panagia will get on with its life and we can get on with ours.'

Inside I knew it was my guilt that plagued me. I was afraid, not really for my neighbours, but for Hugh. I had met and married Hugh because I thought I had fallen in love with him. I had been a sad and lonely person and he came into my life; picked up this ugly duckling and offered her life as a swan.

My actions over these last weeks, months astonished me. I had given myself so completely to Christo so easily it seemed to me now. But what of my initial love for Hugh? Where has that gone?

If I could discard him so easily and replace him with Christo, was I merely a fickle person, a trivial woman with feelings of no depth?

Evenings alone like this, when I have only my thoughts for company, I sit on the terrace looking out to sea. The lamps in the house behind me dimmed, the warm air of evening holding the stars high. Sometimes I hear a long and sad note in the distance, an animal? A seabird perhaps?

Thoughts of long ago haunt me. The excitement of what I suppose was my courtship of Hugh seem at a distance, so at odds with the person I am now. I had been a shy, gauche creature who moved awkwardly, as though in a body that belonged to someone else. For the first time, I begin to know a growing anger.

It caught me by surprise one Sunday evening when I sat and watched the villagers walk along the road in their best clothes. Laughing children skipping beside their parents, who were visibly proud of their offspring and smiled fondly after them.

Anthi's friend and neighbour Maria went past with Yorgo's Aphrodite, and I heard part of their conversation. They were discussing the speed of the growth of their daughters, and Maria said, 'Athena is growing so quickly now, I need to make her skirts longer almost every month.'

Her tone was soft, and I could hear the pride in her voice. Aphrodite looked at her daughter Mika and said, 'They are children for such a short while, and before you know it they must wear headkerchiefs outside the house.'

I had never known or felt that sort of pride from my mother. I was always sure of being only an embarrassment to her. One afternoon leapt uninvited into my mind. I had opened the door to yet another of her rich, heavily perfumed bridge cronies. Her name eludes me, but I recall the withering look she gave me.

'My dear,' she said to my mother as she sat down, nodding her head in my direction, 'I am *so* sorry.'

'I know,' my mother sighed, 'ghastly, isn't it? But try as I do, I can't make her look anything like a girl.'

I remember, for barely a moment, wondering what I did look like if not a girl?

Mrs Whoever-she-was said, as she twitched the head of a fox resting on her ample bust, 'Thank goodness you have the lovely Daphne, that must be some consolation, dear.'

Could you only be loved if you were lovely to look at, tidy, elegant and, on top of that, clever as well?

I had always known that Daphne had far more than I could ever hope for. Did that make her happy, I wondered to myself? She wrote to me sometimes, and I always found her letters sad and full of longing. Clearly she was only envious of my life in the embassies. Now I have told her how I found happiness in the village and in the school here, she never writes. To me, so far away, so long ago, it seems only inevitable that I should have accepted the first man who offered me a life.

Had anyone bothered with me earlier, perhaps I wouldn't have been the clumsy child that nobody wanted; skinny with frizzy hair and ladders in her stockings, her fingernails always chewed and with a habit of turning scarlet when spoken to.

It is dusk again now, time for me to visit Christo in his cave. It is three days since we have been together and I am full of longing. Sometimes I think it's only me that counts our days together so closely. Occasionally I wait for hours on the terrace alone and he doesn't come. Twice I have walked to the cave and found it empty. He never gives me a reason and I don't feel able to ask. One evening, after sitting in the chill dark of his cave for nearly two hours, he came and said he had been with friends in the Piperia. He laughed when he saw my face and teased me. 'Am I never to spend an hour or two with my friends playing a round or two of *prefa*?'

I know my face burnt red with shame. He put his hand under my chin and pulled my face towards him. He kissed me firmly. 'Kyria, you are my only lover and don't ever forget it. I was always taught that love is like a flame: smother it and it will die. Leave a little space, a little air around it, and it will burn long and strong.'

I pack up my art work; today a picture of a twisted olive tree. I smile – it's actually not at all bad!

I will call to see Aphrodite and Yorgo and their children as I pass and take them some of the cheese that Irini has made for me. This is the week after Easter and I know any additional food will be well received. Yorgo's cousin and his family will be staying; extra mouths to feed. They have been so kind and found me a donkey to get around a bit better, Lotto. He is quite elderly but seems to like me

Their house is quiet and I tether Lotto outside.

Usually when visitors are here there is music, dancing, laughter spilling through the windows and doors. Tonight there is just a lonely echoing silence. Aphrodite opens the door herself and hugs me.

'Welcome. Have you seen Anthi? Or perhaps Christo?' I shake my head. I cannot tell her I am on the way to his cave now.

'Then you won't know what has happened. Sotiri and his family have not come. There is no word from them, and they should be here now. We heard that they left their home in Tirana days and days ago. Something must be terribly wrong. Yorgo has gone to the Piperia to see if there is some news on the wireless set.'

I try to offer reassuring words, but it is difficult to know what to say.

A familiar voice speaks behind me and I spin round, unable to prevent myself smiling at my lover.

'Aphrodite,' he says, merely nodding acknowledgment at me. 'Yorgo not back yet?' There is no need for her to answer. 'He left the Piperia ahead of me, I thought to come straight here to you.' He shakes his head. 'It's not good news, I am afraid. On Good Friday, Italy landed troops in all the Albanian ports and marched on Tirana. Within twenty-four hours they had completely occupied the country and declared it part of Italy.'

Aphrodite draws in her breath sharply and, grabbing my arm, begs the Virgin Mary for help. Tears are forming in her eyes. Her girls, sensing there is something wrong, flock around her now, hanging onto her skirts and whimpering, 'Mama, Mama, what's happening? Where is Papa?'

Yorgo finally appears home late, as he had stopped everyone he met to pass on the news. Many people around here have relatives in Albania. He is not alone when he comes in, Aphrodite's aunt, Yanna, is with him, a plump woman whose breasts slope like pillows down to her now non-existent waist. She carries with her always the sweet smell of baking bread mixed with the scent of lavender and acacia blossom that grow in profusion around the pale stone walls of her tiny house in Kato Panagia.

The soft white skin of her face is creased and damp with tears. As Aphrodite gathers her in and pours a large glass of what I take to be brandy, Yorgo says quietly to me, 'She has three boys, all in Albania. She has heard nothing from them for weeks. Salin, the eldest, is certainly in the army, so it is possible his brothers have volunteered to fight as well. The two younger boys are twins and were coming home for their name day next week.' He is shaking his head sadly.

I feel a slight tug on my arm and spin round to see Christo. He looks so serious. His usually bright, laughing eyes are dim. 'I will take you home, Heavenly, this is a place for family tonight. You and I should not be here.'

I am about to protest, to tell him I will leave and perhaps he should stay, but he is already moving to the door with my sleeve still caught in his grip so I can only go with him. Once outside, having called a hasty goodbye, he says, 'This is a bad day for many here.'

'I will go home. I can feel you would like to be somewhere else just now, not worrying about me.'

His smile is brief. 'I will go back to the Piperia and see if I can help in some way there.'

I untether Lotto and, waving briefly behind me, I ride through the still night air to my house.

The days lengthened slowly, oh so slowly, into spring again and while the news from abroad filtered gradually through to us, all of it bad, at least the promise of a better year for food came in with the sun, offering survival at least.

I am reminded constantly of the harshness of life here and, by contrast my own good luck. Easter this year was early and the cold winter days seem long. The school had a small amount of money from the state and there is no shortage of wood for heating or food for the pupils. They would come each morning with a collection of aunts, uncles or grandparents who lingered by the stove, their clothes steaming and odorous, looking hungrily at the bread or stew that was provided for their young, until the professor would usher tham out of the door and close it firmly behind him.

There were mixed feelings in the village when it was heard on the radio that Greece would be celebrating the fourth anniversary of Metaxas rule.

'What are we to celebrate? A fat dictator, who cares more for the olive stone he spits on the ground than for the people of these villages!' Anthi was vociferous in her condemnation of the leader.

We were walking home, weary from a long day in the school.

'Oh, I wish I had brought Astrape. Old and lame as he is now at least the children could ride and they would be quiet with it.'

It is rare to hear her complain about her girls, but today they seemed more tired than usual and their feet were dragging slower and slower, and every word spoken seemed to be a complaint.

'Manolis had his friends in last night, drinking way into the night. It was impossible for the girls and me to sleep.'

'Hugh says that in Athens everyone has come to accept that Metaxas is not really bad and there has been some prosperity in his rule.'

Anthi snorted and laughed, a bitter angry sound.

'Oh I am so relieved that the people of Athens are doing well, 'she said. 'I must tell my Pappous he is quite wrong. Be careful what you say in this village, there are strong feelings around at the moment. Tonight the Piperia will be closed as the men who patronise it refuse to celebrate that man's anniversary.'

I was suddenly uncomfortable in her fury. 'I'm sorry, I don't know what to think. Take no notice of me, I am an ignorant Englishwoman – what do I know of your politics?'

At that moment Voula stumbled and fell. Under her little body her plump legs waved in the air helplessly and she began to wail. I reached her ahead of Anthi and she struggled up and into my arms.

I was wearing a thin cotton frock against the heat of the sun and within moments my shoulder was soaked through with her tears. Anthi pulled her into her arms, and stroked the top of her hot little head, soothing her gently and lovingly: a mother's caress.

Voula was quickly her smiling self with just a grubby smudge on her face. Despina stood stamping her foot impatiently. 'Oh, stop your wailing,' she said to her sister, crossly. 'You are not really hurt, you just want Mama to cuddle you all the time.' She flounced around with her back to Voula. 'And she smells. She has wet herself again.' Turning to me she said, 'She does that all the time. She is nearly four now and still she behaves like a baby.'

'Four is still very young, Despina. Perhaps she can't help it.'

We were moving forwards again now, Voula clasped in her mother's arms, her thumb firmly between her rosy lips.

'Despina was quickly out of her undercloths. She is right, Voula is much slower.' Anthi shrugged as she defended her youngest daughter. 'She can't help it. She is so busy looking each day at something new to her, a flower or a bee or a beetle, that she forgets to relieve herself.'

Despina looked disgusted and marched ahead. I watched her and saw how quickly she was growing. She is over nine now. Her long legs, colt-like in their angularity, could be those of a dancer. She has a natural elegance in her straight back and soon she'll need to tie her long gold hair into a headkerchief like the other village girls. I thought fleetingly, How sad to hide those wonderful tresses. As if she heard me, she turned her head and flashed me a fast smile.

She and I have a warm understanding, I think, looking at her, but I wish I knew what could suddenly cause her to fall into silence. I see Anthi is looking at us and she is smiling now, in spite of the weight in her arms. How lucky I am to have this family as my friends.

Later, when the girls were resting after their lunch, Anthi and I sat under the shade of a flowering almond tree that grew at the top of their garden. In the distance seabirds called to each other, that long, sad sound they make. The silence between us was comfortable and slow.

'Do you think there really will be a war?' Anthi suddenly looked anxious.

'Yes, I am afraid I do, at least across a lot of Europe. Whether it will affect Greece, I can't tell you. Even if it does, it is not certain that it would affect Crete. Hugh can't say much in his letters, but he seems to imply that this is the safest place to be.'

We lay back and looked at the blue sky flickering through the branches. A cloud that had momentarily shadowed the sun passed, and for a moment I was blinded by a sudden, glittering ray of sunlight.

'My Pappous feels that we would not have had the collection of arms unless it was intended to use them.'

'Christo agrees with him about that. You know his friend from Sitia, Kotso? He has convinced him that there is no doubt of war. He says that, across the rest of the country, villagers are preparing for invasion. Whether from Italy or Germany, he seems unsure.'

Christo was spending more and more time with Kotso and told me he thought him well informed. I like him very much. He is small and chunky with stocky, well-muscled legs, a fine moustache and eyes the colour of deep, rich wine, velvety brown. He is always smiling and seems to find humour in everything. I suspect he has guessed that Christo and I are lovers; he is so relaxed when we were all together. What I didn't tell Anthi was that he has persuaded Christo to help form a band of young village men. They are to operate together in secret in the hills and could, at a moment's notice, be ready to fight any enemy.

There was inevitably a danger in these groupings because not all men in a family were sympathetic to them. Christo said it had always been so here.

He warned that families could be torn apart. When I heard this, I remembered that Anthi had told me her grandfather had spoken of this from many years ago: brother fighting brother, father fighting son.

I shivered as if there were a sudden chill; war, fighting, hate, I loathe it all, and long only for the wonderful peace I found in these hills when I first came here.

'Oh I wish we could do something!' Anthi suddenly spoke aloud. Often between us it was as though we shared each other's thoughts.

'I do have an idea,' I said.

'Tell me.'

'Well, why don't I teach the children simple first aid?'

She looked puzzled.

'It would help us to feel we were actually doing something, rather than sitting wringing our hands like the other women.

'Then, I'm thinking, we could all help if the war did come as far as here. Of course,' I added quickly, 'of course it won't, we know that, but there are always accidents of one sort or another and how terrific if the children were able to be prepared and offer proper help. Imagine,' I was getting excited now, 'if there was a fall of stones down the mountainside and someone was hurt by it. Even a child could be useful in bandaging or cleaning a wound.'

Anthi merely gazed at me. 'Is there something you know and are not telling me?' She spoke quietly.

'No, no, I swear, but it is something I could easily do. So could you if I showed you how.'

There was a moment, and then she picked up on my excitement.

'Yes, that's a really good idea.' She was smiling. 'I shall speak to the professor next week.'

*

And that was how we started our hospital and first aid centre. No matter that it was small, the children thought it was wonderful fun in the beginning and started practising shooting each other so there were wounds they could pretend needed dressing.

Luckily the professor thought it a good idea too and found a little money from his government allowance that would pay for a few cloth bandages and surgical spirit. Water, with the addition of red ink, made an excellent substitute for blood.

The children loved this especially and at first were bleeding profusely every day, and limping around the school with a supposedly broken limb. But they soon settled down and slowly began to take it seriously.

They knew their family stories well and most of them had a tale to tell of an uncle wounded in one battle and a grandparent who had nearly died in another.

All this meant that I was spending more time at the school and less at the house. This was painful for me at first, but the busier I became at the school, I told myself, the less opportunity for village gossip about my working with the men. In spite of Christo's reassurances, I was sure there was still suspicion, and I would read hidden meanings into every simple conversation with my neighbours.

I ran the first aid group after school twice a week. The first rush of excitement settled into a small group of stalwarts who confessed to me that being doctors or nurses was what they wanted to do when they were grown up. Many days I took this ragged collection outside and down to the little cobbled square to bandage each other.

Sometimes they persuaded one of the old men who sat on the benches there, in the shade of the ilex tree, sipping their daily ouzo, to be patients. There was no shortage of willing volunteers who would sit with an arm or a leg in the air while telling their 'doctor' or their 'nurse' how they had come by the old scars and war wounds that most of them sported.

I learnt much of Panagia's recent hostile history in this spot during these warm days, by the running water, with the sound of the cicadas chirruping.

For a while, Christo and Kotso thought this was really something of a joke; children learning to dress wounded soldiers? What nonsense! But it was the children who refused to listen to their laughter that soon convinced them to take it seriously. Marina, daughter of the blacksmith, and Anthi's daughter, Despina, had emerged as the natural leaders and came to me after school one day when Kotso and another friend were teasing them without mercy.

Kotso was lying on the ground groaning, his head in Andros's lap. 'Help me, help me,' he called, 'my leg has fallen off, nurse. Please sew it back on.'

Despina pointed to them and said to me, 'Please, can you make them stop?'

I thought it would take more than a stern rebuke from me to finish these two off. 'Even if I do, little one, they will only come back tomorrow,' I said, realising it was a feeble retreat.

One of the old men, sitting hunched over his glass, waved his stick in the air and said, 'They have nothing to do all day, lazy *malakas*, but to come here and torment children.'

There was no answer that I could make to this gibe. I knew, but they did not, that while they may have their days free, their nights were busy tracking paths through the firs on the mountain and making simple safe retreats and hiding places with branches and stones. Locating and clearing old mountain tracks and hideaways disused for years, Christo said, was the best and easiest way to be prepared. Ironic that he couldn't see that the children were, in their own way, also preparing.

The girls came over to me. 'Please, Heavenly,' Marina said, 'why don't you ask our parents to come and we can show them what we are doing.'

'And anyone else who thinks we are just playing,' added Despina, looking directly at the laughing Andros.

And so, on a day when the sun shone blindingly down a motley collection of adults: parents, aunts, uncles, pappous

167

and yayas walked or struggled slowly up through the wooded mountain paths to the little church of Saint Kosmas and Damianos, built a hundred and fifty years ago to house the holy relics of a long-forgotten priest. It was the professor, I suspect urged by his wife Titica, who suggested that we could set up our own little clinic in this church at the top of the mountain.

'It is mostly unused,' he said, 'except one day a year in October, when it celebrates the name day. And it is most suitable. Remember Kosmas and Damianos were two brothers who healed the sick and needy and charged nothing. It will need cleaning, but I am sure the children will help.'

'I will need to get permission, of course,' he continued, 'from the diocese, but I think Papa Costas, who is responsible for St Demitrios, will be happy to support us. I'll have a word with him tonight; he is bringing his wife to eat with us. He likes Titica's cooking better than his own wife's, I think. Look at the figure on the man, you'd think he never ate at all.'

It was true, Papa Costas was a handsome man in his forties, tall – very tall – and stick thin. A sudden anxiety creased my face into a frown. 'Do we need to have permission from Papa Yannis?'

'Oh no, I think Papa Costas is quite sufficient and I am sure he will do what he can.'

The relief not to involve Papa Yannis was clear in the unspoken words between us.

Permission had been swiftly granted to us, and the children and one or two of the mothers had swept and dusted, rubbed and polished, washed and scrubbed, every inch of the inside of the church.

I had asked that Christo make Kotso and Andros come. He had not been easy to persuade. 'I know Yorgo is going,' he said, 'if I come too, that is several hours lost when we could be working on the roof.'

The winter rains have been heavy this year and have shown up the repairs that need doing before the next winter.

I wondered for a moment if he was staying away for fear of

being exposed to the sight of blood. It was not the first time I had this thought. I still felt it an oddity that this strong, brave man had such an irrational childish fear.

We were lying on the rug in his cave. Our love-making had been slow and tender in the heat of the night. I was gently stroking the springy hairs on his muscled chest, my head on his shoulder. He had spoken softly between damp kisses into my ear.

'I know what you are saying,' I said, 'but this is very important for the children, they are, rightly, so proud of what they have learnt. They know, properly now, how essential it is to be prepared and they believe the knowledge they have acquired will truly be useful, not just in a war, but to help anyone in the village who needs nursing.'

I felt rather than saw, that he was smiling now. He had moved to the other side of the cave and was slicing thickly some of the cheese his mother had sent from Sitia. Making love seems always to make me very hungry.

'Oh I do know! Yesterday I was walking past the widow Agalopoulos's house and two of your children were sitting beside her as she lay in her bed. Your deaf and dumb boy was bathing her head with water, and a girl was feeding her something disgusting looking from a bowl.'

'There you are, you see, already they are helping the village.'

'I put my head round the door to see if she wanted me to collect the honey from her hives and when I looked closer, her arm was bandaged and tied up with a stick, and her bed linen was dripping with the spilt water. I reckon by the end of the week, she will have pneumonia and need to go to the hospital in Aghios.'

We were both laughing and I sighed, 'They mean well.'

'I know, and I'll threaten Kotso and Andros with a flogging if they do not come to your demonstration.'

ANTHI

The straggling line of people: mothers and babies, pappous and yayas, climbed slowly up the mountain path for the first-aid demonstration. My Pappous was in front with Yaya on the donkey behind him. Children ran around impatiently on and off the path. Their parents, mostly mothers, tried and failed to keep them in any form of order. Their voices were shrill and cut through the hot sleepy air of the afternoon. I had the sleeping Voula, hidden from the sun under a shawl, on my aching back and Despina clung to my skirts. It was a long trek and the beating summer sun shone down on bare faces and arms. Not many fathers had been persuaded to appear. They should be working the fields but, with wives safely occupied elsewhere, I have no doubt the kafenions are full.

A great wail tore through the air, stilling the laughter, the giggles. We had our first casualty; Vilandis the baker had tripped on a rock and the wicker tray of bread on his head had shed its load over the scrub and patchy herbiage that sprouted from the sandy path. His oaths were scattered to the sky as he tried to decide whether he minded more his flying loaves or the gash already bleeding through his flax breeches. The villagers had no such problem; flying bread was fair game and, within moments, it had all disappeared into pockets or baskets. Vilandis yelled loudly for help, but only his son Jacko stayed to offer him an arm, probably knowing well the thrashing he would get tonight if he didn't.

Vilandis shrugged and carried on up the hill. As he drew

level with me he said, 'Ah well, I was going to give it to them for free anyway.'

'Really? How very kind of you.' I smiled sweetly at him. He had a reputation as a skinflint, so if he thought I would believe this, he was more stupid than his sheep.

The sharp crack of a shot rang out and, beside me, a large bird fell like a stone to the ground. Everyone looked around suspiciously; who had a hunting gun in these days after the amnesty?

Bringing up the rear of the line alone, Petros the blacksmith looked so innocent as he whistled carelessly and strode on that his very lack of guilt condemned him. I think only I had spotted him carefully mark the spot with a cigarette packet.

Then my Pappous drew level with him and I heard him say, 'We will speak about this tonight.'

The blacksmith muttered something under his breath and Pappous, placing his hand firmly on his shoulder, said loudly for all to hear, 'No thank you, sir, my wife does not have need for extra meat, even in these hard times.' Yaya looked just a little sad as she saw the possibility of a game bird or a squirrel or two disappearing.

The air inside the church was cool and sweet. Faint whispers of frankincense and neroli lingered in the old tapestries and drapes. Although the mothers had been here cleaning, the incense of years was not so easily disposed of.

The professor stood at the front, at Papa Costas's invitation, and instantly there was a respectful quiet, broken quickly by Vilandis who limped painfully forwards and lowered himself down onto a bench. He groaned and said, 'I am a true patient today – so here you are, mend my leg.'

The children giggled and looked to Heavenly for guidance.

'Right,' she said, 'Despina and Tika, this patient is for you. What are you going to do?'

The two little girls skipped forward, glowing with pride that they had been chosen to be first. Both were wearing clean frocks and Tika had a headkerchief. I think this was the first time she was wearing one and it had slipped down on one side rendering it useless as her hair kept falling out.

'Shall we wash his leg?' asked Tika.

'Yes,' said Heavenly, 'that's always the first thing to be done, isn't it? Vilandis, do you wish to remove your breeches yourself or shall the nurses do it for you?'

Vilandis, looking terrified, stammered, 'Oh it's not so bad, I think I'll wait . . .'

But Heavenly was swiftly on him and her strong brown arms at work, rolling up his trouser leg gently, and she exposed the angry red gash on his skin.

'Yes,' she said, tucking long wild strands of her hair back, 'this wound needs urgent attention before poison sets in.' At the word 'poison', one or two of the older women crossed themselves. Despina and Tika had filled a vessel with cool fresh water and with swabs of clean cotton were gently bathing the wound.

I was proud of them. They did not flinch or hesitate, although this was certainly the first real blood they had seen since the lessons began. Heavenly smiled at them and whispered something, at which Tika took the dish of dirty water outside and Despina pulled a wad of clean cotton from one of the boxes of dressings we had brought up the hill. Dribbling antiseptic on the cotton, she swabbed the wound clean. She passed the large bottle of ochre antiseptic to me and I stood and showed it to the parents, explaining how it would kill all the germs in the gash.

Within moments Vilandis was standing again, his breeches tidied and a smile on his face.

'I reckon you were born to be nurses, you girls,' he said. 'This leg feels better already.' And turning, he walked back to a place beside his wife, a fat woman who rarely smiles and who merely nodded as he sat down and stretched his leg back and forth.

Standing in a huddle at the side, Christo had somehow persuaded Kotso and Andros to come and Kotso now volunteered for treatment 'for a very severe headache'.

There was laughter as he moved to the front.

'Less raki at night would cure that,' shouted some wit. Meanwhile, Dimitri the deaf mute had slowly and thoughtfully started to bind Kotso's head with a large white bandage. Heavenly was unwinding it before he had finished, explaining in a mixture of signs and carefully spoken words that fresh air and exercise was the best cure for this condition. Dimitri's wide eyes never left her face and he earnestly nodded his understanding as he carefully rolled the bandage up again.

Kyria Titica was passing round cups of cool lemonade she had brought, and the demonstration continued until every child was winding bandages and splints and tourniquets until it seemed there were more patients than in the hospital in Sitia.

There was a disturbance suddenly from a group of women sitting under the big window at the rear of the church.

'Why do they need all this modern stuff; gauze and antiseptic?' someone called out. 'We don't have money for that sort of thing here.' One of the women from Kato Panagia was on her feet, a tiny but aggressive widow I knew as a troublemaker. 'We have always done well enough with poultices we make ourselves from leaves and berries and they are free!' Around her a couple of her cronies called out their agreement.

One, Kyria Pakistrakis, a tall, angular woman with cheeks so hard that the bones above them threatened to pierce her skin, said loudly, 'A potion of gladwin and hyssop heads boiled in sweet wine would sort out his head. Easy, you simply leave it outside—' but someone else called, 'Yes, yes we know all about that, Annis, but we are not here to listen to what we already know, give Kyria Heavenly a chance.'

The professor was already moving to the front ahead of me. 'Did you never lose someone close to you to infection and disease?' he asked. For a moment there was a hush.

'I did,' said one woman rising to her feet; a soft-looking woman, her face like fresh kneaded dough. It was the widow Kariakis, a sad, lonely woman who cared as best she could for her three daughters. 'My husband and my sister died from green leg. The doctor came too late to save them; he cut off both their legs. What use was that? They were dead by the end of the week.'

She was wiping her eyes roughly, the memory had stirred her feelings. 'Buried together they were.' There were murmurs of agreement and sympathy from all around and there was a flutter like birds wings as most of the women were crossing themselves hastily.

'And my sister-in-law,' called someone, 'died from child-birth fever. How could you help with that?'

Heavenly stood tall and firm now, and looked around her. She was a commanding figure in spite of her wild red hair flowing around her face. Her eyes were fiery and determined. 'Of course we cannot perform miracles, but we can certainly try to improve things.' Her face was flushed, but only I could see how nervous she was.

'There will always be a need for home cures and remedies,' she said. 'No one can deny the value and strength of worm-wood, or barberry, and I am sure there are many more, but I intend to have all modern drugs and dressings sent to us from Athens. There is no reason why, simply because Panagia Sta Perivolia is a mountain village in a remote part of Crete, we should suffer from a lack of knowledge that is freely available in the rest of Greece.' There were cries of approval from many in the church now. She had touched a weakness that they well knew: the feeling they were a not a part of civilised Greece.

The professor stood again and everyone was quiet. He thanked us and then added, 'I am pleased to welcome and thank our very special friend, Kyria Heavenly. She has come from many miles away to share her knowledge with our small community. Let us be only grateful to her. Thank you, Kyria, from everyone in our village.' He clapped and within mo-ments most people had joined in. I could see Heavenly was scarlet with embarrassment, but she busied herself with the children in a demonstration of how to bandage a sprained ankle.

By the end of the afternoon some were beginning to shuffle

towards the door when a shadow fell across the porch and, for a moment, the church was in shade. I felt before I saw, a new cold presence. Two men stood there; my husband and his friend, Papa Yannis. A ripple of dislike and fear was almost tangible in the church I thought, but there were one or two calls of welcome as some stood aside to let them pass through.

Manolis's shaved head was hazy with grey stubble, and a strong odour of sweat and tobacco came from the damp, soiled vestments of the priest. The sweet scent of the incense had all but disappeared. The professor stepped forward to greet them. Papa Costas was right behind him, his clean robe putting the fat priest to shame.

'Is it October ninth already, Costas?' puffed Papa Yannis, wiping his sweating brow with a grubby cloth. 'Are we celebrating St Kosmas day so soon?'

Outside, I knew, nothing had changed; the sun beat down, making this the hottest day of the summer so far, everyone said so. The goats lazily roamed the hills, nibbling any small sparse thing of green they could find. The wings of seabirds flapped slowly and almost hesitantly through the baking air, and way down below, the glitter of the waves told of a different world. But back inside the cool shadiness of this church, the goodness that we had all felt throughout the afternoon was wavering.

The arrival of these two men had changed even the very air. I'm certain it wasn't just me that felt it; all the mamas, the pappous and yayas, everyone was now shuffling towards the door, even pushing surreptitiously to get through first. There were few smiles, just apprehension in their eyes and tension in their footsteps. I heard someone mutter, 'I told you we shouldn't be in this place!'

Heavenly moved to my side and I felt the comfort of her hand as it slipped into mine.

'Despina! Despina!' Manolis's voice rang harshly high to the beams. He had spotted his daughter but she didn't move, just stood with her head down. 'Home,' he said. 'Now.' But still she stayed. 'Now!' he commanded.

I called, 'I'm coming, Despoula,' as I saw she was looking helplessly around for me, her eyes dull and downcast. 'I am coming, I promise. Do as Papa says, I shall be right behind you.'

Beside the stone font at the front of the church, beside the icons, beside the sand for holding the candles, the talk between fat Papa Yannis, the professor and Papa Costas was shockingly of sacrilege, the disgrace in using the sanctified church as a meeting place, an extension of the schoolroom.

The priest waddled towards the door as quickly as his sweating bulk would allow, calling over his shoulder, 'This is not the end of it, Costas.' I saw his piggy eyes scanning the group still leaving and I felt sure he would stow away and remember the names of all here.

I was going too, to catch up with Despina, when I saw the curtain to the altar was twitching, yet there was not a whisper of a breeze. I pulled it aside and there was the deaf and dumb child crouched on the floor. He seemed terrified so I took his hand. 'Come, Dimitri.' I had seen his father go through the door just a moment before. I knew what was wrong. There was only one thing that would terrify him like that. 'The man,' I said, indicating someone tall, 'with the priest?' And I drew in the air, a fat, round man.

He nodded quickly and pulled back from me. 'Come, Dimitri, we will find your father. I saw him here earlier. Papa? Yes?' He nodded again. I patted his head gently. 'Wait, wait here.' He seemed to understand so I ran outside and out the door into the hot air calling, 'Manos!' and, oh, thanks to the Panagia, there he was. Quickly I explained and without a word he ran into the church, reappearing a moment later with Dimitri in his arms.

'Thank you, Kyria Anthi,' he said. 'My child will never be at peace while those *malakas* are around.' I felt only shame. He spoke of my husband. I started to apologise but he cut me short: 'Not your fault. But your mother must have no value for you to marry you to that animal. I wish you good day.' He turned away.

I stood, looking after them with an icy heart, the brim of tears close in my eyes. I felt a gnawing sadness, as if my body were falling apart and away from me. He spoke of my husband and I felt nothing but shame.

I walked back in to the church and three women standing in the doorway paused and looked at me. I tried to ignore them and move past but one said, 'Hey, Anthi.' I stopped and looked ahead but didn't answer.

'Don't you agree that a mixture of bryony and worm-seed, boiled in vinegar and water, will make your bones strong?'

'Yes. You leave it at night in the light of a full moon,' said another. 'My mother swore by that, drank it every day and didn't die until she was ninety-three.'

'I won't give it to my Vassilis's mother then, the sooner she gets out of my house and my life, the better!' And forgetting me, they laughed and move away homewards.

It had broken my mood momentarily and glancing round the church, I saw there was only the professor left behind. He was stacking the chairs and humming under his breath.

'No,' he said. 'Don't stay now. Get home to Despina, she needs you more than I do.'

I couldn't speak, I just nodded to him and hurried back out.

Voula had gone home with Pappous and Yaya. I knew she was safe with them, so I started to run down the mountain path towards my home.

I hadn't seen Heavenly at the end of the afternoon, so she must have gone on ahead to her own house and, probably, to Christo. I felt a familiar pang of envy. How good it must feel to hurry home to a man you love.

The late sun spilled into the blue summer evening. The lingering clouds seemed unmoving in the darkening sky and somewhere, carelessly, a songbird sang.

I went through our gate and immediately I could hear

Despina. She was somewhere in the house and crying. Inside there was no sign of Manolis.

I shed no tears when he did not return that night. We did not see him for three days and none of us missed him – even the goats seemed happier.

HEAVENLY

No word from Hugh for ages.

In the darkness of a late summer evening, I was lying limply on a pile of cushions in my living room and trying to persuade myself to stir. Christo had left barely an hour before and I was sleepy, lazy after our lovemaking.

Is it my imagination, or are his visits less frequent? I tell myself that it is inevitable that he will be away with his recruits, *andartes,* in the hills; it is what he must do. But oh, how I miss him and count the hours between our meetings.

Bang! Bang! at the door and someone calling my name, a man.

'Please open your door, Kyria Heavenly, it is important.'

I did, and looked out into the night. It was Stephanos Karanakis, Anthi's grandfather, at my door.

'Excuse me for intruding, but there is news I think you will want to know.' He was turning his magnificent hat around and around in his hands. I couldn't think what he could be talking about. What could he know that I should need to hear? I beckoned him inside. He apologised again for disturbing me at this late hour and then paused as he looked around.

'My word!' he said. 'You have done wonderful work here. It is some years now since I have been in this house and I remember the ruin it had become.'

I quickly offered him refreshment; a raki perhaps or some

lemonade? But he refused and brought his gaze back in my direction. His fingers had ceased the nervous hat twirling.

I was terribly conscious of my state of disarray; too late now to worry about my hair. I hoped he couldn't see my knickers, only half hidden under a cushion.

'Tonight, as often, I was in the kafenion, Il Piperia. You know this place, I expect?'

I nodded. 'I've never been inside, but of course I know of it.'

'You would be made welcome there if ever you should choose. However, tonight as usual, I was listening to the wireless set there and they said that today your Mr Chamberlain has declared war on Germany.' He paused. 'Perhaps you already knew this. Your husband may—'

'No, no, I have heard nothing from him for weeks now.'

'I thought it was something, you would want to know at once.'

'Of course. Thank you. It is so kind of you to think of me.'

'He spoke to England by wireless, they said. Everyone in England will know. Wonderful days we live in when you can inform everyone in the country, even in the world, at the same time. Here, you know, we should have seen the signs.'

I must have looked puzzled, for he continued, 'Oh, there are plenty of warnings of things not right. An old man like me knows what to look for. We shouldn't need to wait for major pronouncements from those in power. Several of the village elders have spoken of trees blasted as if struck by lightning. Perfectly healthy on a clear moonlit night and the next morning – dead, burnt to death. And my wife says she saw a lemon growing on a vine that has produced a fine crop of healthy grapes!'

Again, my face must have shown puzzlement for he said, 'Oh yes! She is not wrong. A vine suddenly taken over by an alien fruit. Unnatural happenings indeed, Kyria, but adding up to bad news.' He nodded sagely. 'Ill-tidings, all can be foreseen. If you know what to look for, that is.'

He left shortly after, still refusing any hospitality. I watched his donkey walking back up the path to the road. I felt only numb as I tried to take in the significance of what he had told me.

Slowly I walked through the house and out onto the terrace. There is a full moon tonight, another sign of change. For a moment I wished Hugh were here. I needed him to explain to me what this all meant; a declaration of war. I closed my eyes and thought of my home. Vividly I pictured my mother and sister, the nurses on the ward all sitting around wireless sets, absorbing this terrible information. I knew times were bad, but another war?

I don't know how much time passed before I went back inside into my house. My house! My responsibility now to myself and to all the generations who had lived here before me.

The wooden stairs creaked beneath my feet as if in warning, and I felt a sudden fear as if to say, 'Be careful, Evadne, not careless.'

I lit a candle and as I made my way to bed I heard something overhead, a scuffling in the roof and along the walls. Squirrels, perhaps, or hawks or bats? I told myself it was of no importance.

I reached the door to a small room; a storeroom, a room unused and untouched, at my request, by Christo and Yorgo. Although I walk past it several times a day I had forgotten about its existence until now.

The door stuck as if it were latched shut, but it was loose enough not to hold. There were so many ancient doors in this house: one downstairs to the cellar, others to closets or storage rooms.

I put the guttering candle down to the floor and tugged at the door. It gave almost immediately and, picking up my candle, I stepped inside.

There was a foul odour. The roots of the old vine grow across the window, pushing out any fresh air or light. I saw immediately what was inside. How strange to rediscover it now.

Hugh's things were scattered here: some of his clothes. Here was an ancient summer shirt and a tie, for heaven's sake, its livid stripes telling me it was his school tie. And there was his old school hat, a boater. As I looked closer, picked it up, I saw one side is frayed away. Again, the scratching sound from somewhere and a feeling of not being alone. I jumped back, afraid.

My sudden movement almost knocked the candle over, almost, but not quite. There was enough light for me to see it was not frayed, this hat, it had been chewed, gnawed. I dropped it in horror. What had been here?

I instinctively curled up my bare toes in my sandals, and found I was gripping my body so tightly it was difficult to breathe freely. Was that a sudden movement of something out of the corner of my eye or did I imagine it? I urged myself forwards, inch by inch, hauling my long skirt up and under my elbows.

Ahead of me was a small pile of books, brought with us from the embassy library in Athens: *Three Men in a Boat* for Hugh, and for me two Tolstoy classics, I had hoped to find the time to read. There was the dark mulberry cover I recognise as *War and Peace* and I picked up the other. This one was blue once – now it's mildewed and wrinkly.

As I recognised its cover, I saw it had been eaten out inside into the shape of a nest. It was full with chewed-up paper and small black droppings. I lost my balance and this time my tread did extinguish the flame. I was in darkness, but I had seen the book's title: *Anna Karenina*

There was little sleep for me that night. I kept thinking of the storeroom with its vile secret life. Locked again and barred for the present, but my beautiful house felt tainted and poisonous. Rats, it had to be, had chewed their way in and nested into the story of an adulterous wife. The irony was not lost on me as I turned and tried to sleep. But then I kept thinking of the news from England. I thought of a steely grey London morning, red double-decker buses moving majestically along rain-spattered streets, towards Westminster Bridge, the Houses of Parliament, and a great wave of homesickness washed over me.

I thought of my family. Would they be thinking about me? They rarely wrote. I'm sure my mother thought good riddance to me.

The chickens woke and the cocks crowed and the long, lonely night was at last over. Another day began. It was a warm, whitish sort of day; the air damp with the feeling of rain to come. I walked through the tall grasses, now gone to seed. I was wearing an old linen skirt with a long-sleeved top, far too hot as I was already damp with sweat and prickly heat. Thorny vines caught me; a wild rose hidden in the grass. I would have to clear this away or it would take over. Above my head, a sky still as pale, this early, as a watercolour wash. On the horizon, a faint sepia shading into blue; it would, after all, be another golden day.

ANTHI

Manolis came home laughing.

It was a while before I understood and my first feelings were far from joyous. It was Aphrodite Babyottis who told me at the spring, Yorgo had heard from the wireless set at the kafenion that England and Germany were at war. All the women there this morning gathered around and some said, 'So what is that to us? As well come and tell us that Albania is at war with Italy.'

My first thought was of Heavenly. It is not a school day; I must go and see her. But she was not in her house, only Yorgo working alone, clearing out a storeroom. He greeted me with a complaint. 'Rats here, apparently. Upset the kyria.' He shook his head. 'I had to stop work on old Bagordakis's coffin and get down to it. Goes on like this, they'll be burying him this afternoon and his coffin next week. I'm supposed to be a master carpenter, not a rat catcher.'

There were days when Yorgo liked nothing better than to complain about everything and this was one of them. 'If my wife saw a rat she would chop it down with her bare hand, not get the nearest carpenter to do it for her.' He stopped, but only for a moment. 'She was upset, though, the kyria. I'll agree to that. She was crying this morning. Never seen her cry before.'

He was off again, now on a rant about Christo. 'I think he's started to take me for granted, you know? I reckon he forgets it's me who gave him the job as my assistant, remember? Now he's off to I don't know where, without asking. And if you

184

want to know, the kyria has gone down to the beach "for a walk".'

He was shaking his head vigorously now. Sometimes the logic of the human race is too much for him to handle.

What were they up to, my friend and her lover? It was too much of a coincidence for them both to have vanished at the same moment. It was only a short time before I learnt the significance of that day. And it was from an unexpected source.

My sister came to my house to tell me that tomorrow was my mother's name day. This was a fact I knew well, but just as she had ignored mine since my marriage, so I ignored hers. This time, however, I was summoned to attend what mother called the 'Celebration Feast'. I almost laughed aloud. Feast? That would be a lumpy cheese pie and a pickled apricot then.

'Please bring your English friend,' said Ririca.

'And my children?'

'Mother said, if you have to.'

I was so tempted not to go, to simply ignore her precious name day but, rather viciously, I thought it would irritate my mother more if I did attend, and with my children. So at five o'clock the following afternoon, I dressed Despina and Voula in their best clothes and with Heavenly alongside, we walked through the village to my old home.

I come here as little as possible, and as I walked through the garden I remembered why. It was somewhere that, for me, was only full of sad memories. Every trace of my beloved father had gone. There was the plot where he grew the best leeks in the village, now filled with tidy flowerbeds, most of them half dead.

'Show me a flower we can eat,' he said, 'and I will grow it.'

Here was the place where potatoes, green beans and onions had once grown in profusion, now flattened and covered with small stones. No colour, no smell, no anything.

My mother came out to greet me and, just as I knew she would, frowned when she saw the girls. 'Best behaviour, you two, this is a party for grown adults really, not children.' She spoke with such distaste, I thought she would prefer people to emerge from the womb fully grown. How she had ever coped with the mess of childbirth, I can't imagine.

I ignored this and said, 'This place is so bleak and empty now. I still miss the wonderful smell of growing garlic that used to hit me when I played here as a child, just past the cedar tree.' She laughed icily. 'You mean the stink of garlic, I think, Rodianthi. You were the only one to like it.'

'And Papa,' I said quietly. 'He loved it and said it always reminded him of the rabbit stews his mother made him.'

My mother shrugged, her thin eyebrows raised high in her white face, and turned to Heavenly. 'It is kind of you to come on my special day, Kyria Timberlake,' and she tried to smile as she took the bunch of wild flowers from her.

'They are really from Despina and Voula. They did all the picking, I only tied them with the string.' My mother held them as though they were poison ivy and thorns. I tried not to laugh as she held them away from her and called for Ririca to take them.

There were not many guests inside the house on this so-special day. My mother is not a popular person in this village and most would find a reason to be occupied elsewhere rather than celebrate with her. Groups of two or three, talking together at assorted small tables ignored our entrance, so I ignored them. I did, however, notice that most of them slyly paused for a moment or two to look us up and down before resuming their conversations.

But one who had made the effort to attend was the person I least wished to see, Papa Yannis. He was sitting alone, but not for long, as my mother pushed us over to sit with him. It was impossible to refuse, so I muttered a greeting and sat as far away from him as I could. Papa Yannis flashed his squinty eyes over my girls as if they smelled bad and rose to clasp Heavenly's hand lingeringly. Knowing his palm would be pinkly moist with sweat I looked pityingly at my friend.

A plate of cheese pies were passed around and to my

surprise actually tasted quite well. Mother must have paid money for some poor village wife to make them for her.

My mother was trying to start an inane conversation about the heat, but the priest interrupted her.

'Do you like to swim, Kyria Timberley?' he asked.

Heavenly sat very still. Too still, I thought, ignoring his mistake over her name.

'Sometimes,' she said slowly, 'if the sea is calm and the weather warm, then I do.'

'You must be very careful in the currents you can encounter in the bay here; awfully deceptive, positively dangerous, to swim alone, I should say.'

Voula had finished her cheese pie and was reaching for Despina's. 'No, Voula, not mine! Ask Mama if you may have another.'

Irritably my mother pushed the plate of pies across the table saying, 'Is she a little backward, do you think? At her age, as I recall, you could have a full conversation. You could, for sure, ask for a cheese pie without difficulty.'

I was about to say that Voula was far from backward, when I saw that Heavenly's face was very pink and she seemed struck speechless. The priest spoke for her, and his words chilled me.

'Just the other day, I saw something very odd on our beach. I was using my binoculars, of course, as I am making a catalogue of the different kinds of birds we have here and their habits. Why, only last week I saw a couple of birds of prey fighting over a small game bird, most unusual. Different species, you understand . . . I digress, my apologies. To my surprise, I saw someone coming from the sea. A woman,' his voice dropped to a hissing whisper, 'I think with no clothes on! Nothing! I was, of course, fearful in case she had been in some sort of accident and was alone and needing my help, so you can imagine my relief when I saw there was someone else coming out behind her – also naked. Of course I looked away at once, so I couldn't be sure. However, they were laughing. Clearly nothing wrong then.'

His red tongue was darting backwards and forwards, lizard-like, between his full wet lips. It was obvious that he was excited by the images he was creating. My mother sat with her mouth open in astonishment. Despina seized the moment to escape and, grabbing Voula and a couple of cheese pies, vanished outside.

Papa Yannis was not going to let his story pass with no reaction.

'What do you think of that then, Anthi? Kyria Timberley?'

Heavenly and I exchanged glances and she said softly, 'My name is Timberlake, Papa.'

'Oh, of course, how silly of me.'

I rose to leave, saying '*Chronia Polla*' to my mother, although I wanted to say that I hoped she didn't live long enough to have another wretched name day.

Taking Heavenly's arm and pulling her to her feet, I turned once more. 'You have no need for concern, Papa Yannis. It was me you saw swimming with Kyria Timberlake, we sometimes go to the beach together.' As we reached the door, I turned again. 'As a matter of fact, I saw you watching us, your glasses were reflected in the rays of the sun. I guessed it was you. In Panagia who else would have such things?'

And we were gone before my mother could shriek about nudity or propriety or the children, where were they whilst I was frolicking? Before she could voice any of her mean little complaints, we were away.

We barely spoke as we started for home, the girls using our arms as swings and darting and running in eager relief to escape my mother's chill, unfriendly house.

As we approached her house, Heavenly finally said softly, 'Thank you. He's a slimy odious beast, isn't he?'

'Remember this day and use it to remind yourself all the time how close you are to danger.'

She started to talk about rats and war and how wonderful Christo was and how he understood her so well.

I let my fury, pent-up inside until this moment, loose. 'Does he also understand the danger he is placing you in with this stupid public behaviour? It's fine for him. If all comes out, what does he have to lose?'

She didn't answer me, so I continued, even though I knew she wanted me to stop.

'Sweetest nothing, that's all. He will take himself home to Sitia and be able to boast to his friends of his conquest of the beautiful and RICH English woman in Panagia.'

She started to protest. 'Oh, it's not like that, truly. We love each other.'

I was so angry I could barely walk further. I wanted to shake my dear friend, slap her.

'I am sure you do, but if the both of you don't take the greatest possible care how you behave, you can wave him goodbye. You will lose everything; your house for a start, and then your husband. You may not care for him just now, but believe me, when you are outlawed by the silence of the entire village . . .' I broke off and shook my head; she was openly weeping now.

'I am so sorry, I know you are right. You are such a wonderful friend I couldn't bear to lose you. Everything you say is true, I know.' The girls were looking at us now, bewildered.

'And why do you enslave yourself to him? Sometimes I see you watching for him, waiting for him, and it distresses me so. Where is your pride, Heavenly? Don't forget what he is – a young, good-looking Cretan workman. I see you, so independent when we met, so admirable, run around him. "Christo says this, Christo says that." He is a man. A man, not a god!'

'Thank you for rescuing me today. I promise you will never have to lie for me again.'

'You know how much I care for you, you know I don't want to lose you. But you still believe only in the goodness of everybody here. Carry on as you do and you will fast learn how evil they can be when they feel threatened. And if they find you out, every woman will ignore you, lest you go after their husband as well. What were you thinking of, letting the priest, of all people, catch the pair of you naked?'

She shook her head. There was nothing to say.

We walked on in silence. The late afternoon sun shone down on us. The air was sweet with the scent of wild thyme and bees buzzed lazily around.

We parted at the crossroads and, for a moment, I watched her walk on, her long skirt flowing around her. She turned as if she could feel my gaze and waved her hand once. Then she was gone.

HEAVENLY

Hugh's letters are few and far between, and so heavily censored that sometimes only a few inane words survive. Often I find myself wishing the house wasn't finished and Yorgo and Christo were still here each day.

The atrocious heat of the summer has taken many of the older villagers, and it seems each day there is another funeral.

The still, hot days of autumn called me to walk the nearby hills. There was no school, but some days a child or two would appear at my door asking for lessons. At first I was flattered until Christo pointed out that if their parents thought they were learning with me, they would let them off helping in the fields or gardens. Each day the sun burned through, unfailingly heating the waiting earth, although it was already baked hard. Everyone prayed for rain, but each morning dawned hot and clear.

For me, in the old Orfanoudakis house that looked down to the clear mountain spring, time moved differently than it did elsewhere. Not in short sharp bursts that grew out of glittering sunshine, but seemingly in great wide waves of change. You could not see the edges; where they began or how far they extended and where they would end. These days ceased to be measured by the seasons, the crops and the harvests. Hugh's letters, sporadic and censored as they were, gave me some insight into where the world was heading and it was impossible not to be shaken or afraid. Even Christo, my untroubled lover, seemed always to wear a frown these days.

Nightly he went to the Piperia and would tell me a little of what he had gleaned – it seemed there was trouble across most of Europe. He was spending a lot of time each day with Kotso and Andros. Sometimes strangers turned up in the village looking for him and he would then disappear for a day or more at a time. There was never an explanation, but I knew they were working secretly to prepare what they could in case the war did come this far, although no one else seemed in the least concerned.

I longed for some word from home. The war in Europe was rarely mentioned, and I was alone with my anxieties. Christo and I were together whenever it was possible. I'm sure he stole an hour or two away when he felt it safe to do so. He took my fears seriously now; understanding that discovery was my worst nightmare. Late evenings we would try to find each other, just to be together, to be close. The fierce heat of our early lovemaking had gradually turned into the slow, sweet strokes of a more mature passion. He taught me the joy of tenderness.

I longed to go down to the sea again and begged Anthi to come with me with her girls. 'We could swim,' I said. But most days she was in her fields, preparing for the coming winter. Her husband somehow expected her to keep the olives fresh. With no spare water she told me, this was next to impossible. Occasionally she would accept my offer to help, but Manolis made it more than clear that I was not welcome when he was around. It was only when he took the resin to sell in Sitia that I could go there.

Looking back, it seems extraordinary to me that we were so ill-prepared for any war that would come. Most people here believed that Crete was their country and Greece was somewhere else. The village had itself to look after. There was enough to concern us all every day. Failing crops, lack of food, even, it seemed, a shortage of wood for fires, so over the winter those old people that had survived the unrelenting heat of the summer began to die from the cold. Several died both hungry and cold.

The shepherds fared worse. Out on the hillsides there were

several deaths just in the course of one night. An unexpected blizzard took six, their bodies lying hidden in crevasses and under rockfalls until spring.

This far south it was unheard of to have to face weather like this. The women spent most evenings in prayer, believing they must have angered the Panagia in some way. I offered help where I could. My house had space and plenty of wood. I tried to persuade Anthi to bring her girls to me until the spring. She laughed. 'Manolis would have us out of there in five minutes, you know that. Or move himself and Papa Yannis in, as well, and any other of their friends who liked the idea.'

She was right and I knew it.

Christo and Andros were now openly recruiting any of the village men they could to join them. They had a makeshift camp in a cave in the hills, far, far up and somehow Christo had acquired a two-way wireless set. He was rather mysterious about where it had come from and I didn't press for an answer. He proudly showed it to me one night, but it only made crackling noises. Frustrated, he hit it with his fist and loud Greek music filled the cave. It was impossible not to laugh and Christo took my hand and led me in a dance. I was filled with a happiness I hadn't felt for weeks. We whirled and twirled to the music, dipping and gliding until we fell to the ground in a heap, gasping. We lay exhausted, panting for breath, and then we were kissing deeply and passionately and we pushed our clothes off to one side and made love until we came together swiftly and noisily. We hadn't made love like that for a long time. Usually our stolen moments together were quieter and gentler. We knew how to please each other and Christo had taught me how to make our pleasure last as long as possible.

No one ever went near the little church of St Kosmas and Damianus on the mountain top any more. So Christo suggested we keep it as the 'hospital' we had created for the first-aid lessons in case there ever is really a need. I didn't argue, although in my heart I still found it difficult to believe that here, tucked away in the mountains, we would be bothered by invaders. What did we have to offer? Foolishly I didn't think of the food and sustenance that any army would need, or the very ownership of the land where, so far, Cretans had walked proud and free.

One day during this time, I went to the spring to join the village women to do my laundry and found them all in a huddle around Adonis's wife Cassandra, who was weeping her heart out. Her large rolls of fat were quivering with grief and her sister turned to tell me her sad story.

She has only one son, Baco. A year or so ago he left home, travelled across the island and joined the crew of a steamship. It was to take him round the world, starting from Port Said. 'A new life for them all,' his aunt told me, her small hands clasped so tightly together, the wedding band on her ring finger almost drew blood as it cut into the other hand. 'And now, nothing, everything gone.'

'Why, what has happened?' I asked, almost afraid of her answer.

'His ship has been sunk by an Italian submarine,' she said, 'everyone on board is missing. *Panagia mou,*' and sad, slow tears brimmed over from her eyes, 'help us now.'

Hugh may write of major negotiations between governments and foreign powers but it is here in our village and other small communities like it, where the pain is felt. Where the sinking of a ship, the invasion of a territory, the slaughter of a battalion, will be felt only as the ending of a young life.

The promise that came with the birth pains extinguished in a fragment of a second and only a bleak future for the elders left behind. For those young there is nothing else to come. Or maybe it is the broken family left behind, when the news comes that an uncle, a brother, a father, has been declared missing, presumed dead.

This time was what I thought of later as the end of the beginning, certainly the end of innocence.

The aggression around Europe that was to invade and change all our lives seemed to start then. Later, Anthi would say that it started before that for the villagers of Panagia Sta Perivolia.

The heat of the long summer turned slowly into the shorter days of autumn again and, with the full, rich sunsets soon to disappear into the briefer days of winter, the news in that time seemed only bad, even the harvest was poor. Money was non-existent and many, especially the old and weak and the newborn, did not live to see if there was news that was good.

In the winter Panagia seemed empty and cold. Huddled figures would hurry through windy deserted streets, perhaps scrabbling by the wayside for scraps of wood. In houses families shivered by tiny flames that flickered briefly and then faded, and relief was the most prominent emotion when a baby or an elder died. One less mouth to feed: grief was short-lived.

And then one morning a letter from Hugh arrived and this time it was not just about the weather or his lavish embassy dinners, but contained a phrase to really puzzle me, and more, confuse and worry me.

I had woken feeling slightly sick. Last night Irini had brought me in a dish of her rabbit stew. It tasted rich and gamey and, sitting alone, I had greedily eaten every morsel, together with a glass of Yorgo's red wine. I think I had indulged myself too freely and this morning I was paying for it.

I couldn't say when Hugh had written this letter, but it was carried up the mountain from Sitia as usual by a man from the offices that governed our region in Lasithi. It could be days, weeks, or even months old, and told me little that I didn't know already.

Until the last paragraph.

'My darling,' he had written, 'at last I can tell you that I may be with you sooner than we hoped. I can say almost nothing for fear of interception, but I have been requested to arrange the safe passage to Crete of an important package.'

Oh how I wished then that I could speak with him, I hate hints and mysteries like this.

'I may be with you sooner.' Does this imply that he would be coming here, to Crete? To this village?

I decided to talk to Anthi. She would, of course, know nothing about all of this, but she is so sensible that at least I could share with her my feelings, my confusion.

Determined, I jumped to my feet and as I went towards the door, a wave of nausea swept over me and I staggered to the cushions to sit down again. I forced myself to breathe in slow, deep, cool breaths as I read again Hugh's words. I think I must have slept a little, for when I opened my eyes I could tell from the shadows that it was later. I felt better, stronger, and pushed myself to my feet. I would walk to Anthi's house and hope the clean fresh spring air would clear my head.

But as I reached the path, I realised I still felt so weak that I had to clutch hold of a hanging branch to steady myself; but several deep breaths set me to rights and I walked slowly onwards.

ANTHI

Despina is silent again.

Three days now and she has not spoken. Inside I feel sad and desperate. If she would answer me only, I could bear it. But she just nods or shakes her head; and that just the smallest gesture. I believe her face shows fear. Her eyes dart around the room, looking for what? Oh my happy, laughing child, come back to us. Sometimes I hold her close to me, burying my face in her hair, telling her I love her. But she stands rigid in my arms. One day, her father noticed she wouldn't answer him, and he cuffed her on the side of her head.

'You behave like an animal, you will be treated as one,' was all he said. That day he left for Sitia with the resin.

This morning I have tended the bees and checked the goats' feet for infection. I had heard from a woman at the spring that there is a different kind of hoof rot around, and many goats are falling over with it. If they are not able to go out to pasture there is a real risk they will die. I have fed and watered the chickens and sent Despina off to collect any eggs. A stew is already bubbling in the pot and the house is beginning to smell of the garlic and herbs I have put in with the meat. Now I must go up into the fields. Walking, of course. I keep Astrape out of use as much as possible to let him rest.

Along the path uphill I saw that the figure coming towards me was Heavenly and, as always, I started to smile. But she was not smiling and we only exchanged a quick greeting before walking onwards together. It was impossible not to notice how pale she looked.

'I'll come to the fields with you,' she said, and even Despina almost smiled.

'What's wrong, Heavenly? You look like a bowl of milk. Sure, the sun has skimmed your cheeks, but I know you, you are not yourself. Are you ill?'

'Oh, it's nothing.'

Walking briskly along, I could see she was not really up to it; stumbling and tripping over stones. By the fields, I spread myself at the edge, our lunch basket and stone water jar marking out the space. Despina placed herself by the hedge alone and kept her head averted.

Heavenly looked at her and then at me with her eyebrow raised, questioning. I put my finger against my closed lips and shook my head.

Voula laid herself down with her head on my leg, thumb in mouth.

'Tell me what is wrong,' I said.

'I think Hugh may be coming back. Look at this letter.' And she handed me a scrappy piece of paper with thick black ink crossing through much of it. I read the few words that were visible.

'See, he says a package? What do you think he means by that? I can only think that he means he is on his way here.'

I nodded slowly. 'Maybe.' We sat in silence for a moment or two. I know that, for my part, I was thinking, 'Well, it was bound to happen one day, why not now?'

'My head is so muddled and my heart is split in two. I'm sorry, I had to talk to someone about this and try and make sense of my feelings. And there is only you.'

'Is this the reason you are so pale?'

'No, I think Irini's rabbit stew didn't agree with me and now I feel rather ill.'

I looked down at the paper again. I had no idea what it could mean, except that her husband was coming here.

'What am I to do?'

'You will do nothing, I think, but wait and see what happens.'

I looked at her again, closely. She was drawn and ashen-faced. This letter had disturbed her more than she will admit.

I realise that it was some time now since I had seen the old Heavenly, the woman who laughed and sang and danced and was always happy. I know these are worrying times for all of us. Not that you could tell that from a casual glance at the villagers. Their attitude is to shrug and water their gardens or pick their produce and get on with their lives. My Pappous despairs of persuading anyone in this village to understand what is happening in the rest of Greece.

Heavenly sat now, her shoulders hunched beside Despina who, locked inside herself, seemed not to notice.

'You look so tired, are you sure you are not ill?' She shook her head.

'Is it your monthly time come round?' An intimate question. I would never ask it of any other woman.

She closed her eyes, suddenly motionless.

'Heavenly, I only wondered—' But she raised her hand, silencing me.

'What day is it? What month?' It was a whisper.

'It is October, early, I don't know the number. It's about the middle of the week, I think. Why?'

But as soon as the question was asked, it was clear to me why it mattered.

She was shaking her head, her expression one of panic, fear.

I took her by the shoulders. 'Why? Tell me. When is your monthly due?'

'I don't know, I can't remember. I haven't . . .' and her voice was barely there, I could hardly hear her words.

'This is very important. You must remember, you MUST.'

She turned to me, her face like stone.

'I haven't had my monthly for ages. I thought perhaps it was just worry; about the war, about my home, about Christo, about Hugh . . . do you think? Tell me, what do you think? You don't think my sickness is, is . . .'

What could I say to her? This was no time to be kind or gentle or reassuring. Just looking closely at her now, I knew with complete certainty that she was pregnant. There is something in the eyes, the skin, the features. Some people can look at a woman and know immediately from her face that she is carrying a baby, and I am one of them. The glow, that at first I thought of as sunshine, gives it away. There was not a glimmer of doubt in my mind. How could I not have seen it earlier?

'Tell me, are your breasts tender, enlarged?' She didn't answer but, just like Despina, nodded mutely.

'You were a nurse, surely of all people you must understand what is happening to your body?'

She nodded again. 'It's true. Of course it must be true, I am carrying a child.' She sounded puzzled, uncertain, but she looked up at me, her eyes deep and sparkling, and there was no way she could sound unhappy. A smile was playing around the corners of her mouth; wonderment, as if she had been given a much-longed-for gift.

'Do you want to keep it or lose it?' I said coldly. 'You have no time for indecision about this. You are pregnant with the child of a wandering mason. And *your husband* is on his way here. What do you want to do?'

I could only be brutal, for part of me wanted to weep and if I was a true friend to her, this was no moment for celebration.

'I don't know. Tell me what to do.'

'How can I do that? This is trouble, serious trouble, and you must decide *now.*'

She was lost to me for a moment, I could only think she was away in her head somewhere. A place where there are no problems. A place where babies laugh all day and sleep all night and never cry or get sick or soil their underclothes. Where neighbours, friends and husbands, smile warmly on a new life and never, ever ask questions.

I clapped my hands together loudly, furiously, so that even Despina looked at me in astonishment and Voula rolled over in her sleep and settled into a new comfort.

Heavenly slowly turned her head to me and repeated, 'Tell me what to do.'

I hesitated and said, 'Let me think for a moment.' Even I was undecided how to advise her. I knew she longed for a child; she was born to be a mother. There is so much love inside her, but, I am certain, not this way and not now.

I opened my mouth to speak and I was struck suddenly by the look on her face. Her eyes were full of longing, hope. At the moment it was not possible for her to feel anything but delight. I knew that when she was thinking properly she might be able to make a decision, but that was not now.

'Right,' I said, 'go to your house and rest. Don't think about this just now. You are not feeling good; rest and sleep is what you need and don't speak to anyone of this. Do you understand? Not anyone.'

She looked at me, her eyes vague and slightly puzzled. 'I must tell Christo,' she said simply, as though we were speaking of the weather.

'No, not Christo, especially not Christo.'

Her face clouded with disappointment. 'I don't understand. Why can't I tell him?'

'I think this, this happening, has made you lose your mind, your sense. In a moment you will be telling your neighbours.'

Where had my wonderful, admirable, sensible Heavenly gone?

My own mind was a whirl of anxiety and concern for her.

'Promise me, my dear friend, you will just go to your house now and rest and speak to no one.'

She sighed. 'Of course, if you say so, but until when?'

'Until I come to see you tomorrow. If I can, I will come tonight. Go now, ignore your neighbours and avoid Christo until we have spoken later. Do you have an arrangement to meet him?'

She shook her head. 'These days we can't make plans. We never know what he will be called upon to do.'

'Good. But swear to me, if you see him you will not speak of this.'

She didn't answer me. 'Swear to me now.'

She sighed again. 'Of course, if you feel it so important, I will swear not to speak of this to anyone. Does that satisfy you?'

She was obviously depressed with this conversation and rose to leave. I hugged her to me hard.

'I love you, dearest friend, trust me for the moment. I will come and see you tonight or tomorrow and we will make a plan.'

At last she smiled. I gathered my girls to me and we set off in the opposite direction. The crops must wait for tomorrow. There was absolutely no doubt in my mind what was to be done. She cannot keep this baby. But now was not the time to persuade her to think of anything sensible. She was strong, young and she would produce a fit, healthy child, unless I helped her. I shuddered at the thought of what I must do.

I took the girls to Pappous and Yaya. They were so happy to see them. Yaya was worried about Despina's silence and as I helped her wash the wild greens for salad, she asked me about it.

'There is nothing I can say. This is the third or fourth time she has descended into this state and she will speak to no one.'

'Poor child,' said Yaya. 'It is as if she has a devil inside her that takes her words away. I've heard of it happening before, just once, in Agropoulos.' This is a village along the sea road, high, high up in the mountains, usually lost in the clouds, it is so high. I have never been there and no one we know lives there.

'A passing tinker told us all at the spring one day. It must be thirty years ago, perhaps more. He said that the priest had intervened and cleansed the child, ridding her of the devil she carried.'

'What happened, after? Did she speak again?'

'Yes, yes she did. I remember the story well because it happened to all the girl children in the village, one after the other.'

'Only the girls?'

'Yes. That was what was strange. Agropoulos has only a few families, only nineteen or twenty people there, and every family had at least one silent child.'

'Plenty of work for the priest then,' I said.

Yaya smiled and shrugged as she cleared the stone sink. 'Always plenty of work for them; forgive me, Panagia mou,' and she crossed herself three times. 'It is not good to speak like this, but the priests are the last ones to starve in hard times.'

I noticed that today Pappous was quieter than usual, and I asked him why.

'The news from the wireless last night in the Piperia is very worrying, Anthi. The fighting in Albania is getting closer and closer to Greece. Yesterday, a port very close to the frontier was blown up and the Italians are saying it was the work of the British or the Greeks.'

'Is this dangerous for us, Pappous?'

'Of course, child. Not here in Crete yet, but they said the Italians are really pushing aggressively forward, and this sort of thing is just the excuse they need to attack Greece.'

'But how could they prove it?'

Pappous laughed. 'You think they need proof? If they decide that the Greeks need teaching a lesson, BOFF! In they come with all their weapons ready and that's it.'

'Enough, enough! We have the children with us, a rare treat, and you spoil it with all this talk of war.'

'Can the children stay with you a little this afternoon?'

'Of course, child. Despina can help me with my needlework while Voula rests.'

Despina visibly brightened at the thought of sewing with her grandmother and within moments they were together on the balcony and Pappous was already rocking in his chair, his pipe alight, Voula curled on his lap, her thumb firmly in her mouth.

I needed to be alone to do what I had to do for Heavenly.

First I went home and collected Astrape, who seemed suddenly lively at the prospect of an outing alone with me.

The paths we rode slowly through that afternoon took us out of the village and up into the hills above. I passed ground scorched and burnt from recent fires. Bare, sad olive trees and fields where usually wheat and corn would flourish, empty, deserted now, and only dry earth scattered with a sparse few weeds. On the sides of the hills, thin sheep scrabbled for any blade of grass they could find. I paused as one fell to the ground, trembled feebly for a moment or two, and I think died as I watched. There would be little meat from that carcass.

Above, a couple of vultures, which had been hovering swooped immediately, followed at once by others, and I knew, when I returned later, there would be only the remains of a picked skeleton.

It took half an hour in the warm autumn sun to reach the group of hovels I was looking for. A small cluster of dwellings in the curve of the hill showed little signs of life at first but as I paused and waited a moment, a child, a boy, ran out through a broken doorway and, thumb in his mouth, stared at me. For a moment I stared back. He was not pretty, there was no hair on his head and his scalp was scabbed and, in some places, bleeding. His face was a mess of healed and healing sores. The pox.

'Kyria Glykeria, is she here?'

He didn't answer, just continued to gaze at me.

'Her daughter, Tassia, do you know her?' I thought he was merely going to stare at me for the rest of the day, but eventually he nodded and pointed to the first house in the dilapidated and crumbling row.

I climbed down from Astrape. He was so tired, there was little point in trying to find a hitching post, so I left him untethered and, with the child still staring after me, walked towards the midwife's door.

It creaked open as I approached and the small, wrinkled

brown hand that had pulled it propped it back so that I could glimpse the interior.

The first thing I noticed was the smell. A rank, thick odour of stale bodies struggled against a rich, over-sweet aroma of cooking flowers or fruit.

'What do you want?' Well, she wasn't going to waste time with polite conversation, clearly. I was about to answer when a small cry came from inside and, clutching my arm, she pulled me over the threshold and into the darkness.

There were no windows here, nowhere for the warm, cleansing sun to shine through, and a thin candle, guttering in the breeze that came as the door opened, threw little light.

'What do you want?' she wheezed again as she sat down beside another shadowy figure, close to the thin flicker from the hearth. It was from this that the cry had come and as I looked, Glykeria's daughter Tassia held up a thin bundle of rags. She shook it and said, 'Baby, baby,' with a fond smile.

'Why are you here?' Glykeria said and, before I could answer, she rose from the stool and poked me in the stomach with a sharp finger. 'Nothing in your belly, then. No little monster boy for your dear mother to bury in some forsaken graveyard?'

I closed my eyes against the memory of my only son and pushed her dirty hand away from my body.

'It's for a friend I need help.'

'Too proud to come herself then?'

'No, no, she lives near Sitia. Too far to travel.'

Kyria Glykeria is not only the midwife here, but I remember Aphrodite telling me she also makes potions from herbs to hasten on the monthly bleed.

'What will you give me?'

My mind raced frantically. What could I give this hag? Food of some sort, she'd want food.

As if she heard she said, 'You have plenty of sheep, I know. Everyone knows.'

If I slaughtered one of our sheep, Manolis would know at

once and that would be the end of our marriage. I didn't care, but it would quite possibly be the end of my life as well.

'I will give you a goat,' I said. I had no idea at the moment how I could do that, but it would be less obvious a loss than one of Manolis's precious sheep.

'*Ne!*' She nodded, satisfied, and I immediately thought I should have bargained harder. Offered some honey, maybe, or some eggs, but in my heart I knew she would settle for nothing less than several weeks' supply of good meals.

With the promise now of succulent meat, she got to her feet with surprising alacrity and reached for a rusty iron pot lying on its side in the hearth. She hawked and spat on the side of the pot and with her sleeve roughly polished it. She gobbed again on the inside, and rubbed that out with her raised skirt.

I shuddered and hoped my face didn't betray the disgust I felt.

She was muttering now, more to herself than to me, I thought.

'Angelika, pennyroyal, cotton root . . .'As she spoke she was plucking dried herbs, hanging in bundles above the fireplace. These all went into the pot. She pulled a lethal-looking knife from a pocket and grabbing Tassia's arm, quickly made a small slit near her wrist. Blood instantly surged up and holding the arm of the whimpering girl high she dripped it onto the herbs in the pot. Glancing up she saw the look of horror on my face and muttered aloud, 'Virgin blood.'

She was reaching for more dried-looking twigs and snippets and these were pushed into the pot. 'Stop your snivelling,' she said to Tassia who was sucking on her wrist, 'and get me some night primrose and some tansy.'

Tassia looked at her blankly. 'Go now!' she said to her harshly. 'And be careful with the tansy, you know it's dangerous.'

The girl scampered away through the door, her shoulders hunched over, giving her the look of an old woman already.

'What are you waiting for?' Glykeria said to me. 'You'll get nothing without payment.'

I nodded at the pot. 'When will it be ready?'

'An hour, two hours, maybe, and then it must be drunk fresh. So you had better bring me your goat as quick as you can, hadn't you?'

I left at once. The boy was waiting outside by Astrape. I saw he was gently stroking the horse's nose and speaking to him in a quiet voice. Astrape whinnied with happiness and I smiled at the child. 'He likes you,' I said and the sad little face lit up with pleasure.

'You are lucky,' he said simply and turned away.

I was back within an hour or so in the fading afternoon.

With Manolis away, it had been easier than I had thought to catch one of my young goats and I urged him along on a piece of string behind me, but it was my horse that refused to move any faster. The child was waiting for me and Tassia was beside him, holding up her bundle of rags. 'Baby, baby,' she said again and the boy laughed.

Glykeria appeared in her doorway, in her hand a small hessian sack. She seemed cleaner than before, more like the midwife who had attended my births. But I felt only relief; there was no need to go back inside that stinking house. She snatched the string away from my hand and with her clawlike fingers scrabbled through the soft goat hair.

'Hmm,' she said, peering at her fingernails, 'clean.'

She handed me the bag. By its shape and weight it held a bottle. 'Your friend must drink this before tomorrow dawn. It will ripen the womb and she will lose whatever she has hidden inside.' She turned away and dragged the goat behind her, into that foul kitchen. Gently kicking Astrape around, I waved to the children and rode off again into the hills, leaving a cloud of dust behind me.

Each of Astrape's tired steps seemed endless as we struggled through the darkening sky. I dismounted and walked beside him. There was a breeze in the evening air. October is a lovely month with the last lingering days of summer still here, but sometimes there are chill moments that surprise.

My feet were tired and sore from treading the rocky mountain paths in my worn shoes. I should have worn Manolis's old clogs; my feet would have been protected more by the wooden soles.

It seemed like hours had passed, but the sinking sun told me that, in reality, it was only about forty minutes since I'd left Glykeria. At last I could see the wisp of smoke from Yaya's chimney.

She was standing in the doorway with Despina and Voula hugging her legs. Voula clapped her hands and laughed when she saw me, but Despina's eyes were as blank and empty as when I left her.

'I hope they didn't cause you trouble, Yaya?' She shook her head. 'Never,' she said as we turned to go inside, whispering, 'but Despina has not spoken to me. I tried, but,' and she shrugged her shoulders, 'nothing.'

Sitting on the table as though awaiting our arrival, was a dish of steaming *pastitsio*. My mouth watered as I smelt its rich fragrance and I realised I had not eaten, except for coffee and some rusks early that morning. Seeing my face Yaya said, 'You will, of course, eat with us before you go?'

The three of us were seated, waiting before she reached for a spoon to serve us. 'Where is Pappous?'

'They came for him early, to go to the kafenion. You must eat now – I can see you are hungry. I will eat with him later.'

'For cards?'

'No, no.' She was shaking her head, no longer smiling. 'Worrying times,' she said, cutting deep into the *pastitsio* and placing the full plates in front of us. The garlicky steam rose deliciously and even for a moment, Despina's eyes seemed brighter.

We were wiping our plates with bread, scraping them clean, when Pappous came in. His step was heavy and there was no smile in his eyes, even for Voula who clapped her hands together at the sight of him.

He stood, silent, in the centre of the room.

'Here,' he said slowly, 'here is everything that is good, precious in my world.' His mood was transparent. Things must be wrong, bad.

'The Italians have invaded our country.'

Wise Yaya had already poured him a raki and he drank it in one gulp, holding out his glass to her for another.

'Early this morning, apparently, they crossed the border. The army has been mobilised, what is left of it. It is war.'

He sank back in his big chair, by the flickering flames of the fire and swung Voula onto his lap. 'Of course, we will fight back. There is already talk of casualties in the far north.'

Yaya crossed herself three times and I remembered her sister had married a merchant from north of Athens. I hastily crossed myself too and stood up.

Through the open doorway the sky had darkened now to the colour of tarnished silver and I made to leave. They did not try to stop me, their thoughts were elsewhere this evening.

I think I expected the world to have changed in some way with this news, but outside everything was as before. The sky was darker, sure, but the night was clear and there were no clouds across the moon that hung like a lamp above.

The path was stony and my feet still hurt me. Overhead a hawk shrieked. I knew the sea glinted below, even though I couldn't see it, and from the path as we slowly passed along it I soon saw Heavenly's house in the distance, her outline lit by the shadowy lamp sitting on the terrace.

Voula waved and shouted, 'Helly, Helly!' but Heavenly was lost in her own thoughts and didn't turn. We were almost at her door before she realised we were there and rose slowly to her feet and stepped towards us.

I let the girls go ahead. Voula's stubby little baby legs beside the skinny, slow limbs of her sister.

I looked at my friend and, for a moment, saw her as I had the first time; that coltish girl lying so awkwardly on the ground. The months and years had served her well, only softening and rounding the edges: that girl was now a woman. Her smile was warm and wide as she reached down, clasping Voula in her arms and swinging her high above her head.

A chill that had nothing to do with the weather flashed through me. How was I to persuade this woman with so much love to give, not to welcome motherhood?

HEAVENLY

I had sat alone for much of the day, stroking my body, imagining the baby growing inside, feeling my breasts, heavier now I was sure, pressing my nipples to get a little pain, a feeling of tenderness.

My mind felt numb; unlike my body, that seemed to be fizzing with excitement. I know that I must think clearly about this. I must think of all the alternatives, all the problems, but I told myself that, just for one day, I can revel in the excitement of a child growing in my body, can't I ? My body, my child.

I hadn't admitted it to Anthi, but I knew Christo was coming here today; he promised. I kept looking at my watch. Moments like this, I wish it wasn't working so well.

Nine. Five past nine. Twenty past nine and, at last, I heard the soft footfall outside and the next moment he was here. I ran in from the terrace in a flurry. Heart beating too fast. Then I made myself go slow, in a calm way, and smile gently.

'Can I come in?' From the doorway. 'I'm sorry to be late.' And then I was in his arms and there was no time. It had stopped now we were together. It always does.

The temptation to tell him my news was all but unbearable, but in fact he had come here only to tell me what was happening throughout Greece, he had no time to spare for me tonight.

'I must leave again at once,' he said. 'Kotso and Andros are waiting for me in the Kanavakis barn. We are trying to raise some interest from the villagers in what is happening today.'

'Tell me.'

'The Italians have declared war on Greece. They are using any excuse they can, but this is what they have wanted for a long time. The invasion of Albania should have shown us all what was coming. There is already fighting in the north. They are supposedly angered by Metaxas's decision to allow the British to build military bases in Thessaly, and there is some ridiculous talk of a Greek spy they caught. If they are determined, and they are, and their army advances across the Greek borders, as they have done, what more do we need?'

It was rare to see Christo so aroused, so angered. I had got up quickly as he arrived, but a moment's dizziness sat me down again. He didn't notice. He was pacing up and down the terrace, his boots clattering. I put out my hand to pull him to sit down beside me, but he ignored it absentmindedly and only continued to stride back and forwards.

'I've heard on the underground network that the Greek army is in tatters in Albania and the only soldiers are the reservists from the hill villages in the north. I would guess there are barely a hundred or so of them and they're mostly over seventy.'

'What can we do here?'

'Nothing. Just now we are helpless, we can do nothing but wait to see what happens next. No one can see a reason for Crete to be attacked just now. But I still feel we should be on our guard, prepared to help how we can.' He gave a bitter laugh. 'You should have seen the men tonight in the Piperia. They turned the wireless set down as the news was distracting them from their cards! That was my Uncle Yorgo, he shrugged it off as unimportant. Only old Stephanos Karanakis insisted we listen. But even he could only persuade Petros and Vilandis the baker to take it seriously.'

He cupped my face in his hands; roughened and blistered as they are from work, they were like silk to me and I nuzzled my cheek into his fingers. He reached down to kiss me, but I gently pushed him away. 'We can be seen here on the terrace.'

He sighed and stepped back. I was about to tell him of my letter from Hugh, at least I could share that part of my news with him, but he was already moving to the steps, down to the inside of the house and speaking again.

'You understand my anxiety, don't you?'

'Oh course I do. We must all be aware of what is happening, you are right.'

And with a wave behind him he was gone.

So Greece is already at war. How long can it last? What will happen now? The people here may think only of Panagia and their crops, their harvests and their animals, but I grew up in England, I was an infant when my country was at war, always afraid that the next piece of news would be of the death of someone we knew, a neighbour, a cousin or a friend killed in action.

To me those three words were the most hated, the most feared of any. I would hang on to my mother's skirts as she stopped in the street to talk to someone already in tears as they spoke. My sister and I would whisper to each other, 'Killed in action, he was killed in action,' and shake our heads solemnly.

At first it was a game. We called it 'action'. We thought it was a fearful place, Action, somewhere on the outskirts of London where men would go and die. Sometimes there was a variation and they would 'go missing' there. In my imagination it was a dense underground jungle with giant thorn trees and vines; snakes and huge lizards lived there that would grab anyone foolish enough to go there and swallow them up.

My sister once asked my mother why they went there if they were going to be killed and she gave us the usual answer: 'Don't be so inquisitive. These are not things little girls need to know about.' I don't remember when I first learnt what it meant, the true tragedies that families suffered at the violent loss of someone they loved. But I do know that I quickly understood the futility of war. I knew the awfulness for young men, it always seemed to be young men, trying painfully to cope with missing limbs or some other disability.

In the ward, even ages later when the war was long over and we were promised there would never be another, we saw so many struggling to live a life like everyone else but without sight or hearing, or worse, hideously deformed by burns that oozed and dripped into dressings that had to be changed daily or even hourly. And what was achieved by all this? I never understood that. Streets filled with silver bands and bunting and balloons and shouting and cheering and words like 'hero' and 'valour' and 'bravery' tossed about constantly, as familiar as raindrops on a spring day. And then there would be another war somewhere else in the world that apparently wasn't so important because they weren't Englishmen that were killed.

And now, Panagia is my home and Greece is my country, and Greece is at war. I feel the acute sadness of a loss that I haven't yet suffered.

I was deep in these thoughts, rocking myself gently in my chair, when I realised the breeze that had arrived with the first stars was bringing goose bumps to my arms.

'Helly, Helly!' and little Voula was struggling up the steps and running to me. I was so happy to see her. Like any child she has a wondrous innocence that radiates from her, offering pure love. I held her to me with one hand, reaching out my other to her sister. Slowly Despina took, it but her grasp was limp and her head turned away.

'Shall I make us coffee?' It was Anthi calling from inside the house.

'Can I have a mountain tea?'

'It's your house, you can have whatever you choose.'

We were all back inside now and Anthi had a pan of water set over the ashes which she had brought back to life with Yorgo's neighbour's old bellows. The puffs and squeaks they made soon brought flames and Anthi rubbed her hands down her front.

'I'll join you in a *dictamus*, I think,' she said, 'but why no coffee for you? You seldom drink this village tea, you tell me it tastes like stewed bird's nests.'

'I haven't a taste for coffee today. I realise that for the last week or so it has nauseated me.'

Anthi turned away, saying, 'Well, you know why that is, don't you?'

Of course! I could only smile as I thought of the baby inside me, rejecting coffee and showing me it preferred *dictamus*. Despina had wandered over to the corner of the room to the old wine press and was already unwrapping the brightly coloured scraps of velvet and silk I keep there for her. Her grandmother has taught her to sew and with tiny, neat stitches she patches together many pieces of the soft cloth to make a usable length. Before she became silent she told me, whispering, that she was making a skirt for her mother 'like yours, she loves these coloured things you wear. It's a secret, a gift for her name day'. But Anthi's name day has been and gone and the skirt is not finished and her daughter is silent still.

Voula had toddled over to join her now and with care was stretching out each piece of cloth, smoothing it down and making separate little piles according to colour. We sat at the opposite end of the room, Anthi and I, sipping at the hot mountain tea. It has a sour, bitter taste, I think, and I sweeten mine with honey.

'Have you heard the news?' I asked.

'You mean about the Italian invasion?'

'Yes, what else?'

'We came here from my grandparents and my Pappous gave me the word from the wireless set. Do you think it is true?'

'I'm sure it is.'

'How did you hear?' And she gave me a strange look, eyebrows raised. 'Oh no, don't tell me, Christo was here,' she added, sounding thoroughly disapproving. 'Say you didn't tell him about, about—'

And I cut her off sharply. 'Of course I didn't mention the baby.'

'Hush, keep your voice low, the children . . .'

'I'm sorry,' I said quickly, my hand over my mouth.

'I told you earlier, no one must know, no one.'

'If you could guess just from looking at my face, don't you think my neighbours can do the same?'

'I think none look at you as closely as I do,' and she turned away, her cheeks reddening, 'and none care as I do.'

I put my hand out and took hers in mine. It's like Christo's, a man's hand, rough and hardened from the work she does. Calluses blister on her palms, but it's a dear hand to me, and a reminder, always, of the differences in our lives. Even when I worked on my house with the men, each night I would rub cream or oil of some kind into my fingers. The sweet-scented creams I had brought with me from Athens had long ago finished, but I had devised a mixture of petals from flowers and oil from the olives and a few drops of that at night softened the skin of my working hands.

I had tried, on several occasions, to persuade Anthi to do the same, but she just laughed saying, 'If I had a man in my bed I wanted to touch, maybe I would, but until then, I won't waste my time, thank you, Heavenly.'

She was watching her daughters now, as she took a hessian-wrapped package from under her skirt and handed it across to me. 'Take this,' she said. I held the package in my hand, curious. 'You must drink it tonight before you sleep.'

'What is it?' I opened the rough sacking and took out the flask inside. It was almost full with a dark greenish-brown liquid. Taking out the cork stopper, I sniffed and immediately held it away from me. 'It stinks. Are you trying to poison me?'

'It'll be good for you,' was all she said.

I had a dark suspicion suddenly. 'What will it do to me?'

She sighed. 'Oh don't ask questions, please let me help you.'

'It's a purge, isn't it? I've heard of stuff like this.'

'It's what the women use here when their monthly bleed is late.'

'My bleed isn't simply late, it isn't going to come again for months. You know that, you know why.'

'No, I know nothing.' Her face was hard, clenched, she was blinking rapidly and couldn't meet my gaze.

I held the bottle out to her. 'Take it away, I don't want it. I don't know where you acquired it from, but if it has cost you money I will give you money. I know what this stuff is and I know what it does, and I don't want it anywhere near me.'

She knew I was angry, very angry. I raised my eyes a moment to look at her daughters but they were oblivious to any tension from this end of the room and were happily absorbed in the scarlets and greens and peacock colours of the scraps.

'You know . . .' and I knew she was going to plead with me. She loved me, as I loved her. I knew that she had acted as she did because she cared for me.

'Please, let me help you. You don't seem to realise the trouble you are in.' She held the bottle of vile liquid out to me again. 'Many women use this here. It's not dangerous, it's not a poison, it just helps to put right any little mistakes.'

I sat back. I had to try and make her understand.

'This is not a "little mistake" as you call it, my dear friend.' I put my hand across my stomach. 'This is my baby. My baby and Christo's baby.'

'And how are you going to tell the village? You think they will believe in a virgin birth?' She was kneeling in front of me now, and crossed herself three times. 'They did that once upon a time, but it won't happen again and you know it. They will be delighted to have a whole new piece of gossip and then they will start to wonder who the father is. They will, of course, suspect Christo first, then perhaps Yorgo Babyottis.'

My face must have expressed the horror and disbelief I felt as she said this.

'Oh yes, believe me. Yorgo has been here for months, often alone with you. Then they will look for any errant husband who has spent too many nights drunk late in the kafenion. What do you think our friend Papa Yannis will make of this? Naked swimming is nothing compared to a bastard pregnancy.'

'Oh stop, stop, please, please stop.' I knew tears were pouring down my face now and my heart was beating fast.

She was scarlet with emotion and breathing heavily. 'Oh, *Panagia mou*, how can I make you understand?'

'Dearest friend, I know what you are saying to me. I know in some ways you are right, but I have to make this decision for myself, don't you understand? Allow me just a little time to be happy with my body, please, please. I have longed for this moment for so long, thinking I would never be a mother. From the moment I married Hugh, I have looked with envy at every woman with a swollen belly. I look at Voula and Despina and long for them to be mine, to feel that love, that special love, that I know you have for them.'

There was a sudden yell from the end of the room and Voula ran to us, sobbing. She was clutching a piece of emerald silk tightly in her little fat fist, saying, 'Mine, mine.' Anthi was on her feet, her arms open to her child, consoling her. Despina stamped her foot by the wine press and, with her hands on her hips, stared towards us. Even from here you could see the fury she was feeling.

'I must take them home, they are exhausted. Take this,' and she handed me the bottle again. 'Of course, you are right, it is your decision,' her voice was flat now, 'but I would be no friend to you if I didn't help you to make the right one.'

I held the bottle as if it would scald me. Roughly I wiped my eyes with the back of my hand.

'Thank you. I understand all you say, but leave me to think. Perhaps tomorrow . . .'

But with her girls clasped to her side, she was out on the steps now, her face turned away from me. 'Tomorrow is too late. The medicine will only be effective for a very short time. You must make up your mind.'

'Please, don't leave like this. I need you to be my friend.'

'I am your friend, I will always be your friend, whatever you do. But don't throw away your life for a moment's thoughtless pleasure.' Her face was lit up by the moon and I saw that tears were glistening on her cheek. And then she was gone.

I sat for hours alone on the terrace. The cooling wind had

died and the evening sky was clear, the air warm. Large moths batted fleetingly across the surface of the lamp and a night bird sang a lonely song. A line of ants seeking food marched in formation across my bare foot and off to vanish down a crevice in the wall. They would find the way back in some-how, I felt sure, and feast on the honey I had left out in the kitchen. I didn't care. Tonight there were more important things to worry me.

I put Anthi's bottle on the top of the terrace steps and sat back and looked at it. Of course I was afraid. When I was doing my training as a nurse I saw young girls and women desperate to end an unwanted pregnancy, trying all manner of ways to expel whatever they were carrying in their bodies. The results were always dreadful, whatever they did. Some did it with a bottle of gin and hot baths. Some took pills or potions from helpful chemists eager to exploit a girl in trouble. Some pressed thin wooden sticks or knitting needles into themselves. Sometimes their bleeds were induced, but always in great pain, and in the end they usually lost what they were carrying sooner, or worse, later.

But however much I filled myself with fear and dread I knew that Anthi was right. To keep this child was madness. And how would I keep it? I would be forced to leave the village, I had no doubts of that. And where would I go? With Greece at war how could I live in the wild, a pregnant English woman used only to the fine things in life? If I could by some miracle get myself to Athens, what then? I could no longer trust that Hugh would be there. And if he was? What would he say to my arrival with the bastard child of a Cretan builder inside me?

There were no choices, no decisions for me to make.

I looked at the bottle. I picked it up, shook it gently. A residue already forming at the bottom spread in an oily fusion through the liquid.

I took out the cork and without a moment's pause I put the bottle to my lips and drank, drank it down.

ANTHI

Manolis had been away for three days and came back silent and sulking. He kicked the door open, came into the house and kicked his dog. He had no words for any of us. Voula tried to climb on his lap saying joyfully, 'Papa, Papa.' But he pushed her aside. Despina sat in a corner with a schoolbook and didn't look up.

The evening of the day was warm, airless, the saffron sky clouding. Perhaps there would be thunder? A storm before nightfall.

It is two days since I have seen Heavenly. I feel I must leave her alone just now, although my mind is desperate with anxiety. There is nothing more that I can do for her. I saw Aphrodite this morning at the spring and asked her, as casually as I could, if by chance she or Yorgo had seen her. She shook her head although she added, 'Yorgo has to collect a saw from Heavenly's house, so he may go there tonight.'

She was carrying her youngest child strapped on her hip as she worked through her laundry. It was a boy with a shock of dark hair sticking up all around his face. His deep-brown velvet eyes looked out at the world with humour, a twinkle, and he smiled as I stroked his soft brow. Even I could feel an empty broodiness in my belly, so I knew well what Heavenly was feeling.

That night it was dark when I heard the tap at the door and a soft call of my name. Manolis had gone out hours ago and as usual had given me no clue where he was going or when he might return.

I opened the door and Yorgo Babyottis stood outside, peering nervously behind me.

'My husband is not here just now, come inside.'

He shuffled across the threshold looking around him. 'You are well, Kyria? And your children?'

'Thank you, all is well here. Will you take a raki?'

'Oh, I don't plan to stay, but if you insist, a very small one.' And he was sitting in Manolis's chair, his feet stretched out to the dying embers of the fire as if he lived here.

'A raki glass is a raki glass, Yorgo, not smaller or larger.' And I poured him one, moving to the table to slice him an orange as I spoke. Funny how he changed when he realised Manolis was away from here. If Manolis returned now, depending on his mood he could easily cause a fight. He hates Yorgo, I have no idea why, calling him 'the coffin maker'. He has a morbid fear of death, my husband, so that is probably why. He detests funerals and won't go near the dying. He probably assumes that a man who makes coffins carries death with him, like an infection.

'It is, of course, a pleasure to see you, but is there a reason for your visit at this hour?'

'That is a fine piece of wood you have here,' he said rather unexpectedly, looking across to my bridal chest. 'Ash, I believe, quite old but very fine.'

'My grandfather made it.' I really didn't want a conversation about my furniture just now. 'Is there something you want with me?'

'Hmm?' He sounded puzzled, his fingers now stroking the arm of Manolis's chair. 'Ah yes, Kyria.' He was not to be hurried.

I breathed audibly; surely he could see my irritation? This slow, polite conversation would drive me to despair very soon but it's likely he would start chatting about my children and animals if I tried to hasten him along.

'You keep a beautiful home,' he said, slowly looking around. 'Your husband is indeed a lucky man.'

He was sipping from his empty raki glass rather showily,

having drunk the contents down in one, so I reached for the flask and filled it again.

'Thank you. Is there something special that brings you this way tonight? Of course, I am, as always, very happy to see you here.' I tried a last desperate measure. 'Perhaps it is my husband you wish to see? He will be here very, very soon.'

He was on his feet at once, draining the glass and moving towards the door. 'No, it is you my wife told me to see. I had to pass by Kyria Heavenly's house tonight, to collect some tools, you see, and I told Aphrodite and she said I must come and tell you. She is clearly unwell.'

'Aphrodite is ill?'

'Not Aphrodite, of course, let me be clear, she is in fine health, but your friend. In fact she could hardly stand, she is so weak. I found my tools, it was my good saw, you know, I use it whenever I make a coffin and tomorrow I have to prepare the wood for old Peridakis, he who lives up the mountains. Only seventy-three and already through three wives—'

I had grabbed my shawl, wrapped it around me, and was halfway out of the door. I paused only to say, 'I'm sorry, I was wrong, my husband won't be home until much, much later. You are quite safe here. In fact, I would be glad if you could stay for an hour in case the children wake. I'll be back so soon, I promise.'

I couldn't hear whether he agreed to stay or not, as I was already running through the yard, the garden and along the road. *Panagia mou*, keep my husband away tonight! I was panting as I arrived at Heavenly's house. The door was unlatched, moonlight softly slipping under it. I called her name as I ran in but there was only silence. I went straight down to the bedroom. It was dark, I guess the lamp had long emptied.

'Heavenly,' I whispered, 'it's me.' Still silence, but I could see through the shadows her shape lying on the bed.

There was a strong smell of sickness and I almost kicked over a bucket as I approached. A quick shaft of unease ran through me. Heavenly's bedroom is always sweet with the scent of wild flowers.

'I'll find a candle.' I went quickly back upstairs, taking the pail with me. In one of her ramshackle cupboards was a packet of candles and a heavy silver cigarette lighter. It must be one her husband had left. Certainly Christo had nothing so fine as this. I ran outside and emptied and cleaned away her vomit.

With the candlelight downstairs, I could see her clearly. She was hunched around herself like a baby. Her face was chalk-white and her eyes, closed as they were, deeply shadowed in purple.

Oh, *Panagia mou*, what have I done to her?

HEAVENLY

I remember Anthi coming. I remember her being here and I remember her leaving. And then, the utter silence of the house bore down upon me, welcome and sedative, silent as thought and I drifted again into sleep. But within barely an hour I guess, I was awake and burning with fever – my bed was on fire. Outside cats howled insistently.

In my head was a bitterness and for some reason, perhaps I was half in a dream, I recalled an argument I once had with Hugh, about money. A subject he considered of no importance. I tried to move my lips, but my mouth was parched and I drank deeply of some water Anthi had left me. The cats had stopped fighting and in the quiet, I slept again.

When I awoke I lay for some time without moving. The cramps I remember feeling were still gripping inside me, but nothing so severe as in the beginning, when I had first tasted that wretched poison. I recalled then, in a haze of pain, how at first they had doubled me over, crippled me it seemed, and I remember Anthi's words about the tansy, how it would contract and empty my womb. I was shivering, my teeth chattering, and I hugged the blankets round me. I felt as though I had no command over my body, that if I stood I would fall over or float away. I had to try and I swung my legs over the side of the bed. Beneath my feet, the floor was cold, icy. I stood motionless for a few seconds and then looked down and around me, glancing dizzily back into my bed. Protectively I put my hand on my abdomen.

This was not, I was sure, a dream. My stomach felt hollow

and vaguely I knew I must not dehydrate, so I drank again. A spasm, a contraction, caused me to bend over, gasping with the pain. Was this it, then? But nothing happened, it slowly stilled and I stood up straight again. I was giddy at once and clutched at the bed head for support.

I was aware of feeling suddenly chill and shivered. My head hurt. Medicine, I thought, and took the bottle of aspirin from the drawer of the bedside table carved, it had always seemed to me, with affection by Yorgo. I tossed a couple of the small, white tablets into my mouth but it was so dry again they merely crumbled at the back of my tongue and the crusty bitterness made me retch. I drank as deeply as I could of the water left in the glass but there wasn't enough and I coughed hoarsely as they tried hopelessly to dissolve. I retched again. The empty pit of my stomach contracted wildly and I staggered towards the bathroom but it was too late and I vomited a stream of clear liquid with shreds of the aspirin onto the floor. I yearned suddenly for a cup of mountain tea but knew, even without trying, I was incapable of so much action without falling. I sank back down onto the bed and within moments, I slept again.

When I woke it was daylight. I think I was still feverish but not the fierce fires of the night. My head throbbed and I ached in every joint. I felt so weak, thirsty and underlying that was a tight wad of anxiety. My breasts were enlarged and still ached heavily. A contraction caused me to lie rigid, motionless but it was certainly fainter, less sharp than before and faded away almost immediately.

I was happy just now to be alone. I could groan and mutter as much as I like. I must recover and think.

Slowly, slowly I managed to get to the kitchen by holding onto the walls as I passed. My head was spinning and I paused often. Then I saw the fire had died as I slept, so I couldn't heat water for my tea and I almost wept.

My memory is hazy and I cannot precisely recall the sequence of what happened next. I think I slept or dozed for most of that day.

Once, when I awoke Anthi was there, or was that yesterday or last night? Her girls were with her, that was clear. I know she washed the floor and I think the branch of sweet briar that fills the room with a scented freshness was placed beside my bed by Despina, who stroked my head gently with a cloth and was imitated move by move by her sister. They both smiled a little as my eyes flickered open. They reached out to the tumblers of water on the cupboard and both tried to persuade me without words to sip. Whether I did or not, I can't recall as I must have slept again, and when I woke in darkness, the house felt still and empty.

I lay for I don't know how long between sleep and wakefulness, but I think it was the sound of scratching on my bedroom window that pulled me back fully into the world. I turned my head in the direction of the sound and said feebly, 'Who is it?'

By answer there was only the soft whisper of my name, 'Heavenly, Heavenly.' It was Christo and he came down and sat beside me on the bed, taking my pale shaking hand in his strong brown one and, for the first time in ages, it seemed, I felt safe. His deep, dark eyes peered closely into my face.

'How . . .' I started to ask, and 'Anthi,' he answered.

'She is a true friend and she came here to look after you every day.'

'Every day?' My voice was barely a whisper. 'How long have I been unwell?'

'Most of the week,' he replied and I sank back down again, deep into the pillows, my mind racing with all the questions I needed answering.

Christo lay beside me on the bed and I welcomed the closeness of his body. His arm stretched over my middle and his hand stroked me exactly, I imagined, where our baby lay dormant. Unless, I thought bleakly to myself, Anthi's potion has killed it.

Tears filled my eyes. I was weak from the fever and felt only

226

like weeping. Christo lifted his head from the pillow, sensing my sadness, and gazed at me with concern.

'What?' he asked. 'Why? Why so sad?'

'Oh, I'm just weak and silly,' I said, 'ignore me.'

He laughed then. 'That is the one thing it is impossible for me to do, ignore you. What can I do? How can I help you? Perhaps I could give you a bath to make you fresh? Would you like that?' And all at once that was what I wanted more than anything else just now; to lie in clean scented water and soak the remains of whatever it was out of my body. I knew I was too helpless to do it alone. I had a sudden thought. 'Could you wash my hair?' My fingers reached up and trawled through my lank and greasy mop.

Christo stood, stroked my cheek and said softly, 'I will do anything for you.'

As he reached over to help me out of bed, I said swiftly, 'I am not very clean, do you mind?'

He laughed and said, 'Then the best thing for you is a bath, my love.'

As I pulled myself upright I asked, 'What is happening with the invasion, the war, is there news?'

'Later,' he said, 'I will tell you what I know later. There is not a lot to know.'

With his arms around my shoulders he managed to get me out of the bed. The sheets betrayed me with the sour odour of sweat and sickness and I shuddered involuntarily as I smelt my unclean self.

Christo caught my eye and smiled. As though he could read my thoughts he said, 'I love the scent of you. Every thing about you is wonderful to me. I am lucky that you trust me with this intimacy.' And with his arm firmly around me, for a moment he buried his face in my breast. And we made our way together, slow and stately, to the bathroom.

In the warm, sweet water, I luxuriated and thought that I may never move again.

First Christo ran back and forth with pans of hot water. He had rebuilt the fire and I knew the flames would be burning

227

fiercely under the large zinc jars. Then he knelt beside the bath on the floor and, with the olive oil soap one of Anthi's neighbours made, his hands slipped slowly and easily over every bit of my body, leaving each part soft and clean. He took a cloth and slowly swept it over my face.

'Lie back now,' he said and I slid lower into the water.

'Like this?' I asked as my hair floated out and around me like seaweed. He held each strand gently in his fingers and threaded the silky soap through. The sweet fragrance of the rose petals in the soap filled the room and carefully Christo massaged my scalp clean. I looked down at the now grey water around me and started to apologise. He stopped my words with a kiss so tender my lips parted and I felt his dear familiar taste in my mouth. I was instantly aroused, weak as I was. Especially as his hands were once again on my swollen breasts. I felt my nipples stiffen under his touch, but all I could think was if he would notice my body was different.

His closed eyes opened slowly and he smiled. 'Come,' he said, 'time to get out before you are cold.'

I could barely make it back to the bedroom and I did so only by clutching onto his arm and going very slowly. Each step an achievement. He had changed the soiled linen on the bed and bundled it into the corner. 'I will wash these tonight,' he said and, feeble as I felt, I managed to laugh.

'You will give everything away if you are seen washing my sheets. I will ask Anthi to help me later, there is plenty of spare linen here.'

As soon as I lay on the bed, my eyes closed and, within moments, I slept again.

As before, I had no idea of time passing and when I awoke it was again dark and Christo was standing by the door. 'Are you coming or going?' I asked him through dry lips.

'Neither. I am simply here. Yorgo came an hour or so ago with some broth from Aphrodite. Do you think you can manage that?'

I felt suddenly hungry and my stomach rumbled in antici-
pation of food. Surely a sign I was getting better?

Christo went to the kitchen and reappeared shortly with a
bowl steaming in his hands. I could barely wait to take it from
him I so wanted to eat. It was delicious and I managed to
swallow all the savoury goodness of it. I thought that I would
be strengthened straight away, but Christo laughed at me
when I said this aloud.

'Soon,' he said, 'soon, but first we must discover what
made you so ill.'

I closed my eyes and beneath the sheet I crossed my fingers
and said, 'Just something bad I picked up from one of the
children, I'm sure. I don't think they wash their hands from
one week to the next. They can't see why they need to and
their fingers are always filthy.'

As I sank back down again, luxuriating in the sweet-
smelling sheets my eyes closed. I was exhausted from the
effort involved in eating and talking. As I did so, I notice that
he had one of the large hammers in his hand. 'What is that
for?' I asked, puzzled.

He looked at it himself. 'Oh the hammer,' he said. 'Well,
every time Irini or one of your neighbours comes to see how
you are, I bang at a wall. They know I am not a doctor, so
why am I here?' I smiled.

'Do they come often, then?'

'Your kitchen is like a market! Of course they always bring
a gift, every time they visit, but it seems everyone in Panagia
cares about you and has been by to send you greetings.'

Sometime later, although how long I don't know, certainly
I was alone again, I managed to rise from my bed and,
holding onto walls as I passed slowly by, went into my
kitchen. It seemed to be filled with sweet-smelling herbs and
flowers. Vegetables and fruits were piled beside plates covered
with bread and biscuits and jostled for room beside cheeses
and bowls of yoghurt. My heart was full and I blinked away
tears as I recognised the generosity of my friends and
neighbours, these very people who have so little themselves,

and this year especially, when the sun has baked and burnt every drop of much needed moisture away.

I was suddenly breathless as though I had run for miles and, turning back again to the bedroom, I managed to struggle drunkenly down the stairs and sank onto my bed where I slept yet again.

This time when I awoke it was to see Anthi sitting beside my bed. I reached to hold her hand in mine. Hers felt cool and strong and I know my hand was moist and shaking.

'The purge you gave me, it made me so ill.'

Her face was suddenly stricken. 'Oh, my dearest friend, I am so sorry to have made you so unwell, can you forgive me?'

I smiled weakly by way of answer and reaching to the floor she fetched a cloth and a bowl and bathed my face with cool water.

'You have been ill for many days. I have been so worried about you. Tell me what has happened?'

'I thought I should lose everything inside me, I was very sick, vomiting so badly I thought it would never stop.' She flinched and closed her eyes. I knew she was going to tell me how guilty she felt and I must stop her. 'Don't, my friend. I know you had to do this and I knew it would be bad.' We sat together in silence for a little, holding hands. 'I'm sorry I was stubborn,' I continued, 'but it seemed the biggest decision I have ever made in my life. I had to think about it properly, accept the responsibility alone.'

'Oh course you did. I understand.'

My head sank back on the pillow again and I closed my eyes. 'I wonder when I will know if the purge has worked,' I said quietly.

She sat very still on the side of my bed. 'What do you mean?'

'I mean, when do you think I will have bleeding?'

'Are you saying there is no blood yet?'

'Oh no, none. I had great cramps for hours, but no blood. No discharge of any kind.'

'You should have had blood with the cramps from the beginning. That is what the tansy does. It contracts and tightens the womb. Are you sure there is none?'

She stared at me, anxiety on her face.

'You have been ill for five days now, there should have been blood immediately,' she repeated emphatically. 'It can't be possible that you have been so ill but have resisted the final outcome. Many village women have used Glykeria's medicine. My neighbour Maria has used it twice. Aspasia in Kato Panagia has used it more than once. I know the strength of it; its action is fast, almost immediate.' She looked stricken now, my dear friend, desperate.

'I'm sorry, Anthi.' I felt my eyes closing again with a great weakness and within moments I was asleep again.

All events at this time run into each other and days fall into nights and nights slip into sunrise. And here again, Christo is with me.

'Would you like to go to the terrace?' he asks. 'It's a beautiful evening.'

'If you will help me,' and together we make our way slowly, arm in arm, like an elderly couple. It is a balmy soft kind of night, more like spring than October.

I pause on the way out of my bedroom and catch sight of myself in the mirror on my dressing table. I'm grey with fatigue; my eyes are hollowed, with deep purple rings around them. My hair, although now sweet-smelling and clean, is unbrushed and stands out around my head, like the mane of an old lion. I am not particularly vain, but I can even frighten myself with the ghastly ghostliness of my image.

Christo tells me news from the outside world. Sometimes, a man comes to listen to the wireless set in his cave. He's hazy about the details.

But the man is not Greek, he's English and the news he receives comes straight from the Greek High Command. 'I was wrong about the Greek army being fragmented and weak,' Christo tells me. 'They are fighting hard in the north and have forced the Italians back across the Albanian border. There are many dead, many casualties but, they say, the will is strong. There is also news of the British. They are in Greece, here in the north of Crete, and have created a strong base in the bay around Suda. Your navy will help with our defences there.'

'And my home in England?' I ask. My brain feels as weak as my body, but I need to know. 'Do you have any news from there?' But he shakes his head. 'I can tell you only a little about the Greeks and Italians. But I have heard that the Greeks in the north think of the English as some sort of heroes, already coming with their ships to help us.'

A sharp lurch of nausea makes me suddenly aware of my condition.

Christo looks at me, a question in his eyes. 'What is troubling you? Aside from this wretched sickness, you are not yourself.'

'There is something I must tell you,' and he doesn't speak, just sits on in stillness while I tell him about Hugh's letter and what I believe it to mean.

His face betrays nothing of what he might be feeling, but he slowly drops my hand and I see a new distance in his eyes. Gone, with the soft crack of my words, is the easy intimacy we shared.

Oh, what have I done? Anthi has tried many times to warn me, to wake me up to what I am doing and I refused to listen. So carried away was I in the wonders of this new love that I have created a scorpion's nest of lies and deceit. I behaved so carelessly with lives and feelings, including my own, and now the man I love more than my life is broken. And the man I married is coming back and I am carrying a child who can never know his father.

I barely notice that Christo is on his feet again.

'I must leave you.' Without another word or glance he is gone and I stand alone on the edge of the terrace watching him ride away into the hills.

I lie sleepless in the cool bedroom. The sheets are pulled

close around me like a shroud. His last words echoing again and again in my head, 'I must leave you.'

What did he mean? Leave me just now, for a short while? Or does Hugh's return mean he is gone for ever? My muddied brain can make no sensible decision.

I slept so much in the sickness that now, when I most need it, it eludes me, hour after long hour. I make myself walk, giddily, round and round my house, trying to tire myself, but every time I lie on the bed, Christo's face swims before me and a great pain of loss pours through me.

My neighbours continued to come, bearing bowls of some mouthwatering stew or broth, and never a day passed without some further proof of their kindness. What of them now? Their innocent trust chides me like hot coals thrown over me. I have returned their affection with lies and deception.

Anthi came with her daughters and while she busied herself with my laundry or cooking, her girls and I would lie in a huddle on the bed and I huskily read or told them stories. Despina sat rapt, spellbound by the excitement of some adventure or other, but she would never read back to me, never speak, no matter how persuasively I tried.

Anthi changed my sheets daily, for I still soaked them through each night with the sweats that lingered after the fevers had gone. These sheets disappeared each day and reappeared starched and clean. And I suspect one of the reasons she scrupulously changed my linen so frequently was to see for herself if there was blood or staining on my sheets. There never was.

Beneath everything I was feeling, the anxiety, the fears, even the guilt, there was one cold fact that try as I might I could not deny: Christo had gone.

There was no word or sign of him. I begged Anthi for any scrap of news of him, but she dismissed my questions, only reminding me each day of the time passing since I had known I was with child: Christo's child.

I had filled out a little in my face. I was no longer afraid to look at myself in the mirror, the dark shadows and lines had all but disappeared and in spite of my health not yet being perfect, I looked and felt more like myself.

And then one night my world turned upside down and splintered into fragments. My husband came home.

ANTHI

I don't know now which is the most worrying; Despina's continued silence or Heavenly's stubborn refusal to reject the child within her. Of course I believe she has tried. I have watched each day her poor body's difficulties in coping with the new being inside her. The morning nausea, the craving of one food over another: one day only green apples, which, of course, gave her the cramps, another, only sweetness would satisfy. I favoured green apples – perhaps the violence of the cramps they induced would help dislodge the growing foetus.

In all my life I have never known that purge to fail before. And, oh, *Panagia mou*, she has been so ill! One night, in her fevers I was sure she would die and it would be I who would be responsible for her death. Manolis was at home that night and I sat with her through the dark hours praying to the Panagia to save her.

I think she was not aware of it, but Aphrodite had sat with her too and once Yorgo came to replace her, but he just sat gloomily wringing his hands together from time to time, lifting his head to call '*mono Theos, mono Theos*' – it is God's will. This was not helpful.

I was there the night her fever broke and that was the moment she started to get better.

Slowly, slowly but gradually, each day saw some small improvement. Her colour eventually changed from grey to a slight rosy tint. Her hands shook a little less and she became able to swallow more than a coffee spoonful of broth.

The weight had fallen off her and her arms and legs were

like sticks, but there was still no blood, no pains producing anything other than a thin yellow stream of foul-smelling diarrhoea.

These fluids oozed from her, but she seemed unaware of the evacuations into her sheets. I changed her linen once, if not twice, each day. I was frightened that I had caused her harm with Glykeria's potion and that, far from losing the child within her, she would give birth to a monster.

This was my worst nightmare; in the beginning she looked so thin and ill there could be nothing healthy about this unborn child. But as she improved, sometimes by only a tiny bit each day, I tried to reassure myself that if she carried this child to term it would at least be normal. But it was small consolation.

Each day everyone prayed for rain and the occasional small shower gave us hope for an hour or so. It took but one dark cloud for the village to look hopefully upwards, hands out, palms up in case we missed a single drop, but every morning dawned bright and clear and glum faces greeted each other everywhere we went in our fields and gardens. The earth was parched and cracked and vegetables, far from being profuse and ready for the winter, withered and died before they had a moment's life. The grapes on the vines hung wrinkled and bloomless, drying into sour raisins before they were even picked.

And then, one day I woke up a little later than usual and Despina had disappeared.

I thought at first she was off around the garden with the goats and chickens and ran outside to call her, but she wasn't to be seen. Manolis had been out drinking even later than usual the night before and was still snoring in his bed. Voula was banging on the floor near her bed with an old hammer. How anyone, even my husband, could sleep through this noise I couldn't imagine, but he did. I pulled the hammer away from her and asked if she had seen her sister. But she looked blankly back at me.

Then she climbed under and over Despina's bed calling her name loudly and turning to laugh at me, thinking this was some sort of game. It was a holy day and there was no school. I had told Yaya I would take the girls and go with her to church.

At first we walked slowly round the garden calling 'Despina' into the hollow air.

Clouds chased each other across the sky, but the sun was trying to come through them and with a little wind to help, it would be another fine day. Little Voula was like my shadow, imitating my every movement and sound like an echo.

The sweet briar that sprawls loosely down to the bare earth underneath is a favourite hiding place, but this morning it showed no sign of disturbance; Despina had not been there.

'Come, Voulamou, we must look elsewhere. We shall ride on Astrape.' Voula brightened visibly. She knew, in the absence of her sister, she could have the best seat in front of me, not clinging to my back as usual.

We released Astrape from his stable and I lifted Voula into the air. She swung her leg easily over the heavy old horse. She has a natural agility I've never seen in her sister. We called first to Maria's house, to see if Despina had taken herself off to play with Athena, but it was deserted. As usual all the doors and windows were swinging open. Like most of the villagers, she has no fear of intruders.

Today, a school holiday or not, makes no difference to the usual workings of the village, and the fields were occupied by farmers and their families. There were no cheerful greetings today as I passed through; everyone worries how they will survive the winter.

Each year is the same, I remind myself, always the worst winter, the worst spring, too much rain or too little. Cretans, certainly Panagians, are natural pessimists, and hope and good cheer seem always to evade us.

We arrived at my grandparents' house and there was still no sign of Despina. I rode Astrape round to the back lane behind the house. I could see the whole village spread out below me from here but it would be impossible to spot anyone in particular and, as if to confound me, clouds that had been hidden for most of our ride appeared over the horizon, scudding quickly across the sky and causing a haze that fell quickly across the village. Yaya came at once to the door, her face anxious. Her silver hair was hanging to her waist. She must be distracted as I hardly ever see it out of its restraining plaits, bound firmly around her head.

'Thank the Panagia you are here,' she said, crossing herself. 'I was thinking I would have to come to you, and that would be difficult. Despina has been here this hour past, come and see.' She turned back into the house and I followed her quickly.

'There is something wrong and I cannot get her to speak to me at all and she won't move from here.' She pointed into a corner near the fire.

I was on my knees in front of my daughter in a moment. She was huddled on the floor like a wounded animal. Her hands covered her face and her haunted eyes peered up at me through her fingers. I wound my arms around her, instinctively rocking her to and fro, murmuring her name over and over. Whatever was wrong must be bad. Her eyes were dry, no sign of tears, and the corners of her tightly closed mouth were turned down, her lips pressed fast together as if to prevent herself speaking or crying out.

'*Koritsaki mou*, my baby, my baby,' I said repeatedly as I rocked her in my arms. 'Oh, Despina, talk to me. Tell me what it is.' I felt helpless. Every time she has these silences it seems for a little time afterwards she will slowly become something of herself again. But then whatever it is that brings them about comes again and attempts to destroy her. It is two years now since the first time and the pain she feels is almost physical: it dulls her eyes, takes away the upturn of her laughing smile. I weep for her.

'Despina, Despina,' I whispered, my lips to her ear. I think Yaya had nursed her in the same way as her sweet young hair smelt of cinnamon and honey.

The only sound she made was a low keening from deep in her throat, as if to comfort herself as no one else could. At first, she was rigid in my arms, her eyes darting about as though looking for danger in every corner. Slowly, slowly, she grew limp and, at one point, as her humming ceased, I wondered if she had fallen asleep. But as she saw Yaya with Voula clinging tight onto her hand, her eyes darted wide open again. Voula ran to her sister calling, 'Spina, Spina,' and, when she got no response, almost fell down beside her and stroked her knee with a small closed fist.

The four of us sat there for a while, not moving more than the gentle rhythm of our comfort.

'Will you tell your mother what is wrong, my child?' asked Yaya and when there was only silence, she repeated the question. But Despina sat unyielding as though she hadn't heard.

We sat for probably an hour. The only movement was from Voula, who offered her sister the best form of comfort she knew: her thumb. But Despina tightened her lips together in resistance and shook her head, pushing her sister's hand away. Voula looked at me sadly and Yaya reached down from her rocking chair and patted her on the head. 'There,' she said, 'you are a dear and good girl and your sister loves you, but I don't think you can help her just now. Best to leave her alone.' We sat on, the four of us as if in a vigil.

'Church?' I whispered to Yaya but she shook her head quickly.

'Pappous will go, I expect. Just now he is at a meeting of the village elders.'

And after a little, Pappous himself came in, singing loudly, startling us all.

'What have we here?' he said, standing in the doorway. 'Is this a wake? Has someone died?'

Yaya shook her head at him. 'Hush, Stephanos, your humour is out of place here.' Rising quickly, she led him out of the room.

Voula had sat still for long enough and was struggling to

her feet. Her chubby little legs must be cramped now from sitting so still. For me, I would hold Despina for the rest of my life if it would help her, but one of my legs was already numb and I knew I must relieve it.

Pappous came back through the door again. 'Go to your Yaya, child,' he said to me quietly, 'I'll watch Despina for you.' But as I rose stiffly and went towards the door, Despina gave a piercing cry and I turned back to her. 'Go,' he repeated, taking my arm, 'your Yaya needs to speak with you.' At the same moment, agile as a young goat he was down on his haunches and had taken my place on the floor. Eighty-seven years old and as nimble as a boy. The sheer strength of his presence seemed enough to soothe Despina and she whimpered softly, her only protest.

I waited a moment or two before tiptoeing from the room. Beyond the door was the kitchen and Voula sat at the table there surrounded by hundreds of bright spots of colours. My Yaya is a fine seamstress and had always made dresses for Ririca and me when we were children and this, her button collection, was the envy of Panagia. It contained a hundred years' worth, or more, of buttons in all shapes, sizes and colours.

Counting these buttons into little piles was one of my girls' favourite pastimes. Just now, Voula was lost in another world with big buttons here, small buttons there and scarlets and yellows, blues and greens in separate groups. Silver or gold, often rescued from old military uniforms, merited lining up in rows at the back of the table.

Yaya took my hand and led me outside to the terrace. The haze had cleared and below us the village was bathed in the warm golden sunshine of mid-morning.

'I must ask you something very private,' she said slowly and somewhat awkwardly. 'Has Despina started her monthly bleeds?'

I was startled. 'Of course not, Yaya. That is not private between us. She is much too young; you will be the first to know when that happens. Why do you ask?'

She paused, her face puzzled, her eyes anxious.

'I wondered if perhaps . . . You see she was bleeding a little when she came here this morning.' She looked away. 'There was blood on her leg.'

'Oh, I'm sure she fell or cut herself on a bramble or thorn, even a stone. It's always happening to Despina. She never looks where she is going and often tumbles. Her arms and legs are covered in scratches.' I faltered; Yaya was shaking her head slowly, her eyes downcast.

'No, this was different.' She paused and I stroked her arm, thin under the lively green of her jacket.

'Different, what do you mean different, blood is blood, isn't it?'

Her lips tightly together, she shook her head quickly, firmly.

'She must speak to you. She must tell you what is wrong.'

'Oh, Yaya, you think I haven't tried? I would do anything to hear her voice again. Anything.'

At that moment Voula ran out to us, buttons tumbling everywhere from her little fists and I bent quickly to the floor to pick them up. 'I think we should leave, Manolis will be awake and about and I must prepare food for him. For all of us.' I hugged her to me closely. She was limp in my arms, her eyes closed, her silver hair moving softly in a sudden breeze.

'Come on, you worry too much. Let me fret about my girls. I'm sure this will all be over soon and we shall forget Despina's silence.' But even I knew my words were false and my heart was heavy with anxiety.

'There are times, and this is one of them, when I feel a million years old. This day there are things in the world that I wish with all my heart I didn't know about.' She turned to face me and smiled. It's a smile so full of warmth that has always lightened my life, but today that same smile was a mask for sadness.

'Tell me, is there something you are trying to say? What is it you are trying to tell me?'

The harsh cry of a seabird far overhead came with a sharp

and sudden chill. Over in the village the church bell rang its triple call, again and again, and the village faithful walked in their best clothes to church, to celebrate this day. Some, seeing Yaya on her terrace, her hair untended, called out a greeting and one asked, 'Is all well, Giorgia?'

She didn't answer, but pushed the air away in front of her, as if clearing a passage. And then Pappous was out on the terrace with Despina and Voula beside him and, with heavy steps, we left to return to our own house.

HEAVENLY

The days are shorter now and the nights seem endless. Gradually, my body clock has readjusted itself; night is no longer confused with day, supper with breakfast. I am nauseous in the morning, and only then, and of course I know why that is. I examine my body closely for signs of change. The shadows under my eyes have faded and the pupils are bright. My breasts are heavy and darker around the pronounced nipples and my waist has thickened, but only a little.

Each day when I wake I smooth my hand across my belly in wonder – there is a new life in there! I am no nearer a decision about my future, or what to do for the best, and every time I start to try and think of alternatives, my mind wanders off and I can't concentrate. I cannot help myself being full of joy.

Still, I have heard no word from Christo and each morning, with the sickness, comes a longing and a sadness that I try and cheer with a hope; perhaps today he will come?

He never does.

In spite of myself, each night I fall into a deep sleep, my dreams vague and troubled. It was on one such night when a sound bruised the air and I was quickly awake. My heart was racing, my eyes wide with alarm. It was a voice, two voices, then laughter, loud, ragged and indistinct. Then one started singing. They were here, close by my house, too close. I recognised the song, not the words, but the sentiment: love, the love of a good mother. Always it's the same.

I swung my legs over the side of the bed and slowly got up;

too quickly and I may fall with giddiness. It was Yorgo's voice, Yorgo and a second man. There was more laughter, a scrabbled, raw chorus now, and then a loud pounding on my door. I ran up the stairs as fast as I was able calling 'Wait, wait.' I opened the door hastily. Yorgo and another, who had been leaning on it, fell into the room and landed in a pile at my feet. They were struggling around untidily, legs tangled with arms, trying to get up. I was blessed if I was going to help them. Let them struggle! One arose, and one lay helplessly, still wriggling. Yorgo, upright, stood straight by clinging onto the wall beside him. The stink of alcohol from the pair of them was so fierce I almost retched, and I reeled back.

'Kyria,' muttered Yorgo, 'Kyria, look who I have here. A present for you.' And he started to giggle. 'A present! Get up my friend,' and he staggered to lift the recumbent figure at his feet. Yorgo wore his old grey jacket and patched *vraka* but as the other finally rose to his knees and looked blearily round through his tangled hair, I could see immediately that his garments, although the same peasant clothes and mended, patched and filthy, were of a superior quality.

He was a tall man and even though he was crouched just now on all fours and swaying dangerously, with his head hanging low and moving from side to side I could see his limbs were long.

'Come on, You,' said Yorgo hauling on one arm to raise his companion upright. His face was streaked with grime and sweat and his hair hung greasily over his brow, but I knew in a moment's clarity that this was, of course, Hugh, my husband.

Years later, when I think back to this moment, I only remember how every part of me stopped, rigid. Not just my arms, clasped by my hands in front of my body, not just my legs, stiffly refusing to let me move forward to offer help, but my face, in a rictus of a half smile, my eyes, dry but unblinking, my mouth half open, in a protest.

I knew then, that even my heart, the organ that is supposed to change our every mood, take us from love to despair, from happiness to sadness had stopped any function, except to work on automatic: pushing my blood around my still body to keep me alive. But I might as well be dead.

Looking at my husband now, for the first time in, how long? Two years? Three? More? I felt nothing. Certainly not pity for this helpless wreck of a creature. As he managed with great difficulty to get up, to stand and lurch towards me, I instinctively backed away from him. Yorgo grabbed his arm to steady him, saying rather piteously, 'This is You, Kyria Heavenly. I found him in the Piperia.'

'Thank you,' I said, 'I am very grateful to you. Perhaps you should leave him here now and go home to Aphrodite. It is late and she will be worried.'

'Of course! You will want your reunion.' He laughed but couldn't quite manage it and almost fell, shaken with hiccoughs. Turning, he pushed the door open and staggered through it, into what remained of the night.

Hugh looked vaguely around him, his eyes puzzled. 'Is this the same old house?' he managed to ask, then, 'God, I'm tired,' and before he could fall again, I took him firmly by the arm and pushed him slowly ahead of me and down the stairs.

There, he saw the bed in front of him, tumbled forward to fall on top of it, groaned and passed out.

For the rest of the night I sat on the terrace.

Above me, the stars in all their many constellations glittered sharply down. The sky was quite clear and the three-quarter crescent of the moon stared coldly. As dawn began to crack open the dark, I grew very cold and took a wrap from the living room.

By first light Yorgo, and anyone else who had been in the Piperia last night, had spread the word of my husband's arrival around the village. I had almost to fight off the callers. My neighbours made one excuse after another to visit me, each one peering around me trying to catch a glimpse of him. They needn't have bothered. He was dead to the world, until even the cocks had finished crowing and the sun was high in the sky.

As my days were still so shapeless, I had no routine to throw myself into. I wanted so much to be busy, to go to the school, do my laundry, see Anthi and, more than anything else, at the end of the day wait for Christo's arrival. But the rhythm of my days just now was only about sleeping and waking with nothing in between: There was no school, I had a chest full of clean laundry, thanks to Anthi, and a kitchen full of good food, from the neighbours.

Eventually, from downstairs there was coughing and grunting. The loud heavy snores had stopped and I guessed that Hugh was awake. I was as nervous now as the gauche schoolgirl I had once been. Slowly, cautiously, my heart beating fast, I went down the stairs, but, dark as the room was with the shutters closed, I could see nothing until my eyes were accustomed to the gloom.

He was standing in the half open doorway that led outside. His back was to me and from the sounds that came from him I realised, to my horror, he was urinating on the stone floor of the lower terrace.

He was humming and turning slightly from side to side. I realised that he was trying to direct the stream into the large stone amphora that stood beside the door. Mercifully, it was the one that harboured the young bougainvillea. If he had aimed for the one on the other side, he would have saturated my winter store of potatoes.

It was a while before he heard me, finished what he was doing and turned around. His face had aged and he was much thinner than I remembered. He looked drawn, gaunt, not as robust as when I last saw him.

'Hello, Evadne,' he said. 'Dear daughter of Poseidon. Oh, it's so good to see you, come here and let me hold you.' And he stretched out his arms to me. But standing as he was, his body was inhibiting and I couldn't move. I looked at this man, once so familiar to me, and he was a stranger. He glanced down at himself, smiled wryly and said, 'Don't worry, I'll clean myself up and then we'll see, eh?'

I managed to force a smile to my lips, but I knew I couldn't make it reach my eyes. 'We have a bathroom now,' I said, over brightly.

'Do we?' he said. 'A bathroom? Fancy that.'

That day is frozen in my mind, each moment fixed, unmoving, like tableaux. We didn't know, I think, either of us, how to treat each other so we skirted around like two cats, stalking.

I wanted to wind myself back, to that last time we were here together, when everything was easy and each day brought a fresh excitement, but that girl, naive and innocent, had gone for ever.

Like a puppet, I walked Hugh around the house and saw everything through his eyes, fresh as he was from the lavish richness of embassy design. He tried, I think, at first, but couldn't completely hide his immediate disappointment and as we slowly went from room to room together, even I began to feel the colours I had so lovingly chosen seemed garish and brash. The old furniture that I found traditional and comfortable, happily given by neighbours, seemed coarse and old-fashioned. The painted floors that I loved for their simplicity seemed, today, rough and plain. He didn't need to use words; a slight sniff, the way he ran his fingers over tables and chests was enough for me to feel sad and embarrassed.

'So this is what you have made of the drawing room,' he said, and as he smiled, I squirmed inside. Where I could smell the rich fruitiness of the drying apples, pomegranates, oranges and lemons lying in careless design at the foot of the wine press, he could only push at them with his foot as though he thought they were a mistake. And even to me, they suddenly appeared shrivelled and old.

When we got to the bathroom, so simple, so unostentatious, he asked, pointing to the tub, 'Do you bath in this?' I saw the scratches and marks on it. All were the remains of its long, slow progress on the back of a donkey up the mountain. I remember how many times it had fallen and poor Yorgo had to keep getting one of the shepherds to help him reload it. He, Christo and I had laughed so much that day.

I nodded in answer to Hugh and was about to tell him with my usual pride that it was the only one in the village, but I thought that would be of no interest to him.

Beside it the Thomas Crapper lavatory, that Christo had boasted of to Yorgo, looked sadly out of place. There is no plumbing here to sustain it and I had to confess to Hugh, through pursed lips that it was for decoration only, so far.

The biggest shock to him, clearly, was his wife. He tried, I could see he did, but it was impossible for him to disguise his distaste at my appearance.

My skirt, the one I was so proud to have made from old curtains, he pointed to and said, 'Village fashion, is it?' It was not said unkindly, but I knew he was thinking of all the fancy frocks I had left behind; the silks, laces and fine linens he had bought me. How foolish and useless they would appear here.

At one point he touched my hair and I think almost visibly flinched – I knew it felt rough and untamed, too long to control. A fast image flew through my mind of Christo lovingly washing it in the bath. Shaking a little, I lifted my hand to it myself and felt its wiry coarseness.

He stretched his arm out to me, silently inviting me to take his hand and gingerly I held one of his fingers, but only for a moment and then I moved away from him.

'Why don't you use the bathroom, and I'll try and find some fresher clothes for you?'

'I feel I must apologise, for turning up here like this. I must admit, I thought you would be pleased to see me, but I suppose my arrival last night was rather inauspicious. I lost my bearings, you see, and went into that café place up the road for directions. Old whatsis name insisted on bringing me here himself. Sorry about that, bringing a stranger in with me, and a drunken one at that.'

'Yorgo is as familiar to this house as I am. He was the senior workman, in charge of the renovations. I wrote to you about him. He is a fine carpenter; all the wood you see here is his craft.' Oh stop! I said to myself. I sound so pompous and over defensive.

We were on the terrace and Hugh was unthinkingly running his hand over the railings, carved by Yorgo. They had been a labour of love for him and at the foot of each he had cut a tiny flower and his initial, invisible to most people, including Hugh, but not to me.

'Oh good, jolly good,' he said. 'Well, I'll take a bucket of water from the kitchen and go and sort myself out.' And whistling cheerfully he walked away. I watched him go. He was moving around the house as if he had lived here for years, taking it all for granted. He called out, 'Chuck me a towel will you?'

Of course he left the bathroom door open, why would he close it? There was only me here, his wife. As I took a towel from the press, he called to me again, 'Any chance of some soap? Or do you use some sort of plant or something, here?' and he laughed.

Averting my eyes from his long naked form standing, dripping water to the floor, I pointed to the wooden ledge over the bath. 'There is the soap, actually. It's hardly Harrods' finest, but one of my neighbours makes it from olive oil and flower petals. I like it.'

'Of course you do, my darling. You love all this village stuff, don't you?'

Suddenly the emotions I had kept bottled up inside for weeks welled up all at once and I found I was shaking with rage. Yes, rage! I didn't want him here. I didn't want him walking around the house as if he belonged here, as if it was his! And I didn't want to face the savage truth in this, so, turning on my heel, I walked out of the bathroom, my head in the air.

'Oh, Evadne,' he called after me, 'didn't I leave some clothes here? Be an angel and fish something out for me, will you?'

An hour or so later he returned to the terrace. He certainly smelled fresher. I had left an old suitcase of his outside the bathroom door and he had retrieved some crumpled shorts and a shirt. I remembered seeing it in the cellar room the night of the rats and this morning had hastily dragged it out for him.

'That's a bit better,' he said, smoothing himself down. 'But I could certainly use a shave.'

I looked up at him. He had grown a moustache and, grudgingly, I had to accept that it rather suited him.

'Any chance of some breakfast?' he asked as he sprawled out on one of the old chairs. 'Or is that something you don't have any more?'

'Of course,' I said quickly, jumping to my feet. Inside I put a pan of water on the fire and then I remembered that I had thrown out his percolator. I made the coffee as I now took it, thick and sweet like the Greeks. I hoped rather desperately that living in Greece himself he would do the same. I put some of the hard Cretan rusks on a plate with a glass of fresh water, arranged them all on a tray with three of Irini's little cakes and took it out to him.

He took one of the sweets and bit into it, but left everything else.

Well go without, then, I thought miserably to myself, and mercifully he didn't ask for his percolator.

'I really am sorry about last night. I didn't mean to arrive in a state like that. I completely lost my way, you see – it was rather foggy and then there was a light and it was that Pepper Tree place and they were all so kind and all over me and I'm afraid I rather let them overwhelm me with their hospitality. You know what they're like here, of course you do. Frankly, I was exhausted and that raki went straight to my head.'

My rage had subsided into a seething ache now, a knot of tension under my ribs. Somehow or other I had to get through this.

'How long are you staying?' As I said it, I realised how antagonistic that sounded. He sighed and I quickly added, 'I mean, how long can you stay?'

'Only two or three days, I'm afraid, and the really bad news is that I can't take you back to Athens with me.' He looked at me. 'I'm so sorry. I want to do that more than anything, but it just isn't going to be possible this time.'

I tried to show disappointment, but inside I was jubilant. Surely even I could cope with a couple of days.

He settled comfortably back in the chair and started to tell me how and why he was here. The war was escalating daily and it was expected soon that Athens would be taken.

'I'm here to find a safe hiding place for the royal family,' he said, obviously thrilled to have been entrusted with this important task. Even I could see it was an honour and said so. He flushed. 'It was too good to be true, to come to Crete, the perfect opportunity to see you.'

'Why Crete?'

'Well no one thinks the Germans will bother with Crete. It's too far from the seat of power, Athens.'

'In the village everyone hopes and prays that to be true, but they don't really believe it. They think Crete is the centre of the world.' I laughed and my laughter sounded shrill to me, like coins in a tin can. 'Mind you, I'm not sure how thrilled they will be. There's little love lost for the royal family, in these villages.'

'This must remain a complete secret. No one must know, understand? No one. Why do you think I dressed as a peasant? I was chosen because my Greek is better than any of the others and I can travel undercover.' He pointed to his face. 'I didn't grow this great fungus for fun, you know,' and he laughed. 'That'll be shaved off as soon as I'm within sight of the Acropolis again.'

And I had liked it, thought it suited him.

He was telling me about the base the British had created at Suda Bay, 'Miles away from here in the north, but we wanted people to see our presence, feel the security the British will bring. That's the most likely place for the King. The Prime Minister, Tsouderos, will be with them. Funny bloke, no charisma, nothing. I always find him a rather meek sort of chap, wouldn't say boo to a new-hatched goose.'

He reached across and took my hand. 'I so want you to be

back with me, I miss you terribly. I thought at first this was the opportunity to get you out of here, but it's far too dangerous a journey for you at the moment. I came over from the mainland on one of the last flying boats but I'll probably go back on a ferry.'

I couldn't help but feel there was something inherently unstable about my husband, treating this whole thing as a lark. Perhaps that's how people like him cope with the horrors of war; all a bit of a jape, an adventure. It's very different to my villager friends here, who face the grim reality of disaster every winter, every spring. They certainly don't feel that life is one long adventure from birth to death.

He was in full swing now, enjoying his story. 'Amazing journey across the mountains here. It was good to give it a try, undercover, as it were. I thought I'd better practise that. If and when we bring the royals it'll be a secret.' He sat back in his seat. 'I did rather well, I thought. I stopped several times to rest and always people treated me as one of the villagers; gave me food, et cetera. I think I fooled them!'

I made my face crack into a smile, to prove to him that I was interested, impressed, even admiring, but he didn't seem bothered by any reaction from me.

'Not a word of this outside these four walls, old girl.' I nodded agreement. 'But how about this for a tale? We've got two-way radios set up in one or two key villages across the island and one of them is at the very top of Panagia! Right here! They each have an operator and, you won't believe this any more than I did, but the chap here is young Bingo, Foxy's brother!'

My mind buzzed. Of course that must be the man Christo had spoken of.

Hugh was on his feet now and striding round the terrace. He stretched his arms high into the air and breathed deeply, in and out, in and out. Newly invigorated, he turned to face me. 'I don't think you met Bingo, did you, darling? We were all at school together. Of course Bingo's younger than Foxy and me, but in spite of being a squit he was a good sort, even then. And the best thing is, it meant I had a perfectly legitimate excuse to come over to this side of the island. Which meant I had the best possible reason to find you.'

I was smiling and nodding and trying hard to show interest, but then I managed to ask what I really wanted to know.

'Tell me what is happening in England? I can get some news of Athens, even Albania, but news of home is impossible.'

'It's not good. Hitler is determined to conquer Britain, but don't worry, Mr Churchill is equally determined to keep him out.'

He told me some of the things he knew that had happened; the Germans had occupied France, and my mind filled with pictures of the little streets and markets of Paris that I had walked daily. He told me that Goering had sent hundreds of bombers to try and destroy London, but now, it seems, many people have built shelters in their homes or gardens and those that haven't go down and sleep in the underground train stations at night.

'We won't give in to the buggers! Your old hospital at Greenbridge and your family will be fine, they're out of London and the Hun don't seem interested in anywhere outside the cities. Well, airfields and that sort of thing, naturally.'

'You say that, but your friend Lady Troutbeck lives near Greenbridge and you wrote and told me she was going to Egypt.'

He laughed. 'Oh good old Dora! Any excuse for a trip abroad and she's off. Don't take her as typical. Anyway, let's not go on about all this gloomy stuff. I'm sick of war talk. It's all we get in the embassy. Now I'm here with you and the sun is shining, let's forget about England and Athens and all that, just for a bit, eh?'

He was smiling like a child on Christmas morning. Except that I was the present at the foot of the tree. His arms were around my shoulders and he pulled me to my feet. I made myself meet his gaze. It felt so deep, so penetrating. It seemed to look through me, right to my soul and I felt he must feel me cringing inside, so I willed myself to smile, forced myself to show happiness and he kissed me.

As his lips forced mine open, I couldn't help but cough. The breath issuing from his mouth was so fuelled by fumes of the raki that I almost doubled over, gasping.

He laughed again as he pulled back from me. 'Oh sorry, the one thing I couldn't find was a toothbrush. Do I stink still?'

I nodded, relieved that he had said it before I had to.

'Do you think old diddlyakis will find my bag in the café and bring it round? I'm stuck without it.'

'I'll walk round and get it for you,' I said, backing away from the terrace, any excuse to get out of there.

'Lets go together,' he said, but at that moment some god or other must have woken up and smiled in my direction for I saw below several villagers coming along the path towards the house.

Papa Yannis hadn't waited long before feeling he could pay a visit and he and Manolis waved stiffly as they saw us.

'You stay here,' I said hastily, 'and entertain these people. It's you they want, they wouldn't be here to see me.' And thanking the Panagia like a village woman, I fled through the house and out the door.

But my departure was unnecessary as Yorgo was the next to arrive with what I took to be Hugh's bag; a rough hessian sack tied at the neck with a worn piece of string. He saw Papa Yannis and Manolis and, thrusting the bag at me, scuttled back the way he had come.

The villagers all came by during the morning; sometimes, entire families came in together to look at 'the man with the short trousers'. Of course they all brought some gift to welcome Hugh and mostly these were small bottles of wine or raki or a few onions, cakes or eggs.

Hugh sat in state on the terrace and received all the callers graciously enough. He even allowed one or two of the children to poke his bare arm or leg. Those that were this bold giggled and soon ran swiftly away.

Hugh knew the rules of Greek hospitality and poured glasses of raki for all the men, each time filling a glass for himself. In the kitchen, I chopped fruit and shelled nuts to provide the *meze*. At least it gave me something to do.

The story of Hugh's arrival had spread around the village and from his greeting to each one and the answers he gave to their questions, I quickly learned more than I needed to know of his life in Athens, so far.

There was no time between callers to shave, so his face seemed radiant as the rays of the sun caught the fair bristles on his chin.

When the last visitors left, I finally felt that my house was restored to me. Hugh had gone outside to wave them on their way. He was quite drunk again and had propped himself in the doorway. I could see that only by holding on tightly to the lintel, could he manage to stand upright.

'Go and rest, I'll wake you later.'

'Good idea, old thing,' and as he staggered down the stairs he called up to me, 'I gather that chap you took on to do the house is a bit suspect.'

I stood rigid as he spoke, unable to move or speak. He went on, 'Bit of a communist, by the sound of it. The priest and the bald chap were telling me. You must be very careful who you hand the work out to, money going into the wrong hands and all that.'

There was a great belch and a thud as I guessed his body hit the bed, and then silence. I slowly breathed life into myself again but I knew I was in great danger of weeping and I longed for solitude. I left the house and walked down to the spring, deserted at this time of day, and slowly onwards to the little church of Panagia Sta Perivolia, the virgin in the garden.

Inside, its cool walls welcomed me and within moments I felt the calm I always experienced here. Then, exhausted myself, I sat down and, within moments, slept.

When I got back to the house Hugh was awake and sitting on the terrace. He looked relaxed and at home. He smiled to see me and held out his hand. I took it in mine and sat down beside him. We sat in silence for a little and, with my new-found calmness, I knew I would feel guilt when he was no longer here. What a hell of a mess I had made for myself.

'Are you hungry?'

'Ravenous. What will you make for dinner? I poked around a bit in the kitchen and you seem to have plenty of provisions.'

'That's the neighbours,' I said. 'Oh, I wish you could understand how good every one is here. How kind to me. I was unwell recently, nothing serious, and they came with food every day, did the laundry, made delicacies to tempt my appetite. Anthi, of course, my friend, was the kindest of all. You remember Anthi? She saved my life when I fell over and twisted my ankle, before you left.'

He laughed. 'Oh, do you mean that rather dumpy little woman? She's your friend, is she?' I was nodding and smiling now. 'It's only her that has made my life here so memorable, so liveable. She got me teaching at the school – I wrote you about it, remember?' And once I started it was impossible for me to stop. My life in the village here was a subject that would never tire me and I told Hugh all the details. How I got the house finished, how well the children were learning English, how they loved it. And the first aid! I told him about the little clinic hospital we had made of the old church. 'In fact,' I said, 'if you think of going up the mountain to find your friend, you could look in and see it.'

He nodded and got to his feet. 'Tell you what, we'll both go when you've cooked us up some of that stuff. I've spent too long away from you to want you out of my sight for a single moment.'

I went to the kitchen and started to prepare a stew of chopped aubergines, courgettes and tomatoes. He was whistling cheerfully now. I had a jug of herbs by the sink and felt sure I could make something every bit as tempting as he was used to. Irini had brought me some of the dry Cretan bread a day or so ago. And I thought if I soaked it in Anthi's rich green olive oil and seasoned it with salt and pepper and put it on a pretty plate with some local cheese, he would find it irresistible.

We were both on the terrace, the tray of food before us, when he said, 'You *are* pleased to see me, aren't you?' He was peering at me under a fringe of hair and I remembered that wistful look he did so well; it had always irritated me, just as it did now.

Briskly I said, 'Of course I am, why would I not be?'

'Oh I don't know. You seem to have your own life sorted out here, teaching and all that stuff. I can't help wondering where I fit into it.'

'Let's take each day as it comes,' I said, knowing I sounded rather desperate. 'After all, I can't come back to Athens with you, you said so. Probably just as well I have something to occupy me here until . . . until . . .'

He had hardly touched the food, it was getting cold as he sat there and even I could see it must now look unappetising. The oil had gelled on the plate and a bruise on the surface of one of the courgettes gleamed darkly through the tepid juice, showing it had been far from fresh when I prepared it.

I piled everything back onto the tray and carried it into the kitchen.

He followed close behind me and when the tray was safely stowed I felt his arms slide around me, his lips nuzzling into my neck. I could smell the fumes of his laboured breath. He pulled me around to face him and started to stroke my breasts, his hands squeezing their firmness. I felt a sudden ache, a sharp pain. They were so tender, the slightest brush against them caused me to wince.

'I had forgotten how firm and wonderful you are; let me love you.'

And before I could speak, he was pulling me with him down the stairs and towards the bedroom. His hands were tearing at his clothes. Age and mildew served only to render the fabric of his shorts to shreds as he tugged at them.

My heart was pounding, fast and heavy inside me. A wave of horror passed over me, like dirty water. The moment I dreaded was here and I must act as though I was happy to be part of this desire.

I was slow to remove my clothing, my old curtain skirt and a grubby chemise. My fingers were numb, senseless and I fumbled with every fastening. I felt his fingers digging into my shoulders, lifting me onto the bed. He was rough, eager and pushed aside any clothing that was reluctant to come off.

I breathed in the scent of his heated body; all the details of him I would try to erase from my mind; his springy underarm hair, his soft, white belly, his damp crotch. Shutting my eyes tight I tried to think of something else, anything, but I failed. He was my husband and he was here in his house and his bed and I was as nothing.

I loved you once, I said to myself, when I knew of nothing else.

Paradoxically, I felt a kind of relief that this dreaded moment was here at last. It would be over and I had allowed it. But I need not have worried. Hugh, never one to waste time on readying me for his pleasure, tried at once to push himself inside me, but too late; he gasped hoarsely and his seed gushed around us, soaking into the white linen of the sheet. He rolled onto his side with a cry and, curled round like a baby, buried his face in his hands. I could hear him faintly muttering 'sorry, sorry, sorry'.

In spite of my relief and my feelings of despair, I could only feel sad. His face was streaked with tears as he looked up at me, and I stroked his back and across his shoulders. I tried to speak, but my throat had shut tight.

Fiercely rubbing his hands across his face, he sat up.

'I can do it, you know, it's not always like this. I think I was just rather too eager today. You know, not seeing you for so long and you are such a beauty.'

His eyes ran over my body but I got to my feet at once and clutched my skirt around my nakedness. I felt raw, exposed, as his eyes continued to travel over me. 'I think whatever it is you live on here must do you some good. You've really rounded out, you know.'

It was as though he was talking of the shape of a horse. Stepping into my skirt and pulling my blouse over my head I felt composed again, only wondering at 'I can do it you know.' He must have taken other lovers. I felt nothing.

The man he called Bingo looked remarkably like Foxy, just younger. He leapt to his feet when we stumbled our way into the cave. 'How wonderful to see you! I heard through this thing,' and he banged his hand on the box receiver, 'that you were coming. My brother got word to me. Oh God, it's good to see a human being.' He looked past Hugh in my direction. 'Oh, sorry, madam, no disrespect intended.'

'None taken.' But I didn't smile.

Hugh was hugging him and chuntering on about his journey. I stood awkwardly, glancing around me. I knew every corner and shadow of this place so well. In the few weeks since I was last here, Bingo had taken occupation thoroughly. He was explaining now to Hugh how hospitable the villagers were to him.

'I'm sorry, Heavenly, you are Heavenly, aren't you? I kept meaning to come and find you but,' he scratched his sandy head, 'I heard you were unwell. I trust you are better now?'

There was a sound of voices behind me. Voices I knew so well and I felt my heart pound harder, faster, and I couldn't move, couldn't look around as Bingo called, 'Hey, come in, you chaps.' And to Hugh he said, 'I'm sure you want to meet this young man, the one I've displaced. He did all the work on your house. This is his home, this cave.'

Christo and Kotso walked in then and without a glance in my direction Christo shook Hugh's hand, saying, 'I hope you are happy in your house. It was a pleasure to restore it.' He spoke in Greek and so Hugh replied in Greek, with a certain formality, nodding and thanking him.

Turning his head to me, Christo said, 'I hope you are

recovered, Kyria?' I couldn't trust myself to speak, so nodded briefly.

I wanted to see love in his eyes; I wanted to see the sadness of his missing me, I wanted to see everything there had ever been between us; but his eyes were those of a stranger; polite, empty. It was a mistake to come. How could I have been so stupid to lay myself wide open to this torture? But I knew why I was here; I longed to see him. I had thought just a glimpse of him would be enough. But this price was too high. I was shaking, giddy and feverish. I stumbled around and made my way slowly to the cave entrance, trying to breathe steadily and calmly.

I managed to say, 'I'll get a little air,' and stepped outside.

Behind me, I heard Hugh say, 'The way up here is rather tough for these frail creatures,' followed by laughter. Christo could do everything I could not. He was easy now talking to Hugh about the house, the village, the villagers, the impending war, all in his casual, easy style. Beside him, only Kotso looked pained, uneasy.

After what seemed an interminable time, Hugh joined me outside and with much jocularity we left the cave and set off downwards. As always I found any journey on the mountain glorious, the air so fresh, clean. To the north was a small craggy peak, outcroppings of granite, dense and convoluted as if to some mysterious purpose. There was a cool breeze in the afternoon air and I pulled my shawl tight around me. Hugh still wore the tattered shorts and beneath the hair on his legs I sensed the goose bumps of a chill.

He was full of good humour as we walked downwards and told me over and over what a decent chap Christo was. He had obviously forgotten all his earlier reservations and went so far as to tell me I had chosen the workmen well.

I was exhausted when we arrived at the house and longed only for my bed. I wanted to sleep for days and wake to find all these events long in the past. But I had a husband here now and although I escaped downstairs telling him I had a headache, he looked so disgruntled that I suggested he walk up to the Piperia and find some rather more cheery company than I could offer.

He did just that and didn't return until two in the morning. By then he was well past the stage of thinking of romance, after the flask or so of raki he must have consumed.

ANTHI

Looking at my eldest daughter beside me, silent as always, I wanted only to hold her, run my fingers through her soft hair, smooth her skin under my hand and hug her so tight that every bad thing she felt, every fear she had, big or small, would be squeezed out of her.

It was impossible to leave her for long. Even a moment's absence when she was sleeping brought shrill cries and she would run to find me. We had to do everything together, Despina and I; we slept side by side in her bed. If I left to tend the bees she was beside me. The hens, the goats, the plants in the garden, I never saw them alone these days. There was no question of school or a social visit to a neighbour. But still she hadn't spoken.

I hadn't seen Heavenly for days, but I heard her husband was back. Everyone knew that and perhaps it was as well to leave her alone just now to cope as best she may. He was the talk of the village within hours of his arrival. His tales of life in Athens had the gossips wagging their tongues non-stop. The laundry had piled high and Manolis had no shirt he considered clean enough, so it must be done. Astrape was loaded down with the dirty linen and we all walked beside him. It was Voula who made me think to call past Heavenly's house. As we made our way to the spring she called, 'Helly, Helly, we are coming.' And looking up at me she giggled and I thought, why not?

We were hardly at the path that led to her house, when

262

Heavenly ran out to greet us, and she was hugging us all with such delight, it was as though we had parted a year ago.

'You are well again,' I said. 'Have you any news for me?'

Of course I wanted her to tell me her bleed had started, but she was chatting to the girls and ignored my question, saying only, 'Everything I have is clean, thanks to you, but I'll happily come with you to the spring. It's good to get out of the house.'

As we approached the crooked pine that edges the path downhill, we heard the laughter of the women at the spring. They were all excited to see Heavenly and dropped their laundry to cluster around her, giggling and gabbling. Aphrodite, who was washing her baby's undercloths in the stone bowl at the end of the row reserved for those things, called over her shoulder, 'Your husband likes the cards then? He is a village man already.'

Turning to the other women she said, 'He is generous also. My Yorgo could hardly stand when he came home last night – and on five-star brandy too!'

Seeing my bewilderment, Heavenly said quickly, '*Prefa*, Yorgo taught him the rules of *prefa*.'

Pounding away at the stained cloths on the stone, her baby tight in the arms of one of her girls, Aphrodite's face was damp and pink with exertion and she puffed in and out in gasps, 'You'll be doing this next year, baby clothes.'

There was raucous laughter at this remark but Heavenly didn't join in, she looked bewildered and turned to me. Before she could say anything, the widow Anastasia called across to us, 'You'd best tell him to forget the cards. No time for them if he's going to work at becoming Papa.' There were cat-calls and even a whistle as everyone joined in the tease.

When the women gather together there is little of the reticence or modesty they display with their husbands. I saw realisation move slowly across Heavenly's face and she blushed, as she finally understood the jokes. There was a lot of amiable chat aimed at her, her husband's return, his short trousers, and even comments on his fine legs. When we had finished and turned to walk away, Aphrodite had the last word. 'You still look tired, after your illness. Get home and rest – you'll need all your strength for your husband.'

Back on the path, the girls ran ahead and I was glad of the chance to speak to Heavenly alone. 'The Panagia must smile on you, my friend. You are surely blessed with all the luck in a single day that the rest of us would be happy to see in a lifetime.' She looked puzzled so I said slowly and clearly, 'Now the village expects you to be pregnant. Surely you see? Aphrodite has answered all your problems.'

Her face cleared at once. 'They think I will carry my husband's child? Is that what you are saying? That I can pretend this,' and she stroked her belly, 'is the result of Hugh's return?'

I was nodding with excitement. 'It's the answer to everything for you.'

But instead of her smiles, there were tears. 'Oh,' she said, 'if only life were as simple as your dreams. How can this be Hugh's baby? Tell me, how can I make it happen?' She told me then what she had never told me before, that her husband is not able to make sex with her. He has almost never been able to. 'That is one of the reasons why Christo has changed my life. He taught me everything; all the things I never knew I could feel; passion, desire, tenderness. Oh, you know well what I mean, everything that is felt between a husband and wife, lovers.'

The girls were transfixed by a hawk that soared up and then, wheeling around, swooped down on the next hillside. The air filled for a moment or two with the shrieks and cries of the small animal it had chosen as prey then silence as, stately and proud, it flew off to its nest with its prize.

'I wouldn't know.' I was blushing now like a schoolgirl. 'I've always believed that what you describe was for men to feel. Women suffer what they are given and bear the children. I'm not the one to ask if there is anything more than that. From what I hear the women in this village say, they get all that . . . that . . . business over as quickly as possible. It's their duty, no more nor less, it seems to me.'

My mind was busy and full of thoughts as we continued our journey back to Heavenly's house. When we arrived, there was no sign of her husband, just a note pinned to the door telling her he had gone up the mountain again to find his friend in the cave with the wireless set.

'He leaves tomorrow,' she said as we followed her in.

'You have tonight, then.'

She sighed and her eyes were cloudy with distress and anxiety. 'To do what? What can I achieve tonight that I have never managed before?'

'You can't give up hope. You can't be defeated like this.' I shooed the girls to the other end of the big room. 'Go and play,' I said. 'Get Heavenly's fabrics and make something, GO ON!' They ran more in fear of my rage than eagerness to play, I think, but just now I didn't care.

'At least,' I said, 'at least now there will be no surprise in the village that you are with child. No one will point and question and stare and gossip. What could be better? Your husband came home and you made a baby together, hoorah!'

'And then? Then, when the baby comes and the war is over and Hugh comes to take me back to Athens? What then?'

She was determined to think of everything that could go wrong instead of seizing the possibilities that all could be right. 'He may be many things, my husband, but he is not a fool. The village may believe that he and I have happily made a baby together, but he will know full well that it cannot have happened, cannot be his child. I am sorry to say this to you, but when he sees his seed spilled in the sheets he knows it is not going anywhere else.'

I blushed again at her directness, her openness, in sharing these secrets with me. I seized her hand in mine. She was hot, trembling and her fingers shook as I clutched at them.

'You have tonight, still, dear friend. Maybe it will be different. You must help him, make it good for him, not

265

hasty. Slow, slow, sweet and easy. You must try, so much depends on it.'

'And if it fails?'

'Oh, you are not talking like my English friend now!' I was angry and let myself go on when perhaps it would be wiser to stop. 'You are planning this to be a disaster, listen to you. You must prepare for him, as you would for . . . for your lover. Bathe yourself, smell sweet, wash your hair; put flowers on your bed, anything. Give him warm sweet wine, just a little, mind you, not a lot. And love him as you have never done before.'

The children were back now and Voula was tugging at my skirts. They were hungry – we must leave now. At least she was smiling as she walked with us to the door.

'I hear what you are saying. I will try and do what you say, I promise. I loathe deception but maybe . . .'

'Loathe deception? It is a little late now to worry about such niceties.'

She winced at my words. 'I will come and find you later tomorrow, when Hugh has gone. Wish me luck.'

That night I slept uneasily. I thought of Heavenly trying to coax her husband into making love to her. What an irony! I longed only for peace from mine. It is some months now since he bothered me at night. Frequently he slept in the chair by the fire, his dog at his feet. Or didn't sleep at all as he was elsewhere.

Did he go with prostitutes when he went to Sitia, I wondered? I could not care less. Unless he spent our hard-earned money there, but what could I do? Tell him not to? What a thought!

Voula was fretful and I had to rise and go to her more than once. Despina slept peacefully on.

At about three o'clock I took Voula downstairs and, cradling her in my arms, tried to talk her back to sleep. The night was stuffy and airless. A low-lying mist gave an eerie silence to the world. Like everyone, I longed for the freshness of a rainfall, craved the coolness of a breeze on my skin.

I whispered to Voula that if she wished we could visit the newborn kid and see if the mother was giving it milk. Once or twice, I have hand-reared these young goats if their mothers reject them and both the girls love to help me. 'Poor Voula,' I said, 'I think you have a painful ear. Will it help you to forget it if we feed the baby goat?'

Thumb in mouth she nodded and we went into the garden and down to the goat hut at the end, past the vegetables. I keep this ramshackle old wooden building as a kind of nursing shed for any of the animals in need. Manolis has no patience with them and has often suggested throwing them to his dog and burning the wood of the shed.

The mist was clearing now and in the sky the moon was full, casting long shadows across the trees. It was fresher out here and Voula slid to the ground and, still sucking her thumb, ran to find the baby goat and its mother. Sure enough, the kid was bleating pathetically, the mother stretched out lazily beside it, blinking with one eye and otherwise ignoring its pleas. I guess we were there for half an hour or so, but my little one had surely forgotten her earache and fell asleep in my arms as we walked through the garden to the house.

I paused for a moment before going in. The clouds that had earlier fogged the sky had mostly cleared and the stars shone so bright again, it was like a sky full of candles. There was the evening star, the brightest of all, directly over the roof.

The windows looked blindly back at me and the air was so still, I fancied I could hear the rustle of an owl's wing in a nearby cypress tree.

There was no sign of Manolis in his chair. His dog lay across the foot of the stairs and growled as I pushed past it. Slowly, I went up the stairs and into the girls' room where Voula slept alone these nights. She didn't stir as I laid her on her bed and pulled the blanket up to her chin. I sat with her for a moment or two, my eyes heavy and tiredness sweeping over me.

And then, what sound was that?

There was a soft shuffling, then a creaking from elsewhere. Something was moving where there should only be stillness and silence. A whisper of a gasp, was that it? Was it Despina perhaps? Was there a low, hoarse, breathy noise? A rhythmic sort of murmur? Or was I imagining sounds where none should be? But I felt strange, uneasy and a shiver ran through me.

Silently I crept along the few steps of the landing and paused at the door of my room where Despina slept now. It was closed. I clearly remembered leaving it open lest she woke. Slowly, gently, I pushed at the worn wood panel of the door and it swung silently open. Manolis, with unusual alacrity, had oiled the lock and latch at my request barely a week ago. The skylight in the beamed roof and the open dormer let the moonlight shine in in folds across the floor and over the furniture. Then, as it went behind a cloud, there was only black darkness.

As my eyes grew accustomed to the shadows any sound in the room had stopped. So still was it, I found it eerie, frightening. Then there was a sudden low sound like a breath, then silence again.

I could not move as I saw what was happening there, what had caused the noises I had heard. For a moment only I froze, even my eyes unblinking and then I flew like the wind across the room to the bed, grabbing Manolis by the back of his neck and the collar band of his jerkin, pulling him off our daughter and throwing him to the floor. I do not know where my strength came from. I knew by instinct to be silent, lest Voula hear.

'You animal,' I hissed, as I reached down and pulled Despina into my arms. Her eyes stared up at me, almost blindly. Her nightgown was pulled up exposing her thighs and the lower half of her body to the moonlight. Her budding womanhood was bruised and reddened.

Over my shoulder I saw my husband scrabble to his feet and leave the room.

'Oh my baby, my little Despoula.' I rocked her in my arms. Our tears mingled as they fell. Her small mouth opened and she gasped in breath after breath of air. I could only repeat over and over, 'My baby, my baby.'

I think I could feel every bone in her thin little body. She was so vulnerable, this child. I carried her across the room and heard a slam from down the stairs. Manolis had gone.

I bathed her as gently as I could with the cool water in the basin. There was no blood. The time for that was clearly well past. How long had she suffered this, my baby? I shuddered and forcibly pulled myself together. As I laid her down she clung to me even harder.

And then, 'Mama,' she whispered, 'Mama.' The first words she had uttered for weeks, and I had never heard a sweeter sound.

HEAVENLY

I reached across and slowly, tentatively, touched his arm. He was awake and reached for me within a minute.

The first part of the evening I had spent so deep in the planning of how to seduce my husband that eventually when we lay in the bed, he went to sleep almost at once. I had prepared a meal that I thought he would like – goat begged from Irini, fresh and quickly roasted on a bed of autumn fruits – and he ate it greedily. To me it tasted like roast lamb, and the leaves of mint I had chopped and sprinkled across the top served to complete this make-believe English dinner. The wine I served was from Anthi's Pappous, rose-tinted and fragrant, it was the best of last year's harvest and, heeding Anthi's advice, I hid the second bottle so that we shared the one flask between us.

I bathed and washed my hair and dressed in one of the last frocks I had that had come to the island with me; pale, ashes-of-roses silk and although the moths had made a start on it, it was mostly intact. They had nibbled away at the neckline so that it appeared to plunge and leave the tops of my, now, full breasts exposed. As I slipped it on I had a sudden panic that it was something other than moths that had feasted here; could moths eat so much, so neatly? But tonight there was no room for thoughts of past horrors. Thank the lord it fitted, just. The little rounding of my belly had been compensated for by the weight I had lost during the sickness.

I tried to think of Christo, but I hated myself so much for

that deception that I stopped and thought only of Hugh. Hugh as I had first known him, first fell in love with him.

It wasn't so easy, he had changed; he had had more years of rich-living in Paris and Athens than I, and it had not been kind to his face or his body – he had aged more than his years. If I looked closely, his hair was thinning now and there was an odd, downward turn to his eyes.

He had eaten the kid eagerly and asked for more. So busy was he feasting he didn't notice that I ate almost nothing. 'You have become a fine cook,' he said. 'I suppose needs must here, eh? No servants around. I must say I would miss that side of embassy life; no one to clean your shoes or press your clothes. There's a lot to be said for it.'

He rose from the table and reached out for my hand to lead me out onto the terrace.

If we were looking for romance, this was indeed a wonderful night for it; the air soft as a whisper, the filmy gold light of the moon and the sky full of stars. In the distance I heard the call of a night bird and the last cicadas of the summer crickety-cracking away.

'I wish you hadn't chucked out my old coffee pot,' he said, cutting through the sweet atmosphere. 'I can't abide that thick, gluey stuff you drink here.' And he belched softly.

We sat for a while in silence and then Hugh started to speak of the early days of our courtship. He remembered so many little things, details I had long forgotten; the Copper Kettle, the films we saw, the meals we had often snatched between my shifts. He made me laugh tonight, just as he used to do. He said, 'You have probably long forgotten all these silly things, but lonely nights in Athens are when I think back to all that fun we had together, just the two of us.' He turned to me and his face, with all these memories, seemed to lose years in the telling; his smile as jaunty and flirtatious as it used to be. And looking in his eyes I saw all the love he had given me over the years. Impulsively I reached out, took his hand and held it to my face, shielding my eyes lest he see my tears.

'The sun here has brought your freckles out and added some, I think.' I tried to smile at him. 'Truth is, it was one of the things I loved about you, your freckles. And your hair. And how you used to fall over or trip up at the slightest thing.'

I looked at him in surprise. 'But they were all the things I hated about myself.'

'I know. But they were some of the things that made you so different from all those other girls. What did you call them?' I opened my mouth to tell him and he put his fingers on my lips. 'No, don't, I've got it, the Minky, Mouse and Boo girls. Don't cry,' he continued, 'no need to be sad. When all this . . . this nonsense is over, this stupid war, we'll have each other again, we'll be together and get on with whatever life has dealt us.' And then we left the terrace and went down the stairs to bed.

For a long while in the bedroom we lay together holding hands, I think each of us lost in our own thoughts, and then slowly I realised he had fallen asleep. I was instantly wakeful; I gently stroked his arm and he woke at once and reached for me. Within moments he was touching me between the legs and my body responded automatically – I wanted him. But he stopped, too soon, and eagerly mounted me, calling my name aloud, pushing insistently to try and enter me. But he failed and came at once, sadly, wetly, spurting once again onto the stiffening sheet.

We lay side by side in the rumpled, sweaty bed. I felt I should apologise to him, make this my fault. Surely his despair would be less if he were not to blame? But he laughed, a harsh, dry laugh, turned away from me and then wept into the pillow. It had been an awkward, urgent, graceless act, nothing more.

I put my arm across his back and my hand stroked him up and down, up and down. He accepted my comfort and took one of my hands, kissing it softly, saying again and again, 'I'm sorry, I'm so sorry.'

Poor Hugh; such a brave-talking figure of romance and here between ourselves he was enfeebled and helpless.

We lay for the rest of the night mostly sleepless, at first side by side. There was nothing to be said, so we didn't speak. Once, I reached again for him, but it was so obviously in desperation he gently pushed my hand away without a word.

And then, 'My dear wife, dear Evadne,' and he took my hand in his. 'We have been apart too long. I should have . . . I wish . . . If only . . . too late now. But soon, eh? Together, properly together. Out of this place.' And as he spoke he raised my hand to his lips.

The mechanics of preparing for his departure took up most of the morning. He dressed himself again in his villager's clothes that I had washed as best I could and dried in the sun. But they seemed stiff and uncomfortable to me. I gave him bread and fruit, some wine and a flask of raki and then suddenly he was ready and there was nothing else to do to keep him here. We were both so awkward with each other. I was full of sadness, with reasons more numerous than I could say, and it was with a voice breaking with emotion that I said goodbye.

He walked to the steps and then, all at once, he turned to me, holding out his hands, and there was such a pleading in his eyes, I took him in my arms.

'Take care,' I said, and pushing me slightly back from him he said, 'I love you, Heavenly. Try and remember that. I've never loved anyone else and I miss you desperately. My life in Athens is empty and lonely without you.'

And he was gone and I was alone and all that I could think at that moment was that, for the very first time, he had called me Heavenly.

ANTHI

It was weeks before I saw my husband again. I learnt he was staying with his brother Stelios.

Despina's recovery was slow. Sometimes there were days when she didn't say a word. Some days she was locked so tightly inside herself that even her eyes were like blind eyes, unseeing. I tried to speak to her about her father, about what had happened, but that only served to lock her further away. It was obvious she wanted to bury it somewhere deep inside. What didn't change was that she seemed never to leave my side. She became my shadow, and soon I didn't even notice that any more.

The rhythm of my life changed daily. That was as usual. The sun came and went, sometimes it rained, sometimes it was dry. Winter came in slowly that year and crept away again and it was spring almost without our noticing.

I performed my seemingly never-ending tasks in a grey haze of misery and fatigue. It seemed sometimes I didn't even have the strength to fear what would become of us, my girls and me.

Every day, I thought I would speak of this to Yaya and Pappous, but every time I was with them and opened my mouth to say the words, I stopped, changed my mind again and again. I wanted him dead, and I knew my Pappous would kill him, shoot him without a thought if I asked, but such an act would set in line a chain of events that would surely ruin all our lives, so it seemed too horrendous to contemplate.

Heavenly knew there was something wrong. We had come

to know each other so well, she and I, that I couldn't hide any secret from her. In the first days, when all I felt was a terrible icy rage, I stayed away from her. School had started again and we met there, but I avoided going to her house, and she kept away from mine. From time to time she gave me a quizzical look and sometimes even a hug in passing. I was grateful for that. And then one day she said, 'Remember I am your friend now and always will be, I hope. You have been so wonderful to me. I will always be here for you.'

She was increasingly obviously with child. All looked at her, but few spoke. Until one day Aphrodite at the spring, where else, said, 'So your husband didn't come from Athens for nothing, I see, Heavenly.'

She blushed and smiled but didn't answer.

Eventually I asked her, 'Was it successful, your seduction?'

Her face crumbled. The smile had gone and she closed her eyes tight against the world.

'I don't know what I am going to do. No, everything was as always with Hugh.' She stroked her hand across her swelling belly. 'This is Christo's child and mine and I have a few short months to enjoy that and then I don't know what I will do.'

But then Manolis was back and I could think of nothing else. He walked in one night as though nothing had happened. Sat at the table and banged a knife up and down. He was waiting for food. My mind raced, supposing I refused him? Say I ignored him completely and left him to do his own cleaning, cooking? Tend his crops and fields and sheep and goats, what then? He would throw me out of the house, that's what. And my girls?

I felt sick to my heart, as I realised he now had a use for them, so he wouldn't let me take them, would he? The image of him with Despina would never leave me. Every night when I closed my eyes he was there behind my eyelids. And Voula would be next. I couldn't bear it, so I gave him food. I washed his clothes and I tended his flocks and looked after his garden and waited on him as I always had, but inside I knew I must find a way out of this. And soon.

Despina turned her back to him and sat hunched over herself in the corner. Thankfully he ignored her too. But Voula was pleased to have him back and ran to him laughing. He ignored her, concentrating only on his food and chewing each mouthful, slow and ugly. Voula tugged at his shirt. He stared at his plate. She looked puzzled and backed away. Then she ran up to him and clapped her hands. 'Woof woof,' she barked. His old dog pricked an ear but nothing else. Again and again she barked, nothing. It was a sad sight. I wanted to weep. She only wanted his attention. She mooed like a cow, miaowed like a cat. Manolis finished his food, pushed his plate away and then reaching down he grabbed her up and into his arms. She giggled and wriggled but he held her tight, and a slow smile creased his face. 'My Voula,' he said, and a sick, cold chill ran through me.

Despina and Voula and I all shared the one bed now. When he was in the house my two little ones were never out of my sight; Voula, especially, was so full of energy, she ran everywhere. By the evening of each day I was exhausted, but I only slept for an hour at most. I would jerk awake, then look around in fear, hold my girls and try and think myself back to sleep again.

Sometimes I could hear him moving about in the night. I smelt the burnt tang of his tobacco in the air. In the mornings smeared, greasy dishes littered the table, smelling of strong wine and cheese. Sometimes, as I lay in bed sleepless, I heard him pacing the floor beneath me, the squeaking leather sound of his fart.

One morning I came down as usual, Despina tight by my side. Voula had scrambled down ahead of us, full of giggles and eager to start the day. His eyes followed us around the room as I prepared their food. I poured a bowl of coffee and placed it at the end of the table. My hand was shaking. Standing, he drank it down in one and walked to the door before turning briefly and saying, 'I'll be back.' And he was gone.

Yaya was busy baking when we arrived at her house that

morning. Voula ran straight to her and dipped her finger into the bowl to lick the dough she was making. 'Not for you, little one,' said Yaya gently, pushing her fingers away. She looked at me momentarily as she began to knead the pastry.

'These are for the funeral gathering later,' she said. 'Did you know the widow Bigorakis died last night?' She shook her head. 'Not many will mourn her passing, she was a miserable old witch after her husband died.' She crossed herself hastily three times. 'Forgive me, Panagia mou, but I speak the truth.'

She took a bunch of green tansy from the side table and, clearing a space, started to arrange the plant for chopping. Pulling off the bright yellow button-like flowers, she put them to one side. 'Tansy biscuits,' she said. 'Not many remember now, but we always used to make these for a funeral. Dangerous stuff, tansy – if you eat too much before the funeral, you will end up sharing the box with the corpse.'

I remembered suddenly Glykeria's potion for Heavenly. I knew it was potent, but not that it was dangerous. 'How much is too much?'

She indicated the flowers she had cast aside. 'If I used all of those with all of these,' and she pointed to the reddish stalks she was chopping finely, 'it would be enough to kill a strong man. I only make these biscuits occasionally now. I'd hate to give convulsions to half the inhabitants in Kato Panagia.'

'Stop, miss!' and she pushed Voula's hand away.

Within minutes the tray of moulded biscuits was in the oven. I stopped her arm as she swept the remains of the tansy and the flowers into her apron. She looked up.

'I have many of these growing with my vegetables, they have a good smell; like rosemary.'

'You should dig them up and burn them lest the children get at them; they're certainly pretty and sweet-smelling, but they can be lethal.' She saw my face and mistook it for puzzlement, saying, 'I'm serious. Carelessness with something so toxic, so deadly, could be fatal.'

'Of course,' I said, but with her words my mind was already far away from here.

It was a glorious spring day, good to be alive. We walked across the hills towards home and it seemed everywhere I went I saw those same yellow flowers of tansy. To my mind the scent in the air was heavy with them. Did everyone know how dangerous it was?

But in my garden I didn't cut them back, as Yaya said. I stood and looked at them and my mind filled with dark thoughts. I shivered, although the day was hot, and ushered the girls inside. In the house I made a vegetable stew; there was not much meat around, no one was killing. Waiting for Easter. As I was chopping the leeks and root vegetables small, my eyes kept going to the open window. A thin breeze seemed to fill the air with this heavy smell of the yellow flowers, so I added some garlic to my pot and that had its own pungency.

'Shall we take Heavenly some eggs, Mama?' It was the longest sentence and the most positive idea Despina had had in weeks.

We met Heavenly on the road to her house. She was coming to see us.

'I must walk every day,' she said, 'or I'll be as fat as a pie.'

So together we walked. The girls were carrying the eggs in their aprons so our progress was slow, but we did arrive eventually and sat on Heavenly's shady terrace. She fanned herself with a leaf. 'I have five more months and twenty days to call this baby mine. After that, when it is born,' she shrugged, her face stricken, 'I have no idea what I will do. It's a boy, I am sure. He kicks hard already.'

'I wish I lived here, I hate our house,' said Despina suddenly. 'Can we live here with you, Heavenly?'

'And me, and me!' said Voula, jumping up and down.

I was still, silent.

'You can stay here whenever you like. I would love to have your company, you know that.'

And then a thought came creeping into my head and for a moment I shivered.

'Perhaps just for one night then,' I said hesitantly.

'Oh yes, yes,' said Voula.

'Of course,' said Heavenly and Despina looked at me, a smile whisking over her sombre little face.

'Tonight?' she said. 'Oh please, Mama, tonight.'

'Tonight, tonight, yes!' giggled Voula.

'Is Manolis home just now?'

'Yes, but it won't bother him whatever we do. I'll go and . . .'

'. . . get some things,' Heavenly finished the sentence for me. 'We'll be fine while you're gone, won't we, girls? You can help me do some cooking, for our supper.' They were pushing her towards her kitchen as I left.

I pulled a few of the girls' things together when I got home. I went to the hearth and stared at the cast iron pot on its heavy iron hook, the lid covered in embers. The vegetables inside were almost cooked.

It was as though I was in a dream. My head was in a whirl and my hands were shaking. I stood there as the sky slowly darkened.

I don't know how much time had passed before I left the house, ran through the garden, along the path and, breathing heavily, finally arrived back at Heavenly's house, the warm feeling of safety sweeping through me.

HEAVENLY

Manolis Manadakis died on the day the Germans entered Athens.

Well, that was the day his body was found. He had been missing for two or three days. But as his movements were never consistent, no one could be quite sure. The night Anthi and the girls stayed with me was the last time anyone remembered seeing him alive.

I heard that he was found at the bottom of a ravine, less than a quarter of a mile from his house. Yorgo, who of course made a coffin for the burial, was eager to tell me as many of the gory details as he could, with plenty of his own imaginings, I felt sure. It was his cousin who had found the body. 'Rabbiting, he was, and his dog brought back a bit of a man's hand. Covered in dried blood, just the one finger and a piece of the palm. All gnawed up by wild animals—'

'Stop!' I said, 'Anthi is my friend. I don't need to hear all this.'

'Nasty business,' he said, determined not to cut short a good story. 'They saw him in the kafenion the night he went missing. Sick he was, terribly sick and not in his right mind. Talking gibberish. Looked dreadful, they said, like a corpse already and he'd fouled his clothes.' He shook his head. 'They reckon he was taken bad, lost his footing on the way home and fell down the path. It's dangerous over there if it's dark and there's a lot of cloud. Of course,' he crossed himself three times in quick succession and lowered his voice, 'I'm sorry to say he wasn't much liked around about. He had his own little

280

group of royalist friends, including Papa Yannis, but not many others.'

I sat out on the terrace knitting; Aphrodite had shown me how and gave me wool she had gathered from her goats, washed in the spring water and spun into fine soft yarn.

There had been only one short note from Hugh since he had left. I knew that he had arrived back in Athens safely, little else. Although it sounded as though it had been a hard journey, with many escapes.

Anything I knew about the progress of the war came from the wireless set in the Piperia. Yorgo knew that I was always hungry for news so he came here most days, to give me bulletins.

I guessed the royal family were in Crete now. But was Hugh with them?

I dropped a stitch and pushed the thought from my mind. I couldn't follow this through. In the village no one seemed to think we were in any danger; except Anthi's grandfather who said it was only a matter of time.

After Hugh left, I was alone with my secret for days. I had very little sickness, fortunately, but I was tired all the time. I wanted to sleep and sleep. And then, just at the time I calculated I was three months pregnant, I started to be full of energy all day, every day. And then Christo came.

I was sitting where I always sat these days, on the terrace.

It was one of those glorious spring days when everything seemed full of the promise of good things to come. I was knitting. I didn't hear him arrive, or come in through the house. Suddenly he was there in front of me, standing very upright and his eyes met mine and it was as if I could see in them everything there had ever been between us; all the love, the laughter, the tears. I stood up and took a step towards him. He didn't move and I thought, I can see all the things I want to see but can I also see fear? Sadness?

I whispered his name. 'Christo?'

'Am I welcome here?' he said.

'Do you need to ask?'

'Yes, I think I need to ask.' And he took a step backwards,

away from me. 'I want you to know I am here to bring you news of the war. Unless you know all that is happening from your husband?'

'I know almost nothing,' I said.

'I understand from my uncle's wife that you have every reason to be very careful of yourself.' He was turning away from me now, his eyes flickering around the terrace.

'You understand only a little of what is true then.'

At last his eyes were still, looking at me, quizzical slightly. 'Are you saying you are not with child?' And then he looked away from me again. 'I apologise to you, I have no right to ask any questions, especially not of such intimacy.'

'Look at me, please,' I begged. 'I cannot bear you to look away from me, speak to me like that, as if . . . as if we are strangers.' He turned his head towards me just a little and I moved in front of him, close. He could not avoid me now. I was so close I could feel his breath. Smell the warmth of his body. I willed him not to step away from me. He stayed.

I lifted my arm just a little and touched him. I breathed deeper.

'You are not wrong,' I said quietly. 'I am carrying a child, and I am careful with myself because this child here,' and I took his hand in mine and lifted it to my body, 'here,' and I pressed his hand close, 'is our child. Yours and mine. And nothing is more precious to me than this.'

I had imagined this scene many times; in my dreams we were sitting by the embers of the fire and I would say, 'I am having a child and it is yours.'

I waited for him to ask me how I knew it was his; question me about how I could be so sure. But he didn't. From the moment I told him, he believed me.

Later, of course, when we did sit by the fire together, when night had fallen and a spring chill shivered the air, we talked. I told him a very little of Hugh's visit but he asked nothing, wanted no details and I was grateful for that.

We spoke of his family and mine. As he lay at my feet, his head in my lap, he told me for the first time of the sadness of his sister. The irony not lost on either of us, her longing for a child and her seeming inability to bring one to term.

He spoke of Bingo in his cave. How he had come to really like and admire the young man, his determination to be in the front line of any action and his frustration at staying in the backwater of Panagia. Still he didn't mention Hugh's visits there. He was keen to give me such news of the war as he had. He told me of brave villagers dying in the north of Greece as they struggled to fight the advancing German army. He is convinced that Crete will be invaded.

'I can smell it in the wind, the threat of occupation. The men in my village, my family, we always know. We have never been wrong before. My grandfather was butchered by the Turks when they came and no one listened when he tried to warn them. He knew!'

Bingo is involved in some new secret intelligence and has promised to share any news with Christo and Andros. 'We shall resist, we are ready to fight here whether it is the Italians or the Germans who come.'

We sat in silence for a while. For me it was joyous to simply be with him again. Night fell and through the open terrace door we could see the stars, then the moon, full and rich. We made love and it was just as it had always been. He was so careful of me, so gentle, tender.

'I won't break,' I protested, 'this is not an illness, you know.'

We made love again; this time full of passion and I felt my womb contract a little as I came. It was a thrilling feeling and I made him put his hand quickly on my belly. He seemed in awe of my breasts. I am indeed very proud of them! They are swollen and tender and the nipples turning darker still, 'ready for our child to feed from,' I told him.

'How will we . . . ?' I stopped him asking any questions that began with 'how'. Or 'when'. I have no idea how we are going to cope with any future life together as a family; so best not to speak of it. I know we should, we must, but not just now, not yet. He was so kind with me, gazing with such love in his eyes.

'Every moment of every day I will be with you in my heart. You and this, this . . . little person of ours here.' And he stroked my growing mound. 'I will never leave you again. You know that, don't you? I smiled, nodding my head. 'Yes I will be gone sometimes when I must, when there is no choice, but I will always come back to you.'

And then, only days later, Yorgo came, puffed up with the importance of his mission, and told me he must escort me to the 'Englishman in the wireless cave'.

He said to tell me he had information for me. 'It's so important and secret,' said Yorgo, 'that even I must not know what it is.' As if Yorgo was usually the one person in the village to be informed of every important development. I hid a smile as I walked quickly after him and along the path.

There was no sign of Christo or Andros, just Bingo sitting alone, cigarette in his mouth outside in the warm sunlight. He jumped to his feet as I approached and stamped his cigarette out, fussing around me. He was a good-looking young man, in that very English way; wide-eyed, innocent with a warm grin always ready. His sandy hair was ruffled and in need of a cut and his face was freckled, like mine, from the sun.

'Oh, Mrs Timberlake, er, I wasn't sure if I did the right thing in dragging you up here?'

'If you have some news, you did absolutely the right thing and why don't you call me Heavenly like everyone else?'

'Oh, yes, thank you, Heavenly. There was a communiqué from the British Embassy. Actually it was from my brother, you know him, I think?'

'Foxy? Of course!' And as I said his name his face flashed into my mind, so like his brother here. I felt a pang, a passing moment of missing him, Hugh and all of them. I felt that so rarely these days it took me by surprise.

'Actually, Hugh is back here on Crete. He has been escorting some . . . er . . . some really important . . . er . . .'

'It's OK, Bingo, you don't need to say it. I know what you are referring to.'

'You do?' He was clearly relieved. 'Oh right, well those people, they all got out of Athens and here to Suda Bay. You know it's—'

'Yes, Bingo, I know what it is.'

'Well they may have to move on; possibly to the house of that archaeologist chap, Arthur Evans. Foxy said no one was quite sure where they would end up, but Hugh is there with them and he wants you to know that he is safe. They all are but he can't leave them. Not even for a short time. They must be prepared to travel at a moment's notice.'

Poor Bingo, he was getting a bit pink now. 'So he, Hugh that is, sends his love and, er, says he misses you.' I smiled and thanked him.

'I hope I did the right thing?' he said. 'But Foxy said you were sure to want to know.'

'Oh I do,' I said. 'Thank you so much.'

I sat on for a little. A hawk on a branch high above sat motionless, watching the details of a small world getting smaller; a brilliant butterfly, scarlet and blue; moths flickering over bending grass stems; shadows which belong to nothing. I got to my feet again clumsily, thinking, If I'm moving like this now, lord knows what I'm going to be like in a few months time.

So Hugh had come back here with the King and presumably the royal household and the Prime Minister. It really was such an important job; I was happy for him and, yes, proud. He wouldn't be entrusted with something so vital for Greece unless he was really highly regarded in the embassy. I was grateful that it would keep him occupied. It would be disastrous if he came to Panagia now. I was beginning to show and I was foolishly miles away from any decisions.

As I walked slowly back down the mountain it came to me that nothing would ever be the same again. Nothing ever is; I suppose it's called being alive.

ANTHI

There was such a lifting of my heart that I had to fight to keep myself from smiling every day. I wished I could pretend to feel any of the grief I should show. If I looked at Voula, I could catch her sadness, her bewilderment and that helped. The poor little girl was barely old enough to understand her beloved Papa was dead. It was all a mystery to her. When I told them Despina simply said, 'What will happen to his dog?' but Voula at first looked puzzled and then said, 'Mama, when will he come back?'

'Never, stupid,' said her sister. 'He has gone to the Panagia, if she will have him, and no one ever comes back from there, do they, Mama?'

'Yes they do! The Panagia's son Jesus came back after three days.'

Despina laughed scornfully at her. It worried me. It was too harsh a reaction and unlike her usual kind self. She was a changed child.

'Be careful with her. She had no reason not to love her papa,' I warned her.

Manolis's brother Stelios came as soon as he heard the news and I sent him to Papa Yannis's house, to view the body.

When Manolis was found, at the bottom of the ravine, I hoped at first that he had simply got drunk, stumbled and fell. It would not be the first time someone had died that way. But I could not fool myself for long. They told me he had nothing to drink in the kafenion that night, that he was ill already when he arrived there; complaining of stomach cramps.

Papa Yannis took the body. It was so badly mutilated it would not be fit for the children to see. I think he was genuinely upset by the events; certainly he wept enough for both of us. Stelios and my mother helped him wash and prepare the body for the burial.

My mother immediately took charge. She loves ordering everyone around and there is nothing like a death to bring out the worst in her. She provided the grey hemp shroud he would be wrapped in; does she keep a supply of them, always ready?

She came to tell me the coffin would be sealed at once and there would be no viewing of the body. I was cleaning the house when she came. She exclaimed and snatched the broom from my hand. 'What are you doing? You must never do this so soon after a death, you will sweep his soul away!'

Voula, thumb in mouth, silently followed her around the house as she closed windows and pulled the shutters together. She emptied all the vessels and jars of water, throwing it across the yard before she refilled them. 'Thanks be to the Panagia,' she said, 'that he died on the twelfth of the month. One more day and she would never take him.'

She opened the cupboards, sniffing in jars and containers. I said nothing. I knew what she wanted. 'No sweetmeats, Mother,' I said

'We must talk about your future, and what you are going to do.'

She was such an interfering old witch! Sometimes it was hard for me to be polite to her, even after all this time.

'I shall manage well enough alone, thank you.'

'Huh, you say that now but you'll be complaining soon enough. Take those beads off too, you are in mourning, remember.' My hand went to my neck and the necklace of carnelian pieces that my Yaya had given me on my name day.

'You know nothing of customs, do you? You have always

gone your own way. Well, there will be plenty of talk if you forget the rules now.'

The next day, the day of the funeral, was one of those grey days when the darkness never seems to lift entirely. After days of warm spring sunshine it seemed fitting that the sky should be filled with heavy cloud and rain threatened all morning. At first light I took the girls to spend the day with Yaya. Pappous was to accompany me to the service and together we went to Papa Yannis's house. At noon, the bells started to toll in the church and under lowering skies a thin line of mourners stretched silently outside the priest's house.

I looked quickly round. Although Manolis was liked by few when he was alive, nonetheless it was the duty of everyone who knew him even slightly to attend his burial, and most of Kato Panagia was there. I kept my head down and pulled my kerchief forward to hide my face. Pappous thrust a large white linen square into my hand. I looked at him with curiosity.

'For your tears,' he said quietly. I nodded quickly, wiping my eyes and blowing my nose loudly.

As is the custom, Pappous walked with the other village men at the rear of the small procession, just ahead of my mother, my sister and me.

My mother was one of the few who wailed noisily with grief, but as we got to the church several others joined her.

Papa Yannis was cantor and intoned the prayers for the dead as we approached Manolis's family plot. Just before the coffin was laid into the freshly dug pit, the priest placed a piece of stone on it with the words, 'Jesus Christ conquers' etched into the surface.

My mother peered closely into my face as she wailed on. She would get no satisfaction from my tears, I determined, and turned my head aside.

There were no flowers for the grave, but Voula had picked some wild blossoms this morning and I threw them on top of the coffin as it was lowered, clumsily, into the grave by six village men.

'For Papa,' she had whispered as she gave them to me. Dear child, she knew and understood more than I gave her credit for.

Stelios wept silently at the side of the pit and fell to his knees whispering prayers, presumably for his brother's soul.

At last it was over and outside the church everyone washed their hands and shook them dry as they exchanged news and gossip; their grief quickly forgotten. My mother had prepared the funeral feast although these were lean times. When we got to her house I quickly scanned the table where a few biscuits and cakes were spread out, with some of Stelios's wine and raki. There were no tansy cakes here.

I watched them eat and drink and chatter together; they were quickly emptying their glasses and coming back for second measures.

This could go on for hours, I thought. I walked among them for a little time and overheard various snatches of conversation, none about my husband. It seemed he was already forgotten.

My mother bustled over to me. She was dressed, of course, in deepest black with not a single adornment. I reached to my neck as she approached and boldly pulled out my beads to sit comfortably under my own black collar.

The rich amber of the carnelians caught a ray of light from the door and it seemed they glowed. 'Ignore me if you want, you wilful girl. You'll be grateful enough when I find you a new husband. You will need help come the winter.'

'You did harm enough for one lifetime with the husband I have just buried, so don't bother yourself further, thank you.'

I pulled on Pappous' arm and we turned towards the door, about to leave, when Papa Yannis bumbled over to us, a large glass half empty in his hand.

'Anthi, dear Anthi,' he said, 'a sad day for all of us. Manolis was a good, wonderful friend of mine and I am sorry to raise the subject of money at such a time, but we must be ready for what comes next.' He glanced at Pappous, trying to hide his dislike of him and failing miserably.

I knew it was mutual and Pappous pushed me through the door ahead of him, saying over his shoulder to the priest, 'I will see that you will be paid for everything, but today is not the time to start harassing widows with small children to look after.' And we were gone.

Outside, Pappous shuddered. 'I have a feeling the Panagia will forgive me for my dislike of that odious priest. It's possible she has little time for him herself, but just in case . . .' and he crossed himself three times.

He took my arm as we walked and gently removed the white linen square still clutched in my hands. He shook it out; it was dry as a sun-bleached bone.

'Not too many tears then?'

I looked up at him, 'No, not too many.'

He was puffing a little as we walked up the hill; then paused and mopped his brow. Although fit, he was not as agile as he used to be, my Pappous, could he finally be getting old?

'These are bad times,' he said as we walked on, a little slower now. 'I suspect that if the Italians hadn't made such a mess of their attempted invasion, the Germans might have left them alone to get on with it. As it is, the mainland has now been savagely taken by the German army and many, many Greeks have lost their lives trying to keep them away. Not just soldiers, mind you, but peasant villagers, women, even children.'

We walked on through the grey gloom of the early afternoon and he paused under a tangled arch of bare brown trees that cornered a piece of dead waste ground, its earth blackened by a recent fire.

'We are supposed to gain things as we get older in return for the things we lose, but what have I gained?' He laughed but it was a sad, dejected sound; 'Wisdom? Not much of that. And what have I lost? So much, child, so much; youth and peace, the possibility of hope and optimism. Innocence? Ah that is long gone! As our future shrinks away our pasts grow longer.' A twig cracked under his foot and he kicked it away. 'And now it looks as if we face another invasion and how

290

many more of my friends will I bury? In 1896 and then in 1905 we thought each time that was it, that was the end of it.' He gave a deep sigh. 'We must find courage in our history again; Saracens, Venetians, Turks, they have all been seen off. Cretans have been martyrs for a thousand years. And now . . . ?'

So it was not only the funeral that had made my Pappous so gloomy today.

Back at his house, the girls had helped Yaya prepare a meal for us all. No reference was made by any of us to the burial, and in spite of Pappou's general air of gloom we were able to laugh at Voula's antics as she imitated the animals she had encountered in her short life – and invented some that she hadn't.

It was with a lighter step that I returned to our house that evening, hand in hand with my girls. As we approached it, Despina squeezed my hand in hers and looked up at me. I thought I could see peace in her eyes, but perhaps that was just my hope. Now this place held nothing for any of us to be afraid of, it could be a proper home.

I couldn't know it then, but soon our world would be so completely changed for us that nothing else was thought of; not Manolis's death, nothing at all.

HEAVENLY

I didn't go to Anthi's husband's funeral. In my condition it was easy to be excused and Anthi told me to stay at home. She seemed a different woman now, relaxed and calm. I warned her she must be careful. Nobody liked Manolis, but they expected to see his widow grieve. It was her girls I was most worried about. Sure, Despina was in so many ways back to normal as she was speaking again; but there was a knowing look in her eyes that I didn't recall seeing before, a hard coldness. I'm sure something happened to her during the last year, something that changed her. I'd no idea what it was, but it was strange that she seemed to accept the death of her papa with no tears.

Voula also, she seemed somehow older. The grief she felt for the loss of her father was almost tangible. She spoke of him often and her pretty eyes filled up with tears at once. Despina had no time for this and quickly and, I feel, quite cruelly, snapped at her to be quiet.

Stop pretending to cry,' she said. 'You don't fool any of us with this display. You're just trying to get attention.'

I never asked, never let my thoughts, my doubts ever come to the surface, but certainly each day that passed I felt a little shiver of wonder at the convenience of Manolis's death.

But then everything was swept out of all our minds; deaths, births, nothing mattered, except what was happening to our island.

*

On a glorious morning in May, a day when rightly we could expect a cloudless blue sky filled with singing birds, butterflies, the puff of a dandelion clock, instead, at early dawn, while the haze of night was lifting over land and sea like a veil and the red rising sun hovered over the horizon, a cry ran through the village: 'Umbrellas! Umbrellas! Come and see!'

And the weeks and months the Cretans had spent in denial were over, finished.

Later I learnt that in villages all over the island everyone ran outside to look up at the sky, shielding eyes against the early sun.

These were not umbrellas. Instead, the flying wings of the parachutes carrying German airmen came down, hundred after hundred after hundred, and then more. All the morning the air filled with the evil sound of the first bombs, swiftly followed by the terrible sad wailing of injured men, women and children. Dogs barked, animals ran wild with fear. Chaos. We should have known, should have been prepared.

Later, isn't it always later? With hindsight we realised the broadcast Christo had heard telling of the exile of the King to Cairo meant that Crete was no longer safe. It would be months, years before we knew the full extent of the tragedy that started that morning. Here in Panagia we were blessed, it seemed; we hardly saw a German. Of the few that landed here, the flyers must have escaped over the mountains with speed.

Instead, the Italian navy landed at Sitia and although their purpose was to move northwards to support the Germans, they did what they could to occupy our province and they proved, for the most part, to be enemy enough.

All that day and the next I sat on the terrace. Anthi came with her girls and we sat there together not speaking. Even the children seemed to understand that something momentous, something terrible, was happening on our very doorstep.

It took just eleven days for Crete to be occupied.

It was said that never had a people struggled so fiercely against an aggressor. Christo told me this. I hardly saw him; he and Andros and their compatriots from Panagia and nearby villages were part of the strongest resistance movement in Greece: the National Solidarity group, which offered food and relief to villages up and down the country besieged by the occupying forces that were looting and destroying wherever they went.

And all this, remember, with so few weapons! The arms amnesty that General Metaxas had declared had left the people of our province, and others, with so little for our own protection. But our village men fought with sticks and stones and the branches of trees, anything they could lay their hands on.

There were plenty of tales, rumours and gossip; in the beginning we could speak of little else. Aphrodite told me one morning of her cousin, Marina. We had gathered as always at the spring, even more often than usual, I think; we needed to be together to share the stories that we heard were happening elsewhere on the island.

Marina had been captured trying to help an Australian soldier and was thrown into a makeshift prison where she was made to listen to the cries of her brother as he was tortured in the room next door.

Aphrodite wept as she spoke. 'She was desperate for water and when one of the German soldiers spilt some, laughingly on the floor outside her cell, she was forced to take off her headkerchief and mop the water up with it and suck it out. Can you imagine that humiliation?' She wiped her face on her apron and we all understood and shared those feelings.

Everyone had a tale to tell; in one village they hanged dead Germans from trees but Angeliki said that her mother and aunt in Paleochora had found the body of one enemy soldier. 'He was a young man, barely out of school, they said, and while my father and uncle urged them to throw him in the sea, they refused, saying he was some poor woman's son.

They washed his body and wrapped it in one of her dowry sheets and dug a pit with farm tools in the churchyard.'

At first we appeared to be safe, unbothered by any enemy, and gradually a kind of normality returned – at least to the women – and talk was starting to be about such mundane things as my pregnancy.

They liked nothing more than to fill me with horror stories of endless days in labour, babies dropping to the ground in fields as mothers worked with the crops, One poor woman, apparently, gave birth in a graveyard as she tended her husband's tomb: 'She left the baby too long alone in the grass and it died, right there on her husband's grave!' Well that was what Aspasia told us one morning and no one offered a contradiction. Such were their tales that it seemed to me a miracle that anyone ever survived here.

The men gathered every night in the Piperia and listened to the radio. Everyone now was hungry for news. War, war and more war; it seemed it was everywhere, with German warships sinking British destroyers. War was bombs and killing. Women were not allowed in to listen; it was all about aggression, death and fear. War was unpredictable and therefore ugly. Not suitable for women and children. This enraged Anthi.

'Even Pappous tells Yaya and me to get on with other things! While our island is invaded we are expected to speak only about tomatoes and chickens, I suppose.'

They learnt from their broadcasts that the royal family and the prime minister and most of his government had fled from the capital and, escorted to safety by the British Embassy in Athens, it was suspected they had sheltered for a while in Crete. Their island! Although most of them despised the royals in peacetime, come the war all that was forgotten. Apparently Hugh had been singled out for mention in one bulletin. Of course I was proud.

But overall, I felt a sense of despair. Crete had been taken, occupied, and in spite of the incredible bravery of every Cretan, there was no longer a feeling here of safety.

What else might happen? We were all used to the anxieties of the approaching seasons, the harvests good or bad, the weather favourable or not, but now there was an underlying horror that was felt by every man, woman and child; what will happen tomorrow? How long will we be left alone in peace?

As it turned out, it was three weeks, two days and a few hours. Twelve o'clock on a warm and sunny morning, cocks crowing, a low-flying hawk, the song of birds winging nearby. In the baker's garden his bitch gave birth to a litter of six puppies. Anthi's goat, the one she had reared with Voula's help in her yard, gave a cry of surprise, pushed, and produced just one kid. Yorgo and his cousin Petros were preparing to set off for a day's hunting; the children had come from the school, running homewards with paint-spattered hands and grubby, smiling faces. The square was unusually full that day, that time. And then through the narrow streets of Kato Panagia came the sound of marching feet.

I was back from the spring, washing just a few things today, blowing sweetly in the gentle breeze. I had strolled to the square to meet Anthi and her girls. We were planning a picnic. And then we all heard the regular clack-clack-clackity-clack of boots on stone and we froze to the spot.

Dust rose in a cloud that made it difficult to see how many there were, but it seemed at least a dozen and a half men were coming down the hill in formation, two by two. At the front I saw immediately were Kotso and Bingo. They were tied to each other, roughly around the ankles and were stumbling, nearly falling as they walked. They looked proud and unafraid. The sun caught Bingo's fair, tousled hair and although I then saw both their hands were bound together, he bent and with his elbow pushed his fringe to one side leaving his freckled face open to the air. For a moment suddenly he looked about thirteen; not old enough even to smoke a cigarette or drink a glass of beer. Every time they tripped, the soldier behind pushed his rifle harshly in the back of one or other of them, and his fellows laughed and jeered.

No villager moved. Not a muscle twitched; everyone had, it seemed, taken root where they stood.

'*Kalimera*!' shouted the soldier in front. As the dust settled, I saw he had some medal or other on his grubby uniform. '*Kalimera*,' he shouted again. Angrily, he stamped his foot and said, in heavily accented Greek, 'Answer me when I speak to you, when I wish you good morning, villagers.' And then he swore in Greek and you could hear a faint shocked intake of breath from one or two men in the small crowd.

'*Kalimera*,' whispered a few voices.

He merely nodded in response. And then spoke rapidly to his men.

None of us understood, but it was soon clear what he meant as two soldiers stepped forward and, roughly shoving everyone aside, started tying Kotso and Bingo to the cross that stood in the square. The cross that was there to show anyone and everyone how many Panagians had died at the hands of the Turks in the early years of the century.

From the back of the square there was a sudden disturbance and one or two heads dared to turn to see what was happening. Coming to the front murmuring, 'Excuse me, excuse me,' to anyone in his way, was Anthi's Pappous. He was a magnificent sight. He was always a handsome, imposing figure, but today he shone with the air of a man in command. His *vrakes* were, as always, tucked into his high boots, that gleamed with the polish he could only have applied this morning.

His silver moustache glistened with oil and turned up at each corner as if in greeting to his splendid flat hat and draped red silk scarf hanging over his ear. In his hand he held the blue and white tissue-thin cotton of the Greek flag. He held it high and, tattered and old as it was, it moved just a little in the faint breeze. A brave and magnificent gesture from a proud man.

I could just see his wife, still at the back, anxiously watching his every move.

Within moments he was at the front and facing the soldier

with the medals. He was no taller than him but, even so, he outmeasured him in every way. He was our general, our leader, and I'm sure everyone there could feel it.

With authority he spoke: 'How may we assist you?' Ignoring his words, the man with the medals instead spat on the ground at his feet then smiled around him. 'We are looking for traitors here.' And idly he raised a booted leg high and lowered it, savagely kicking Kotso and Bingo, once, twice.

He was a thin man with a face like a diseased vegetable, crevices in his cheeks and a forehead filled with grime and I knew how he must smell: dirty, unwashed.

Tears sprang to my eyes as Bingo whimpered, like a child in pain. Beside me Anthi gripped my hand, hard. Instinctively we both felt that I was in great danger at this moment, because of who I was.

Clearly they were hunting the English, these men, and in Bingo they had found the only one I knew of for miles.

Anthi's Pappous stood tall and unmoving, although I could see his hands clench and unclench. 'Who are you?' he said evenly, his voice clear and calm. 'And on what authority are you here?'

The officer spoke. 'Aah, poor old man,' he said. 'Have you not heard? Your village, your country now belongs to us?' And he laughed in his face.

That was too much for Pappous. He had fought and survived many occupations of his country, he would not be humiliated by this piece of trash. It was written in his eyes. And with no thought for his own safety, he raised his arm and waved his flag high in the air.

'Crete is Cretan,' he said, 'and always will be so!'

Later Anthi and I would talk of this moment endlessly. We both felt the terrible inevitability of what happened next.

Furious, the officer turned and spat out the order to his men, 'Take him! Now!' and two soldiers rushed forward and grasped Pappous by the arms.

There was a horrified murmur from the villagers and one lone cry rose from the back, 'No, Stephanos, NO!' Then

Anthi's Yaya was trying to push her way through to be with her husband. Her friends and neighbours acted together with one thought – stop her – and they held her back. Anthi looked at me for a moment, desperation in her eyes and without another thought I pushed her away from me towards her grandmother. Everyone cleared backwards and she was beside her Yaya in a breath, holding her, whispering into her hair, comforting her in any way she could.

Voula, beside me, shrieked, 'Mama, Mama,' and I gathered her to me at once. Despina reached out for her sister and between us we held her tight and close.

The officer in charge looked around, a small smile playing around his thin lips.

'Kneel!' he said, but Pappous didn't move, he held his head high staring ahead.

'Kneel, kneel!' said the officer furiously and when nothing happened he looked at the two soldiers holding him and said, 'He will kneel, NOW!'

The two men shoved and kicked Pappous forcibly to the ground.

And as I drew in my breath, the officer pulled out his pistol and shot Pappous twice in the head.

Mighty creature that he was, Pappous slowly and sound-lessly crumpled into a heap and, without a murmur, I think he had died before I could breathe out.

A terrible wail rose from the crowd. I have never before and hope never again to hear such a sound; such pain, such feeling.

On the cold grey stones of the base of the cross a thin stream of blood dripped slowly downwards. Kotso and Bingo were spattered where they were tied.

'Silence! Silence,' shouted the officer in command, and the crowd gradually stilled and hushed. There was just one lone cry now, Anthi's Yaya, her voice ragged with grief: 'Stephanos, my Stephanos.'

'I hope this will make you understand, all of you, who is in charge here now.'

But we knew that whatever happened, whatever they did, there was no victory for these soldiers today, not here, not now. They could kill and destroy the bodies, but the spirit of men such as Pappous would never be crushed.

ANTHI

It took those monsters but five minutes to leave the square.

They dragged Kotso and the wireless operator with them.

No one followed them. Not even one person followed with their eyes. They were pieces of shit and everyone there wished them dead.

As I looked slowly down to my Pappous, I remember thinking there seemed such a little, little bit of blood from such a great man. But as I looked, it spread slowly out from beneath him: a dark crimson stain.

My thoughts then were only with Yaya. Surrounded by her neighbours and friends, I took her from the square and home. Behind us, every man of the village who had been there that day surged forward to carry Pappous, my beloved brave and noble Pappous, to his home.

Heavenly waved just once in my direction and then I saw that she had gathered Voula up into her arms, taken Despina by the hand and gone. I hoped they would be safe with her for as long as I needed.

Apart from her savage first shout as Pappous was taken, and her instant cry of pain as he fell, Yaya had not uttered a word or a sound. What was there for her to say?

The path to their house was shaded and cool as a breeze whispered through the olive trees. Our steps were slow, measured. We walked arm in arm as though we had walked for hours, exhausted. We paused as we entered their house. He was everywhere here. That was his chair by the table; the carved sigma for Stephanos, his chair. On it the cushion she had made as part of her dowry forty years ago, still bearing the imprint of his body. His thick winter coat hung on a nail from the door and the sleeves stuck out a little at an angle as if waiting for his arms to push through. On the table the dry crumbs of a piece of Cretan bread were scattered by his cup holding the dregs of his morning coffee.

Only her close neighbours and friends pushed through the doorway now, over it hanging the branch of cedar wood to keep the moths at bay.

On the wall the photograph of them on their wedding day looked proudly down. He was smiling, his arm around his beautiful shy bride. His son, my father, the only other face on the wall, and next to them all the iconostasis with the nubs of burnt down candles.

None of us in the room that day was prepared for this. The rituals of death, although familiar to us all, seemed inappropriate here, now.

Yaya glanced quickly round and seeing so many gathered in her little room looked at me for help. 'Anthi, will you, can you . . . ?'

I felt only the need for privacy here, and as I turned to look at the gathering, they took the message clear in my eyes and slowly left us alone. There were mutters of '*Mono Theos, mono Theos.*' Hard to believe in a god if this was his will, I thought.

Forlornly they drifted away. I knew they would return later to grieve with Yaya, but for now they all knew she needed only her family.

We sat side by side, she and I, waiting. We knew that the men would carry Pappous back here and we must attend him.

I reached across and took her hand in mine. The papery-dry skin clutched my fingers and with my other hand I stroked her softly. I knew no other comfort.

And then outside we heard the sound of the men coming up the path to the house. They were singing quietly as they walked, an old Cretan lament. The words lost to me but not to Yaya who whispered along with the men as they carried Pappous into his house for the last time.

Later that night, I left her briefly to see my girls. Heavenly opened her arms as I arrived and I crumpled into them and then the tears came. Despina and Voula sat crouched by the hearth and as I wept, so did they.

'Why, Mama, why?' asked Despina, and Voula sobbed, 'Is everybody going to die?' And for a moment I remembered she was still feeling the pain of her father's death.

Roughly I rubbed my eyes and gathered the girls to me. There were things to be done, decisions to be made and much as I would have liked to stay here, safely, turn the clock back and play with the children, I had no time for tears.

Heavenly said, 'Let me keep the girls here with me just now. We won't leave the house, you know they will be safe here.'

There was hope in Despina's eyes and, all battles forgotten, she said gently, 'I will look after Voula, Mama. You must go to Yaya.'

Is this what war did? Turn children into adults? For her words had a wisdom beyond her years so, thanking Heavenly, I kissed the three of them and left.

The streets were deserted as I walked through. Every door was closed; windows were shuttered and barred. Even in basements the animals were locked tight in their stalls – our village was a ghost of itself.

In Yaya's house, Irini, her closest friend and neighbour, was sitting beside her. Upstairs I knew Pappous lay on their bed. Yaya and I had washed him with fresh water and her tears earlier. We had dressed him in his best shirt, his neatest *vraka*. His boots bore the shine of the morning's polish. We had cleaned his head of the blood; in his forehead two small holes that he would carry to his grave tomorrow.

We three sat downstairs in silence. At some point Irini left and I think I must have dozed upright in my chair. I woke to the sound of a night owl and in the far distance, an angry dog barking. There was no sign of Yaya. I walked quietly through the house and then up the stairs to the bedroom.

She lay beside him on the bed. No tears now, just her arm over him as if to protect him. There was nothing left to protect him from.

I crept away and sat through the night at the table until the chill grey dawn came and the first cock crowed.

The funeral was a very different affair to the burial we had given my husband. Yorgo had stayed up all night to make the coffin and it seemed like a work of art. He had carved his name, Stephanos, simply at the head, but he had used the finest wood. He had oiled and polished it and it gleamed golden in the rays of the rising sun.

As we led the procession to the church, it seemed the entire village had come out to join us and even the strongest men were openly weeping.

I had urged Heavenly to stay at her house today – she had to remember she was in danger. I held the hands of my girls as we walked slowly along beside Yaya. She alone was silent. She would shed her tears in private.

Even though the coffin was open, I knew the body inside was not the Pappous I remembered. This body was merely trying to imitate him; my Pappous would live on in all of us here. Papa Costas officiated at the funeral. The small, white-washed church was filled to the rafters with the mourners. The Papa spoke warmly of Pappous' love of the countryside and his understanding of traditional ways. But it was outside afterwards, where the villagers waited in line to embrace Yaya and Marie Elena, Pappous' sister, that his fierce patriotism was spoken of.

The few who were from families that had disagreed with him from way back made a hasty exit from the churchyard, but most of the village, certainly all the elders, stayed to speak with Yaya and each other of his wonderful spirit.

I heard 'He was a true Cretan,' said over and over again.

These friends stood around the grave, the open coffin resting on three strong boards.

Panos, one of his closest friends who had played *prefa* with him every night for as long as I could remember, stood on the edge, looking down into the coffin. His hat clutched in his shaky old hands, he sang a *rizitiko*, a mournful, sad dirge of love and loss.

We stood on the damp soil looking down to the bright sunlit sea below. He had never left this island he worshipped, only rarely had he left this village, and nor did his only son, my father. I thought to myself, And neither will I, but as the boards were removed and the coffin lowered into the new-dug earth, I renewed my vows to give my daughters everything I had never had – the chance to travel and learn away from home.

HEAVENLY

Christo comes to me now only under cover of darkness. His face betrays his tiredness and it seems he has aged ten years in a moment.

'They have taken Bingo and Kotso over to Sitia, 'he had told me the first night he came. 'Bingo was captured on the hillside a good half a mile from the cave. At least they didn't discover the wireless. So I try and tune in at least once a day.' He was pacing backwards and forwards in the living room. I had rarely seen him so restless.

'How well do you trust your neighbours?'

I knew why he was asking. As the only Englishwoman in the village, I am under a great threat.

'Is anyone likely to betray you?'

'I can't think of anyone who might,' I said, but as I spoke a memory of Papa Yannis's fat face swam into my mind and I said his name aloud to Christo.

'You must leave this house, immediately,' he said.

I shook my head. 'No, Christo. I will not be driven into hiding. I will speak to the father. If I am honest with him, I can't believe he would give me away.'

Christo's reply was a harsh laugh. 'Now you are speaking like a fool. If he is offered safety for information he will not hesitate to tell them of the Englishwoman living here.'

I nodded, helpless.

His dear face was furrowed into a frown. Suddenly I forgot what his smile was like. Would I ever see it again?

He left, but was back within a moment and hugged me roughly to him.

'Always remember you must be so careful. I will find out what I can of their movements, how they operate and I will be back.'

He was gone and Despina and Voula ran to me. They were still shy in his presence and mostly hid behind the furniture when he was here. We sat on the floor, all of us huddled together, and we were still sitting like that in the evening when Anthi came. We gave the girls food and then put them to bed together in my big bed. They slept within moments.

Anthi is here such a short while each time; she stays with her Yaya. I have offered them both room here, I have plenty, but she always refuses and I understand why. It is important for Yaya to live in her own home where she had lived with her adored husband all the years of their life together.

These last nights I have slept in a pile of cushions and blankets, sometimes in the living room and sometimes in my bedroom. The first night, I climbed in with the girls and slept fitfully beside them. But I get cramp now that I am bulky and cannot turn over so easily. Best to let them rest alone. Often little Voula cries herself to sleep and Despina holds her. They share their grief. It is a private thing. I have tried to help; my instinct is to cuddle them to me, but at these moments they honestly only need each other and I must respect that.

The days all run into each other now and I think it is the same for everyone. We no longer seem to notice rain or sun; birds sing into the empty air. Flowers bloom and fade, grass grows over paths once trampled daily. Except for necessities, everyone stays in their homes.

The soldiers come from time to time, but only in groups of two, sometimes three. They need food and they take what they want, no questions asked, no answers given. We have never seen the one with the diseased-looking face again; Pappous' murderer. These soldiers stroll through the village, their guns stuck in their belts, their uniforms scruffy. They steal what they can find: eggs here, flour there; always wine and raki or brandy when it is to be had. Stories abound of their doings. Anthi told me that in Kato Panagia, several of the women hide their hens together, in the cellar of one of their houses, and so far they have evaded the raiders. She told me that in one house, in the search for food, they came across the rich linens the family had saved for the daughter's dowry and took those.

'Imagine those murderous bodies sleeping in little Stephanoula's embroidered sheets.' She paused and I took her hand in mine as she wept.

It is from Kato Panagia we learn that over there, the Italians, for the most part, are kind and respectful to the girls and the women. Openly flirting with the girls and hunting with the men, letting them use their guns to shoot rabbits and hares for food. Here our experience is less than good and we are more suspicious.

I stay in the house. My only exercise: walking on the terrace each day, back and forwards. I am big now with my child; I am sure it is a boy as he kicks me fiercely, especially when I am resting. I talk to him sometimes. Softly I whisper stories I remember from my childhood and, I'm sure, he is soothed by them. Thank goodness for Hans Christian Andersen! I'm sure by the time he is born he will know them by heart. But I make my thoughts stop there; I still don't know what I will do when he is born.

Anthi tells me the professor has been to see her and told her what is happening in Pano Episkope and other villages across the hills. The schools have their doors all tightly closed. The only lessons the children learn are how to hide and what to say if any stranger approaches. But he thinks one day, before long, they will open again. 'How can we teach our children to live in a peaceful world, if we don't educate them?'

One evening she said, 'I saw Aphrodite today, she came to me at Yaya's. She said she spoke on behalf of all the women in Mesa Panagia. They want us to know, you and me, that they care for you like a true woman of the village and you are safe here. They will never speak out against you. You are a woman much admired in all of Panagia, they are proud you chose to live here.'

I was moved almost to tears by her words. 'I have no right to expect their trust.'

'Maybe not, but you have it, like it or not. What happened here has shocked everyone to their roots. If any good is to come of it, let it be that it has united us. We have a common enemy now; there is no place or time for bickering or petty quarrels. Even with my mother and my sister.' She paused and almost laughed. 'They came to pay their respects to Yaya and to drink her coffee and eat the cake I had made, of course, double helpings mind you, and they wanted to tell us that they appreciate your kindness to my children and they will never reveal your presence here. If what has happened serves to unite my family in my favour, then I will start to believe in miracles.' Then she laughed like the old Anthi. 'But not if it means she expects me to behave like a daughter. That would be too much after all this time!'

The sky was peppered with stars, so many there was scarcely room for the dark to come through. We sat in silence for a while. I stroked my swollen belly and felt a small, hard lump move under my hand; a foot, perhaps?

'Christo will come to see you later,' she said. 'To tell you that I have asked him to take me with him when he goes out with the *andartes* at night. They are going to hunt out and finish the group of *malakas* who came here. And I want to be part of it.'

She raised her hand in the air as she saw the look of doubt on my face. 'No, don't even think to try and dissuade me. Christo has already spent hours doing that. I know every possible objection, including getting too cold.'

She stood up. 'I am a woman. They think I am too feeble, weak. But all over Greece women are fighting alongside their men. Christo let me listen to a report on the wireless set and it made that much clear.'

I sighed. I knew Anthi in this stubborn mood. And Christo

knew, as well as I did, that if she was intent on going with him, nothing would stand in her way.

'What of your girls? What will become of them, if you are not here for them?' I couldn't say the words 'if you are killed' aloud; too shocking even now.

'I've thought of that too. Aphrodite and Yorgo will add them to their family and I trust you and my Yaya to make sure that in the years ahead they will have all the things I didn't. The only thing I really worry about is that if I am not around, my mother will try and make some kind of marriage for them. Run away with them! Take them with you to Athens or England. Give them a proper chance of life away from here.'

I hugged her to me. Her arms tight around me, I knew she was weeping silently into my shoulder. She pulled away, scrubbed her eyes with her crumpled sleeve. 'I must do this, you understand, don't you? I must. I can't just let him die like that, like an animal, for nothing.'

Silence. Staring into our separate darknesses we sat there. Behind us stretched the past; the shared warmth and love of our friendship that had grown so strong, meant so much, I believe, to us both. Ahead of us, a future holding we knew not what.

I had to be strong. This woman had done everything for me, given me a life and helped me to learn to love. In all the time we had been friends, she had asked nothing of me. My own future without her flashed before me for a moment. What would I do? How would I bring the child I was carrying into the world without her beside me, without her wisdom, her knowledge? But I knew this was not the moment to raise my own doubts and fears.

'I understand. You must go, and take my love and my friendship with you. Of course you will be back! We shall hardly miss you before you'll be here with us again. Running our lives as you have always done. Go now!'

I watched from the top of the stairs as she whispered her goodbyes to her girls. They were deeply asleep, sprawled across my bed, the only sound the contented suck of Voula's thumb. She kissed them both and came back up to me.

'Look after Christo for me?'

'Do you need to ask?' she said. 'He is a changed man, even I admit it. He is a man who has learnt to love.'

We hugged and then, without a backward glance, she was gone.

ANTHI

I hadn't been completely truthful with Heavenly. Christo had done more than try and dissuade me; he had forbidden me. I knew that he had recruited Andreas the iron worker to the *andartes* and I reminded him of this. He had laughed. 'Andreas is six and half feet tall, a giant of a man. Look at you! What will you do, travel in his pocket?'

I begged, 'I am small, yes, but I am strong too. My size means I can get into spaces you and Andreas can't.'

In the end I suppose my persistence wore him down. Reluctantly he agreed to let me go. I knew the mission was to try to track down and bring back Kotso, and even Bingo. Of course that was important, but I had another reason too, and Christo knew it.

'None of us has quite the spirit of revenge that you have. But don't let it spoil your judgement. You will do only as I say. There can be only one leader. If Kotso were here it would be him. But . . . well, let's hope we can get him back.'

In the last of the fading light before darkness set in, we left the village. Behind windows and doors, closed in spite of the heat, we knew we were watched. Since the occupation, there is no trust here.

I didn't know where we were going, what our weapons were, if any, I could only guess. Christo carried on his back a rough straw pannier, and it rattled: maybe they were in there? But I knew it also contained a couple of water jars and a zinc bread-box.

Christo says, 'The less you know, the safer you are.'

Dusk came quickly, enveloping the olive trees with strange purple hues, but we all knew this terrain well, our animals grazed here.

When I first arrived at the cave there was almost a feeling of shock as the two men looked at me. I was wearing a pair of Manolis's old *vrakes* and I knew in normal times this would not be acceptable; a woman in man's clothes? Outrageous!

We ate together before we set off, sitting on the floor in Christo's cave. I recognised a couple of cushions and a rug from Heavenly's house and as I raised my eyes to his face, Christo smiled at me.

Andreas spoke of the north of the island, 'My sister lives there, in Galatas.' He paused. 'Well, perhaps I should say, lived. Who knows what is still standing there.'

'I'm sorry to tell you, but they say there is almost nothing left,' said Christo quietly.

'I heard reports on the radio that it was the last place to fall before Chania.' Andreas bowed his head, crossing himself quickly, his eyes closed. He is built like a mountain. I have only ever seen his ruddy face smiling, until now.

'She had three children. Two boys I've never even seen.'

Christo put his hand on his shoulder. 'I'm sorry, I heard they fought so bravely alongside the British and the Australians who had come from Suda to help them. Many of the enemy were killed.'

'But not enough, eh?'

'No, my friend, I fear not enough. They passed through and burnt Chania almost to the ground. Well, that's what I heard.'

At last it was time and we set off in the early hours of the morning, creeping through the undergrowth in a line. No one spoke. We stayed close together as Christo had told us and slowly, slowly, we moved forwards, upwards.

Progress was slow. After some hours we reached a cluster of trees and the scent of wild thyme was strong under the morning sun. Christo waved us all to a stop. We had what Andreas called a 'duck's breakfast' – a drink of water and a look around. We took it in turns to rest, but even though we were in open country near the top of a steep hill, we were the only humans for miles, it seemed. We slept; the trek so far had exhausted even the strongest of us.

By halfway through the fourth night our life had taken on a certain rhythm; we moved onwards by night and rested by day. We were far from home and it was my turn at the front. I caught Christo's eye as I turned to see where he was, and he nodded reassuringly. He had urged me forward earlier: 'You go ahead, and I'll follow with Andreas. Keep to the goat path across this hill and follow it round to the left when you get to the other side. You will see where we are to go. We are heading for the sea.' He smiled briefly and continued, 'We are going a little way towards my home village, which is on the stretch of land along from Sitia. The Italians have made a camp about a mile from there.'

The path was steep and uphill just there and I was soon winded, sweat matting my hair into knots. Behind me Christo stopped. 'All well here?' he asked. I nodded, gulping down deep puffs of air.

'We'll pause here,' he said. 'Take some water and rest a little. We have one more village to pass through and then down to the beach. We need to keep our strength for then.'

We sat down. I leant back against a tree and closed my eyes. I thought of Despina and Voula as I had last seen them, sleeping so peacefully in Heavenly's big bed and I felt a great ache in my belly. Was I doing the right thing? Would all this really make any difference? It wouldn't bring my Pappous back, that much I knew. As I thought of him and his great courage, I wanted to weep. But Christo was urging us onwards again.

'Enough rest for now,' he said. Beside us was a stream that was rushing down the side of the hill and he told us to fill our water bottles. I was filthy. The men didn't seem to notice but I could smell the stink of my sweat and of theirs. I stripped my clothes off and plunged into the stream. It was heaven! The men, hearing what I was doing, paused to wait for me, their heads turned away. I put my whole head under the water and it was the best feeling. I rubbed myself clean in all my private places; under my arms and between my legs. Feeling better, I dried myself roughly with my shirt and we went on.

I found it hard to sleep during the day. The fierce sun beat down on us relentlessly and I lay with the others on the scratchy undergrowth, tossing and turning. When I did drift off it was to wake suddenly with insects tickling in my hair or ants crawling down these itchy trousers. I wondered how much easier I would find it if I had worn an old dress. At least I would be cooler underneath skirts.

Then at last, a village.

I looked at Christo but he shook his head. 'We're not there,' he said, 'not yet.'

It was dusk. We crept forwards in the half light, finding our way to the edge of the houses as Christo had taught us to do. CRACK! One of us had stepped on a twig and a dog barked. We shuffled slowly forward.

The silence of this village was eerie; just that one lone pitiful howl. Not the sweet silence of peaceful sleep. It was something else. Nothing stirred as we moved slowly through to what must be the centre. Every house seemed empty, and shutters creaked and swung open. From one house, a wisp of smoke rose into the air, but not from a chimney.

Christo paused and behind him we stopped. A sudden breeze sent a terrible smell in our direction.

'Death,' said Christo softly. 'That's what we can smell here, violent death.'

As he spoke, an ancient memory stirred. Once, as a child, I went to a neighbouring farm with my mother. While she talked to the women I ran around the animal houses. The pigsty was open, the gate creaking on its hinges and I crept inside. I loved pigs. It was the smell that hit me first. I was six and curious. A large sow was lying on her side, her piglets suckling desperately from her teats. I ran in and bent to stroke her head. It was then I saw that her throat was open; ripped out, I learnt later, by a wild dog come down from the hills and hungry for food.

I remember standing rigid, appalled at the sight of so much blood. I turned, vomiting as I ran away. My mother jumped up, took one look at my soiled dress and yelled her displeasure. I had embarrassed her and that was never forgiven.

That sow sprang into my mind now, overwhelmed by this truth here.

'Stay here,' said Christo, his face white and drawn, but we couldn't. We moved forward, looking in through every door with an appalled fascination. Some houses were empty as we thought, but not many. Bodies were lying everywhere in grotesque mimicry of life. The stink of death hung over everything, overpowering our senses, nothing moving or living.

In one hovel an old couple lay side by side in bed, butchered as they lay sleeping. In another a whole family of men, women, children and even a tiny baby were gathered together in their kitchen, lying in a heap on the floor – all dead.

Beneath our feet, the loamy soil inside these dwellings was enriched with shit and fear. We covered our mouths and noses, but the stench trickled through.

A sudden scratching and I gasped as a bare skeleton of a dog loped past us with who knew what clutched in its jaw, trailing, dripping, on the ground.

These pitiable bodies seemed no longer to be humans but monsters; tongues huge and black, faces distorted, eyes glaring. The only living things were fat bluebottles, their iridescent wings bucking as they feasted on the dead.

And in the corner of one room, a fat toad slipped under the bodies of a mother and child hugged close together; their faces not so much flesh any more as jellied fluid.

In the village centre, set apart from the houses, bodies were piled together in and spilling out of a water trough. Christo bent over them. I think he feared to find Kotso or another of his friends slaughtered here.

Nearby lay the body of a young man, no more than seventeen or so. He wore what I would come to recognise as the uniform of the German airforce; a swastika on his shoulder. A shock of bright fair hair swept across his brow, his eyes were open, staring milky and sightless at the sky.

It was impossible not to think of a mother like me, somewhere, waiting daily for news of her son.

We walked together to the end of this village. Neapolis, it was called; a common enough name hereabouts, but one that would mean only desolation to me for the rest of my life. In front of me, suddenly, Christo paused and then his face blenched, and grey, he turned aside and doubled over, vomiting. Retch after retch until surely his guts would fall. He straightened up slowly and panting, his arms, his hands quivering like a leaf in a breeze. I reached out to him by instinct and he waved me aside. Ignoring us, he walked as firmly as he could onwards. His lapse had never happened.

Daylight was breaking on the far horizon. Over that terrible place the birds sang as sweetly as ever, a goat rang a lonely bell and another glorious summer day dawned. We walked onwards, huddled together. For a short moment no thought of our need to hide, the birdsong broken only by the terrible sound of Andreas weeping.

At the first clutch of trees we came to, Christo stopped. He was ahead of us by several paces now. I sensed he needed to separate himself. We didn't speak; what was there to say? He sat down his back against an olive tree. Dumbly we sat too. We were exhausted but no one slept.

It was later that day, when we were getting ready to move on again, before any of us spoke, and then Christo said, 'Do you want to stop now, go home?'

We shook our heads.

'There's no shame if you do. This is not to admit failure or defeat.' He looked around. 'You have seen here what is happening all over Crete; villages taken, every living thing killed and abandoned. It is worse in the north. The bulk of the occupying army is there. Down here, for the most part, the Germans leave their Italian lapdogs in charge; they are pretty feeble and just steal our food; interested only in their own survival. Occasionally they feel the need to prove themselves and take a village, as they did in Panagia.'

It made no sense to me, and I said so. Christo shrugged. 'It's called war; they can do what they like with us, they are in charge now. But believe me, everywhere they go, they are met with fierce resistance. Everyone says they have never before found an enemy as brave or strong as the Cretans. They will wish they never came to this island.' His laughter was just a crack in the empty air.

Through the scrubland and gorse we struggled. The weight of what we had found in Neapolis hung heavy on us. Andreas seemed not to be able to move onwards with the same vigour as before. He caught up with me at one point and, our arms swinging side by side, it seemed natural for him to take my hand in his. He gripped it hard and I realised the tears had not really left his eyes.

'I can only think of my sister's village like that,' and he waved behind with his free hand. 'In my head, I keep seeing her children left like the ones there. No one to bury them decently, their flesh and bones left to rot in the sun until the buzzards pick them clean.'

'Stop! You will only drive yourself to lunacy if you think like that.' But his words were echoing in my head and I thought of my two girls and shivered. I don't think any of us will forget what we saw today.

Ahead, Christo waved us to a stop on the edge of a small olive grove. There was a shack beside it. I guessed it was an overnight hut for the goatherds or shepherds in spring at birthing time. A good keeper will not leave his animals to give birth alone.

We sank into the shade and I drank deeply from a water bottle before passing it to Andreas. 'We will meet Kotso here if he has managed to keep his freedom,' said Christo. His casual words gave no sign of the dread he must feel.

But there was only the empty silence of birdsong and the wind rustling through the olives.

I could feel my eyes closing as I relaxed. Andreas, on one side of me, slumped low, his head in my lap, his eyes lidded. My mind was drifting when I realised Christo was on his feet, listening. There it was again. I had thought it was birdsong, but it was a distinct whistle, sharp and clear.

Kotso had found us.

At the time, I thought I would remember every detail of that night. Every step was cut onto my mind; every sound and reaction. The sharp call of the owl which seemed to have followed us across the island, the dips of the moon and the clouds that scudded past it.

Christo seemed strengthened by Kotso's arrival and I realised the responsibility of taking two untried revolutionaries, one of them a woman, alone across the hills had caused him serious concerns.

Kotso looked awful. His eyes were hooded and drawn with exhaustion. He walked with a limp and I could see bruises wherever I saw skin.

He said he and Bingo had been dragged across the island to the small encampment we would see later. They were questioned daily. 'Every time it seemed that we'd persuaded them that we knew nothing,' Kotso told us. 'But every morning they would start the same questions over and again. The only use we had was that we knew the terrain. Well, I did anyway. They used me as a guide. They seemed convinced that Bingo had information on the whereabouts of the king and the prime minister. They gave him a very hard time.'

At his words I thought of Heavenly – she knew his family.

'I escaped only yesterday. '

It was later that I discovered that it wasn't just affection for his friend that made Christo come to find him. Kotso led us to another shack, this one sturdier. Empty now, its roof was in shreds. But under a metal plate in the floor that Andreas heaved up in a moment, there was a cellar. 'Anthi, you are the only one who can get through this.'

I scrambled down into the evil-smelling space and as my eyes grew accustomed to the dark, I could see a rough canvas sack in the corner. This was what they wanted, and I pulled it over and hauled it up before wriggling out.

It was guns. There were four, one each. Christo made us clean them, handle them, look through the sights. We had all handled guns before. The rabbits and wildlife we eat have been shot with something like these, hunters' guns. I held one, ready for use. It felt strange; partly right, but also the unknown feeling to me of holding a weapon intended to kill a man.

But overall I felt exhilaration. I was so close now to why I was there.

In the middle of that day Kotso shook me awake. My sleep was crawling with dreams and I was happy to leave them behind.

The wild dogs were howling outside the hut; a pack of strays seemed to have bonded together. Grey shadows of dog shapes, big and small, passed at the bottom of the mountain. We heard the faraway rumble of battle and a lone Stuka flew low across the sky. I know now that it was the same as the multitude we saw on that first day.

Then we heard the cry. It was a terrible scream of pain, and my blood turned to ice in my veins; it barely seemed human.

We could see the beach at the edge of the cliff and there was somebody there.

'Come back,' said Christo in a whisper. 'We will be dead at once if we move now. That's what they want us to do. We must wait for darkness.'

So we returned and then followed Kotso down the steep goat path, inch by inch, until we gathered in the shadows at the base of the cliff. It was Bingo lying there. He was still alive, I think. His hands were tied behind his back, his feet bound. He was covered in blood, fresh and bright from the cuts and slashes they had inflicted in many places. They had given him no chance.

I reached down to sweep his hair back across his forehead, but Kotso pulled me back. 'Into the caves quickly,' he said, 'they have put him here as a lure. They know we will come to find him.' He raised his eyes upwards and I saw the sky was full of birds of prey waiting hungrily for their feast to die.

Christo looked swiftly around and then, lifting Bingo's head, gave him water.

It was a long day until sundown. We hid behind rocks and in crevices, our bodies cramped and sore. No one slept. Kotso and Christo took turns to look out, and to move out to give water to Bingo, but aside from that far rumble of battle and the occasional plane, nothing.

It broke my heart to ignore Bingo like this. Surely he could not live without help. What would I tell Heavenly?

But as the last rays of the sun disappeared over the horizon, we knew we were not alone on the beach. Softly, stealthily, from the bay at the end they came. Two uniformed men. They were armed and as they neared Bingo's body, a shaft of moonlight lit up their faces. One was the killer of Pappous, a face I would never forget. They moved silently, looking around. One raised his foot and kicked Bingo over.

When I look back at this moment later, in my mind is only confusion – which of us fired the shots that brought them down, I cannot be sure.

The four of us rose as one, took aim and fired. With barely a cry they dropped like stones in a pond. Christo pulled Bingo behind a rock and I know that Kotso dragged me away. I was shaking from head to foot. I expected to feel jubilant. We had achieved what we set out to do, hadn't we? I could tell Yaya I had taken vengeance for Pappous' death. But all I felt was a dreadful, sad weariness. Somehow I felt diminished by yet another senseless killing.

Later, after we had all slept an exhausted, anticlimatic sleep and I was awake, Christo said, 'It is time for you to go home.

You and Andreas have families, responsibilities. You have both been part of a day you can be proud of.'

We didn't argue. As we made ready to leave, he took me aside and said quietly, 'Look out for him, he has been badly affected by all he has seen. You proved your worth,' he added. 'I'm glad you came.' And he hugged me.

HEAVENLY

Every day I counted out the time of my pregnancy. I spent hours stroking my belly and talking to my baby inside.

Sometimes I fantasised about the future. My favourite dream was to think maybe I would leave Panagia, go to the city. Athens, London, Thessalonika. I would get an apartment. 'Near a park,' I'd say to my little chap inside. 'I could be a teacher and we will be together all the time. Christo could finish his training as an architect and design beautiful buildings. There will be a need for that after the devastation of the war. We'd never be lonely.' I sat with my hand on my belly, my eyes closed.

Harder than the physical changes to my body were the unexpected sweeps of emotion. When I was caught up in the great net of these feelings, tears poured from my eyes and I felt so helpless and often frightened. How could I leave Panagia? I remembered that I hated cities, couldn't cope with city life. How real was it to think of Christo miles away from his roots, his family?

These were just dreams.

This morning the weather changed; it had been a pounding summer rain, with us for three days. It wore the skies out with its relentless drizzle. It flooded the ditches and the sewers, primitive as they are. It made running streams of the streets and there was a great pool in my bedroom downstairs. Then, as suddenly as it had come, the sky cleared, the sun blazed and a cool wind dried all the surfaces.

'Hullo, are you here?' It was Aphrodite. She pulled her

plumpness up the steps and I met her at the door. I was happy to see her. Anthi has been gone for days now and while her girls are company, the sight of Aphrodite was cheering.

It was unusual in these times for her or any of the village women to visit me. They had occasionally come in for a cup of *dictamus* or a coffee, but these visits had become less frequent.

I now dressed as a village woman all the time. My fancy clothes and curtain skirts had long been locked away. If I was honest, I was happy these days to climb ungracefully into worn, drab shift dresses; they concealed my belly as well as my identity. A dull grey or brown headkerchief kept my wild hair, now cut short, out of my face.

And any villager who passed me unnoticing, said '*Ya*'. Even *kalimera* seemed too cheerful these days.

Aphrodite paused to catch her breath and glanced around. She spread her hands wide and shrugged. 'Look, empty-handed, you must forgive my rudeness.' I smiled and told her it was her presence that was welcome to me, not her gifts.

I led her through to the terrace and she peered all round before sitting down; everyone is nervous now. I offered her refreshment but, '*Tipota,*' she said: nothing.

She admired my knitting, but laughed at the clumsiness of my dropped stitches and ragged ends. She chatted on a little and asked for Voula and Despina.

'With their yaya,' I said. 'She is making walnut cake today and she lets them crack the nuts and stir the mix.' At her look of surprise, I remembered the tradition so I quickly explained, 'It's for the girls,' I said, 'she will not keep the cake. It is for them.'

She nodded. 'No widow will make sweetmeats for her home.'

'They miss Anthi painfully,' I said. 'So do I.'

'I come about the priest,' she said, 'Papa Yannis.' I frowned. She waved her hand in the air. 'No, no, I don't come here to alarm you, not to worry you. But I think you

324

can help him.' She must have seen how puzzled that made me, my thoughts whirling.

'He is sick, did you hear?'

'What's wrong with him?' I tried to sound sorry for him, but part of me was pleased. He was the biggest threat to my safety.

'He fell last week. He was coming back from a thirty-day service. He had been at the family's house.' And she named them, notorious drinkers, all of them. Apparently in the dark, very late, he tripped on the steps up to his house.

'He lay there for the rest of the night unable to move. Next morning my Yorgo and our eldest two were on their way to the fields and heard him cry out. Yorgo said he was blue in his face, his leg all twisted up under him. They got him inside but he was in great pain. Sophia, you know, his sister? She gave him a ragwort infusion with a calendula poultice. But today she came to us and asked Yorgo and me to persuade you to go and see him.' She shook her head. 'Not good. Yorgo went over there and said the poison is weeping through the wrapping and it smells bad.' She waved her hand in front of her screwed-up face, as if the odour was here in the room.

She continued, 'He's dying, and he knows it. He can hardly speak, but he asked for you. He knows you are his only hope. There's no chance of getting a doctor up the mountain, even for the priest.'

There was a long pause. I had kept my fears hidden, only Anthi and Christo knew of them. Could I say them aloud?

As I was about to speak, Aphrodite went on, crossing herself three times as she said, 'Forgive me, Panagia, but between ourselves, if he was not the priest there are many who would cross the street at his approach. Because of this, we all know why you might feel in danger from him at this time.' She lowered her voice to a whisper, 'He is the only one here in Panagia who would sell his mother to the Germans for the right price.'

I tried to smile, it wasn't easy.

'Listen to me. If you help him now, he knows that he must never, CAN never, betray you.'

'What makes you so sure?'

'Because he is afraid, terrified of dying. He has lived a life far from innocent and he lives in dread of meeting his maker. Every time he gets drunk he weeps out his fear to anyone who will listen. He has made my Yorgo hear his confessions a thousand times.'

Her hands were flying back and forwards across her heavy breast in an endless flutter of crosses. 'Papa Costas has heard him tell of his sins, many times, and but for this war, would have reported him to the Patriarch in Constantinople. Now he knows how near to death he is, for sure he knows that a calendula poultice and a few herbal infusions will do nothing to save him.'

She sat back, looked at me and wiped her brow on her sleeve. 'I know it's hard for you. But you are in danger whatever happens.'

Oh, how I wished Anthi was there now. I missed her painfully all the time but, right then, I needed her wisdom so badly. I stood, crossed to the edge of the terrace and looked out. To the sides, the mountains, to the front, the dark-blue sea.

Where are you, my beloved friend? What would you tell me to do now? Oh, come home safely, Anthi, and come home soon. But I knew I had to decide this one on my own. And I thought of my friend and I thought of her Pappous and what they would tell me. Then I turned again to Aphrodite. 'Do I have a choice?' I asked.

Slowly she shook her head. 'Since you took everyone up the mountain and showed them your modern medicine, everyone here thinks you are wonderful, you know that. They believe in you. They are all waiting to see you bring Papa Yannis back from the edge of death.'

'And if I fail?'

'Then they will know you tried. None of them will ever

betray you and the only one who would, will be dead.'
Another trio of crossings flew across her breast.

Her simple logic was hard to resist. 'I'll do it,' I said.

I had never been in the priest's house before. Always I hurried past, but many times his piggy eyes would be watching through his window. Aphrodite led me there. She had a quick, balletic walk, her steps tiny and precise, belying the bulk of her comely body.

She crossed herself as we entered the unlocked door and called out. There was no reply. She looked back at me and shrugged. She closed the door and we were plunged into immediate, stifling gloom. We stood for a moment until our eyes grew accustomed to the dark, but everything there was still shadowed deeply. Large cupboards and chests loomed at us darkly through the shade. Everything was from a bygone age, heavy and ancient.

I grabbed Aphrodite's sleeve and she guided me through to Papa Yannis's bedroom. I followed closely and immediately wanted to turn and run. The room smelt of sickness and decay, with an overlying thick veil of incense.

We stood by the bed and I looked at him. A stub of candle flickered, another in front of the oversized *iconostasis* above it. There was no other light. He lay on his back with his hands crossed on his belly. The damaged leg lay outside the heavy, burgundy damask cover. This was where the smell came from.

Aphrodite looked at it, closed her eyes and uttered a prayer under her breath.

Through the airless gloom I could see his cheeks were brilliant, his eyes glazed. I put my hand onto his brow. His fever was so high he was dry with its heat; his lips were vivid, bruised plums and his breath short. I felt for the pulse in his wrist – it raced unsteadily. He was very ill.

He was trying to speak, but his voice had cracked to a fragile whisper, and I had to lean in close to the circle of his sour, rank breath.

'What can you do for me, Kyria Timberley?' His voice wavered between a whisper and a croak. There was little point in correcting him. What he called me was immaterial.

'You must do as I say, and I will try to help you mend. Firstly I must look at this leg.' Aphrodite had retreated to a corner of the room and I called her back to the bedside. 'Will you help me?'

She nodded, panicky. 'Oh, I'm not good at this; you'll have to tell me.'

'Of course I will. First, get some water boiling and find something we can use for bandages. Sheets, linens, anything clean that we can tear up.' I had brought with me my dwindling medical supplies, so I gave him some aspirin and made him sit up and drink some water. To do this I had to hold him in my arms and ease him upright. I repressed a shudder. I had dealt with worse cases on the ward; not many, but it helped.

Aphrodite came in with a zinc basin of steaming water and over her arm a couple of fine linen sheets. His eyes flickered round and widened in horror when he saw what she was carrying.

'What are—'

I put my fingers over his lips. 'We are going to try and help you but we cannot do it if you resist. We must make bandages and dressings with whatever you have.'

Suddenly I was no longer afraid of this man. Bullies like him are always frightened of strong women; they were brought up by iron mothers, and governesses who were strict and zealous: they fear being bullied themselves. So be it, I could be fierce too.

'You will do as I tell you, you understand?'

Head on the pillow, his eyes were closed and he faintly nodded.

'Right. Next, Aphrodite, please open the shutters and get some light and air in here.'

She did so and within a moment the room was transformed. It still stank. I suspect the rotting decay was the result of years of filth and neglect. His life was all prayers and piety with little care for cleanliness. He would have clean hands and face and a white surplice, but underneath, filthy drawers.

As the first fresh air for, I suspect, years came whispering in, his eyes filled with horror and he clutched the sheet to him, 'Don't let that chill air touch my skin!'

'It is the first and most important part of the treatment to make you well. It will blow away germs and disease. Now we will take a look at your leg.'

He sank back and made no more protest. I called Aphrodite and between us we unwrapped the bandage from his leg. It was stuck tight so I splashed it with the water to loosen it. A groan escaped his lips as I pulled, but he knew that it was pointless to protest further. Slowly, slowly, the wound was revealed. It was a horrible sight. I turned my head away, breathed deeply and felt around it firmly with my fingers. It was festering and suppurating but no bones were broken underneath. It was certainly black and blue and green with bruising; there would be no chance if I didn't get it clean soon. In fact, with the lack of medicines, that was about all I could do and hope that I wasn't too late.

Well, everyone will see that I tried.

Aphrodite and I worked as fast as we could; neither of us wanted to be in this unholy place longer than necessary. As we worked together his brows knitted and he worked his jaws in little chewing motions. I remembered that loathsome habit he had of flicking his red tongue back and forth, back and forth, through wet lips. I think he was praying; well, that may help him now. I thought of his vile life stretching behind him and wondered what horrors it contained. Let his maker deal with him in his own way. Frankly, nothing less than the fires of damnation would be just. And I smiled grimly to myself at the thought.

Aphrodite told me his sister would be in later and stay the night here. Under her breath, she whispered, 'I don't think she likes him any more than the rest of us, but she has little choice.'

'You are to leave these shutters open until I return to-morrow, do you understand?' I spoke loudly and firmly and Aphrodite looked surprised. On the pillow he gave a faint nod.

'If you close them I may return to find you dead in the morning.'

As we left, Aphrodite said, 'You certainly know how to control him, don't you?'

I returned the next day and the next alone. The shutters stayed open and the sound of birdsong drifted in. By the end of the second day the smell of rot and decay was going from the room, but I was having a hard job bringing down the heat of the infection. I had clean bandages and dressings and iodine, but nothing stronger than aspirin to counteract the fever. The only way I knew was to clean out the wound each day and this caused him great pain. It was sited on the shin where there is little flesh to bring healing blood to the skin.

By the fourth day, I was not winning. I brought Aphrodite with me and she peered down at his leg, drawing in her breath as she gazed at it.

'Oh, *Panagia mou*,' she said, 'that's bad.'

There was one thing I could try but I dreaded it: cutting it open further and forcing the pus to the surface and out. It was how we treated leg ulcers in Greenbridge. One problem, I had no scalpel. I left him with Aphrodite and went to my house. In the kitchen I knew there was a little fruit knife that had belonged to Hugh's grandmother.

Back in the priest's house, I sent Aphrodite into the kitchen to boil it. It would be sterile at least, but would an implement used to cut apples be sharp enough to act as a surgical knife? I had no alternative. I also had no ether. But there was a good supply, I had noticed, of spirits. Papa Yannis certainly liked his drink.

I poured him a great slug of brandy and Aphrodite watched in surprise as I persuaded him to drink it down, and fast. As soon as the glass was empty, I filled it again and then again. After four large measures, his eyes were glazed and rolling and he could barely lift his head to take the liquor.

'You'll have to hold him down,' I said to Aphrodite. She did what she could and as soon as he was still, I attacked the wound, slicing into it as though it were a watermelon. It worked and a great stream of pus and blood spurted out like a geyser. The papa screamed and Aphrodite jumped into the air, but within seconds the pus was gone and rich, healing blood flowed freely.

Papa Yannis fell back onto the pillow and passed out. I put a thick, clean linen pad over the leg and held it firmly, until the blood gradually stopped flowing.

I gave him aspirin before we left, but I sent Aphrodite home. She'd seen more than enough for one day. 'I don't know how you can do these things,' she said, shaking her head in wonder.

That day I stayed until Sophia arrived. He was so drunk I could not risk him choking on vomit if he was left alone. She was a timid little mouse of a woman, a natural victim. How she survived with this creature as family, I couldn't bear to think.

The next day was the first I knew he would heal. 'Well,' I said to Aphrodite, 'I can tell you his leg will be better, but as for his soul . . .'

Now I had to persuade him out of bed and moving around. But first I had to make him clean. The fevered sweat had left greasy runnels in his skin and what condition his body was in I couldn't imagine. Filthy, I suppose. He had never looked to me like a man who washed himself with any regularity. He used an ancient commode in the corner and I imagine Sophia emptied it each morning and evening. At least I did not have to do that.

I persuaded him out of bed while I was there on the third day, and I brought in a zinc basin full of warm water. Sophia had been stoking his fire, so there was water easily available for me to use.

I watched him remove his nightshirt and stagger naked

into the bowl in front of me. His legs and arms were skinny and wasted from the sickness, but his drooping belly was fat, round and white like a frog.

He tried to cover himself with his shaking hands, but I couldn't help seeing his genitalia were like small purple and brown prunes that dangled uselessly down. I washed him with a cloth but couldn't touch that part so I handed it to him and took his arm in my hand to balance him while he whickered delicately around them himself. I thought, If I had my way, I'd cut them off, filthy *malaka*.

ANTHI

The carnage we had seen, and the sorrow we felt, made everything else seem so simple and unimportant and, coming slowly through Panagia, I took a deep breath of air. It seemed scented with blood, ancient lives and old dreams.

It was late in the day and the sun fell thick along the edge of the mountains and heated the scored, grey trunks of trees that swayed out over the path.

I felt as old as these hills myself today and even the thought of being home with my girls again could only raise a whisper of pleasure. Kotso had a young girl, no more than fifteen or so, Agni, working as a runner with our band of *andartes*; a tiny, nut-brown girl with cropped hair, like a boy. She had acquired us a mule, old but sturdy, and Andreas and I took turns in riding. He never spoke now, just shook his head when I spoke to him. He was lost deep in his thoughts, and I guess of all of us he was the most changed by what he had seen. I knew his wife Marina would have little pleasure in his return, and I thought I would talk to her when next I saw her at the spring, help her understand.

It was as we were coming down the path past Papa Yannis's house that I saw Heavenly. She was coming out of his door. What was this? She looked up when she heard the steps of the mule and her face broke into a great smile as she saw me.

'Oh, my friend,' she said. 'You're home.'

I passed the reins to Andreas and jumped down, running and nearly falling straight into her arms. She held me tight, saying, 'There, there,' as if to a child.

As I rubbed my tears away on my sleeve she was looking round. 'Christo? He's not with you?'

'He's safe. He will be back soon. What you are doing here?'

'Oh, I'll tell you, don't worry. Lots to talk about. Your girls are fine. They're with Yaya just now. She has been wonderful.'

With a single wave Andreas moved on up the path. I linked arms with Heavenly and together we walked to her house. She was bulky with the child and moved heavily.

Doors and shutters were closed tight as we passed, just like before. So, in spite of the heat, no one here risked exposure. I was sad to see my friendly village closed and changed. The only sound of life was dogs howling and thin chickens scrabbling in yards for scraps of grain. This was what war did; filled everyone with fear and drove them away from each other. I said so and Heavenly nodded. 'Don't worry,' she said, 'come to the spring – the women don't stay indoors so much, it's mostly their men.'

We went directly to Heavenly's house and on the way she told me a little of what had happened to Papa Yannis.

'Leave him to die, if you want to know what I think,' I snorted.

And then we were there and as we went up the steps, I heard the laughter of my girls and my Yaya's voice saying, 'Mix and rub, that's what you do, mix and rub in your fingers until it looks like crumbs. That's right.' She sounded almost happy.

'Being with the girls has helped her grief to heal,' Heavenly said, 'and she's turning Despina into a fine cook.'

She paused, puffing a little. 'Oh, my dear friend, it's so good to have you back.'

We walked up the steps and Heavenly put her finger to her lips.

'Guess who is here?' she called, and little Voula ran out of the door first.

'Is it Pappous come back?' she shrieked, her voice high, excited.

A flood of disappointment and sadness flowed through me, but it lasted only a moment and when she saw it was me, she ran towards me, her arms open wide.

'Mama, Mama!' she said, her voice a squeak of excitement. I hugged her and lifted her high in the air, burying my face in the sweet, girlish scent of her hair, her skin.

Despina stood in the doorway quite still and quietly. 'Mama, welcome home,' she said. She looked older than her eleven years and her voice was low. Suddenly I saw she was a young woman. Our eyes met and she smiled. I realised what the events of the last year had done to our children. I would see later that all the children in the village had seen things that no child should. They seemed to have lost their childhood, their innocence, overnight. That hideous image behind my eyelids reminded me that Despina had suffered more than most and there were things she would never forget.

'Come, Mama, come and see what we have cooked for you,' and Voula was tugging at my hand. It was that moment they all saw what I was wearing – Manolis's old *vrakes* and Voula shrieked with excitement: 'Now you are Mama and Papa too!' she said.

Yaya appeared in the doorway behind the girls, smiling at first, and then, as she cast her eyes down my body, she gasped and covered her mouth with her hand.

'Oh, *Panagia mou*, my child,' she said, 'What is this?'

I had shocked her. Suddenly I was like a child again myself, incurring her wrath.

I blushed. 'Forgive me. It seemed the best thing . . .' My voice tailed away.

She was shaking her head. 'You must do nothing, nothing, to make them notice you. Walk through Panagia like that and everyone will stare and if the army is patrolling and see you, that is the end. Besides, you are a widow now, you seem to forget that.'

She was dressed in deepest black and would do so for the rest of her life. Of course she would expect the same of me. But those cheerless, drab shifts are not for me.

The next day I learnt that lesson the hard way.

I was with the women at the spring. There were maybe five of us, six, no more. Marina was amongst them. She told me that Andreas hadn't spoken since his return. 'He sits in his chair all night, Anthi,' she said. 'He ignores the children. Every time I pass him, I rub his shoulder, his back, all the things he likes me to do, and nothing.' She lowered her voice. 'He weeps. All the time, his eyes fill with tears and he doesn't even brush them away. Slowly, slowly, they fall down to his lap. I tell you, it is a terrible thing to see a man like Andreas cry.' Her own voice was breaking. 'This bloody, bloody war. Why do they come here? What have we got?'

The other women were nodding, it seemed everyone had a story of horror they had seen. It was at that moment that we heard the sound of heavy footsteps approaching. Our men never come here. We stopped, our hands half in the sinks wringing out the clothes, scrubbing. We kept our heads down and nobody spoke.

'Stand up, women,' barked the one who seemed the leader. 'Come over here. NOW! Make a line.' He spoke bad Greek in a thick, heavily accented voice, hard to understand.

We shuffled together to do as were told but we were stumbling and clumsy. They had guns, these men, and although they had uniforms of a sort, they were stained and dirty. Collars open. They looked like rubbish with unshaven chins and greasy hair. Soldiers of the Cretan army would be ashamed to be seen turned out like that. Curiously, that thought gave me strength; I felt superior.

The leader shouted something; it sounded like an order, but none of us could understand. He repeated it, furious that, in front of his men, we couldn't tell what he was saying. Then he pushed forwards and seizing the nearest woman roughly, tore her blouse from her body.

It was Marina. She screamed and tried to cover her bare breasts.

He waved his arms in a gesture that included all of us. 'You and you, all of you,' he shouted.

I thought, We are not deaf to be yelled at like dogs.

My fingers were slow, my buttons stuck. We were all clumsy, our fingers damp and thick. We looked at one another in fear. What did they want with us to make us undress? I could think of only one thing. My hands trembled and I could see from the corner of my eye we were all filled with the same thought.

We were down to our shifts, our blouses on the ground, soaking up the pools of damp scum from our laundry.

'Quick, quick!' yelled the one in charge, his rifle pointed at us. He then said something I didn't understand and the men smirked and sniggered. We moved, slow and clumsy, until we were exposed, half naked. I closed my eyes not to see my friends' and neighbours' shame. We had never seen the like before, and next to me Marina was muttering a prayer under her breath. Her breasts were full and proud before her. Panos's wife, Myrto, older than the rest of us, was openly crying and trying to cover her sad breasts that drooped, withered little sacks to her waist.

'The shoulders!' screeched the leader, and this I did understand. 'Look at their shoulders. Have they carried guns that cut into them?' and the men walked up and down the line peering at us. For sure, it was not only our shoulders under examination there. Marina closed her eyes and held her head high.

They stopped in front of each woman. It was the young ones who interested them most and they could not resist squeezing breasts and pulling nipples.

They kept us standing like that for half an hour or so in the full heat of the morning. I glanced sideways, we were all sweating and Myrto looked about to faint. I knew I was the only one who had been near a weapon, but for such a short time it left no traces.

And that was it. That was all they wanted to know; had we carried rifles, were we *andartes*?

They cleaned their boots in our sinks and used our linen, lying carelessly there, to wipe them. Then they were gone.

As they disappeared under the cypress trees I spat on the ground. '*Malakas*,' I said to their backs, and one by one the women took it up. '*Malakas, malakas*,' and they spat as I had done.

Filthy rubbish!

HEAVENLY

There is a curfew now, the same all over Greece. Enough resistance fighters have been tracked to the hills and fought back. They travel by night; darkness their only cover.

For days there has been no word from Christo. Exhausted by the worry, my pregnancy and the heat, I couldn't sleep and sat on the terrace watching the moon and stars, listening to the cicadas and the bullfrogs and trying to plan for a hopeless future.

When Anthi was back, we went together to the little chapel on the hill, St Kosmas and Damianus, and cleaned it. The only thing I knew for certain was that it was the place for my baby to be born, away from the eyes of the village. We swept and tidied. I took blankets and sheets there and the dwindling remains of my medical supplies.

Despina and Voula came with flowers and decorated it with twigs and branches and old bits of ribbon and lace. It became a little more cheerful in moments.

And then Christo came back to me.

He came under cover of the night and I could see he was exhausted and changed by what he had seen. Just as Anthi had creases round her eyes now and lines of anxiety around her mouth, so Christo looked in some lights like an old man. It was as if his youth had been stolen away.

We lay on my bed and he told me some of the things he had seen. I guessed he gave me a censored version. His eyes were closed as he spoke, but he told me they would be part of his life for ever now. He would never get away from those images of death and destruction. 'In the centre of the island,' he whispered hoarsely, 'I saw a village burnt to the ground. Men, women and children shot and chucked into pits roughly dug from the earth by their killers.' He kept stopping and clearing his throat, and his hands trembled ceaselessly. 'At the very hint that anyone was harbouring one of the *andartes*, their house would be flamed and whoever was inside lined up and shot. Those bastards even raped the women.' He was whispering now and I strained to hear. It seemed important to know. 'In front of their men and their children. How do children ever recover from that?' His voice was tight with emotion and anger. 'And often, they'd just be carelessly kicked aside like an old dog and left there without any hope of surviving.'

I stroked his head but there was no comfort for him tonight.

If he could only weep, I thought, it might give him some release from this terrible pain inside. I thought he drifted into sleep as I held him, but he was awake again within minutes.

'They won't defeat us, Heavenly. Cretans have always fought back harder than anyone in the world, I think. Not everyone gave up their guns or their old hunting rifles, thank the Panagia, and those that have them have still taken them out of hiding. They crawl on all fours, day and night, through thorns, cistus bushes, stones and streams. They are full of nervous energy and every single one of them is determined to be rid of yet another *malaka* trying to take over our island, our Crete.'

'Who are they all, these fighters? Where do they come from?'

'They are all mountain boys who have lived in the hills shepherding their family flocks since childhood. There are hundreds and hundreds of them all across the island. They'll do anything, whatever is needed. And I tell you, Heavenly, it's not only the men and boys. It's the women too! I think anyone who is able or who is not running the home is out there. One night I was following a group crawling through gorse and when we got clear, I saw the leader was an old woman – she must have been ninety. She had a great curved knife tucked into a belt, ready for action. It seems they can sniff out the enemy wherever they are, and they hide in caves or under rocks or bushes, determined to fight to the death.'

I shook my head in wonder. 'We have nothing like this in England,' I said.

'England has never been invaded, totally under the command of an enemy power. If it were . . .' His voice tailed away into thought.

I was pleased that he had stopped trembling. Speaking of his *andartes* had cheered him.

'In between fighting, they are messengers carrying information from one group of our friends, our supporters, to another. British, Australian and New Zealanders can only operate with this undercover help. Agni, remember? The girl that works alongside Kotso?'

'Of course! I never questioned who she was or what she was doing. I suppose I assumed she was Kotso's girlfriend.'

He snorted with laughter. 'She is one of the best runners on the island. Kotso may wish she would warm his bed for him, but she's far too busy helping the *andartes*.'

He stroked my belly and within moments he slept. There seemed little peace in that sleep. He cried out often and once sat upright and pushed the air away in front of him with a violence that in him was new.

'Hush, hush,' I whispered to him and stroked his brow, damp with sweat.

We woke with the birds; their sweet calls like a murmur of close friends nearby.

Christo left before sunrise. He turned to me, took my hand and said quietly, 'In all the horror I have seen, and I know all the tragedy that must lie ahead, there is one thing that keeps me sane, my Heavenly. It is you and this,' his hand caressed

341

my belly, 'the child of our love, here. I never lose sight of that. It is what I live for, now.'

And he was gone again.

I knew we would meet later at dusk in the hospital chapel. He and Kotso had brought Bingo and a New Zealand boy, a soldier, back with them. They were badly in need of attention.

It seemed the Germans had left Bingo for dead on that beach and, with the help of the girl Agni and her mule, they had journeyed by night back to Panagia. A perilous trip made possible only because of the clouds over the moon giving them darkness.

In the full morning I wanted to go immediately up the mountain, but as I was about to leave to collect Anthi, Aphrodite came.

'You must come with me to Papa Yannis,' she puffed, patting her chest with her hand as if to increase the intake of air.

'Oh, why? He is mended now and Sophia is there for him.'

'He wishes to thank you in person.' And she collapsed panting into a chair. 'I think you must come this one last time. He has something to say to you.'

I heaved myself up, and went along the path resenting every second that was keeping me away from the mountain and the wounded men there.

He was sitting in a chair, waiting for God or me, who knew? The flush had gone from his face, his hair seemed thinner, but the flesh on his cheeks and throat had thickened, coarsened. It was a face in decay, falling and sliding down from its bones, sprouting veins and moles and fat greasy blemishes. I could see an old man there already.

He held a shaky hand out to me and gestured for me to sit.

I did so cautiously. The stool he offered was too low and small to accept my bulk with any comfort so I hoped he'd get this over with fast.

'I owe you my life, Kyria Timberley. And I shall never forget that.'

I thought, longer than you remember my name, perhaps.

'I have not lived a blameless life, you know.' I tried not to snort with the disgust I felt at this. 'But as I faced death I knew I must make my peace with God. I have prayed for redemption, Kyria, and I know if it is to be granted to me I must be a good, a better, person from now until the end of whatever life is left to me.'

There was more in this vein but I was thinking that if there was a god and it was as easy as that to pay for your sins, it was a strange world we lived in. I was getting cramped from this wretched stool and the baby was playing football inside, so I wriggled and stood up.

Aphrodite looked quickly to me and raised an eyebrow. I knew that the papa had had a visit from Papa Costas, days ago, and Yorgo said he had never seen him so afraid in his life. I made myself shake his quivering old hand, his tongue still darting back and forth wetly out of his mouth, but I felt I was safe from his betrayal at least and I made my farewells.

Outside we went our separate ways, but I had barely reached my house before Yorgo arrived. He was puffing and panting along the path just like his wife.

He was fatter now than when he had worked on my house. It seemed while the rest of the village suffered the deprivation of war, Yorgo thrived.

'Come, Heavenly, Kyria Heavenly, I mean. Aphrodite says you must come at once, please. The tinker has arrived at our house.'

'Oh please, I have no need of the tinker today. I must go to the chapel on the mountain, there are sick men there.'

'Oh, Kyria, just a few minutes, please? 'He was flustered, gabbling. 'Aphrodite says I must bring you and I must do as she says.'

The man inside their house was a stranger to me. He was old and his donkey seemed even older. His nut-like face was wrinkled and brown, a man who lived in the air, the wind and the sunshine. Yorgo told me he was a tinker like his father and grandfather before him. He travelled around the mountain villages, scouring copper pots, sharpening knives and even sometimes mending shoes. I knew that wherever these travellers went they collected snippets of gossip or sometimes meaty chunks of scandal to pass on from village to village.

Since the occupation his travel, like all the cobblers, coopers and tinkers had been curtailed. Travelling was difficult around the mountains now with the strict curfew. But he had news from Athens where his brother had been earlier in the year and this was what they thought I should hear.

It made terrible listening. There was starvation in the poorer districts of the city. Bodies lined the streets, thrown from houses for public collection. It sounded medieval in its horrors. The swastika was flying now over the Parthenon. Official buildings were closed; the museums, council offices and embassies bolted and shuttered tight, although there was looting and most of them had been broken into anyway.

'Shocking, shocking,' said Yorgo. But I felt unable to have much concern for antiquities, however priceless. It seemed trivial in the face of human suffering.

Then he gave us news of the royal family.

Some months ago he had travelled through a mountain village in the north of Crete, Therissos. There was much excitement there as the king and the royal family and even the prime minister had come and sheltered before heading off across the White Mountains.

The king and the prime minister slept in the dairy and most of the others under the trees, huddled up together in sleeping bags or tattered blankets.

The women of the village had scorned them when they first arrived. Who were these men who weren't away fighting? When they realised they treated them like, well, like royalty.

'These days everybody loves the king,' said Yorgo as he offered a basket of bread to the tinker.

They were a strange party: New Zealanders, Greek soldiers, local police and Cretans, young and old. With them came prisoners from the gaol in Aghyia: freed by the invaders and left to roam. But they were forced to stay behind when the king and his party left the next day. The tinker said the women were not so civil to them and chased them out of the place waving brooms and sticks. And then he told us he had heard that some 'handsome English man' dressed in village clothing had arrived the next day and escorted the group to Agia Roumeli and then to Sphakia.

'From there,' the tinker said, 'they were to go by ship, to British territory, Egypt. They even asked if any villagers wanted to go with them for safety. But, of course, everyone wanted to stay and fight.' He drank deeply of the wine Yorgo had poured for him and wiped his mouth on his sleeve.

When he had gone, Aphrodite said, 'That Englishman he described, Heavenly, that must be your husband!' She was so excited the words came tumbling and falling drunkenly from her lips.

'Of course, of course it was You,' said Yorgo, vivid with the thrill of all this news. It was almost as though he had crossed the White Mountains himself. 'What a brave man is You,' he said. 'Fancy that, a man from this village, our friend, escorting the king across those dangerous peaks in winter. What do you think of that then?'

I shook myself back. I had been lost in thoughts of Hugh in Egypt.

'Well, that's good news of course. When do you think all this happened?'

'It was cold, so that sounds like winter. Mind you, up in the north it's still cold in May and you can see the snow on the mountains there right through until the vine harvest, so who knows really?'

I had heard all I needed so I excused myself hastily and hurried on.

It was impossible not to feel a pride in what Hugh had achieved. I imagined him now in Cairo regaling Lady Troutbeck and her chums. He would be proud of himself, and rightly so. He had shown the courage of a hero. I was happy that he had achieved such distinction – the stuff of legends.

I found Anthi and the girls on the path. She had seen Kotso, learnt what was happening and come to help. The doors and shutters were open, but there was a smell of sickness inside our little hospital.

I could only remember the day when we had come with the children and their families and played at being nurses and patients. The memory was oddly shocking in the face of the reality that greeted us just now. Two men were lying on the makeshift beds. They were filthy. They had travelled without stopping across the country. No place or time for bathing or clean clothes. They were alive, but barely so.

Anthi sent the girls to prepare bowls and pans of clean water. We had no means of heating it so it would have to be cold. We looked quickly at the New Zealander. He would survive and I sent Anthi to clean him up.

I went to Bingo's side and knelt clumsily there. His dear boy's face was cut and bruised, his hair matted with dry blood. His eyes were puffed and swollen and he could barely open them. When he saw me his poor face tried to crease into a smile.

'Hullo, Nurse,' he said. 'Excuse me if I don't get up, will you?' I put my hand gently on his shoulder.

'Don't think of it,' I said. 'We'll get you mended and up and about and then we'll work on your manners.'

'That's the ticket,' he whispered through cracked lips.

He was having difficulty breathing; gasping for air and wheezing. I feared pneumonia had already set in. It's usually the way with neglect. He had needed help long before this. I turned my head away not to show the anxiety and fear I felt. I wasn't at all sure how much I could help him and the thought made tears well up.

'Pull yourself together, Tyler,' I thought.

'Nurse,' he said, 'Nurse, I'm cold, nurse.' He was shivering with the rigors of his fever.

'It's Heavenly, Bingo, remember?'

'Nurse, nurse, so cold, nurse.' He didn't know me.

346

I called Despina over with some water. She crept towards me on tippy toes, trying hard not to spill a single drop.

I wasn't sure how much to involve her, how much to protect her from the darkness of this young man's condition. But as soon as she was with me she knelt down beside him. I watched her for a moment. She soothed his coarse hair back from his face with fingers so gentle. He closed his eyes and I could feel a calm move through him. She stroked him so gently that her little face creased with the effort of not hurting him. Quickly I took one of the strips of clean linen that Anthi and I had prepared and wrung it out in the water.

'Good girl,' I whispered, 'you remember perfectly what to do.'

I glanced across quickly towards Anthi and the other lad. He seemed peaceful and cleaner already. Her hands moved quickly, efficiently. Beside her, Voula looked across to her sister and, seeing what she was doing, moved her hand across the New Zealander's forehead in the same movement. Her free hand was raised to her chin, her thumb firmly in her mouth.

Slowly and as carefully as I could, I washed Bingo's face. Looking down, I knew I would have to cut his shirt off and see the rest of the damage underneath. As though she knew what I was thinking, Despina gently started to undo the buttons. Her fingers were so quick and dextrous. His chest was soon revealed to us and I flinched, but she seemed not to notice the wounds. She eased the sleeves back and looked at me. I nodded and she was up and moving like a gazelle, crossing the floor to the pile of linen in the corner.

We worked on together like that, squeezing the water through the cloths. Every few minutes she would lift the zinc pan up and stagger across the chapel with it to the door, chuck it outside and fill it again from the spigot on the wall.

But the fever raged through Bingo, and however much we bathed him down with cool water, nothing would cause this heat to leave him. He was drifting in and out of consciousness and his skin had the blueish tint of death.

Although I tried to lift his head I couldn't persuade his lips to stay open long enough to get him to drink.

A spasm of cramp shot through me and I stretched my aching back up and out, but nothing would shift it and I had to stand and walk, move around somehow. My belly had never felt heavier and I clasped my hands under it to help take the weight while I walked back and forwards and back again.

Despina had found a large leaf from somewhere and was stirring the air over Bingo's face, trying to cool him.

I went over to Anthi and the other young man.

'This is Jack,' she said quietly.

He looked up at me. 'How d'you do, nurse,' he said. 'Am I in heaven already, or are you angels living down here these days?'

Anthi had done a good job of cleaning him up and although bruised pretty badly, he already looked considerably better than when we had started.

I smiled when I saw that Voula had curled up at his side now and was fast asleep. 'She's like one of my puppies,' he said, his hand now stroking her hair as she lay. 'We just had a litter when I got called away. My old mum cursed you lot, but I said to her, "Mum, I gotta go and give old Mr Hitler a good seeing to, you'll have to get 'em going on your own."'

While he was speaking, Anthi had pulled back the blanket covering him and I saw his legs. One was mashed up badly and she had cleaned that too. There seemed to be no sign of infection and I knew if we kept it clean, with luck, it would heal. I nodded and she covered him again. He had drifted into sleep so Anthi stood up and stretched her own aching back, looking anxiously across to Despina who was now singing softly, sweetly to Bingo.

'She's fine, Anthi, 'I said. 'She's doing a good job.'

Jack slept on for most of the afternoon. Sleep was the best cure. I yawned and Anthi persuaded me to rest too. Nothing would make Despina leave Bingo's side. She sang softly on, fanning him with no sign of weariness.

I must have dozed but jerked awake at a cry. Swiftly I rose

and was at Bingo's side at once. Outside the sun was slowly leaving the sky and falling back over the edge of the mountain as Voula played with the doll she had carried up here.

'There, there,' she said, 'better soon.'

But the cry was from Bingo and as I sat down heavily beside him, I saw there would be no better soon for him. The fever racked his body and he was struggling in desperation for each agonising breath. The rattling in his chest grew louder and his breathing was laboured.

'What can I do?' Despina looked up at me, her eyes troubled, reflecting pain.

'Nothing more than you are doing now, little one.'

Death was not kind. It came slowly. His eyes flickered open for a moment and he reached out with his hot, dry hand. She took it in hers and stroked it tenderly.

'Nurse, nurse,' he whispered urgently. And then, 'Just smell those roses.'

There were no roses.

He struggled, gasping for a breath, smiled a moment. 'Lovely roses, Mother,' he said, and breathing deeply just once, he was gone.

'Has he died?'

I answered her gently, but the words almost caught in my throat. 'Yes, he has.'

'Everybody here dies now,' she said bitterly, and ran outside.

A day or so later, in a troubled sleep, I was woken by cramps. They started gently but, within moments, were insistent enough to wake me thoroughly. I had been lost in a dream and at first I didn't know who or where I was. Was it night? Day?

At that time sleep washed over me at all hours, but sometimes a long night passed where I barely closed my eyes. The sun was high on the horizon, so I guessed it to be about five in the afternoon. I was living in Christo's cave. It was no secret.

I had given up toing and froing from my house to the

hospital, I needed my energy just to live and help any of the sick and wounded that were brought to us.

The day I left my house was one of those perfect days. Early sun from across the mountains, a soft breeze, a golden, precious day.

That morning I walked slowly around the house that I knew now as home. I remembered that first day I'd seen it. How instantly I had fallen in love. How I knew I wanted it to be in the years ahead with our children, Hugh's and mine, running around and through it. They were, of course, in my dreams, always laughing.

Now there I was, gross in my belly with Christo's child and no thought of my future at all. There, by the old wine press with the sweet, amber scent of dried pomegranates heavy in the air. Tears of sadness filled my eyes for this house, still known throughout Panagia as the old Orfanoudakis house, where I had grown up. Every other place I'd lived in through the years faded beyond memory.

This was where I had left Evadne. This was where I'd found Heavenly.

I lay for a little, drifting and dozing, but the cramps this time were growing stronger and my belly was tightening and seemed to be pulling me down. I stood up and that simple movement released a flood, a torrent that fell from me. It soaked my night shift and left me standing in a puddle of water. So, it was time.

I had given up counting the days as I kept forgetting where I had started. But I was huge and felt I had been so forever! Each interminable day seemed never-ending, and a little cramp here, a spasm through me there, had me on my feet at once, day or night thinking, This is it, this is the moment, only for everything to settle calmly again – another false alarm.

I had to think quickly, what should I do? New-found independence I may have had plenty of, but I didn't want to bring my baby into the world alone.

Anthi and Christo, I needed them both, and as if my prayer had been heard there was a soft whistle from outside. Christo! Not waiting for an answer he came in, gently calling my name.

'I'm here,' I said.

I hadn't moved and he stood in the entrance, taking in what was happening. Crossing over to me, ignoring the puddle, he put his arms around me and nuzzled softly into my hair. 'Is it now?'

We had spoken often of what we should do when the time came. Now it was here my mind was a blank. Except for one thought, one anxiety.

'Can you help me, Christo? Can you really be with me?'

He looked momentarily puzzled. 'Do you doubt I can help you?'

He had never voiced his feelings about blood; I had never asked. I thought it was private, for him alone to know. Anthi had told me of what had happened when they were away. How he had vomited. 'It was terrible there,' she'd said, 'we were all frozen with horror. But Christo, our brave leader, seemed, somehow, to take it more personally. I don't know.'

I had told her what Yorgo knew about his mother. She nodded. 'I suppose so, I guess that's it.'

Now he looked at me and slowly nodded. 'It's natural you should be worried. But I've thought about this moment and all I feel is excitement. In all the horror that is going on – something good, something beautiful, will come out of it. My child, our baby, and I will be part of its arrival with you.'

The pains were stronger now, regular, about every five minutes.

'I have the mule here, Agni's mule. Anthi is at the hospital. I've just come from there. It's quiet today, not much happening there or anywhere. I think everyone is trying to get the last of the harvest in before the threatened storms come.'

He half pushed, half lifted me into the saddle and I winced at the hardness beneath me. I saw his hand shaking as he grasped the reins.

Our journey up the mountain took twice as long as usual and every movement, every jolt, sent another spasm through me and I couldn't help the groans that fell from my lips.

I don't think Christo had been near a woman in labour before, why would he?

He looked at me and there was fear in his eyes. 'Is it bad? What can I do?'

Between contractions I managed a smile. 'Nothing, it is normal. Don't worry.'

At last, the small bell-tower of the whitewashed church was in sight and I begged Christo to let me walk the rest of the way. But each remaining step caused me to groan and much as I tried to stifle each one, I could see Christo was now rigid with alarm. He had one arm around me and the reins clutched tight in the other. Under his breath I could hear him whispering to the Panagia for help, something I had never known him do before.

'Mama! Mama! Come quickly, Heavenly is here and she is injured!' Standing in the doorway, Despina was the first to see me. I tried to call but the effort was too great and I found I had dropped to my knees, weak and faint.

'Despina, take the reins,' I heard Christo call through the haze that seemed to fill my mind and before I could speak or look around I was lifted high in his arms and carried in through the door.

ANTHI

Heavenly's baby, a boy weighing the same as a sack of figs, was born in the heat of August on the night of the full moon.

Christo stayed beside her, but I think it was hard for him see her in pain. She was lying on one of the makeshift beds, a sheet thrown over her bare body and her cramps were coming fast now. She knew what to do, of course, and panted hard with each new spasm. I offered her some *dictamus* tea and she managed to sip that in between times.

Every now and again she got off the bed and, to Christo's astonishment, she crouched down on all fours, still panting. I remembered my own time and, try as I might to think only of Voula, little Constantinos kept coming to my mind. It had been seven years and not a day passed without my thinking of him, imagining how he would look.

Mercifully, the worst heat of the day was over. A tiny breeze scented with sage and wild thyme whispered in and she took great gulps of that air as though it were a soothing drug. We were alone. Christo and two villagers took the last of the injured away yesterday. No more Bingos, no more dying; well, not yet, not here.

There are thousands and thousands dead all over Crete, Christo tells me. Remembering Neapolis as I do every day, to know there are other villages similarly savaged is the fabric of my nightmares. More wives made widows, more children without fathers, more mothers without sons and more grand-children left without their beloved Pappous.

Christo stayed beside Heavenly, she was gripping his hand,

biting her lip in the effort not to cry out. On the other side was my Despina. Nothing would keep her away. 'I know what to do, Mama, and anyway I am as strong as you.'

'I doubt that, *koritsaki mou*, but we will let Heavenly decide.'

'She said I could, Mama! I told her that if I am a good enough nurse to help people to die, surely I can help them to be born? And she said there was no answer to that.' She was now bathing Heavenly's face with cool water. Voula was keeping company with my Yaya. The girls had rescued her from a lonely old age, though for how long, I could only wonder. She lived with the savagery of Pappous' passing and the horrors of that seemed etched on her face. In spite of the girls, she rarely smiled and the deep black of her mourning did her no favours.

I couldn't bear to think of what would happen to this baby.

At the time Heavenly was living in Christo's cave. It was closer and she was in the hospital most days. It made sense, in fact it was Aphrodite's idea, and so the women at the spring could only agree. Heavenly could do nothing wrong in their eyes; they knew how hard she worked with the *andartes* and they saw her bring Papa Yannis back from Heaven's door.

Everyone knew Christo had vacated the cave for Bingo the wireless operator and slept wherever he ended up each day.

'Don't you mind being homeless?' I asked.

'Heavenly is my home.'

Jack, the New Zealander, was one of the last to leave. He mended well and stayed around to help us. Voula adored him, following him like a shadow, and even Despina smiled more easily when he was around.

She taught him backgammon with the set Pappous had made her. In return, he showed her conjuring tricks. He made us all laugh and Heavenly, and even Yaya, said it was a long time since they had seen me looking so well.

'Even happy,' said Heavenly. Well, it's a long time since anyone paid me a compliment, especially a man. Jack's blue eyes used to crinkle into a smile and he called me 'angel'. 'You two are Heavenly and Angel,' he said one day and it stuck. He wasn't very tall, but he was certainly strong and full of a barbarous energy. He wasn't quite the boy I first thought; he was a man, probably older than me. He wouldn't let us lift or carry anything heavy or awkward.

'Well, Heavenly carries the baby and you, Angel, carry the world on your shoulders.'

I tried to tell him that I had always done it. 'It's the life,' I said, 'I'm used to it being this way.'

'Well not when I'm around. You're too pretty to do all that stuff.' I knew I was red, Heavenly told me so: 'You're blushing, Angel,' and she laughed.

He was a brave man. He had little fear for his own safety and Christo said he was a good runner for the *andartes*. He seemed as at home in the mountains as he must have been in his own country. 'You would love it there, Angel.' The night was full of stars, the gibbous moon sitting hunchbacked in the sky. Voula was asleep beside him, her head was in his lap and his hand was stroking and soothing her hair. He had strong hands.

'I've worked with animals all me life,' he said when I commented on them. 'A thousand sheep and counting. One day at a time, Angel, I know.' I had often said this to him, many times when he told me of his fanciful dreams. 'But I can only hope. Let's get this ruddy war over, get them dirty Krauts back where they belong, and who knows, eh?

He had made us some more beds out of old doors we found in the village. They were rough and ready but, covered with thick grass matting, they were better than nothing. Aphrodite and her neighbours and friends had begged us some blankets and linens from the villagers. 'What use is a dowry if you are not alive to use it?' one said.

Jack went down to stay in one of the caves by the sea. His New Zealand regiment, the 22nd Battalion, had left Suda Bay to return home. 'Probably thought I was dead,' he said cheerfully. Yaya gave him some of Pappous' *vrakes* and an old sailor's cap. He grew a fine beard, mostly black, but speckled with grey, and he passed for a fisherman, 'as long as no one expects me to open me mouth, I'll do. See you later, Angel, I'll be back.'

I missed him dreadfully.

But still the war went on. Those who had thought that it would only take three weeks, three months, for the Hun to be sent back home, all finished by the olive harvest, are not so cocky now. We coped with it at first as though it was a bad dream.

So when one night a small convoy of casualties – five or six men on lice-ridden stretchers, with appalling wounds, moaning softly, dismally, for their mothers or their wives – arrived silently in Panagia, brought from God knows where by the *andartes*, then the reality came to us.

Suddenly everyone was very quiet and came slowly out of their houses to look at them, these shadows of men. The women clasped their hands together tightly, biting their lips. I think everyone felt helpless and ashamed as, for sure, they were all glad it was not their husband or son lying there.

It took hours to get them up the mountain to the chapel. How much quicker, someone said, to keep them here in one of the village houses. 'And have them dead by the end of tomorrow,' Christo said. We knew he was right. The enemy sent patrols frequently and with no warning, foraging for food. No, the chapel and the nearby caves were the only places with any chance of safety. It was such a trek to get up there, so far they had been ignored.

Word of a little makeshift hospital had spread like a fire through the *andartes* in this part of the island, but none knew where it was. It was a tightly guarded secret. Somehow Christo had acquired a large box of medical supplies and he and Yorgo lugged it up the mountain, disguised by straw on one of Yorgo's donkeys.

I came up here most days. I thought my girls had seen enough sickness and death to last them for ever, but Voula seemed not to notice and Despina wanted to help. And she did. She bandaged efficiently and was not bothered by the sight of a bloody wound. She also, along with Jack, fetched and carried fresh water for hours each day from the mountain stream that flowed alongside the chapel.

Aphrodite and Yaya, even Irini, offered help, but we kept them away. They had more to do in the village than they could cope with anyway. With many of the men away with the *andartes*, the women did all the men's work as well as their own and neighbours happily helped each other.

Yorgo tended all our gardens, mine as well as Yaya's, watering and cutting whenever there was need.

A loud cry from across the room and Heavenly is nearly there, I think. I push Christo away from her and take his place. 'No place for a man,' I say, and laying a kiss on her damp forehead, he reluctantly goes to sit outside the door. So it's just Despina and me. She is pale with fatigue, but will not leave, and her eyes sparkle at the miracle happening in front of her.

Heavenly smiles up at me for a moment, her face wet with sweat, her hair spread damply wide across the pillow. She kicks away the sheet I have pulled up for modesty.

'Aahhhh,' and her face is a mask of freckles and crinkles as she strains to push. She is panting with exhaustion, but even in the throes and indignities of childbirth she is beautiful. 'Harder, harder,' I tell her. 'Nearly there.'

'Look, Mama, look.' Despina's eyes are wide with wonder – there below is the very top of the head just coming into the world. There is a whisper of damp, dark hair and with one final great cry from Heavenly, the baby slithers wetly out and into mine and Despina's clasped hands.

'You were right, it's a boy.' There was a roaring great yell from this new little person. His eyes opened milkily and through long, black lashes he blinked at us all. His blue colour flushed red as he took his first breaths.

Heavenly couldn't wait. She grabbed hold of the wet,

slippery, bloodstained little chap and put him naked to her breast and laughed and cried all at once.

Christo ran back inside and, modesty or no, he gazes down at his son and his lover. We are all weeping together with the joy of this moment.

Constantinos she has called him. 'For you, my dearest friend, Angel.'

And so we have a Constantinos with us now. He is a beautiful, healthy baby and he is surrounded by love. All the love my own Constantinos was never allowed.

But I have to ask, have to know, and even through the great joy you can almost feel in the air of this little hospital, this church, what now for Heavenly? What now for Christo, the father, unacknowledged though he is? And what now for Constantinos?

HEAVENLY

We have not seen Christo here in the cave for nearly a week. The runner Agni simply shrugs if we ask for him. Her frown worries me, but then what is there to smile at outside this place?

And then, late, he is here and in the glow of the oil lamp I light in his honour, I see how gaunt, worn and tired he looks. He limps too, painfully, but waves me aside when I ask him why.

He sinks to the floor and as our baby smiles at him, he holds his arms out to take him.

I think Constantinos knows his smell, just as I do. The scent of the mountains, the thyme and wild garlic, the rosemary and the cypress trees, all are here in this man, along with the rough sweat of his labours.

Every time he is here now he talks to me, tells me of some of the horrors he has seen. I encourage him to do so. It is devastating to hear, but I like to think somehow it relieves him to share it with me.

This week another village burnt to the ground and all the men over fifteen were lined up and shot. He has heard there are a thousand such villages across Greece. The women are left in the ashes of their homes with the children and no food or water. They have to crawl away to try and find refuge elsewhere.

'Today I found a baby, just like my Constantinos here, lying on the ground, scarcely breathing. His mother gone or shot dead, who knows?' He pauses, his breathing jagged, rough. His lips buried in Constantinos's hair. 'He died in my arms. I buried him as best I could.'

I put my arms around them both and pulled them close to me; my two most loved people.

He said, 'I hope never to bury another child as long as I live.'

And then with Constantinos fed and asleep between us, at last, Christo slept too. He left at dawn with a rough kiss on the head of his sleeping child and a slow smile for me.

And now here it is, our last few hours living in this cave high in the mountains together. It is simple, but it has become our home.

It has been a beautiful red and gold autumn day, still touched at the edges with moments of summertime. And the evening before, there had hardly been a hint of chill in the air. The soft-scented silence feels as deep and endless as the sky.

Constantinos is twelve weeks old today and a chubby, healthy baby. His eyes are blue, just as Christo's, and his black hair is tipped with auburn through the curls. Of all the things to inherit, he has my hair! When I bathe him and wash it, it dries to a frizz just like mine. His smile is like his father's: it seems to light up the air around him. He rarely cries; if he does, it is a sound to break my heart.

It's too dangerous to take him to the village, to leave from deep inside these mountains, so we move between the cave and the hospital. Constantinos is always on my hip or my back. Anthi had brought me the length of strong, brightly coloured linen that her Yaya first wove to strap her father to her back and then passed to Anthi for Despina and Voula. All that time ago, when I first met Anthi, that was how I remembered her.

But mostly my Constantinos was in my arms. I couldn't bear to put him down. Although I did, of course, when I was nursing any casualties that had found their way to us. Mostly they were the *andartes*, the village boys and men who left their wives to tend their flocks and worked together with fire in their loins and often little else.

All of them paused when they saw my baby son, fingered him under his chin or gave him their thumb to clutch tightly, which he did happily. Then, in spite of their pain, they always, every one of them, smiled.

'I think he is better than all our medicines,' Anthi said one day. 'He is the future. It is for all the baby Constantinoses everywhere that they are fighting.'

Usually they were with us only a day or so, the longest a week and then they were off, away, and although we never spoke of it, Anthi and I, we both knew many of them would never make it home again and their wives and mothers would be caring for their flocks for a long time yet.

Voula came most days and just sat beside us smiling. She seemed as bewitched by Constantinos as I was. He loved to play with her fingers and she had been trying to teach him to suck his thumb. But this was not for him. He pulled it out from between his lips and blew a bubble or two instead to make us smile.

He seemed to need no other comfort but my breast when he was hungry and, from time to time, a clean undercloth.

I thought I knew love. I had loved Hugh and oh, my Christo, how I love him. But nothing in my life had prepared me for this magic, here and now; my baby, my son, my Constantinos.

Sometimes I caught myself forgetting to breathe, so carried away was I by the thrilling intensity of my love for this little one, and a moment of dizziness brought me sharply back to earth. I took in the soft, damp, warm sweetness of him with a gulp of air. Grown inside me, inseparable, he was me.

That day I knew would be the most difficult and painful day of my life: I had to say goodbye to Constantinos. Christo was coming at daybreak and then I knew I would never, could never, see him again.

How could I do this thing? I didn't know if I could bear it.

But the only thing I could give my son was a life, so I had to do it.

I remembered from Greenbridge the girls who came to have their babies and leave them for the orphanage or adoption. Matron said it was easier for them never to see the baby at all and they were removed and placed in the nursery within minutes of their birth. And I remembered the pain of those poor girls, who would weep piteously through the nights, begging to be allowed to hold them, just once.

Never to see Constantinos, never to hold him, never to feed him from my breast, would that have been easier than this?

The only people from the village who knew that Constantinos lived, apart from Christo and me, were Anthi and her girls. Together we cared for him up the mountain, in the cave. Despina and even Voula knew and understood that our Constantinos was a secret baby. Despina, of course, at twelve, understood secrets. Anthi had finally told me of the horrors that sweet child had known.

As for Voula, this war and the terrible things she had seen had aged her beyond her seven years. She said to me one day, 'I dreamed of the Panagia and she told me I must never ever speak to anyone of Constantinos, even if they shoot me. And I won't, Heavenly, never ever.'

Christo and I had talked long into many nights and this was what we had decided for our son.

Anthi wept when I told her, but I think they were tears of relief as well as sadness. It was she who warned me from the beginning of the impossibilities of any alternative. If he lived here with me, if we survived the war, we should have to leave when it was over. This was Hugh's house and Hugh knew he had no child.

If I left with him now and took him away from there, how would we live and where would we go? Imagine, an Englishwoman and a baby in the wilds of the Cretan countryside? The enemy was everywhere. We would be captured and killed without a moment's thought.

Could I take him to England? I have asked myself that many times.

But there would have been no place for him. All I had there was my mother and she would not even have allowed me through the door with the bastard child, as Anthi said, of a wandering stonemason. Besides he was Cretan, like his father, and I would be denying him everything I now believed important. I wanted him to grow up in this wonderful island. Its history, his inheritance. I wanted to give him the sunshine to light his days. I wanted to give him the warm Aegean sea to swim in. And I wanted him to run in the olive groves and reach up into the cypress trees and shelter in the pine forests, and love this place as Christo did and as I did. And if I kept him I could give him none of that. He was going to be brought up in a village along the sea, past Sitia. It was not far in distance, but the two mountain ranges between us could be crossed only with great difficulty. His mother was going to be the happy wife of a fisherman there. He would be her only child and her brother, his Uncle Christo, would see him every day and watch over him for the rest of his life. At his baptism Christo would be his godfather and would never leave him.

Christo's sister and her husband longed for a child. But she had suffered many miscarriages and seemed unable to conceive. Her friends in her village would be told she had taken in an orphan of the war. There were many, and mostly they died, unless they were adopted into homes such as hers.

The day after Constantinos was born, Anthi went down to the spring. All the village women were gathered there. 'More for their mutual comfort than to do the laundry,' she said. There had been another raid at dawn the day before, another lesson to be taught to the villagers. This time the savages were from the German army. Christo said that he had heard they thought the Italians, who were the bulk of the occupying force around this end of Crete, were too soft on us! Soft? Was Pappous' death a game? So this was as much to shake them up as us.

They had marched into the village square and three men had been bound hand and foot, lined up outside the community centre and in the very place Pappous had died, they were shot by a firing squad.

One of them was Andreas. 'He died for nothing,' said Aphrodite, weeping. 'What lesson do we learn from this?'

'Only that none of us is safe,' said Anthi, tears falling from her own eyes.

Andreas's wife Marina was a shivering wreck of a woman these days and could barely find tears enough to weep. 'The things he saw happening on this island almost killed him already,' she said. 'To be honest, I think he was happy to die.'

So although they expressed their sympathy for me when Anthi told them my child had not survived, they were so occupied with their own grief that they could spare me barely a thought. 'A quick prayer to the Panagia and a promise to light a candle for you, no more. It's the Cretan way,' said Anthi. 'You know they have no time for other's illness, others problems. They are still so rooted in old superstitions they think they will catch bad luck if they come too close. No, Constantinos will be safe.'

So, a few weeks after his birth, I went back to my house, alone, leaving Constantinos with Anthi and the girls. I walked around, showed my face and offered sympathy.

Papa Yannis came to visit and fawned ingratiatingly. He was thin as a bone himself now and Anthi told me that the supply of luxury foods that had somehow always found a way to his door had dried up. 'His bribes and blackmails no longer work.' she said. 'There is so little for everyone to share they ignore him now.'

I barely gave him the glass of water he asked for, fanning his face with a far from clean handkerchief. I stood myself and didn't offer him a seat and he puffed and sweated his way back down the steps and was gone.

Although most days I went to the hospital, there were no further casualties needing my care for a while. Mostly the beds were used for the *andartes* to rest. Some of them were far from their homes and had nowhere to sleep.

Christo protested once, 'They are perfectly used to taking a blanket into the shade of a tree.'

'Not while there are empty beds here,' we said.

But Christo's cave was where I was to be found every day. Constantinos slept well and peacefully in a wooden tomato crate lined with Despina and Voula's old baby shawl. I sat beside him for hours at a time, gazing down at his glorious perfection. When I was not there the girls watched over him. He was never alone. Any tiny cry and one or other of us picked him up. I fed him every four hours; my breasts were heavy with milk and Christo loved to sit and watch us when he could.

Now, as I wait for Christo to come by, my breasts are aching and tender. But I must ignore them and wait now for the milk to dry up; my breasts no longer useful.

Christo's sister has found a wet nurse in her village. A woman she knows and likes who has plenty of milk for two.

Sophia, that will be Constantinos's mother. A lovely name and I try hard not to resent her. I must think only warm and good thoughts of her, for Constantinos and Christo's sake.

One thing I don't know, oh, Christo my love, and have asked him not to tell me, is if he will come back here when he has settled his son in his new mother's arms. If I am truthful to myself, I think, if he is to be the godfather to Constantinos he has promised to be, he will stay over there.

And I know I have to return to being Hugh's wife. I must think of him as my future. I try to remember the morning he left. He called me Heavenly and I hope that with my help he can change. I will think of how I loved him when we met and that has to carry me on to the future. But just now I can barely think of life without the two of them, my son and my lover. The loss of my son is enough, but I have told Christo it is not for me to choose and he knows there is a part of me that wants him to stay there, for Constantinos's sake.

Christo also knows there is a lot of work to be done if the people of our island are to survive, and there is plenty for him there where he comes from, just as much as Panagia.

The night has been long and every moment I try to recapture another memory to hold with me for ever; his birth, his smile, the tiny blister on his lips from sucking, the sweet almond scent of his hair and that wonderful, extraordinary feeling of feeding him at my breast. But now I hear the steps of a mule and in the low moonlit dust of the mountain path I can see Christo approaching. And now he is here.

We kiss and for a few precious moments I hold him tight in my arms. And then I hand him our baby, Constantinos, already wrapped in the shawl and sleeping peacefully.

And then they are gone.

I stand on the mountainside in the chill air of dawn and watch them ride away. Christo in the saddle with one hand resting protectively on our baby in front of him.

I have to be strong. I have to be brave. There will be no tears. There will be no tears. I stand still until they are far out of my sight and then I turn, alone, each movement a knife in my heart.

It was time for me to say goodbye.

AFTER WORDS

Tauranga
North Island, New Zealand

JANUARY 1972

ANTHI

I keep in touch with Panagia Sta Perivolia when I can. Aphrodite writes to me and tells me that she and Yorgo will come and visit one day soon. But she has been saying that for years and always something comes up with one of her children. I know that they have busy lives. One is a heart surgeon in Athens even!

I have a happy life here now. We live on Jack's family sheep farm. His father died some years ago and his brothers wanted to live elsewhere so my Jack keeps it going. I work beside him, there's a lot to do. We employ over twenty drovers and plainsmen and he says it's time I relaxed more. But he's said that ever since the day we met so he should know by now that I just shrug and say, 'It's the life,' and keep going.

I find it impossible to sit and do nothing. I read a lot but never during the day, that would feel like a sin.

We have three children. Despina and Voula, of course, but we also have a son. Jack said I should call him Constantinos, Costas, but I couldn't. That is all far away in the distance now. Besides, there is another Constantinos, isn't there?

My son's name is Stephanos, after Pappous, of course, but everyone calls him Stefan, which is fine. He started to go to agricultural college in Tasmania but got fed up after three months and came back here. 'I'll work beside Dad,' he said. 'I'll learn a whole lot more that way.'

My girls have done well; everything I ever dreamed of for them. Despina is a Professor of Medicine at Harvard University in America. From those days in our little hospital she longed to be a doctor, it was natural to her. And she rose steadily upwards in her profession – she is a clever girl. She comes home to us here once a year. She is a serious young woman, well, not so young any more. She is not yet married. It doesn't surprise me.

Voula is a teacher in Auckland. She loves her work, but has somehow found time to have four children, all girls. She married a paediatrician, a Cretan, Yannis, who came here from Heraklion to study, met Voula and never went home. They come here, all of them, every year for Christmas and Easter. I love the girls dearly and Jack spoils them terribly. He can never say no to them over anything, so it's not surprising they seem to love coming. Jack has given them a pair of fine horses that we keep stabled here for them. They live happily alongside the farm horses and my own stallion, Astrape. I couldn't resist calling him that.

Voula and her family go back to Crete every couple of years, but mostly to the north of the island. I sometimes wish she would go over to Panagia, just to visit, but why would she? Panagia is a place only of memories for her and so many of them sad.

And what of the old days?

Jack managed to live the life of a fisherman until the war ended. He came up to Panagia when he could and we gradually got to know each other better. I, who thought never to look at another man in my life, began slowly to realise that the pleasure I got from Jack's visits was becoming greater, more than simple affection between friends. I missed him when he left each time and counted the days until his return. The girls clearly loved him too. So when Yaya died just after the war, there was nothing to keep me there. Well, there was, of course, my mother and Ririca. They didn't care for me, they never had, and moved to live in Chania. I assume they live there the life of two miserable old women. Whether they are alive or dead, I have no idea.

Papa Yannis died, a lonely man, before the war ended. His

sister found him one morning dead in his bed. Good riddance!

At first it was hard to leave the village, but I had always
promised myself that I would give my girls a better life, away
from there, so for their sake I left. Well, if I'm honest, it was
for my sake too.

After the war, Panagia, like all the villages that survived,
would never be the same again. The Germans surrendered to
the British, they couldn't face the Greeks, I heard. When all
Europe had fallen, England and Greece had been left facing
the enemy alone. Jack bought me a book, which I treasure, a
New Zealand history book about the war in Crete. He said
he'd been told not to bother looking in the English books as
they didn't even give us a mention.

It seemed impossible to believe that six thousand on both
sides had died along with Pappous, Andreas and Bingo. And
more, too numerous to mention. But we who were there will
never forget them.

It seems that the spirit of hope and love, that Pappous had
always taught me was the future, was killed along with all the
casualties. For barely had we pushed the last German off our
land than Greece dissolved into civil war and once again
brother fought against brother, father against son. All that
sadness, all that pain and nothing changed.

And then there is Heavenly.

Ah, my dear, my beloved Heavenly.

She came to our little hospital just about every day and
went home most evenings, back to Christo's cave. I went over
there once and found her sitting in the entrance gazing up at
the stars, her cheeks wet with fallen tears. She was holding one
of Christo's cushions clutched to her belly, and wrapped
around it one of baby Constantinos's shawls. I hugged her to
me and something inside her seemed to give way, to spill over
and she cried and cried until I thought her heart would break.
My girls were with Yaya that night, I think. I know that I
stayed with her until dawn. Holding her and stroking her
back.

Christo did not come back to Panagia. I knew that he wouldn't. He told me so. He could not bear to be with Heavenly knowing that she would have to return to her husband at the end of the war. But also he had promised Heavenly he would be there for their son. And he was.

Whether she ever recovered from the loss of so much love in her life I never really knew. She seemed able somehow to keep herself going day by day. There was a constant stream of casualties needing our care. Kotso had taken over running the *andartes* in and around our hills and then the professor opened the school again and we worked side by side there as well. I know she had aged considerably by the end of the war and grief and pain were etched in fine lines on her face.

Hugh came back, something of a hero. Although, in a moment of intimacy and laughter, Heavenly told me he'd had a good war for the most part in Alexandria in Egypt. Of course she went with him back to Athens. They were there for some years and then they went to Thailand. I had many letters and postcards from her and I treasure them all.

The one that surprised me and, I suppose, pleased me the most came from Panagia. She and Hugh had a child, William. So that gave her the reason to stay there for some of the time while William grew up in the village. Eventually, of course, he went away to England to Hugh's old school. And then later she had a daughter whom she called Angel.

'She named her for you,' Jack said, but I told him not to be so silly.

She continued to send me photographs and news and gossip from the village. Everyone there had long forgotten her first pregnancy. I think they had forgotten she was English! So she could stay happily in Panagia as much as she was able.

And then, two weeks ago now, came the letter from Aphrodite.

'I don't know if you know this,' she wrote, 'but dear Heavenly died on September twenty-first. She had, it seemed, been ill for a year. Hugh, William and Angel were with her. She was buried in the morning in the little chapel of St Kosmas and Damianus at the top of the mountain. Remember it used to be your hospital during the war?

'A sad day that one, because in the afternoon we had to go over to Sitia for the funeral of Yorgo's nephew, Christo. He died suddenly of a heart attack. I know you knew him well when he lived here. He never married.'

I wept for days. I felt I had lost half of my soul. I had always loved her so much. And Christo's world was empty without her.

I try to be positive. I try to look forward, for somewhere there is Constantinos and, of course, William and Angel.

It is the life.

the house
of dust and
dreams

Reading Group Notes

In Brief

When Evadne Tyler marries Hugh Timberlake in the late 1930s, she thinks he's saved her from a tedious existence. But in fact life as a diplomat's wife is as dull and passionless as her marriage, and Evadne craves excitement.

She finds it when she and Hugh arrive in Crete, where Hugh has been despatched on temporary diplomatic business. They stay in an old, run-down house that belonged to Hugh's family which Evadne (renamed Heavenly by the villagers) loves, although Hugh longs to escape. She's befriended by Anthi, a village woman forced into marrying a man much older than herself, a bully with very different views to most of the villagers.

When Hugh is recalled to Athens, Heavenly stays behind to oversee renovations to the house, and it is only when Hugh leaves that Heavenly really begins to live. Not just working with Yorgo and his young nephew Christo, but also starting

to work with Anthi at the village school, teaching English.

Heavenly and Christo develop a strong friendship as they work together on the house, and she enjoys learning new skills. Soon, they become lovers, although she is racked with guilt and often thinks about her husband. But Christo has opened her eyes to the kind of relationship she could only dream of with Hugh.

The Italian invasion of Albania brings the threat of war closer to the Cretan villagers. Anthi's grandfather, who has previously resisted the call to lead the village, takes on the mantle of mayor. Anthi, who has guessed what is going on between Heavenly and Christo, is very concerned, and urges her to keep the affair secret or risk being run out of the village.

Heavenly begins spending more time at the school, and she and Anthi develop first-aid lessons for the children, aware that if war is to come it will be useful to have shared this skill. But some of the more traditional villagers don't like the modern medicine being practised. In particular Manolis,

Anthi's husband, is very unhappy with what is going on.

Shortly after she receives news that England has declared war on Germany, and that Hugh is on his way to Crete from Athens, Heavenly discovers she's pregnant. Meanwhile, Christo becomes involved in the underground resistance, determined to help protect his beloved island, as the situation in Albania and Greece deteriorates. When the island is invaded by the Germans, Anthi's grandfather is shot dead in the village square as a lesson to all the villagers. Desperate to help Christo and avenge her grandfather's death, Anthi joins the *andartes*. She goes out with Christo and another villager, Andreas, and they see for themselves the atrocities the Germans have committed against people across the island.

Meanwhile, Heavenly is called upon to use her modern medicine to save Pappa Yannis, the corrupt priest who is the only person in the village likely to betray her to the Germans. Shortly afterwards, Heavenly's baby Constantinos is born. But what future can there be for Heavenly, who

must return to her husband in Athens after the war, and what will happen to her baby and her one true love?

About the Author

B renda Reid's career began in television, as a script-editor and as a producer on a wide range of BBC productions before becoming Head of Drama at Anglia Television. She was nominated for a BAFTA for the drama *Drums Along Balmoral Drive* and shared an EMMY award with David Putnam for *A Dangerous Man*, starring Ralph Fiennes in his first screen role, as Lawrence of Arabia.

Other credits include *Ballykissangel*, *Chimera*, *Goldeneye* and *Unnatural Causes*. She has also worked with, amongst others, Alan Bennett, P.D. James, Fay Weldon, Lynda la Plante and Rose Tremain.

In addition to spending time in her village house in Crete, Brenda Reid lives between the Welsh borders and her children's houses in London.

THE STORY BEHIND

The House of Dust and Dreams

I have a love affair with the island of Crete. Years ago we restored a house in a mountain village there. It was the family home of the grandfather of dear friends and, like the house in the book, was known as the Orfanoudakis house. We are there whenever we can be, and friends, children and grandchildren come to the village to stay.

Sitting on the terrace there I am surrounded by the voices and sounds of the village, and the music and the smell of neighbours' cooking (which they frequently share with us). Being part of a life that hasn't changed for hundreds of years inspired me to tell a story. An imagined story with its roots in truth.

I read everything I could find about the battle of Crete in the Second World War. There was little in English history books. And yet it was a defining battle for Hitler – an invasion solely by air. If it had been successful, the British Isles would have been next on his list. And I learned that the Cretan villagers – men, women and children – fought back armed only with pitchforks, sticks, stones and old rabbit hunting guns. It was a truly heroic battle.

But I didn't want to write solely about the war. I wanted a love story, but more than that even. So I sat on my terrace and let myself dream. I imagined a young English woman coming to the village before the war. She would be tall and clumsy like me. And because friendship between women is important to me, my heroine, Heavenly, has a growing friendship with a young Greek woman, Anthi. Two women from different worlds coming together and growing together through good and bad times for Crete.

On that terrace with the songs of the birds, the clicking of the cicadas, the shouts of the elderly

card players from the taverna up the road and the songs of Greece playing through open doors and windows, *The House of Dust and Dreams* gradually came to life.

Brenda Reid

For Discussion

- What did you know about Crete's role in the Second World War before you read this book?

- Has reading this novel made you want to visit Crete?

- Do you think the state of Hugh and Heavenly's house at the start of the novel could be seen to represent their marriage?

- 'I like this Heavenly. I hope she stays.' What do you think would have happened to Heavenly if she had returned to Athens with Hugh and not remained on Crete?

- Does Heavenly make the right decision about Constantinos and Christo at the end of the book?

- Discuss the relationships between the characters and their mothers.

- Did you find the end of the novel satisfying?

- 'I think we must be living in two separate worlds, you and me.' Should Heavenly and Hugh ever have got married?

- 'I went to tea parties with other wives. I took part in endless discussions about hairdressers and dressmakers.' How would you adapt to life as the spouse of a diplomat?

- How do you think the dual first-person viewpoints add to the novel?

- When Hugh arrived in Crete, the villagers were shocked that he wore shorts, thinking them too revealing. Discuss the impact of the culture clash.

- Why do you think the author called the novel *The House of Dust and Dreams*?

Suggested Further Reading

The Island – Victoria Hislop

Zorba the Greek – Nikos Kazantzakis

Ill Met by Moonlight – W. Stanley Moss

Captain Corelli's Mandolin – Louis de Bernières

Crete: The Battle and the Resistance – Anthony Beevor

The Greek Myths – Robert Graves

Four Famous Greek Plays – Professor Paul Landis (ed.)

The Cretan Runner – Georges Psychoundakis
translated by Patrick Leigh Fermor